RED GLC

RED GLOVES

Beth Vaughan

First published in Great Britain in 2008 by Gollancz
An imprint of the Orion Publishing Group
Orion House, 5 Upper St Martin's Lane, London WC2H 9EA
An Hachette UK Company

A CIP catalogue record for this book is available
from the British Library

ISBN 978 0 575 08420 9

3 5 7 9 10 8 6 4 2

Printed in Great Britain by CPI Mackays, Chatham, ME5 8TD

The Orion Publishing Group's policy is to use papers that are
natural, renewable and recyclable products and made from wood
grown in sustainable forests. The logging and manufacturing
processes are expected to conform to the environmental
regulations of the country of origin.

www.orionbooks.co.uk

This book is dedicated to

Patricia A. Merritt,
who read every word and always asked for more

And

Denise Lynn,
who took every phone call, listened,
then convinced me to get back to work

Thank you both so very much.

I wish there was some way to list all the people who helped me during the writing of this book. But for once, my words have failed me. So please know that I am deeply grateful to all of you for the love and support, and please forgive the lack.

But I must say a special thank you to my agents, Meg Davis and Merrilee Heifetz, and my editor, Jo Fletcher, for their understanding, support and confidence in me.

ONE

Water squelched between the fingers of Red's glove as she pounded on the door.

The wet wood seemed to give under her attack, and she eased back a step, cursing under her breath. Best not to be too fierce, seeing as how she was begging shelter for the night.

Her feet squished in her boots as she stepped back. Some water from the roof of the small hut dripped under her cloak and down her neck. She cursed again as the wet chill rolled down her spine under her armor.

Impatient, she raised her gloved fist and pounded again.

Rain fell in sheets around her, obscuring the cleared area around the hut. She cursed the rain, cursed the night and the cold. She glanced back over her shoulder at Bethral, who was holding the horses, her hood pressed against her head by the weight of the water.

Red was certain that they'd never been this wet, cold, and filthy. The horses' heads were hanging, poor tired beasts, their legs and bellies caked in muck. Beast was favoring a hind leg, and Red feared he'd strained it badly. They needed shelter, needed it now. Only the faint trace of woodsmoke had brought them here. There was no other sign of shelter for miles.

She turned back to the door, raising her gloved fist to pound on it again, when the door was pulled back, scraping against the dirt of the floor. A wave of blessed heat and the smell of food and fire pressed against her cold face. The hot air was thick with the scent of stew and spices she didn't know. Her mouth watered.

A figure blocked the door, a big man. Red tilted her head to look into brown eyes flecked with gold, glaring at her, questioning, and full of something she knew only too well.

Pain.

She swallowed hard and her stomach clenched. 'Shelter,' she croaked, her throat raw. 'We ask shelter for the night.'

'We?' A deep voice rumbled softly, and the door swung open wider, as the man peered over her shoulder and out into the rain. A fire crackled on a hearth behind him and the fragrance of his dinner filled her nostrils.

'My friend and I and our horses.' She swallowed her pride and anger, for asking did not come easy. 'We offer peace and honor the household.'

The man snorted softly, as if at a jest. 'Such as it is.' He gave her a long look, then nodded once. 'Bide.' The door closed.

Red snarled, letting her rage bubble up. She backed away and squelched over to where Bethral stood patiently in the rain. Her sword-sister looked out from under her hood and raised an eyebrow.

'The man said to "bide." ' She took the reins of her horse. 'Not sure, but I hope that it means—'

The door creaked open, and the man came out, wrapped in a cloak and carrying a small lantern. He pulled the door closed behind him. 'Come.'

Red took the lead, tugging on the reins to get her horse moving. Beast let his neck stretch out to its full extent before he heaved a sigh and lifted his feet out of the mud to follow. Bethral waited a pace or two before following with her horse.

The man led them around the hut, passed an old stone well, and moved into the night. Red peered ahead, surprised to see a large stone structure appear in the darkness. He moved carefully to open an enormous wood door, sliding it off to one side. She led her horse into the dark barn, far enough to allow Bethral to bring Steel in as well.

They stood there, dripping, and gaped. The man lit three lanterns that hung from posts. The building was huge, with box stalls lining both sides of the wide aisle. The place smelled dusty and disused.

A rustling noise came from one of the boxes and a small white goat stuck its head out, blinking sleepily in the soft light. It bleated softly, as if asking a question.

'Visitors,' the man's voice rumbled. 'Go back to sleep.'

The white head pulled back.

'I've never seen the like,' Red spoke in the echoing darkness as she took off her dripping cloak. 'It's huge.'

'From the days when this was a rich and foolish man's breeding farm.' The man pulled back his hood and hung his lantern on one of the hooks. 'The fool is gone, the barn remains.'

'And you?' Red asked. In the light of the lanterns, she got her first good look at the man. A good strong face, handsome even, but etched with lines of sorrow. Dark brown curls, with traces of silver, and those brown eyes, flecked with gold.

'And me,' he replied, not really answering her question. He gazed at her with tired eyes. Not so old as she'd thought he was, but his pain was.

'I go by Red Gloves.' Red said.

His eyes flicked to her gloves, but thankfully he made no comment.

'My friend is Bethral,' Red said.

Bethral pulled off her hood and gave the man a nod. His eyes flickered over her blonde hair and blue eyes.

'Our thanks for—' Red continued.

He waved off her words. 'See to your animals. Make free with what you find, for I keep no horses. Down that way is a foaling room. There's a small hearth there for heat. I'll bring you wood and such as I can spare.'

'Again, our . . .' Her voice trailed off as he flipped his hood up and left the building, leaving them standing there. She glared at the door. 'Rude pig.'

'We've shelter,' Bethral said quietly, as if that excused the man. She removed her cloak and moved farther down the aisle. 'There's water and buckets.'

'Let's get at it, then.' Red tied off Beast and Steel. 'You water them, and check Beast for me. I'll get the gear.' She pulled off her sodden cloak and tossed it on a hook to dry. 'By the Twelve, everything is soaked,' she swore. 'What do you wager the food is wet and mucked, eh?'

Bethral nodded absently as she pulled two buckets from the trough. The horses stirred, straining as she placed the water down in front of them. 'Easy,' she crooned as they drank.

Well, no point in talking now that Bethral was focused on the beasts. Red grumbled under her breath as she pulled the sopping saddlebags off Steel. She grunted as she took the full weight and lugged them to a nearby bench. Next the saddlebags from Beast, who stomped a front foot as the weight was removed, but never pulled his head out of the bucket.

Bethral was stroking them as they drank and then reached to feel between Steel's forelegs and chest. 'They need walking out.' She kept a hand on Beast as she knelt to check his leg. 'There's no swelling. We'll know more in the morning.'

Red grunted as she pulled the saddle off Beast. 'The cloaks didn't protect much.' She placed the saddle on a rack nearby. 'Leather will have to be worked in the morning.'

Bethral removed Steel's saddle, and racked it as well. The bridles, too, leaving the horses with their halters.

Red untied Beast, who threw his head toward the trough. She pulled his head down, and started to walk him down the long aisle. 'Stop that, Beast. You'll cramp up for sure, and then where will I be? In a goat barn in the middle of nowhere, with a strange goatherder and naught for aid.'

Bethral snorted a laugh as she followed, leading Steel, and for a while there was no sound but hooves on beaten earth as they walked the horses down the wide aisle.

After a few minutes, Red handed off the lead to Bethral and went in search of what she could find. Her voice echoed the length of the barn. 'There's straw.'

'Fresh?'

'Well, dry at least,' Red answered.

Bethral kept the horses moving down the aisle and turned them just out of the light. 'Any grain?'

'No, we'll have to use our own. I did see clean rags, and some bottles and jars, but I can't tell what's in them.'

'Smell them.'

'I'm not sticking my nose in those, thanks kindly.' Red strode back into the aisle. 'They cool yet?'

Bethral patted Beast on his chest, moving her hand down between his legs. 'No.'

Red nodded, giving the wet gloves on her hands a tug to tighten their fit. 'I'll fork down the straw and hay, and get the grain ready.' She turned slightly, toward the ladder to the loft,

4

only to pause at the base of the ladder. 'You still have that molasses in your bag?'

Bethral gave her a look as she turned the horses again. Red shrugged. 'Aye, I know, I said you were spoiling them too much with the sweet grain.' She pulled herself into the loft. 'They've earned it, wading through the muck and mire of that bog for two days.'

'True enough.' Bethral's voice floated up to her. 'But whose fault was it that we were lost in the muck and mire to begin with?'

Red bit back a scathing retort and gripped the handle of the pitchfork she found in the loft. The wet leather of her gloves mushed against the wood; she snarled again, and set to work. First the horses, then themselves. Once she was dry and had food in her belly, Bethral could complain all she wanted.

And would.

Red attacked the straw, flinging it into the boxes below her. She made quick work of the task of the bedding and getting the grain ready. Normally Beast would fidget if he smelled grain and molasses, but he continued to walk with Bethral, calm as you please, as Red made up the feed buckets.

'They're tired and hot.' Bethral said quietly. 'A bit longer and I can let them eat.'

Red nodded. 'I'll see if I can find that foaling room.' She moved down the wide aisle, in the faint light of the lantern.

Sure enough, a door to the side opened into what could almost be another barn, it was so big. An open stall at one end, with a wide barn door, and two bunks at the other end, with a small hearth for heat. It was stale inside, as if no one had entered in some time. But there was a lantern inside the door, and Red took it up and returned to Bethral's side.

'It's there as he said, with a small hearth and bunks. I'll drag down our gear.' She lit the lantern.

'Go. Get a fire started and get yourself dry.' Bethral said softly. 'I'll take care of the horses.'

Red gave her a grateful glance, and took up a bucket of water from the trough. It would be cold, but enough to get clean of the muck.

It took a moment to lay a fire, and it started to crackle at once.

Red pushed the door shut to let the heat start to build in the room, and placed the water close enough to the fire to warm. There was a small copper pot that she usually used to make kavage; she found it in one of their packs and filled it. It sat by the fire, reflecting the light happily, a touch of the familiar in an unfamiliar place.

Her leathers came off easy but the linen padding underneath had to be peeled from her skin. Her nose crinkled as she got a good whiff. She stank.

She fumbled about in her saddlebag and pulled out her tunic and trous, and a spare set of gloves. Slightly damp, but clean. She also found the soap.

With the heat on her skin, Red plunged her gloved hands into the bucket and started to work up a lather. It would feel so good to get some part of her clean and dry. Washing with the gloves on was something she was used to. Better than the alternative, that was certain. She'd dry them well, and oil them in the morning. Wouldn't do to lose her extra pair. Too damn hard to replace.

She heard Bethral's voice, and knew the man was back. She listened, then snorted softly. Her sword-sister was using the same voice she'd use to calm a shy horse. She'd seen it, too, in those brown eyes with gold flecks, seen the man's grief. Knowing her sword-sister . . .

'I'm called Josiah,' Red heard him say through the door.

Red grinned. Frightened animals and people, they all trusted Bethral within a moment of hearing that voice. She chuckled, missing Bethral's next words.

When the door banged open, she looked around in surprise.

Josiah banged through the door without a thought, his arms full of wood. But he froze there, mouth open, eyes drinking in the sight.

Red had turned to look at the door, her expression a question, her long brown hair hanging straight behind her, past her shoulders. The light of the fire danced over her burnished skin, for she stood naked as the day of her birth, except for the red gloves on her hands and the bar of soap she held.

Muscular and strong, with a few scars here and there. A warrior's body, but that only added to her loveliness.

Her look was not astonishment or fear or embarrassment, as he would expect. Rather, her brown eyes sparkled with life as she took in his shock. After the pause lengthened to the point of pain, she arched an eyebrow at him, and planted one gloved hand on her hip. Her breasts swayed, the birthmark beneath her right breast a sharp, dark brown contrast to her skin.

Josiah sucked in a breath and backed away, dropping the wood. He thought he stammered an apology, but he wasn't sure he was using actual words. He pulled the door shut, then stared at the closed door, still seeing her in his mind's eye. Her breasts. Her birthmark.

A sound drew his attention, and he turned to see the tall blonde staring at him oddly, down by the horses. He moved her way, walking quickly, clearing his throat. 'I interrupted her. At her bath. I'm sor—'

Her expression stopped him cold. With a frown and a swift lunge, she was between him and the foaling room, pulling her sword. 'Was she wearing her gloves?'

Josiah gaped at her in astonishment.

'Quick, man.' Bethral pushed him back toward the outside door, her focus down the corridor, as if fearing attack. 'Did she have her gloves on?'

TWO

'What?' Josiah repeated, his confusion growing by the moment.

'Was she wearing gloves?' The blonde was focused on the aisle and the door, her voice tense, her stance protective.

The image flashed before his eyes again: the naked warrior in the firelight. Something stirred in his groin, something he'd thought long dead. The soap glistening on her slick skin, the suds between the fingers of her . . .

'Yes,' Josiah said, clearing his throat to speak. 'Yes, she was.'

'Oh.' Bethral's tension melted away. She sheathed her sword and stepped back to the horses.

Josiah watched her, puzzled. 'She was naked,' he explained. 'I burst in on her.'

'So?' Bethral didn't even bother to look at him. She just shrugged. 'Red won't care.'

Josiah frowned, glancing back toward the door. She certainly hadn't appeared offended. She'd almost seemed . . . interested. Standing there, not moving, except that sardonic eyebrow raised in a question. And the dagger-star birthmark beneath her breast.

He swallowed hard.

The rattle of feed buckets pulled him back. The horses were eager as Bethral put the grain before them. She reached for a cloth then, and started rubbing the horses' legs down as they chomped on the feed, murmuring to them softly.

'I've food to share, some stew and biscuits,' Josiah offered. 'I'll bring it out. To make amends.'

Bethral glanced over, her blue eyes warm. 'There's no amends needed.' She spoke softly, the sound easing some of the tension from Josiah's shoulders. 'But hot food would be welcome indeed.'

Josiah nodded, grabbed up his cloak, and headed back into the dark.

*

'Rude pig.'

Bethral looked up from her task to see Red standing in the aisle, glaring through the open barn door at the rain outside. Or at Josiah's figure disappearing into the mist.

'What was wrong with the man?' Red grumbled. 'Certain sure, there's nothing wrong with me. A few scars, maybe, but I'm decent looking.'

Bethral snorted softly. Red had managed a quick wash and was dressed in her spare tunic and trous, a dagger at her belt, a fresh pair of dry gloves on her hands. Good. That would put her in a better mood. 'Not so rude that he fails to give shelter to two strange women bearing weapons, when he has none.' Bethral turned back to rubbing the horses' legs dry. 'Perhaps he prefers his own sex.'

Red glared out the door and growled something under her breath.

'He offered to share his supper in apology,' Bethral added.

Red gave her a quick look. 'Food?' She quirked an eyebrow at Bethral. 'Well, then, maybe I can forgive his actions.'

Bethral chuckled.

Red grabbed a dry cloth. 'I'll finish this. The bags are wet clear through, but I pulled out your spares and put them by the fire. Go and change. I'll get them watered and bedded for the night.'

Bethral straightened with effort. 'I'll do that.' She paused for a moment 'Red, you need to warn him. About—'

Red gave her a stubborn look. 'I left them on, didn't I? We'll not be here long enough to—'

Bethral held up her hand to stop the familiar argument. 'I'm too tired to argue.' She turned to go, aware that Red was muttering under her breath, but too tired to care. The surge of energy she'd felt before was gone, leaving exhaustion in its wake. It was all she could do to walk to the foaling room.

The birthing stall was large, but what drew her was the small fire by the two bunks. True to her word, Red had set out her clothes to warm.

Bethral heaved a sigh of relief as the warmth of the fire wrapped around her body. She was cold, and ached in every joint. It took the last of her strength to lift her arms and remove

9

her chain shirt. She sighed deeply as the weight came off her shoulders.

She'd heard of elven chain that was half the weight of human make. Said to be as rare as elves themselves. Bethral shook her head. Might as well wish it was magic armor while she was at it.

She sat then, to pull off her boots and peel off her heavy leather trous. Muck and grit had gotten under every layer as she undressed, so she took her bucket and moved away from the fire to splash as much as she wished. The feel of the water on her skin revived her a bit.

Once dressed, she started in on the saddlebags. Red joined her once the horses were bedded, and they sorted out the few possessions they shared. Everything was wet, from their clothes to the provisions.

'The dried meat is fine, but the beans are wet.' Bethral set those items aside.

'We'll need to clean everything tomorrow,' Red grumbled softly, pulling out a pack of spare bowstrings.

'And oil the armor and blades before rust sets in,' Bethral added.

Red lifted her head at the sound of the barn door opening and closing, and footsteps headed their way. The soft tap at the door made her give Bethral an amused glance. Bethral returned it. Apparently their host had learned his lesson.

Bethral opened the door to find Josiah laden with a cloth parcel and a covered pot. He went to the fire and uncovered the stew. A tantalizing aroma filled the room, and Bethral took a deep breath.

'What is that scent?' Red asked, sniffing the air.

Josiah gave her an odd glance. 'Marjoram.'

'Don't know that spice,' Red said, 'Smells good.'

She plopped down on one of the bunks, and Josiah gestured to Bethral to take the other. He sat before the fire, and unwrapped the bundle and started to dish out the stew.

'I don't have three bowls.' He handed Red a full mug and a spoon.

Red dug in, not waiting a moment. Bethral accepted her mug with a smile. Josiah handed them each a biscuit, and for the moment they all three ate in silence. Josiah had emptied his bowl and was refilling Red's mug when he spoke. 'You are not from here.'

Bethral gave the man a long look over her mug. Smarter than he looked, then.

Red shrugged. 'Never said we were.'

'What gave it away?' Bethral asked, curious. They'd worked on their language skills for some time.

Josiah shrugged. 'A faint accent. And that you've not seen marjoram used in stew before. It's fairly common in Palins.' His eyes slid over to Red, and then he looked back at Bethral. 'And other things.'

'We're from Soccia.' Red held out her mug for more. 'Not much work for two mercenaries in a land fat with peace.'

Josiah's face darkened. 'There's no peace here.'

Red nodded, never noticing his dark look as she dug into her second helping. 'Should be able to find work, then.'

Bethral stifled a sigh. There were times . . .

They continued eating in silence. Bethral sensed that Josiah had something on his mind, but she didn't really feel like encouraging him to talk. The warmth and the food made her sleepy, and all she cared was that there was a bed beneath her. They'd sleep warm, dry, and safe, and she was grateful.

Finally, after they'd scraped the pot empty, Red set down her mug and sighed. 'Any more and I will burst. My thanks, Josiah.'

'Mine as well,' Bethral added.

Josiah gathered the dishes into his bundle. 'I'll leave you to sleep, then. There's blankets in the trunk, and you've enough wood.' He stood and cleared his throat. 'I'd ask . . . were you wounded? I saw a mark under your breast and—'

Bethral mentally rolled her eyes. The goatherder wasn't being very subtle. But then she caught Red's eyes shifting slightly, and knew full well her sword-sister was up to something . . .

Red Gloves considered the man before her, then reached for the bottom of her tunic. 'Twelve, no.' She stood and slowly pulled the material up, watching as his eyes followed the cloth edge. She lifted it to just below her breasts, making sure that a bit of curve was revealed. 'A birthmark, nothing more.'

The poor man stood staring, as if poleaxed.

She studied him through half-closed eyes. Oh, he was interested, which pleased her. There was desire there, that was certain. Something else as well . . . how long had he been alone? Not healthy to repress a body that way.

Well, he was about to get his itch well and truly scratched. Red lowered her tunic, making sure her dagger handle was free, but she didn't bother tucking her tunic into her trous.

Josiah seemed to come back to himself. He opened his mouth as if to talk, but Red made a point of stretching, and yawned until her jaw cracked. No sense letting the man talk, after all.

Josiah hesitated, then spoke. 'You're welcome to stay as long as you like. Your horses look in need of some rest. I can provide breakfast, but my supplies will not stretch far.'

'We have some beans that need cooking,' Bethral lifted the sack.

'Let me have them, and I will set them to soak,' Josiah offered.

'Gladly.' Bethral smiled, handed him the beans. 'Goodnight, Josiah. Our thanks again for the shelter and the food.'

Red gestured toward the door. 'I'll walk with you, Josiah, and check the horses.' She tried not to sound too smug.

Josiah gave her a questioning look, but headed for the door. Red followed, and pulled the door firmly closed behind them. She caught a brief glimpse of her sword-sister as the door closed.

Bethral was rolling her eyes as they left.

Red smirked at her. Some men just needed to have the obvious made plain, that was all.

She turned and followed Josiah down the aisle of the barn as the big man blew out the lanterns in the aisle, leaving only the light from the one he carried. The light caught the glints of silver in Josiah's dark curls. One minute she thought his hair black; the next, a dark brown. She wondered whether it curled around his—

They paused by the horses, and Josiah raised the lantern, showing that the beasts were well and fast asleep. He turned toward her, and looked down into her eyes. 'I can leave this with you, if you need—'

Red reached out and caught a handful of his tunic in her gloved hand. Slowly, deliberately, she pulled him closer. There was a puzzled look in those pained eyes, as if uncertain as to her intent.

She smiled slightly as she captured his mouth.

He tasted salty. Or was it sweet? There was a subtle spice to the warmth of his lips.

She felt him move away, and so pressed him back against the stable wall, using the entire length of her body. His body was taut, tense, but she concentrated on the kiss. He opened his mouth under hers, probably in protest, but she just explored further.

A thrill swept through her when she felt him relax into the kiss. His heat was delicious, and she hungered. Even through the layers of clothing, she felt his body respond to her.

Her free hand moved up to thread her gloved fingers through his hair. She shifted her weight slightly, and raised her leg up along his, eager for more. Releasing her grip on his tunic, she stroked down to fumble at the waist of his trous. Josiah groaned into her mouth as she searched for—

Strong hands on her waist lifted her, and set her away from him with a thud.

Five goats' heads emerged between the slats of a stall, blinking at them in the light.

Red stood, gasping, staring at the man who looked flustered and grim. 'I am not fit, Lady.'

Her eyes went down to his crotch. He'd seemed—

'Not fit for a relationship,' Josiah said.

'Who said anything about a relationship?'

Bethral raised an eyebrow when Red stalked back into the birthing room and closed the door with a slam. Red's trysts were usually a little longer than—

She got a good look at Red's face and decided not to ask what had happened.

'Watches?' Bethral asked.

Red's anger faded as quick as it had come. She took a deep breath and shook her head. 'Not sure it's necessary.' She shrugged ruefully. 'Not sure I could stay awake.'

Bethral gave a short nod, then dragged the heavy blanket trunk in front of the door. 'That should give us some warning.'

Red had her weapons on the floor within reach. She checked

the fire, then crawled between her blankets. 'I doubt a small army bursting through would wake me. I am that tired.'

Bethral grunted her agreement, arranged her weapons, and crawled into her bunk. A simple straw mattress, but it felt like the finest down. The blankets warmed quickly, and she felt her muscles finally ease. They'd traveled hard and been lost in that mire for so long, she wasn't even sure of the days. 'That's the last time I follow you into a bog, Red.'

The only answer was a soft snore.

Bethral closed her eyes, and let sleep enfold her.

Josiah ducked his head as he entered his hut, pushed the door closed, and drew a deep breath.

The room hadn't changed. Just big enough for his needs, with a table, chair, and bed. The herbs he had drying in the rafters stirred in the cold air he'd let in the door.

The largest thing in the room was the old stone hearth. The fire he set there didn't come close to filling it, but it was enough to warm the small hut.

Josiah sighed, and set his burden down on the table.

It couldn't be true, of course. They were mercenaries, women warriors out of Soccia. But there it was, below her right breast, the dagger-star birthmark. Clear as day and sharp as a blade.

She'd kissed him.

A tingle passed over his skin at the memory. She'd pressed up against him, and he could still feel her body, her warmth, her mouth. Five years it had been, five long years, since he'd held a woman.

No, that wasn't right. He'd never held a woman like her in his arms. No shy reluctance, no hesitation. Just a warm and very willing woman in his arms, making it very clear what she wanted. She was no lady of the court, full of deceit and treachery, hiding her plans behind words of love.

He looked at the bundle in his hands without really seeing it. It wasn't a dream. He'd eaten with them; the dishes in the bundle were proof they were real.

That and the fact that his pot was empty.

He set about washing the dishes, and took care of the few chores that needed doing. But his hands moved on their own, with no real help from him. His mind was too filled with the possibilities.

His groin stirred, and Josiah drew a deep breath, trying to suppress that urge. No, he needed to concentrate on the other possibility.

Red Gloves bore the birthmark of the Chosen of Palins.

His fire banked and the beans set to soak, Josiah stripped down and crawled beneath the wool blankets of his bed. He lay there, breathing, as the bed warmed around him. He stared up at the thatch of the roof, lost in thought.

After all this time, after all the pain, could this be? Could revenge be that close?

He lay there for a long time as the fire died to coals, his heart filled with a strange mix of hope and fear. In the morning, he'd make some breakfast and talk to the women. Try to learn more, try to explain—

A soft bleat broke through his thoughts.

Josiah's gaze shifted to focus on the small white goat by the bed. She danced closer, and butted her head against his shoulder.

'Is that you, Snowdrop?' Josiah asked softly. He reached out and scratched her between the ears. She leaned into the scratch. The four others bleated softly, coming from the shadows. The two largest settled down by his bed, tucking themselves close. The little white one stamped her foot as the other small ones leapt up on his bed.

'All right, all right.' Josiah shifted to lie on his side as the goats tucked themselves in along his legs and back. The small white one was quick to claim the spot in front of his chest.

Surrounded by the familiar warmth of their bodies, Josiah yawned and curled his arm around the white one. He closed his eyes with a sigh.

In the morning, he'd talk to them. Learn and explain . . .

In the morning, he'd . . .

In the morning . . .

Dawn found Red in need of the necessary.

She grumbled, and left the shelter of the blankets slowly, trying to leave the heat within, for she had every intention of crawling back into them. The fire had died down – only a few coals remained. She took the time to add some tinder. She'd add more wood when she got back.

She grabbed her dagger and went to the door. What Bethral had moved with ease the night before took her a minute more to move from the door. Red cursed slightly as she swung the door open. She walked down the aisle of the barn, pleased to see the horses sleeping in their stalls.

The morning light let her see the goats in the far pen – five, from the look of things. She liked goat, if it was well cooked. She yawned, and opened the smaller door to go outside. The darkness outside was thick, silent, and cool. The rain had stopped, and it looked to be a clear sky above. She grunted as she spotted the small house and made her way to it.

It was when she emerged, with the sun just a hint of pink to the east, that she finally got a good look at her surroundings. She paused, her bare feet on the wet grass, and looked about in shock. The barn, it was big. Very big, and . . .

Red stood in the light of a silent dawn, really looking as the light spread to reveal the barn, the bricks that bore the marks of weapons and the scorches of fire. From the blackened walls, it was amazing the thing still stood solid.

Stunned, she looked further, at the fields around her, at the skeletons of burnt trees reaching for the sky, at ruined foundations where buildings once stood.

It wasn't a farm. It was a battlefield.

THREE

Bethral glared at Red, less than pleased. She'd been pulled from a warm bed to view the land about by a very excited Red. Bethral wasn't at her best in the mornings.

At least, not before kavage.

'What do you think? The damage, it's maybe two, maybe three years old, eh?' Red was looking around, her arms folded over her chest. She'd dragged Bethral out to stand by the well. 'Farmland, from the looks of it. I saw a few foundation stones and some straggling crops growing about. Mostly scrub plants, though. What looks to be the remains of a vineyard, there across the fields. How the barn survived, I don't . . .'

Bethral grunted again, as Red ran on. Not much for chatter, her sword-sister, unless it was battle or the aftermath. Bethral sighed, and left Red standing there as she stomped up the path to the necessary.

'. . . destruction on a grand scale. The trees, stumps of burnt fences. It had to be magical fire, from the scorch marks. Did you see—'

Bethral emerged from the necessary and headed back into the barn. She'd seen all she wished to see. She was more worried about the horses.

'And that hut where he is, it's just wattle and daub, but the chimney is stone. You suppose he built it up against some ruins?' Red followed, still speculating, as Bethral went into Steel's stall.

Bethral was careful to let Steel know she was there, as he was still sleeping when she entered. She spoke softly, and stroked his flank gently before tapping his knee. Without really stirring, Steel lifted his hoof for her inspection.

It needed picking out, what with the mud and all. Not to mention the wet and dirty leather of the tack. Bethral sighed, and dropped the leg. Steel shifted a bit in the straw, but then

17

fell to drowsing again. Poor tired animal. She knew how he felt.

'Beast's fine.' Red spoke again, from Beast's stall. 'They need a full day of rest is all.' She didn't sound upset by the idea.

'And brushed down.' Bethral patted Steel on the shoulder, and made her way to the door of the stall. 'Could be worse.'

'Could be blood,' Red agreed.

'I noticed something else,' Bethral added.

Red looked over at her with a question in her eyes.

'Listen,' Bethral said. 'What do you hear?'

Red closed her eyes and held her breath. Bethral stilled, and wasn't disappointed. Red's eye popped open in astonishment. 'Nothing.' She peered around the barn, then looked up in the rafters high overhead.

Bethral nodded. 'Not a bird to be heard, nor the rustle of a mouse in the straw. Not so much as a barn cat.'

Red's hand moved to her dagger hilt, her eyes narrowing.

Bethral shook her head. 'I don't think there's a threat here, Red.'

'Blackened fields, sparse growth, the ruins of fences.' Red relaxed, but still looked interested. 'Why live in that hut? Why not in the barn?'

'Why so curious about a goatherder?' Bethral asked. 'What happened to "Don't get involved unless you get paid"?'

'There's something about his eyes.' There was something slightly defensive about Red's tone, and Bethral gave her an intent look.

Red was staring at the wall, lost in thought, as she continued. 'Something about his pain . . .' Red's voice trailed off, but then she shook herself and shrugged. 'Something to think about besides all this cleaning.'

'Well, after we've seen to the horses and the gear, we'll spar.' Bethral turned toward the foaling room. 'Three days lost in that bog with no chance to practice. You need a blade in your hand.'

The faint sound of a goat bell came from outside.

'You could clean, I could hunt,' Red offered, as if making a sacrifice of her efforts. 'Our host may appreciate some fresh meat.'

'Don't bother.' Josiah stepped into the barn, followed by the five goats. He held two pots by their handles and had a cloth-wrapped parcel tucked under his arm.

Bethral drew a deep breath. 'Is that kavage?'

Red had her hands crossed over her chest. 'I'm a good hunter.'

'Skills don't mean much when there is no game.' Josiah moved past them, toward the foaling room. The goats made to follow as well, their tails wagging. 'I've brought warm oats and kavage.'

'I've some molasses for the oats.' Bethral offered.

'What happened here?' Red asked.

Josiah stopped dead in his tracks, as did the goats. Bethral was willing to swear that all six heads turned at once to look at Red.

Red hadn't moved, her stance firm, her arms crossed before her. But there was a tilt to her head, and a glint in her eye that Bethral had seen before. One that didn't bode well for the prey she stalked. 'Who fought here? When did it happen?'

The goatherder stood there, silent, his face a mix of emotions Bethral couldn't quite read. But one she knew well, had seen often enough. In the warriors she'd fought with. And against.

Fear.

Red opened her mouth again, but Josiah cut her off. 'Here.'

He thrust the pots at Bethral. She took them quickly, if only to save her breakfast from being spilled. He pushed the bundle into her arms as well.

Josiah strode for the door. 'I've chores to do.'

'I'll have an answer, Josiah.' Red's voice was low and husky. 'Now or later.'

That brought the man to a halt. Bethral watched his back, and didn't miss his hands as they clenched into fists and then relaxed. 'I set the beans to soak. We'll have soup tonight. Together.'

'And answers.'

Josiah looked over his shoulder. There was a long pause as he and Red stared at one another. The goats were clustered by his feet unnaturally quiet. The hair on the back of Bethral's neck stirred, as if a storm was rising.

Josiah looked away. 'And answers.'

He strode off, the goats following, bleating as if in distress. Red watched as he walked away, a satisfied smirk on her face.

'What's he afraid of?' Bethral asked as she balanced her burdens.

'I don't know,' Red answered slowly, still focused on the man. 'But I will.'

Josiah caught glimpses of them during the day, going between the barn and the well, cleaning their gear and their horses. The two women worked hard, he'd give them that.

They'd scrubbed the horses down, picking out their hooves and even combing out manes and tails. Then their gear, placing saddles and bedrolls to air in the sun after being cleaned.

He made sure to stay out of their way as much as possible, since the smaller one, the one named Red, was sure to ask questions. He went about his business, as his mind and belly churned. He'd as many questions for them as they did for him, and the answers would bring back the pain. The thought of talking about what had happened was a lead weight pressing down on his chest. Talking would bring back the memories, and the nightmares. The sights, the smells . . . the sounds.

He had to stop at that thought. Just stop what he was doing, close his eyes, and breathe.

A familiar bleat, and a head butted against his leg. He opened his eyes and looked down into the brown eyes of the little white goat. He gave her a rueful smile, and bent down to scratch her head. 'All's well, Snowdrop. Let's see what we can gather in the old herb field, eh?'

He took up his shovel and an old tattered field basket and started off. The goats followed, as they always did. Brownie, Fog, and Dapple ranged out, but the two smaller ones, Kavage and Snowdrop, tended to stay closer.

The walk brought him peace. Over past the copse of dead trees, and down a hill to the old herb field. He wandered through, harvesting what he could from the survivors that grew wild in amidst the weeds.

These past few years, it had always been a comfort to be out and about on the ruined fields. There were times he could almost feel the land, as if it was trying to absorb his pain. When the rains fell, when the snow covered the hills, it was like he was blanketed as well. Cushioned, even.

A fancy on his part. No – more like a conceit.

Some of the more tender plants hadn't come back from the

ravages. But the marjoram seemed to thrive. He cut a generous amount, and placed the bundles in the basket with his other finds. Some wild onions, a few turnips. They'd add to the soup, that was sure.

It calmed him, as it always had, this kind of work. The sun rose higher, and he took a break to sit in the shade and drink of the sweet water from the stream. He leaned his head back and sighed, grateful to be tired and worn.

The goats browsed nearby, eating the scrub. He'd had some bread and cheese he could have brought, but he'd left it behind. Oh, well, he'd be hungry for supper, then, for the soup and . . . her questions.

The memories flooded in then, and the pain flared up. His stomach cramped, and he wondered how he'd get through a meal without being sick.

It had to be faced, if he wanted answers from her. About the birthmark, about her presence here, now . . . he had to know, and yet . . .

Josiah stood up, grabbed his basket, and strode back to his hut. The goats scrambled behind him, bleating at his abrupt departure.

He'd work to do. And a soup to put on the fire.

He'd just come out of the trees when he heard the laughter. He paused, and looked at the barn.

Red and Bethral were fighting.

Well, Bethral was fighting. With a sword and shield, she was guarding herself close.

Red was dancing.

Josiah's breath caught. Red was leaping at Bethral with two daggers, her long brown hair flying behind her like a banner. Two bright blades flashed, real steel from the look of it. Part of him knew that they sparred, the other part drew a breath as Red evaded Bethral's blade by the merest breadth.

Their laughter was bright, but their movements showed the seriousness of their blades. To his eye, neither was the better of the other, but then he didn't have enough skill to know. All he knew for sure was that Red was alive in a way that Josiah hadn't seen in years. She was fast, darting about, trying to penetrate Bethral's defenses.

A shiver of pure lust passed through him. She was light and joy and a bright beacon. He felt her lips on his, could taste her on his tongue. His mind betrayed him with the thought of her moving beneath his body, naked, awash in passion, their bodies—

Red stopped and stood, breathing hard. Their gazes met across the field.

Lord of Light, he wanted her. Did the sweat bead on her skin like the soap had? What would she sound like, as she—

Even at this distance, he saw the side of her mouth quirk up. She knew what he was thinking.

He clenched his teeth, and wrenched his gaze away, to stare at the barn and the ruins that surrounded it. At the destruction of his joy. He'd no right to feel this way. His path was set: narrow, dark, and straight to the revenge he prayed for. He drew a deep breath, then looked at the ground between his feet, at the moss that had regrown between the stones of the path.

Grief welled up in his chest, but that was good. It allowed him to take a step, and then another, toward the hut.

The two women had broken off, and were sharing a drink as he walked past them. He could feel Red's look on the back of his neck, but he didn't stop. Time enough for the questions later, when their bellies were full, and he could ask as much as he'd answer.

Grief was an old friend. He could bear grief.

What he couldn't bear was hope.

The goats headed off to join the horses in their grazing. He walked into the hut and pulled the door firmly closed behind him.

They'd ended up in the foaling room again, sitting before the fire. Bethral was warm, and tired, the good kind of tired that came from hard work and a good sparring session. With all of Red's speed, she'd landed only two blows on Bethral, and only one would have been lethal. Red might be faster, but strength and patience still counted in a fight.

Red leaned forward like a dog on a scent, clearly interested in their host.

A host who'd walked in with a pot of bean soup and the look

of a man going to his doom. Josiah had placed the pot by the fire, and handed out pieces of coarse brown bread to go with the soup.

Bethral's stomach growled when he lifted the lid off the pot. The scent of beans, salt pork, and onion had filled the small room. The man must have heard it, since he served her first, with a full mug and a spoon.

'What do you know of Palins's past?' Josiah asked.

Red took her mug from his hands with a shrug. 'A civil war rages here, and has for some time.'

Josiah filled his bowl, but he held it in his hands, and made no effort to eat.

'True, and yet not true.' He sighed. 'Five years back, King Everard reigned in this land, with the High Barons on his Council. Each High Baron held his lands in fealty to Everard.'

Red nodded, blowing on her soup. 'He died, with his queen and heir.'

'Queen Rosalyn and Prince Hugh. Everard's only heir.' Josiah stirred his bowl. 'With their deaths, there was no one of the bloodline left to rightfully rule this land.'

'So, civil war,' Red stated.

Josiah shook his head. 'Not right away. The Council was summoned to Edenrich, the capital city, and the High Barons began to discuss appointing a regent until someone with the royal bloodline could be found.'

'"Discuss"!' Red snorted. 'I imagine that went well.'

'A regent was appointed,' Josiah said. 'But discussion turned to dissent, and dissent into discord.' He focused on the fire, his eyes far away. Bethral noted his hands gripped in his lap, the knuckles white. She gave Red a quick look, but Red was focused on the face of the man before her.

Josiah continued. 'From discord to chaos. The High Barons turned on each other, attacking in order to claim the throne for themselves.'

'Is that what happened here?' Red asked.

Josiah nodded. 'Even here. All was destroyed in the name of power.' His voice cracked. 'Now Palins is hard-pressed, its people no longer a charge to be cared for, but a resource to be drained.'

Bethral considered the man in silence. His head was bowed, sorrow in every line of his body.

Red scraped her mug with her spoon.

Josiah lifted his head and focused on Red. 'The mark you bear, we call it the dagger-star.'

'My birthmark?' Red eyed him doubtfully.

'It's the sign of the Chosen,' Josiah said in a hushed voice.

Bethral narrowed her eyes and studied the man, but he seemed perfectly serious.

Red snorted. 'Is there any more bread?'

Josiah handed her the loaf. 'Don't you understand? The prophecy says that the Chosen will claim the throne. Justice will return to the land and its people.'

'Justice?' Red raised an eyebrow as she tore a hunk from the loaf and handed the rest to Bethral. 'Because I have a mark on my chest?'

'Flaunt it in Palins and it will get you killed,' Josiah replied. 'You are the Chosen of the Gods, a child of prophecy, born for this purpose. This destiny.'

Red rolled her eyes and dug into her soup.

Josiah frowned. 'What?'

'Red follows the teaching of the Twelve.' Bethral answered, as Red shoveled soup into her mouth. 'She doesn't believe in relying on gods.'

'Doesn't believe?' Josiah looked at her. 'But—'

Red cut him off, talking around a mouthful of soup. 'They leave me alone, I leave them alone.' She swallowed her food, then continued. 'The mark means nothing.'

'It means everything,' Josiah argued. 'A chance to set things right in a land where cruelty rules, and people are sold into slavery.'

Red fixed him with a stare. 'You care deeply, goatherder, for one that lives alone and apart.'

Josiah shrugged. 'Not so apart. There's a town to the southeast, a day's hard ride.'

'But no one lives here,' Red pressed. 'No one but you, in a hut of your own making, I think.'

Bethral stayed silent, eating her soup, watching and listening. There'd been a time, when she'd been young, when she'd thought to save the world with her sword. To make a real difference. But time and experience had taught her well.

Red, on the other hand, had never been a dreamer. Ever practical was her sword-sister, except about her gloves.

Josiah looked ill, setting his bowl of soup at his feet. 'The goats and I are all that remain of a prosperous land fat with innocent folk. Folk now dead, or taken in slavery, because of a—' His voice broke. He dropped his head and clenched his fists tight.

Red opened her mouth, but Bethral'd had enough. She gestured sharply. Red glared, but closed her mouth.

'Eat, Josiah.' Bethral spoke softly. 'The soup does the bowl no good.'

Josiah nodded. It took him a moment, but his hands relaxed and he picked up his bowl and took a few bites. Red scowled, but went back to her meal. All three ate in silence for a few moments, until Josiah looked up at Red. 'We'd never thought to look outside Palins. You were born in Soccia? Not Palins?'

Red's eyes narrowed. 'I'm of Soccia, so far as I know.'

'But do you know?' Josiah pressed. 'Is it possible that—'

'Possible or not, I do not know,' Red snapped again, putting her empty mug at her feet. 'It matters not.'

'And why the gloves?' Josiah asked. Bethral sucked in a breath as he continued. 'Why wear—'

'You've given of your house and food, Josiah,' Bethral interrupted him firmly. 'We thank you.'

Red had straightened her back, her hand on her dagger hilt.

Bethral continued, a warning tone in her voice. 'How can we return your gift Josiah?'

Red gave Bethral a glance, and spoke grudgingly. 'Do you have work we can do for you? A hunt for your table, perhaps?' Red lifted her chin. 'I can find game, even if I have to go back in the bog.'

'No, no. I've enough for my needs, and am pleased to share.' Josiah rose. 'You are tired. We'll talk more in the morning.' He gathered the dishes into the empty pot.

'As you wish, Josiah,' Red answered.

Bethral gave Red a questioning look as the door closed behind him. 'You were kinder than I expected with that talk of a prophecy.'

Red shrugged. 'He's a good cook. Not his fault that his wits are wandering. Pity, really.'

Bethral opened her mouth, but Red shook her head. 'The horses are rested. Best we be gone and on our way before dawn.'

FOUR

In contrast to the past days, it was perfect traveling weather. Red had found the road that the goatherder had spoken of, and they'd left without so much as waking the goats. Which was fine as far as Red was concerned. She'd have had to hurt the man if he'd tried to stop them.

Pity, though. She'd been interested until he'd shown himself insane.

But now the road was clear before them, and the sun was bright and just warm enough to be comfortable. A cool breeze was at their backs and there were no clouds to be seen.

The trees were just filling out, their tiny leaves a bright green. The forest floor was still clear of growth, and she could see back in the woods for quite a distance, removing a threat of ambush. Though the blackflies were out, they weren't thick yet. Birds flitted from every branch, making their mating calls.

It was spring, and Red was determined to enjoy the ride.

They'd have to stop and hunt soon, since the storm had left little of their supplies. But all in all, Red was feeling damned good. They'd follow this road to the nearest town, purchase what they'd need, and then follow a trade route in search of work. The road stretched out before them, as far as the eye could see.

Bethral was quiet, had been since they'd ridden clear of the devastated area. Red was used to long silences from her. Sometimes Bethral thought too much. It could be a problem, all that thinking. But not often enough that Red wanted to end their partnership.

Beast was moving well, rested and eager to get on the way. Red relaxed in the saddle, about to let her horse's walk lull her into a doze, when she realized that Bethral had stopped. She looked back, to see the blonde dismount. 'Problem?' Red called.

'A stone, I think.' Bethral was digging in her saddlebag for a pick.

Red shrugged and turned Beast back to ride to their side. Bethral pulled Steel's foot up and set to work.

Beast dropped his head to browse the grass at the road's edge. Red stretched in the saddle, taking in their surroundings. Not that there was much to see but trees and road. But the road was quality, that was certain. She studied it for a moment before speaking. 'That goatherder wasn't lying. At one time that must have been a grand place, to have a road like this leading out to the middle of nowhere.'

'I think we should help him.'

Astonished, Red swiveled in the saddle to look at Bethral. The blonde had her head down, looking at the hoof she had braced between her knees. Steel was taking full advantage, leaning his weight against Bethral. Not that Bethral minded. She just set her legs and took the load with no real problem.

'What did you say?' Red asked, certain she'd misheard.

'I think we should go back and help him,' Bethral repeated, prying the muck out of Steel's hoof.

'Your wits are gone!'

Bethral sighed, and kept working. 'Red, what lies down this road?'

Red scowled. 'An inn, with any luck. A hot meal, cold ale, and work for two sword-sellers.'

'Exactly so,' Bethral said. 'We enter a town, seek out work, risk our lives, and wield our swords for a few gold coins. We save some, spend the rest, only to do it all again in the next town.'

'So?' Red fidgeted in the saddle, which made Beast snort and shake his head.

'So?' Bethral echoed. 'What do the Twelve say about a good life, about challenging yourself?'

Red scowled. She hated it when Bethral turned priestly on her, thinking and talking in ways that made her skin itch. 'It's a good life,' Red protested. 'Hard, but good.'

'As it is,' Bethral agreed. 'But the road behind us is an uncertain one, filled with unknown paths and chances. Doesn't that tempt you? The challenge of taking a throne, based on a birthmark?'

'The challenge of staying alive, more like,' Red scoffed. 'You'd take the word of a mad goatherder? Where's the profit in that?'

'Not all profit is gold.' Bethral looked up at her with those blue eyes. 'It would be an adventure.'

'We are adventurers,' Red pointed out briskly. 'A life on the road, going wherever our swords take us. How can this not be an adventure?'

Bethral looked at Steel's hoof. 'Is there anything down this road that you haven't faced before? That you don't have the skills to deal with?'

Red raised her hand and rubbed her temple with her gloved finger, right where it was starting to throb. 'So, it's not an adventure because I'm good at what I do?'

Bethral nodded. 'A true adventure is one that takes your breath away. Where nothing is certain, where—'

'I need to find a bush.' Red dismounted, and walked off into the trees, leaving Bethral to preach to the horses. Best way to end that kind of talk. Talk that made Red all itchy, inside and out. There was nothing wrong with her life, nothing that needed changing.

People on thrones needed book learning, and their letters, and she had none. They needed to be wise and learned, and she'd none of that. Sure there was sword work, now and again, but the idea was to rule a land at peace, and how dull would that be? She shook her head. A birthmark meant nothing.

Red stomped through the woods, kicked at a clod of loam, and found a nice fallen tree to let her do her business. She sat for a moment, taking in deep breaths of spring air and admiring the greenery.

But her thoughts returned to the look in that man's brown eyes. She didn't know what drew her in that direction, but something tugged at her. Mayhap the way he'd pleaded for aid. Maybe the kiss, when he'd started to respond to her. There'd been passion there . . .

He'd been watching her spar with Bethral. She'd felt him, even from that distance. Felt his gaze, and caught him in the act, too. Red smiled at the memory. Oh, she'd felt his desire, his need . . .

She scowled, and pushed the feeling away. Why should she

care? Her caring came at a price, and one that a poor goatherder could not pay, that was certain.

She adjusted her clothing, setting her weapons as she wished, before striding back to the road. A new season awaited, with new work to be done. What more adventure could anyone ask?

Bethral was putting her hoof pick away when Red emerged from the trees. The blonde glanced at her with a questioning look. Red shrugged. 'I'll take the road I know, thank you.' She mounted Beast, then glanced down at Bethral, suddenly uncertain. 'And you?'

Bethral smiled, and pulled herself into Steel's saddle. 'Our roads are one, sword-sister. Never doubt that.'

Pleased, Red urged Beast forward. 'A real bed and cold ale will set you right, Bethral. You'll see.'

Out of the corner of her eye, Red saw Bethral shake her head and follow.

They entered the town toward evening, having made good time on the road. The place was small, but Bethral was pleased to see an open market with quite a few sellers. They'd find employment soon enough.

The people seemed wary, but friendly enough. Given what the goatherder had told them, that was to be expected. There was a wide variety of skin colors here, but that also was no surprise. Palins had been a major trade center before the troubles, bringing people from all over and beyond the seas. There were rumors that Palins had once traded with the Tribes of the Plains, but Bethral didn't put much stock in that story.

The only inn bore a sign over the entry that showed a bare foot missing the last two toes, and a mug brimming with ale. The stables were clean, and the boy in charge seemed capable. Red and Bethral took their gear with them.

'The black bites,' Bethral warned as the boy took the reins.

The lad grinned, showing missing front teeth. 'So long as he doesn't kick,' he lisped.

Red was already striding over the cobblestoned yard toward the inn. Bethral followed, just as eager for a hot meal.

'Welcome to Three Toes's Inn.' From behind a long bar, the

innkeeper, a tall black man, bald of pate and round of stomach, greeted them. 'How may I welcome you, warriors?'

Red stepped forward and slapped down a coin. 'Ale to start.'

'Well enough.' The man pulled two large mugs, and filled them from the keg behind him. Red drank deeply from hers, but Bethral picked up the mug and turned slightly to study their surroundings. The room was filled with tables, stools, and benches, with a large fireplace across from where they stood. A few men sat about, having an early drink.

A movement drew her eye back to the innkeep, who was wiping the wood of the bar and giving them a careful look. As she caught his eye, he gave her a nod, and relaxed. Bethral knew he'd been assessing them for trouble, as any smart innkeeper would. She took a sip of the cold ale, surprised by the nice nutty taste.

'That's good,' Red spoke, having drained her mug.

'I brew my own.' The man pulled her another mug. ' 'Tis the best since the troubles came upon us.'

Bethral finished hers as well. 'If your rooms are as good, we'll have comfort indeed this night.'

'Let me show you, ladies.' The man called out his intent to the kitchen, then limped toward a set of stairs. He gestured for them to follow.

'We're no ladies. I'm Red Gloves. This is Bethral.'

'I'm Three Toes.' He led them up the stairs.

'Big place,' Bethral commented.

'We did a brisk trade when things were right with the world,' Three Toes said. 'I can offer two rooms, if you wish. Or one with two beds, small but cheaper.' He pointed to a door. Red opened it and looked in. Plain, simple, with two beds and a window. A small table and one chair.

'This will do,' Red answered. 'We've two horses, as well.'

They dickered awhile, with Red paying for two nights. Three Toes offered two evening meals as part of the price, and Red was quick to accept.

Once they'd stowed their gear upstairs, they settled at a table near the fire with their suppers and another cold ale each. Three Toes's cooking was as good as his brewing, producing two large rabbit pies. They dug into the flaky crust, revealing a good bit of meat and vegetables.

The room slowly filled around them, with locals looking for their suppers, ale, and gossip. As the evening wore on, the general laughter that Bethral expected didn't appear. Men ate and talked, but there was no banter or mirth.

As strangers they drew a fair share of attention, but a few dark looks from Red had most of the men looking away. Bethral had a fair hope that they'd not have any trouble – until four lads staggered to their feet and headed their way. The boys had clearly been in their cups for longer than was best.

Two of them came to stand behind her. One leaned in, his breath heavy with ale. 'You're a lovely one.'

Bethral didn't look up. 'My thanks, but I'm not interested.'

Red shifted on her stool, moving back to give herself room. The other two had come up behind her.

'That's unkind.' One of the others spoke. 'Vel just wants a bit of company, that's all.'

The other two lads agreed, laughing loudly. Red gave them a sharp glare, but said nothing.

Bethral tried to stave off what she knew was coming. 'No offense intended. Let me buy you a round of ale, for peace's sake.'

'I'd let her, boys.' Three Toes walked by with a tray. 'You're asking for—'

'No one asked you, old man,' Vel snarled.

Three Toes shrugged and moved off. 'There's always them that's got to learn the hard way.'

Bethral looked at Red, but there was no help there. Red's eyes held a deep gleam of anticipation.

'We're looking for peace,' Vel claimed. 'A piece, that is.'

His friends laughed at his wit. One reached out and lifted a strand of Red's hair to his nose. 'You'll do, once we peel off your armor and gloves—'

Red stood, her stool going back onto the floor with a clatter. She drove her fist into the speaker's jaw. The man dropped to the floor like a felled tree.

There was a roar from Vel and his friends, but Red was moving before the shouts passed their mouths. She whacked the man next to her with her mug, and jumped on the table.

Bethral remained seated, pulling her mug closer in to protect it.

The second man was stunned, but not down, so Red clobbered him again with her mug. This time he sagged, groaning as he fell.

That left the two on Bethral's side of the table. They both reached for Red to pull her down. Bethral leaned back as Red evaded them, cackling with glee. She wielded her ale mug, striking at their hands. One made the mistake of bracing himself with his hand on the table, and Red's boot cracked hard on his fingers.

Bethral winced at the man's howls. Broken, to be sure.

That left Vel, who proved himself a fool by pulling a knife and climbing onto the table.

Bethral sighed and eased her stool back a few more inches.

A crowd had gathered round, egging the boy on as he lunged at Red with his blade. Red didn't bother to pull her dagger or sword. Bethral saw her take a better grip on her ale mug as she grinned.

Red dodged, feinting in to make the boy swing wildly in response, taking the kid's measure.

Not that it took long.

Red moved in, and dealt the boy a ringing blow to his head. The cheers of the crowd rose as the lad collapsed to the table, then to the floor.

Red took a bow, and jumped to the floor. Bethral gave her a sardonic look, but that didn't faze Red one tiny bit. 'Three Toes! I need a drink.'

Three Toes arrived promptly with two full mugs. 'Stupid fools,' he muttered as he stepped over Vel. 'Here, now, you men, drag these louts out and throw them in the street.' He placed two mugs down, and took Red's offered coin. 'My thanks for your restraint, Red Gloves.'

Red shrugged. 'He deserved a beating, not my blade. My thanks that you didn't summon the Watch.'

'Watch?' Three Toes grimaced. 'There's no Watch here, nor a lord. Folks have to fend for themselves.' He glanced over at his bar, crowded with thirsty men. 'Your pardon, warriors.'

Bethral glanced at Red as he limped away. 'No Watch?'

'Work for us, then,' Red responded, taking a drink.

Bethral shrugged. 'We'll know in the morning.'

There was no work to be had, much to Red's dismay.

It wasn't that folk didn't need protection. But there were none who could afford private mercenaries. It had taken half a day of talking to possible employers, but none would hire them.

Bethral shrugged, accepting the situation. Red had pressed the point, but had no luck. She finally accepted that they needed to look elsewhere after talking to Three Toes over the noon meal and an ale or two. He'd explained that the town of Orloss might be a better choice for them. It was on a major trade route, a three-day ride away. He was sure they'd find an employer there.

At least they could buy supplies here. The market wasn't big, but large enough to have what they needed. Dried meat, bread, and hard cheese. Some grain for the horses. Bethral found more molasses and kavage. She had the coin pouch now, bargaining for a pound of salt pork and a small sack of flour. Red waited patiently as she dickered, balancing the various packages.

Bethral walked over, well pleased with her purchase. 'Enough for three days, easy.'

Red nodded, taking the packages so that Bethral could tie the money pouch to her belt. 'We can leave in the morning. Tonight a bit of company, eh?'

'We should have gotten separate rooms, then,' Bethral said.

'Who needs a room?' Red asked with a grin. 'There's the stable, the necessary, the—'

The sound of weeping and the clink of chains made them both stop dead to stare at the sight before them.

There was a low wooden platform, with a small crowd of people before it. Lined up on the platform were men and women, most in rags that barely covered them, chained together like nothing Red had ever seen.

They stopped, stunned. Bethral spoke first, her voice a bare whisper. 'The goatherder said there was slavery.'

Red's face was grim.

A long line of chained slaves was being taken away, and it was clear that the sale was almost over as the buyers gathered to settle up and take their purchases home. The crowd was thinning quickly when one of the sellers stepped forward. 'One more, we have one more to offer today, but this one's not fit for more than feed for your dogs.'

The handlers dragged out a man in chains and dropped him to the platform. If man it was. Red had seen better corpses. Skin clung to bone, with every rib showing. The man was naked, crusted with filth, his skull shaved. Naked, that was, except for the welts, bruises, and open wounds, and the shackles tight around his wrists.

Dog food, indeed.

'Come, now. Someone bid and rid me of this piece of shit,' the seller called out. 'Not even a copper?' He bent down and tore the shackles off the slave, leaving bloody wounds at the wrist. 'Of course the copper won't buy the chains.'

Red started in surprise when Bethral's hand moved, and a single copper coin flew through the air to land at the seller's feet.

FIVE

Red's mouth fell open in shock.

'Your dogs will have bones to gnaw on, warrior!' The seller picked up the coin with a flourish.

Bethral ignored him. She just stepped to the platform and carefully pulled the slave to a sitting position. Not so much as a groan to be heard. She eased him up onto her shoulder, paused to make sure she had her balance, and started walking in the direction of the inn.

Blinking, Red watched her go, shook her head, and then ran to catch up. 'What were you thinking?' she hissed softly. Not that she needed to bother. They drew no real attention, even though Bethral had a naked, filthy man over her shoulder. In point of fact, the townspeople were averting their eyes and minding their own ways.

'I'll not leave him in their hands.' Bethral's voice was soft and somewhat breathless. For all that the slave was skin and bones, he was still a dead weight. And a stinking mess, truth be told.

Red shifted the packages in her hands as she walked alongside Bethral. 'What in the name of all of the Twelve are you going to do with him?'

'I doubt he'll last long.' Bethral kept walking steadily, but she was planting her feet carefully.

'Where are you going to take him?' Red pointed out.

'Where else? The inn. He'll die free, at least.' Bethral sucked in a deep breath and kept walking.

Red rolled her eyes. She could just imagine how Three Toes would feel about a slave dying in one of his beds. But she kept her mouth shut. Partly because Bethral didn't have the breath to talk. But also because the hairs on the back of Red's neck were standing up, and there was a tingle at the base of her spine.

Something was wrong. Very wrong. She looked around, without

36

turning her head, and saw nothing different. But suddenly the townspeople who had seemed no threat before were now setting her nerves on edge.

'You feel that?' Red asked. She made sure her lips barely moved.

Bethral gave a short nod. They were both alert and tense, sensing trouble even as they kept a steady pace.

They'd reached the cobblestone yard and the gate of the inn when a shout came from behind them.

Red dropped her burdens and spun on her heel to face the gate, sword and dagger in her hands.

The slave seller was running toward them, holding up a copper coin. 'Warriors, please.' He stopped for breath, looking warily at Red. 'No need for alarm. I made a mistake, warriors. That slave was not to be sold. Please forgive me. I'll return the purchase price, of course, or replace that one with anoth—'

Bethral was slower because of her burden, but she'd turned to face the gate as well, the slave still balanced on her shoulder. 'No,' she growled.

'A simple mistake,' the seller offered, holding out the coin again.

'He is mine, bought and paid for,' Bethral spat.

The man stepped back, taken aback by her response. Red stayed between him and Bethral, weapons at the ready. She caught movement at the door of the inn, but didn't take her eyes off the man before her.

'My master will have him back, warrior.' The seller paused, licking his lips. 'Let me keep the peace. Take back your coin.'

Three Toes emerged from the door of the inn, far enough that Red could note his presence.

'My master will insist.' The seller puffed himself up. 'He will come, with those who will aid him. He will take the slave.'

'Your master can try.' Red took a step forward, and the man fled through the gate.

Three Toes moved close, sweating heavily. 'Warriors, I can't afford this trouble. The slave master will come with his bullies. Please, I—'

'We're leaving.' Red still faced the gate. 'Now.'

'Stin!' Three Toes bellowed. The stable boy popped out of the

37

barn. 'Saddle their horses, boy. NOW.' The boy was gone that quick.

Bethral spoke. 'Our gear is—'

'I'll gather it myself.' Three Toes was already moving. 'The faster you go—' He disappeared, bellowing orders.

Red sighed. 'So much for a warm bed and a bit of company.'

'I'm not company enough?' Bethral asked.

Red snorted.

Three Toes appeared with their saddlebags and bedrolls. He was followed by one of the serving wenches, who started to gather up their purchases and stuff them in two bags. Another man ran up as well, with an old blanket and two water-skins. Judging from his apron, he had to be a cook.

'There are some salves in the sack, with bandages.' Three Toes helped stuff the items in the saddlebags. 'The skins are filled with ale, for your journey.'

Stin ran out, leading Steel. He handed the reins to Bethral and ran back into the barn.

Bethral dropped the reins. 'Stand,' she ordered Steel.

The horse stood straight and still.

'Go, girl. Get inside,' Three Toes ordered. The serving wench scurried off.

Three Toes and the cook helped take the slave from Bethral's shoulder. Red glanced back to see that they were wrapping him in the old blanket, struggling to keep him upright as Bethral mounted.

'Pah,' the cook said with a grimace. 'Stinks.'

'Poor bastard,' Three Toes muttered in agreement.

The slave showed no sign of awareness.

Once Bethral was seated, the two men lifted the bundled slave into her arms. They then strapped the bags on the horse, making sure the load was even. Three Toes hung a wineskin from her saddle.

Bethral settled the man securely in front of her. 'Is there a back gate?'

'Aye,' Three Toes grunted as he tightened a strap. 'Stin!'

The boy popped out, leading Beast, who was snorting his displeasure. 'Done!'

'Open the back gate. Go!' Three Toes ordered. The boy darted off.

'Stand, Beast.' Red commanded.

Three Toes spoke quickly, as he and the other man loaded Beast. 'Behind the stables, beyond the privies, there's a gate. It will take you out a path toward the river.'

Bethral gathered her reins, and gave him a nod.

'They're coming,' Red warned.

Three Toes and his helper ran for the inn door and slammed it shut, leaving them alone in the yard. They disappeared just as a group of slavers ran through the gate.

'That's them!' The seller was pointing them out to a large, sweating, fat man and four armed men. 'They've got him.'

'Warriors,' the fat man gasped, making a show of mopping his brow. But Red noted his eyes narrowing. 'A simple mistake,' he continued, gesturing for his men to move up on them.

'Go,' Red snapped over her shoulder at Bethral. She heard the clatter of hooves on cobblestones behind her, as she turned to meet her foe.

Bethral pulled Steel to a halt in a clearing, and listened for sound of pursuit. But all she could hear was Steel's labored breathing and the pounding of her own heart.

She'd followed a deer path deep within the woods, leaving the inn and the river behind, never once risking the road. There was pine here, enough to shelter them for a moment. Dusk was coming on. That would help even more to hide them.

Steel dropped his head, and heaved a sigh as he shifted beneath her.

'Sorry, boy,' she whispered as she patted Steel's neck. It wouldn't do to dismount. She wasn't sure she could wrestle her burden back into the saddle, and she couldn't do it quickly. Better to stay mounted until she knew for sure that they were safe.

The blanket had fallen over the slave's face as they'd ridden. A tug revealed his face. It was a long moment before she was even certain that he still breathed. There was no spare flesh on those bones, the cheekbones in stark relief, lips dry and cracked. She winced in sympathy.

'What's within you, that they pursue you so?' she whispered.

There was no response.

Bethral shook her head, not sure what impulse had come over her, to buy an abused slave. Anger — that was certain. Disgust that anyone could treat another being so, be they man or beast. Red would have her head for this.

Provided Red was still in one piece herself.

The normal sounds of the woods were returning, with the skitter of small animals and the soft cries of birds. Bethral relaxed slightly, since there didn't seem to be an immediate threat.

With one hand she held the man close, and with the other she reached for the bag that Three Toes had tied to her saddle. There were some bandages, and she pulled one clear with her free hand. It took some effort, but she managed to get the cloth wet from the wineskin.

She pressed the wet cloth to his lips, trying to at least soften the skin. It took a moment, but eventually the lips moved against the cloth, and she heard him suck at it.

'That's it,' she crooned softly. 'Let's get some ale in you.'

She kept an eye and ear to her surroundings as she wet the cloth, and let the man pull as much moisture as he could. She'd look down once in a while, then return to her vigilance.

At last, she pulled the cloth free of his mouth and the man sighed. She looked down, and found that his eyes were open, the greenest eyes she'd ever seen, green with flecks of gold.

'Can you hear me?' she asked softly. 'Who are you?'

The eyes took her in, roaming over her face. But there was little awareness to them that she could tell, and only his eyes moved.

'Sleep,' she whispered. 'You're safe, here in my arms.'

His eyes fluttered closed, and she thought the corner of his mouth turned up a bit, as if trying to smile.

Steel's ears perked up. Someone was coming.

Bethral jerked her head up, dropped the cloth, and pulled a dagger.

A barn owl call echoed through the trees.

Bethral rolled her eyes, and hooted in response. As the brush rustled, she shook her head. 'It's too early for owls to be about,' she said softly.

Red emerged into the clearing, riding Beast. 'It was supposed to be a duck.'

'You never get that right. Stick to scarlets. You can chirp like one well enough.' Bethral relaxed, seeing no wounds on her sword-sister.

'I haven't seen a scarlet since we entered that damn bog.' Red responded sourly, ducking branches as she moved Beast closer.

'Did you kill any of them?' Bethral asked.

'No,' Red said. 'I didn't want to give them a reason to pursue us. I just sliced a few, then got to Beast. We charged through them to the gate and the main road. Beast and I ran for a while, but then we circled back and picked up your trail.' Red frowned, dismounted, and picked up the wet cloth. 'But there's a mounted group on the main road, searching for us. They want him back.' She nodded toward the slave. 'How's he doing?'

Bethral looked down. 'He breathes. Not much more.' She covered the slave's face and tucked the blanket loosely around him. 'Will they follow?'

'Best to think so.' Beast snorted, and they both paused and listened. A breeze was picking up, and the leaves about them rustled. Red mounted Beast. 'You keep going. I'll muddle your back trail, and discourage any pursuit.' She looked at the darkening sky. 'The darkness will aid us, but it will be a long night.'

'Where are we headed?' Bethral asked.

Red grimaced. 'The goatherder's. Where else?'

The pounding at his door brought Josiah to his feet before he was even awake. He stood there for a moment, blinking in the faint light from the coals in the fireplace. The door trembled again, as the pounding started back up. With three steps he was there and threw open the door.

Red Gloves stood there, glaring at him.

'You came back,' he blurted.

'Not my choice.' Josiah gave way as Red shoved past him and dumped two saddlebags by the fire. Bethral was next through the door, carrying a man wrapped in a blanket. She pushed past as well, and placed the man on Josiah's bed.

41

'I'll get the rest of the gear.' Red pushed past again. 'You see to him.'

'What' – Josiah looked back to Bethral – 'what has happened?'

Bethral pulled back the blanket to reveal the man's body.

'Sweet Sovereign Sun,' Josiah cursed. 'Who—'

The frantic bleating of goats interrupted. 'Out of my way, you—' Red shouted at the top of her lungs. Josiah pulled the door open to let her in as she struggled with the parcels, and the goats, who were trying to push their way past her. Josiah kept the goats out as she stomped in with saddlebags and two sacks. He shut the door behind her. 'Who did this to him?'

'Your countrymen, goatherder, and their slavery,' Red snarled as she dropped her load by the hearth.

'No men of mine,' Josiah snapped at her. He glared at the warrior, but her gaze was on the slave. As was her anger, he realized.

'It's a wonder he still breathes.' Bethral knelt, spreading the blanket out over the bed. 'We had to ride hard to get here.'

Josiah took a step closer to the bed and sucked in a breath at the sight of the man's wounds. 'You stole a slave?'

'No.' Bethral's voice was flint against steel. 'I paid the seller his price. But he demanded the slave's return, for a refund of the price, and I refused.'

Red scowled at him. 'We are not thieves.' She went to the door. 'I'll see to the horses. We'll all sleep here this night, just in case.' She yanked on the door, then turned to Josiah and smirked. 'You might want to put on some trous, goatherder.' She pulled the door shut with a thud.

Startled, Josiah gathered up his trous and dressed hurriedly. 'Why all sleep here? There's not much room—'

'They gave chase,' Bethral said. 'We've lost them, and covered our trail, but we should stay together, just in case.'

Josiah sighed. 'Few will venture into these lands.'

'Still.' Bethral shrugged. 'Red will insist that we take no chance.' She glanced back at the man on the bed. 'I'll bathe him, at least. Get some of the filth off him.'

'I've not much in the way of medicines,' Josiah said.

Bethral cast a glance at the herbs drying among the rafters, and Josiah caught the look. 'Cooking herbs, mostly. I've some yarrow and bruise balm.'

Bethral rummaged in one of the sacks that Red had brought in. 'There's bandages here and some jars. I know how to treat battle wounds, but not enough to truly aid him.' She sighed, looking down at the man. 'We may have rescued him only to watch him die.'

'We could get some broth in him, perhaps.' Josiah reached for a bucket sitting by the hearth. 'Maybe a gruel. I'll draw some water.'

Red was watering the horses by the well when Josiah emerged from the hut. She smirked to see that he'd pulled on trous. A fine figure of a man, bare of chest and feet as he walked through the moonlight toward her. Her eyes half-closed, she imagined his body moving under her, filling her—

She turned back to her task. Maybe it wasn't such a bad thing, being forced to return here. The horses could rest up, with a good graze, if the goats would let them. She scowled at the little beasts cavorting around them, getting in her way.

Bethral could see to her slave, and maybe she could lure—

'You are the Chosen, you know.'

Red wrinkled her nose. In the rush, she'd forgotten about his madness. Why was it that all the good ones were insane? Cooled her ardor, certain sure.

She stepped back, to give him room. 'That's as may be,' she answered. 'All I care is that Bethral be allowed to do what she can for that man.'

Josiah began to pull up a full bucket of water from the well, his muscles rippling in the moonlight. 'She fears he will die.'

'She cares over much.' Red responded absently, moving through the goats, shooing them out of her way.

'And you don't?' came the challenge.

Red grabbed the horses' halters to lead them to the barn. 'We'll all sleep in your hut this night.'

'Not much room.'

Red shrugged without looking at him. 'The floor is all the bed I need.'

43

'Red!' Bethral's shout from within had them both running for the croft.

Red was first through the door. 'Bethral, what's wrong?'

Bethral was half-seated on the bed, her arm around the slave's shoulders, supporting his head, a mug in her other hand. Her face was white as she looked at them. 'His tongue's been cut out.'

SIX

'He'll die, then.' Red spoke through her clenched jaw, anger and disappointment flowing through her.

Bethral shrugged, her pain reflected in her eyes. Her blonde tresses had spilled out of her bun, and over her shoulders. 'He's so weak and wasted even broth trickled down his throat would not be enough. I fear he is too far gone for our aid.' She sighed and set the mug down on the floor. 'Why didn't they just kill him and have done?'

Red gritted her teeth against Bethral's sorrow, a pain she was helpless to remedy. 'To make him suffer.' She grated out the words.

'And to prolong the suffering,' Josiah added.

'We should not aid them.' Bethral lowered the man to the bed, and rose. She drew a ragged breath. 'He will waste away then. We should grant him mercy, sword-sister.'

'Wait,' Josiah said. 'I've a friend who might be able to help him.'

Red gave him a sharp look. 'I thought you were alone here.'

'I am.' Josiah looked out the open door. 'I'll send for her.'

'How?' Red demanded.

'I've a way,' Josiah growled. He looked at Bethral. 'If she can't heal, she can at least offer him the last rites of the Lord and the Lady.'

Red narrowed her eyes as she studied him. She'd no desire to be indebted to a madman, but if he could get help . . .

Bethral looked down at the man on the bed, pulling the blanket up to cover him. 'I'd thought to see him healed,' she said. 'But without a tongue, I don't see how it matters.'

Red tilted her head to the side and considered the prone figure. 'How long before your friend arrives?'

'There's time before dawn. If possible, she will be here within the hour.' Josiah shrugged. 'If not, then mid-afternoon.'

'It would take an hour to dig a grave, anyway,' Red mused.

Josiah sucked in a breath.

Red ignored him, and turned to her sword-sister. 'He seems to be resting easier, Bethral. I know you would follow the ways of your mother in this, but wait a bit.'

Bethral gave her a narrow look, and Red puffed out a breath impatiently. 'He's breathed this long, hasn't he? What's an hour more?'

Josiah stood and watched as Red headed back to where she'd left the horses. Once Bethral had agreed to wait for aid, they'd left her with the slave in the hut. Red would finish her tasks and fetch water. Josiah was going to send for Evie.

Had that been a glimpse of compassion he'd seen in Red as she'd looked at Bethral? For a moment he'd have sworn she'd been grateful for his offer of assistance. Odd to think a hardened mercenary would be so concerned.

Of course, once they'd stepped outside, she'd asked where she could find a spade.

Josiah shook his head, and headed toward the ruins of the old chapel. He'd taken the lantern, since his path wove through the trees where the darkness still clung. If he was lucky, he'd catch Evie before she started to prepare for the Dawn Greeting.

There was soft bleating behind him, and then the goats ran up around him, scampering to keep pace. He reached down to scratch Snowdrop's ears. She rubbed against his leg, then danced away, her white coat glowing in the soft light of the lantern.

He took the path as quickly as he dared, and entered the ruined shrine. Not much left, except the back wall. It stood with its stylized sun design, a silent witness to the destruction all around.

The goats pressed through with him, their hooves clattering on the rough stone floor. He kept it swept clean, except for the rough pile of stones in the center. He knelt, set down the lantern, and piled the stones in the pattern that meant he needed aid. Evie usually checked on him before the Dawn Greeting. With any luck . . .

Josiah left the lantern and retreated back up the path until the doorway was just visible in the moonlight. Far enough that it wouldn't cause Evie a problem, yet close enough that he'd see her when she stepped out.

The goats explored around him, sniffing at the plants. He seated himself on the ground, leaned back against a tree, and looked up at the night sky. It would be no bad thing if Red were indebted to him. Maybe he could get her to understand what that birthmark meant, who she really was.

He'd despaired when he'd found them gone, and cursed himself for a fool. There'd been other ways to convince her, maybe, but he'd fumbled it badly. The empty foaling room had brought his hopes crashing down around him. But they'd returned, thank the Lord of Light and the Lady of Laughter. Bethral's impulse had brought Red back to him; he'd not lose this chance again.

How bad things must be, outside. What was happening, that slaves were abused so? He'd known that people were being bought and sold – Evie had told him – but this? Josiah frowned, curious. He'd ask Evie, later. Maybe she was hiding the truth from him.

Dapple bleated, and trotted toward the shrine. The others followed, and Josiah stood, brushing off his pants.

'Josiah?' A soft voice called, and the light of his lantern moved toward the doorway. He smiled as Evie stepped out, reaching to pet the goats. She was dressed in all her finery, with a white robe edged in gold, a heavy cloak with a large hood, and white gloves. The perfect portrait of a Lady High Priestess of the Lord of Light and Lady of Laughter.

'Josiah,' she called again, lifting the lantern. Not that it helped all that much, with her being a head shorter than himself. Josiah stifled a chuckle. Evie was a bit sensitive about her height.

'Here,' he answered, and started to walk toward her.

'What aid do you need, cousin?' Evie asked, worried. 'Are you hurt?'

'It's not for me,' he explained as he swept her into a quick hug. 'Can you come?'

'I've an hour before services. Who's injured, then?' Evie started down the path.

Josiah took her hand to aid her, not sure how he was going to explain. 'It's a long story, Evie.'

She looked at him with concern, but said no more. It was only when they drew close to the hut that she spoke. 'Is that someone by the barn?'

Josiah nodded, as Red headed toward them. 'Yes. I let them bed down in the foaling room.'

Evie stopped dead. 'You went into the barn?'

Josiah ignored that. 'Red,' he called out, 'help is here.'

As Red walked closer, her eyes widened as she took in Evie's finery. 'Where did she come from?' she blurted out.

'This is Lady High Priestess Evelyn, of the Church of the Gods of Palins.' Josiah said. 'Evie, this is Red. She's—'

Red gave him a grim look, and Josiah changed his mind about mentioning the birthmark. 'She's a warrior—'

'She's not hurt,' Evie said impatiently. 'Who is?'

Josiah pushed open the door. The heat of the room washed over them, as did the light of the fire. Evie ducked in under Josiah's arm, and made for the bed as Bethral stared at her in shock.

Once again, Evie stopped dead, staring at the man on the bed. 'Flame of the Sun,' she breathed out. 'Who did this?'

'Slavers,' Bethral responded, recovering her poise.

'This is Bethral,' Josiah said from the doorway.

Evie threw back her hood, revealing her thick white hair pulled back in a perfect braid. She started to pull off her gloves, revealing her small hands and the silver ring that she always wore. 'Josiah, you need to leave.'

He'd expected that. She'd want to get to work as quickly as she could. 'Call out if you need anything, Evie.' Josiah stepped past Red, who looked confused, and went back outside.

Evelyn wasted no time. The poor man needed her help. She cast a quick spell, and set a small ball of light hanging above the bed. It bathed the room in daylight, and let her see the man better.

The two women were startled, but Evelyn didn't have time for their surprise. 'What happened to him?' she asked the warrior next to the bed as she removed her heavy white gloves, careful not to catch them on her ring.

'What hasn't?' the blonde woman answered sadly. 'We're not

sure. He hasn't spoken since we rescued him. We don't know so much as his name.'

'When was that?' Evie asked. She swept off her cloak, folded it, and put it at the end of the bed.

'Yesterday, midafternoon,' the one named Red answered.

Evie frowned. There was more to this story, that was clear. But she'd work to do and not much time to do it. 'Has he moved his bowels? His bladder?'

'No,' the blonde responded. 'He opened his eyes once, but I can't claim he was sensible. He sucked a bit of ale from a cloth, but his tongue has been cut out, Lady.' The woman sighed. 'I do not know what else has been done to him.'

'I will.' Evie sat on the edge of the bed, and reached over to touch the man gently on the forehead. She closed her eyes and whispered a soft prayer.

Knowledge flooded through her, and she set her lips tight against it. Her own body ached in sympathy, but that was the price one paid for this spell. She took a breath and probed further, wanting to know all that she could.

She opened her eyes and looked at the two younger women. Bethral was staring at her with a worried look, but Red was regarding the light ball as if it might bite her. 'His suffering started about a year ago,' she told them. 'Whipped and beaten daily, combined with starvation and a lack of water.'

'Rape?' Red asked.

'I saw no sign,' Bethral offered.

'Everything but that,' Evie said as she turned the man's wrist to study the wound there. 'His body is failing within, beyond the marks that you see.'

'These medicines can't help, then?' Bethral showed her the sack just under the bed.

Evie looked over the contents, smelling a few of the salves. 'Save these for later. Right now, we need to make him comfortable. Clean and warm is a good beginning. You must also try to get him to drink.'

'He can't swallow.' Red reminded her.

'He can,' Evie said. 'It's just very difficult, especially since he is unconscious. Trickle it down the inside of his mouth, and stroke his throat with your fingers. You will feel it when he swallows. Go slow.'

'Why bother?' Red asked, looking away at the floor. 'He's as good as dead.'

'No, he is not,' Evie insisted.

Red and Bethral both gave her surprised looks. Evie just smiled. 'He's not dead yet. We will see what the Lord and the Lady will for him.' They still looked puzzled. 'You've never seen a priestess heal?'

When they shook their heads, she sighed. 'It's rare enough, these days.' Evie knelt by the bed. She stretched out her arms, holding her hands a few inches over the man's belly. 'I'll—'

'Water,' Red blurted out. 'We need more water.' She snatched up an empty bucket, and bolted out the door.

Evie looked at Bethral, who shrugged. 'Gods make Red nervous.'

Evie arched an eyebrow, but didn't waste words. She turned back to her patient and spread her hands over him. The white star sapphire in her ring glittered in the light, the star gleaming on the stone. She closed her eyes and began to pray.

Josiah sharpened the blade of his axe as he waited a good distance from the hut. He'd seen Red bolt out the door, but she'd taken herself off to the barn, and looked to be in no mood to talk.

That suited him as well.

He concentrated on his task, working the blade with a stone. He'd need to cut more wood if they were going to keep the poor wretch warm enough.

The goats lay about him, making soft noises as they dozed. The sun was a hint on the horizon when the door opened and Evie stepped out. Josiah stood, relieved at the sight of her tired smile.

She held the lantern, and he met her on the path. 'Will he live?'

She grimaced then, putting her free hand up to smooth her hair. 'That's in the hands of the Lord and the Lady, Josiah. I think I disappointed Bethral. She seemed to expect him to be instantly healed and spring out of the bed.' Evie looked at the morning sky. 'I am going to be late.'

Josiah stepped ahead of her, heading toward the shrine. 'Did you explain?'

Her voice floated to him from behind. 'I did. All the healing went deep, so he looks much the same as he did. Bethral is going to clean him, and try to get some broth or gruel into him. I'll return, after the services and a good nap. I might bring help.'

'Is that necessary?' Josiah asked carefully.

'Josiah' – Evie was using her 'priestly' voice – 'you know that it is. The Lord of Light and the Lady of Laughter give us the gift of their magic, but it has to flow through me. If I have another here, I can channel more into the patient, without exhausting myself.'

'You will take care,' Josiah stated. 'You will—'

'I will take every precaution.' Evie's voice softened. 'Figure that I will return about midafternoon.'

They had reached the point where they could see the shrine. Josiah stopped, and looked down into her blue eyes. 'Evie, how is it that a slave can be abused so? Isn't the Church doing anything? Are the Regent and Elan—' his voice cracked, and he had to stop to clear his throat.

Evie looked up, and studied his face. 'The Church supports the Regent, Josiah. And the Regent and his supporters do nothing to protect the people.' She tilted her head to the side. 'That's the first time you've even seemed curious about what has happened in Edenrich.'

Josiah looked away.

'So tell me, my "little cousin," how is it that I find you with two young, comely women and a beaten and abused man?'

He turned back to look at her, his mouth open but without any words to explain. It was the glint of humor in her eye that saved him. Josiah relaxed. '"Little" cousin? You have only a year on me, Evie.'

Evie looked up into his eyes and gave him her rare impish grin. 'To think I towered over you when we were smaller.'

Josiah sighed. 'That was a long time ago, Evie.'

Her eyes softened, and she reached out her hand to cup his cheek. She raised an eyebrow, silently repeating her question.

He shrugged, and looked at her feet. 'It's a long story, Evie.'

She puffed out a breath and lowered her hand. 'To be certain. And it would be, when you know that I must not be late for services.' She lifted the lantern, and walked past him toward the shrine. 'But I will want the full tale later, when I return.'

He watched as she walked within the shrine, and noted that the shadows moved as she placed the lantern on the floor. He retreated down the path.

The goats bleated as they came to stand around him.

'She's gone,' Josiah said softly, 'but she will be back.'

They walked down together, and entered the ruins. The area was empty, except for the lantern on the floor.

Josiah lifted the lantern. But before he turned to leave, the light caught the stylized sun on the back wall, and it refracted the light all about, banishing the shadows around him.

Red met him at the door of the hut. Josiah suspected that she waited for him. 'Well,' she demanded, 'did it work?'

He pushed open the door.

Bethral was half-seated on the bed, her arm around the slave's shoulders, supporting his head, a mug in her other hand. Her smile was bright as she looked at them. 'He swallowed.'

Red stepped in behind Josiah. 'He doesn't look any better,' she said. 'Those wounds are still open.'

'Evie said the magic went deep within, where it was needed most,' Josiah explained.

Bethral nodded. 'I'm to get as much liquid in him as I can. She wants him to void his bladder.'

'And soil the bed, no doubt.' Red wrinkled her nose. 'I'd have thought she'd have done more.'

'There are limits,' Josiah growled. 'She will be back later today. I suggest we eat, and take turns seeing to him.'

'We should sleep as well,' Red pointed out. 'We're all tired. We can take watches and share in the burden. There still might be pursuit. I'll watch first.'

'Bethral, get some sleep, I'll sit with him for a while.' Josiah offered.

Bethral smiled and nodded. She stood and stretched. 'I'll curl up here, on my bedroll. In case you need me.'

'Won't that be cozy?' Red snorted, and made for the door. 'Guess I'd better go fill in that grave, then.'

Her words were harsh, but Josiah didn't miss the obvious relief in her eyes just before she closed the door.

SEVEN

'Why did I let you talk me into this, Evelyn?'

Red's lips narrowed as she watched Evie lead a blindfolded man out of the ruined shrine. Josiah had told her to wait here for her, and that she would be bringing help. But Red didn't like the man's looks, or his tone of voice. He was tall, towering over Evie, with long black hair that flowed down his back. He was dressed as a priest of Palins, but his voice was—

'We are only supposed to heal with the approval of the Church.' The man spoke again as he stumbled on the doorsill. 'Are you even being paid?'

Whiny. Definitely whiny.

Evie reached out to steady the man, and took his arm. 'Dominic, you know they can't all afford to pay.'

The man recovered his balance and looked damned arrogant while he was doing it. Red curled her lip.

'Some commoner, then,' Dominic sniffed as Evie drew him down the path. 'Really, Evelyn, you go off to the worst hovel at the first suggestion of a need. All some lowlife has to do is snivel that he is ill, and off you go, no questions asked, no permissions granted.'

Evie looked apologetically at Red as they neared. 'Dominic, you know that is not—'

'Who is there?' Dominic stiffened, sensing Red's presence.

'A lowlife,' Red spat. 'With a blade.'

Dominic reached for his blindfold, but Evie stayed his hand. 'Stop that,' she scolded. 'It's your own fault for being rude. She isn't going to hurt you.'

Red snorted.

Dominic snorted right back. 'It is not rude to speak the truth. You may be one of Evelyn's lost lambs, but you should respect her office. One of the lesser priests, or a lay healer with herbs and ointments, would certainly serve your needs. Certainly not the most powerful priestess in the—'

'Dominic!' Evie tugged on his arm, and got him moving.

Red followed. The man continued his chiding as they reached the croft. His personality did not improve with his speech, as far as Red was concerned. He cursed every root and rock on the path, as if it was a personal affront.

Evie pushed the door open, and Red followed right behind the man. She wasn't leaving him alone with Bethral and their 'lost lamb' for a minute. She crowded in behind, and shut the door firmly.

Dominic was tall enough that the dried herbs brushed his face. 'What—'

'You can take off the blindfold now,' Evie said. She reached up to remove it for Dominic, at the same time he reached up. Their hands met briefly, and Red saw that Dominic's hand lingered on Evie's for a moment longer than necessary.

Then Dominic got a good look at his surroundings. 'Oh, for the love of the Sun!' He gave Bethral a disdainful glance and then looked down at the bed. 'Evelyn, what are you thinking? A slave?'

'How do you know that?' Bethral asked, her hand on her sword hilt.

'Please,' Dominic glared at her. 'Those wounds were caused by manacles, and those are clearly whip marks. Any fool can see that this man is a slave.'

'Dominic' – Evie placed her hand on his arm – 'this man is suffering and needs our help. His tongue has been cut out.'

'Really?' That seemed to give Dominic pause. He reached out with long, delicate fingers and touched the man's chin, turning his face toward the light. He frowned slightly, and Red saw something pass over his face.

'What is it?' she asked.

'He seems familiar,' Dominic answered slowly. 'What color are his eyes?'

'Brown,' Bethral answered. 'He's opened them only once.'

Dominic pulled his hand back quickly. 'Not the man I thought.' He looked at Evie impatiently. 'I suppose you are determined to do this.'

She smiled at him gently. 'I am.'

Dominic slowly smiled back at her, and shook his head. 'Well, then, we will see it done.' His black hair shifted, and the tips of his ears were visible.

'You're an elf,' Red blurted out.

'Half-elven.' Dominic gave her a disdainful look, sweeping her from head to toe. 'Not that it is any business of yours. We need some room for our task. Do you mind leaving?'

'Actually, I do.' Red replied. But she did press herself back against the door, giving them more room.

Evie knelt by the bedside and spread her hands over the slave. Dominic took one look at the rough planking, curled his lip, and moved to stand at her side. He placed one hand on Evie's shoulder and extended his other hand, spreading those thin fingers wide.

They both began to pray, their voices low. 'Hail, gracious Lord of the Sun and Sky, Giver of Light and Granter of Health, we ask . . .'

Red's stomach flipped as their hands began to glow. In her experience, gods were beings best left to their own devices. Beseeching aid was rarely done in Soccia, and was not without its consequences.

The voices continued, and the glow began to drift down from their hands, encasing the slave in light. Bethral was intent on the man on the bed, watching him like a hawk, probably for signs that the magic was working. But Red couldn't see any evidence that it was, and certain sure the slave never once reacted with so much as a twitch.

They began to repeat the prayer, and Red took to counting her breaths. There was no change in their voices, but the outstretched hands were starting to tremble.

Finally, Evie's shoulders slumped slightly. Dominic's voice grew stronger, and the words of the prayer changed, thanking for aid instead of begging.

The glow faded. Dominic dropped his hand and drew a deep breath. He squeezed Evie's shoulder, and she looked up with a tired smile. His sharp features softened as he gazed down at her and offered his hand. 'Well enough, Lady High Priestess?'

'Very well.' She chuckled as she accepted his help to get to her feet.

'Then let us return.' Dominic picked up the blindfold from the rough table, and shook it out. 'I'll need to bathe and sleep before I can preside over the sunset service.' He handed the blindfold to Evie.

'I'll see you back,' Evie said gently. 'But I've some advice to give before I go, and I want to read my patient and see what the magic has done.'

Dominic grimaced, then shrugged. He lowered his head so that she could wrap the blindfold about his eyes. 'As you see fit. But do not waste too much of your strength here.'

Red fumed silently as Evie wrapped the cloth tight, and tied it. A better fit around the man's neck, and twice as tight would work just fine, as far as she was concerned. But she said nothing. She just stepped clear of the door, jostled Dominic hard in her effort to pull the door open, and then silently followed them to the shrine.

Dominic complained the entire way, even as he held on to Evie and leaned against her for support. Red didn't stop at the designated spot; she followed them right up to the doorway. Evie shook her head, but didn't object. She just led Dominic to face the back wall.

'Make sure you are in good time for the service,' Dominic scolded.

Evie gestured at the wall and spoke three sharp words. Red watched in amazement as the wall shimmered before them, like a series of long white curtains moving in a breeze. There was a sound as well, of wind chimes, or maybe a waterfall.

'Thank you, Dominic, for your help.'

Dominic's hand reached out slowly until his fingers found Evie's cheek. 'Only for you, bright one. Don't linger here.' Without removing the blindfold, he walked between the curtains and disappeared.

Evie waved her hand, and the curtains faded away. She turned to Red with an impish smile. 'What he doesn't know is that I traded off my duties for the rest of this day and tomorrow.' She walked over to the corner of the back wall.

'What were those curtains?' Red asked. 'A priestly thing?'

Evie fetched a parcel and a good-sized basket from the shadows. 'Oh, no. My father was a battle mage, and he taught me a thing or two about portals.' She swept past Red as she headed to the doorway. 'Let's get back. I want to change, and I've brought enough for a decent meal for all of us.' She looked at Red over her shoulder. 'Go fetch Josiah from wherever he's hidden himself. Tell him it's time for our talk.'

Red watched the goats cavorting around the horses as she walked toward the barn. The horses paid them no mind as they grazed, completely ignoring their antics. The goats were chasing each other around the horses' legs, butting each other and having a great time.

She walked past the entrance of the barn. Josiah had said that he would be on the far side, well out of sight of the croft. She heard him before she saw him, the sound of woodchopping echoing against the barn.

Josiah had taken off his tunic. Red stopped to admire the ripple of the muscles of his back as he raised the axe and brought it down to cut through the piece of wood on the block. He was a fine-looking man, especially from the back. Nice long torso that narrowed where his trous clung to his waist. Red let her gaze drop, and her mouth curled in appreciation. Certain sure there was nothing wrong with his—

'They're gone?' Josiah asked, throwing the smaller pieces of wood into a pile, and bringing another to the block.

'Yes.' Red carefully moved closer, well off to the side, and sat on a convenient log. 'The Priestess says it's time for your talk. She sent me to fetch you.'

Josiah grimaced. 'Who'd she bring with her?'

It was Red's turn to make a face. 'An arrogant mucker named Dominic.'

'Arrogant, but skilled,' Josiah said. He gave her a quick grin. 'I'd wager he complained the entire time.'

'He did.' Red watched as he split another piece of wood. 'Seems to think we're beneath him.'

'That would be Dominic.'

'Bethral doesn't trust him,' Red said. 'Not sure I do, either.'

Josiah paused in his work. 'Dominic is not my favorite person, but I've never known him to be less than honest. I don't think his arrogance would allow him to lie.'

'There aren't many elves in Soccia,' Red observed.

'Nor in Palins,' Josiah said. 'Dominic would be the first to tell you that he's half-elven. The pure-blood elves rarely mix with humans.'

Red looked up, studying the man before her. Josiah's breathing was evening out, and there was the faintest sheen of sweat on his chest. She gave him a half-smile. 'He's also in love with your Evie.'

Josiah snorted. 'I doubt that. Evie is high-born, but not high enough for Dominic.'

'Oh, I don't know.' Red stood, and walked toward Josiah, putting a bit more sway in her hips than was absolutely necessary. 'I can tell when a man is interested in a woman.' She moved as close as she could without actually touching Josiah. 'It's in his eyes, in the sound of his voice.' She lowered her voice, and half closed her eyes. 'It's in the way his body moves.'

Josiah drew in a deep breath.

'But it's there, all the same. The need to touch.' She leaned in close, bringing her mouth to his, tilting her head just so. 'To kiss.' She closed her eyes in anticipation.

'Red . . .' Josiah's voice was a low rumble. His breath caressed her cheek.

'Yes?' Red drew in the scent of his warm, male body, and opened her mouth for—

'I want to tell Evie about your birthmark. She needs to know.'

Red snapped her eyes open and glared at Josiah. 'No,' she snapped. 'What business is that of hers?'

Josiah turned away and reached for his tunic. He pulled it on silently, his back to her.

Red planted her hands on her hips. 'I am in your debt, Josiah, for the aid that you and Evie have given Bethral. You have my gratitude and thanks for that.'

She took a step closer and ran her hands over those broad shoulders. 'I'd be more than willing to express my thanks in a pleasurable way, one we'd both enjoy. What say you to a bit of bed fun, eh? And call the debt even?'

Josiah turned so that her hands rested on his chest. 'No.'

She snatched her hands back as if burned.

'As lovely and desirable as you are, I am not releasing you.

Come.' Josiah strode off, leaving her standing there with her mouth open. 'They will be waiting.'

Red watched as he walked toward the hut, then closed her mouth with a snap. Even from behind, she could tell that Josiah was pleased with himself.

She should be furious that he'd seen through her, but part of her couldn't help but grin. Oh, she'd concede this little battle, but not the war. She was a mercenary, after all.

Red straightened her face, and followed. Josiah had much to learn about mercenaries and their ways.

And she'd be the one to teach him.

Bethral heard Red and Josiah approach just as the mage light over the bed winked out.

'Bother,' Evie drew back from her examination of the slave. 'That man never remembers.'

The door opened, and Josiah stepped in, an irritated-looking Red on his heels. He looked at Evie and stopped. 'I'm sorry, Evie. Did I—'

Evie smiled at him. 'You did, but never mind that. We have good news! He pissed!'

Red looked over Josiah's shoulder and crinkled her nose in disgust. 'I'll see to the horses while you celebrate.' She vanished in the next moment.

'There's a few old horse blankets in the back stalls,' Josiah called after her. 'Fetch a few, would you?'

'I'm sorry, Josiah.' Evie was still smiling as she finished cleaning the patient. Bethral was fairly certain she had the same smile on her own face, as well.

Josiah shrugged. 'It's just straw and ticking, Evie. It's no great matter.'

Evie flashed him a grateful look. 'Lift him for us, and we'll strip the bedding.'

It took some maneuvering in the cramped space, but Josiah was able to scoop the man up in his arms, and let the women strip the bed.

'Here's a blanket we can use,' Bethral pulled one from her bedroll.

They carefully wrapped the man in the blanket and laid him

on the woven bed ropes. Josiah dragged out the sodden mattress just in time to thrust it into Red's arms when she opened the door. He grabbed the old horse blankets and closed the door quickly as Red staggered off, cursing under her breath.

He turned back to Evie and Bethral with a smile on his face. Now Bethral lifted the man, and Evie and Josiah made up the bed, using the blankets to form a mattress of sorts.

'That will do for now,' Evie announced with satisfaction in her voice. 'He's doing very well.' She gently tipped the man's head back and opened his mouth to look within. 'It's too soon to tell, but I will heal him again before we sleep this night. And we will see.'

'If you're staying, Lady, then I need to warn you.' Bethral spoke urgently, aware that her sword-sister would return at any moment. 'I need to warn you both about Red's gloves.'

EIGHT

'Don't ask about the gloves. Don't refer to them. Don't talk about them. Ever.' Bethral was deadly serious. 'And never try to remove them.'

Josiah could hardly believe his ears. 'She never takes them off?' he asked softly.

'I've never seen them off,' Bethral growled. 'I know why she wears them, and grim was the day that I learned her reasons. I'm thrice oath-bound never to tell a living soul.'

Evie frowned. 'But—'

'No,' Bethral snapped. 'You've been warned. Never surprise her. If you think she has taken them off, don't go near her.' She shot Josiah a look. 'Whether at work, or at play.'

Evie took a deep breath, but Bethral cut her off. 'If you see her without the gloves, run. Run away. Call my name and keep running.'

'How long?' Josiah asked.

'Forever,' Bethral responded. 'I can slow her down but I can't stop her, unless I kill her. And I won't do that.'

'She'd hunt us down?' Josiah pressed.

'How do you think we ended up in the bog?' Bethral asked.

Josiah paused at that, and looked at Evie, who gave him a sardonic look. 'We all have secrets, Josiah. Don't we?'

Josiah looked away.

The door opened, and Red poked her head in and sniffed. 'All clean now?' She looked at them all with her mouth quirked up a bit in the corner. 'Then how's about some food?'

'What?' the High Priestess sputtered, spilling her tea.

Red belched with her mouth closed, and stretched her feet toward the fire, pleased with her full belly and the warmth. She'd claimed the floor as her seat, so that she could stretch out in the small hut.

Bethral was perched on the side of the bed, sopping up the last of the juices with a slice of bread. She glanced toward Red, but said nothing.

Josiah's voice was a soft rumble, but Red yawned and ignored him. Certain sure the 'Chosen' nonsense was going to start. She closed her eyes and yawned again, hoping that it wouldn't take too long. The beds were made up in the barn, and she planned—

'Show me,' Evelyn demanded.

'Eh?' Red opened one eye to look at the priestess, perched on the only chair, right by the hearth. Josiah was sitting on the floor on the other side of the hearth. The hovel hadn't been built for more than one, that was sure.

'Show me the mark,' Evelyn insisted, putting her bowl down at her feet.

Red rose to her feet, casting a glance back at Josiah. She tugged at her tunic, and raised it over her breasts without a word.

Evelyn leaned forward, licked her thumb, and rubbed it over the mark, hard.

'Hey!' Red took a step back, and jerked her tunic down.

Evelyn was looking at Josiah with eyes open wide. 'It's real, Josiah.' Her voice trembled as she raised her fingers to cover her mouth. 'She's . . .'

'I think so,' Josiah responded softly.

Evelyn raised her face and closed her eyes. 'Thanks be to Thee, Gracious and Glorious Lord of Light, God of the Sun, Thou who are the best and the brightest, for sending the answer to my prayers.' Tears were forming in the corners of Evelyn's eyes.

Red looked at Bethral, who shrugged. Red gave her a scowl, then turned back to Evelyn. 'Lady High—'

Evelyn moved her hand, and turned it palm-out to face Red. 'For five years I have worked slowly, patiently, to build support for the day the Chosen would claim the throne.' The tears streaked down her cheeks, but her bright eyes were focused on Red alone. The firelight danced in her white hair, turning it into a crown of light around her head. 'I'd thought it would be years before we'd be in a position to take action. But you stand before me, the Chosen.'

'I doubt that, Lady—' Red answered.

But the pale blue eyes of the High Priestess had sharpened, and seemed to stab her like a blade. 'Who are you? Where did you come from?'

Red sighed, and settled back to the floor. 'I'm a mercenary,' she said patiently. 'From Soccia. Trained in the ways of war and the blade. I know no more.'

The priestess leaned forward, intent. 'Your parents? Who were they?'

Red's anger rose at that and she scowled at the woman, but Bethral jumped in. 'Does it matter, Lady High Priestess?'

Evelyn settled back, still studying Red. She looked puzzled and confused. 'How is this possible, Josiah?' Evelyn asked.

'I don't know, Evie,' Josiah answered softly.

'I've searched for so long . . .' Evelyn was looking at Red with faraway eyes. 'And every time, what did they throw in my face?' Her eyes sharpened their focus. 'Now here you stand. The one who will bring us the support we need.' Evelyn leaned forward. 'Do you know what that means?' she asked.

'No.' Red crossed her arms over her chest. 'No, I can't say as I do.'

'You know of the death of our King, and his heir? Of the Council of the High Barons that was called?' Evelyn asked.

'I know of that,' Red answered.

'Once the High Barons fell to fighting, there was naught but chaos in the land. Iitrus, a merchant of Edenrich, approached the Church of Palins, and with the support of the Archbishop, he managed to be appointed as Regent. But the High Barons remained independent and stubborn, unwilling to swear fealty to him or allow him to take the throne.' Evelyn drew a breath. 'If the Chosen appears at the head of an army, with the support of four of the High Barons, the capital will fall, and the throne can be reclaimed.'

Bethral, felt a need to speak at that point. 'Easy enough to say,' she pointed out. 'But not so easily done.'

'I've been working to build that support, quietly and carefully,'

Evelyn said. 'We need only four of the High Barons to have enough support to win through. Given proof of a Chosen, and a warrior in the bargain, I am fairly certain that Summerford, Penature, and Wyethe will support us.'

'You said four,' Bethral responded. Red was staring at the fire with a look of polite boredom, but Bethral could tell that she was interested, and listening.

'That will give us four,' Evelyn answered. 'After all, we have Josiah.'

'We do, do we?' Red straightened to look the goatherder in the eye, arching an eyebrow.

Evelyn blinked, shooting Josiah a quick look. 'Of course. Hasn't Josiah told . . .' her voice trailed off for a moment as Josiah looked at the floor. 'I guess not.' She cleared her throat. 'Josiah is the fourth. Lord Josiah, High Baron of Athelbryght.'

Bethral lifted her eyebrows at that statement.

'Oh?' Red asked, drawing the word out slowly. 'What kind of Baron herds goats?'

Josiah stood. He pushed past Red, and left the hovel.

Evelyn sucked in a breath. 'The kind of High Baron whose lands were attacked and destroyed,' she answered sharply. 'His people killed or taken, his lands decimated, his herds slaughtered, his vineyards wiped out, his crops burned. A High Baron who cared deeply for the land and his people.'

'So . . .' Red stood slowly, and stared at Evelyn. 'Your fourth High Baron is one with no people or army, a land in ruins, a hut, and five goats to his name. Pardon me if I am not impressed.' She turned, and stared at the door. 'I'll just have a word with yon High Baron.' Red moved toward the door, and Bethral knew that look. Red was on the scent of prey.

As the door shut Evelyn turned to her, a question in her eyes.

Bethral shrugged. There wasn't much to say, and no point in speaking.

Evelyn looked back at the door, and sighed. 'Well, then, let's see what more we can do for your "purchase," eh? Where is that salve?'

As the priestess turned away, Bethral glanced over at the bed, and found two green eyes open and staring.

They were as green as new leaves, unfocused and confused. She drew a breath to speak, but her voice froze in her throat. Those eyes suddenly . . . focused.

Focused on her, pierced her. She shivered, a chill running over her skin as if the man had seen her soul and beyond. But as quickly as it came, it vanished, and the eyes grew clouded.

They drifted shut as Evelyn turned. 'What's wrong?'

Bethral swallowed before she answered. 'His eyes were open for a moment.' She reached out to touch the man's hand, but there was no further response. 'Do you think . . .'

Evelyn handed her a jar with a smile. 'With the blessing of the Lord and Lady anything is possible, Bethral.'

The rough stones of the well caught at the fabric of Josiah's trous as he leaned against it. The goats had run up to mill at his feet, bleating softly. He sat watching the sunset, and waited.

He didn't have to wait long. Studying his shoes, he heard the door open, and her footsteps on the path. The goats shifted, and her boots came into sight, stopping right in front of him. If he looked at her, he'd no doubt she'd be standing there, hands on hips, glaring at him.

'Well?' she demanded.

Josiah steeled himself and looked into her eyes, surprised to find no anger there. Instead she looked serious and curious, and . . . understanding.

He looked away and swallowed hard.

Red made no sound or movement. As if she would wait for hours, patient but unrelenting.

'Behold Athelbryght.' Despite his best intention, Josiah's voice cracked. He cleared his throat and plowed on. 'Once a fair land, fat and prosperous. Our crops were plentiful, our livestock and our people were hale and hearty, and our wine caused bards to weep.'

Red moved to sit next to him on the well. She didn't say anything, but he felt the warmth of her body through his tunic.

'When Father died, I inherited the Barony. Mother grieved so for him that I knew she needed something to keep her going. She loved the Court life, and the weaving of political intrigue, but I preferred the land and its people.' Josiah sighed. 'Mother went to

Court, to represent our interests. I stayed home, and between us we protected our land and our people.

'But then Everard, Rosalyn, and Hugh died under mysterious circumstances, and all hell broke loose. The Council was convened and a Regent named. Mother felt my presence was necessary. But it was no use. The arguments continued, hot and furious, until I grew uneasy. It seemed to me that certain members were stalling, trying to keep the High Barons arguing.

'So I returned here' – he closed his eyes – 'and stepped into a nightmare.'

Against his eyelids, he saw it again: the flames of the manor house, the dead tossed about like broken dolls, the screams as warriors attacked farm folk. 'They—' His voice cracked again, and he dropped his head to his chest, squeezing back the pain.

Red waited.

'I tried to rally the few that lived, and they tried to reach my side. We fought, but with no real skill. Our attackers were experienced and ruthless. They cut through us like a scythe through wheat. I fought, as best I could, but I was no warrior. I took a blow to the head. I remember warm blood flowing into my eyes, and running into the barn . . .'

Red said nothing.

'I awoke in Evie's arms, sprawled in the mud of the yard, damaged in ways I hadn't known possible. To find five goats and the rest in ruins. To learn of my Mother's death, to see the remains of Athelbryght. All dead, all burned, everything blackened, devastated, gone . . .'

His breath caught in his chest, which felt like it was being crushed. Two quick breaths helped control the pain and the horror that threatened to overwhelm him.

Red was still silent, still waiting. The goats were close, pressed against his legs and the wall of the well.

Licking his dry lips, he tried to relax, tried to let the pain go, but—

Gentle fingers touched his chin. He started, surprised, but the soft pressure made him turn his head as he opened his eyes.

Red's eyes held compassion and something more. But he didn't have time for further thought as she moved closer and kissed him.

Josiah sucked in a breath just as Red's mouth covered his. Her lips were warm and firm, and his eyes closed instinctively as that warmth moved over his body.

The wonder increased when she didn't pull back. He felt her fingers cup the back of his head, and slide into his hair. The kiss strengthened and went on, reassuring, comforting—

Without another thought, he wrapped his arms around her and crushed her close. All his pain and his sorrow washed away in the desire for her heat and joy in living. For one bright moment, he dared feel, dared desire this warrior woman. There was no struggle, no resistance. She just melted into him, humming her appreciation into his mouth. It could have gone on forever, as far as he knew, but he broke away at last, terrified at the brief glimpse of hope.

He sat there, breathing hard, shaken to his core. He risked a glance at Red.

The side of her mouth was quirked up. She seemed somehow oddly satisfied. But she was breathing hard as well, and he felt a brief joy at the idea that he could rouse her with his kiss. But then it all came crashing down on him, and he turned away in despair. He had opened his mouth to offer an apology when she suddenly stood up.

He looked up as she took a step forward and pushed through the goats. He half expected another invitation to her bed. May the Lord of the Sun forgive him, but he wouldn't decline it again.

But she just looked back over her shoulder. 'I need more information.' With that, she turned away and walked back to the hovel.

Josiah stood for a moment, then followed, entering just in time to hear Red address Evie. 'How's your patient doing?'

Evie stood, shaking out her robes. 'Well enough. I've done what I can for him today.' She looked up at them with all seriousness. 'Did you two talk?'

Red nodded. 'I did, I need to know more.'

Evie nodded. 'And there's something you need to see.'

'You're going to take her there, then?' Josiah asked gruffly.

'She has to know, Josiah. Know everything.' Evie said calmly.

Josiah took a breath. 'Can we trust her?'

Red gave him a long look over her shoulder. 'I was wondering if you'd think of that.'

Josiah looked at her, expecting anger. But Red just turned back to look at Evie.

Evie stood straight and raised her chin. For such a small woman, she was a force of nature when she needed to be. 'If we can't trust her with this, we can't trust her at all. The birthmark says we can trust her. If we can't trust that, then everything we believe is for naught.'

Josiah sighed. 'Very well.'

'That's all well and good.' Red crossed her arms over her chest. 'But does someone mind telling me where we're going?'

NINE

'It won't hurt,' Evelyn assured Red as they entered the shrine. 'It's like walking through a door.'

'This isn't a priestly thing, true?' Red asked. Bethral had no problem with her leaving, but then Bethral didn't have to walk through the damn thing, did she? Red scowled at the stone floor beneath her feet. Magic she could stomach. Barely. But godly things . . .

'It's a magic spell, not a prayer,' Evelyn chided over her shoulder as she strode ahead. 'You people of Soccia are all alike. So tense about—'

'How far are we going?' Red didn't need a lecture, that was certain sure. She adjusted her sword belt, and then cursed silently for showing her nervousness.

'Far enough,' Evelyn said quickly. 'Now let me work.'

Red narrowed her eyes at that, as she took the basket handle. The priestess was nervous as well, and being about as clear as fog. But Evelyn turned to face the back wall of the shrine, and began to chant. The hairs on Red's neck rose, and she looked away, out the doorway of the shrine.

Josiah was still out there, up the path, holding the lantern. The thrice-damned goats were there as well. He'd walked out with them, but had stopped there, letting them go alone. Red narrowed her eyes again. Something about that wasn't quite—

'There.'

Red turned back to see the wall of the shrine was now a doorway, filled with thin white curtains that seemed to move in a breeze only they felt. She swallowed hard. 'I've heard of this, but never seen it. Is it true that you have to know a place before you can go there? This way?'

Evelyn took the basket from her hand. 'Yes. Ready?'

'I thought only mages could do this,' Red observed.

Evelyn nodded. 'My father was a mage; my mother, a priestess. I can wield some magic that is not of the Gods.' She tilted her head. 'You're stalling.'

'I'm not,' Red said, staring at the curtains.

Evelyn took her elbow. There was a soft scent of incense about her. Red looked down into eyes that held a glimmer of laughter in their depths. 'I'll be happy to explain all about portals. Later.' Evelyn smiled as she spoke. 'Now close your eyes and take two steps.'

Red shook off the touch, closed her eyes, and took two steps forward.

She expected to feel the curtains on her face. Instead, a breeze touched her cheek, carrying the strong scent of pine and a faint smell of manure.

She opened her eyes to find herself in a sun-dappled grove of birch trees, their white bark almost glowing in the light. The grove was a perfect circle, with a second row of pines behind the birch.

Red looked back over her shoulder, to check the portal. But there was only birch and pine. Evelyn stood at her side, a faint smile on her face.

There was a path off to the side, but Red's attention was caught by the stone in the center of the grove, its flat top covered with wheat sheaves, a few dried sunflower heads, and a lump of suet. A bright scarlet bird, startled by their arrival, exploded off the stone, scolding them with loud chirps as it took to the trees.

She stepped forward, craning to look, when a deep voice sounded from the trees. 'Hold, stranger.' The voice sounded oddly forced.

Red placed a hand on her sword hilt but Evelyn gave a little shake of her head, as if in reassurance.

'Who goes there?'

Red frowned. The voice – it was a child's voice, a child trying to sound much older.

'Lady High Priestess Evelyn, and a guest.' Evelyn called out in response.

There was a pause then as the greenery to the right rustled, with some sort of whispered consultation going on in its depths. There had to be at least two, maybe three—

'Is all well with you, Lady Priestess?' The voice faltered a bit in a childish tenor.

'I prefer honey in my kavage,' Evelyn answered.

Three children leaped out of the pines, laughing. 'Aunt Evie!' They piled out of the woods, chattering and running. Red half expected them to vault the stone, but they ran around it and mobbed Evelyn, clutching at her robes, all talking at once.

Red took a step back as Evelyn knelt to return their hugs. The youngest one, a small blonde, was demanding her attention. 'We's guarding, Aunt Evie! We did good, didn't we? Didn't we?' The child turned and looked back at the pines.

Two men emerged, dressed in leather armor and carrying long bows. The elder chuckled, but the other gave the child a cynical look. 'All's well, but for almost knocking over a Lady High Priestess. Where are your manners?'

The child give him an angry, stubborn look. 'But she's Aunt Evie.'

'That she is, but she's brought a guest, hasn't she now, and deserves respect, doesn't she?'

The child puffed out a breath, and swiveled her head to look Red over carefully. The others quieted, and then they all stepped back and performed a bow.

'Greetings and welcome, Lady High Priestess Evelyn.' The tallest, a blond boy, spoke with formal tones. 'How may we serve you?'

Evelyn solemnly curtsied to the children. 'Allow me to make you known to my guest. This lady—'

Red snorted.

Evelyn ignored the interruption. 'This lady is the warrior Red Gloves.'

The children bowed. Red noted the wariness in the men, but they inclined their heads as well.

'Red Gloves, this is Tellen, Cordell, and Brela.' Evelyn indicated each child in turn. 'And their teachers, Oris and Alad.'

Red inclined her head. 'Well met.'

'Another to join the cause, Lady?' Oris, clearly the elder, asked.

'We need to speak to Auxter.' Evelyn answered.

'He's at the forge, Lady.' Oris gave the children a look. 'Your hour of guard duty is done. You may go with the Lady High Priestess.'

The boys quivered, but managed to restrain themselves and gave him a formal bow. Evelyn laughed to see it. 'Enough! Tell me about your lessons.'

The children gathered about her, all talking at once. They smelled of pine sap, and had needles and leaves in their hair. Brela, the smallest, a blonde girl with eyes of bright blue, looked up at Red. 'Why do they call you Red Gloves?'

Evelyn sucked in a breath. Red gave her a look out of the corner of her eye. Bethral had warned them, then. Just as well. But did the priestess think she'd— Red made the look a withering one before looking down at the child. 'I like red gloves.'

'Oh.' Perfectly satisfied, the child reached up with both hands. Red swooped her up into her arms, pleased to see that the priestess looked a bit like a dying fish.

Evelyn had the grace to blush. She took the hands of the two boys, and started to walk toward the path.

Red paused, giving Oris and Alad a hard look. 'And if the Lady hadn't liked honey with her kavage?'

Oris gave her a tight, hard smile. 'You'd have two arrows in your heart.'

'Nah,' Alad said. 'I'd have gone for the thigh.'

'We was guarding.' Brela explained softly.

'That you were,' Red said, as she gave both men a nod and turned to follow the priestess. Sensible, to guard the area, but did that mean that any mage could open one of those things? How did you guard against that, then?

'Your hair is pretty.' A soft hand stroked her head, and Red's attention was pulled back to the child in her arms. Brela was nodding her head in approval. 'It's brown, like my friend's hair. I like it.'

'I'm glad you like it, Little One.' Red said. The pines were thinning, and the path wove between the trees. She could hear Evelyn and the boys up ahead, but had lost sight of them.

The trees thinned then, and she could see Evelyn's white robes ahead where the path emerged from the trees. Red stepped into the sun and blinked at the contrast to the shade of the forest. 'The boys ran ahead?' she asked.

Evelyn chuckled. 'After an hour of guarding, they need to work off some energy.' She smiled at Brela. 'But this little one is more patient.'

Brela giggled and held out her hands to Evelyn, suddenly leaning toward her. Red was caught off guard by the sudden shift of weight, but the priestess caught the child easily.

'Go see Unca 'Siah and Snowdrop?' Brela asked.

'Not today, Bright Eyes.'

Red barely heard. She sucked in a breath at the view. Acres of cleared farmland, some being tilled, some being seeded. There was a large manor house, and all manner of barns, fencing, and livestock within view. She looked in astonishment at Evelyn.

The priestess looked back. 'Quite a contrast, isn't it?'

Red looked back at the scene. 'Why does Josiah stay there, when he could come here? A healthy land, with people . . .' Her voice trailed off as she spoke.

'He can't.' Evelyn started down the path with the child in her arms.

Brela looked over her shoulder at Red. 'Unca 'Siah pops the door.' She spoke gravely, as if that made everything clear.

'Come,' Evelyn said. 'We've a ways to go to get to the forge.'

The boys ran back, chattering at Evelyn, which was fine with Red. She just wanted to take in the sights, and not worry about talking.

Their path took them between fields filled with sheep and frolicking lambs on one side, and cows and calves on the other. Farmworkers, men and women, raised their heads as Red's group passed, but with a smile and a wave of their hands, they returned to work without comment. Red wasn't much for field work, but she knew as well as anyone that the crops needed to be planted as soon as weather permitted.

The breeze now brought sounds to her: a smith's hammer chiming, the sounds of men and animals in the fields beyond.

As they drew near to the outbuildings, Red heard a sound more familiar to her ears. The clash of sword on shield. But Evelyn and the children seemed to have no concern, so Red followed, until the reason why came into view.

It was a practice ring, with warriors sparring and watching. Greetings were called, but Evelyn never paused. She walked right up to the open doors of a forge, where a large man was seated on a stool, watching another work metal at the anvil.

'Auxter,' Evelyn called out.

The seated man turned his head, a broad man with gray hair and thick, bushy eyebrows, and a wide smile on his face. 'Evie! I didn't expect you for another week at least. What does Josiah need? Arent and her cooks baked today, so there's plenty to be had.'

The smith, a younger, dark-skinned man, smiled but didn't stop his work. He was folding white-hot metal, but it was no plowshare he was forming. It was a sword. A glance about showed more weapons than horseshoes along the walls. The boys were fascinated, but they stayed well back.

'Down,' Brela demanded.

'Not in here, Bright Eyes,' Evelyn said. She looked back at Auxter. 'Better double the normal supplies, and double them again. And add some dishes. Josiah has company.'

'Eh?' Auxter was eyeing Red now, giving her a good look.

'Auxter, meet Red Gloves.'

Auxter nodded. 'Another sword for our side, then?'

'Well,' Evelyn took in a breath, and hedged, 'we need to call council. There have been some developments.'

Red mentally rolled her eyes. Best just to cut to the bone. She opened her leather armor, baring her breasts.

Auxter's eyes bulged. The blacksmith dropped his hammer.

Brela, still in Evelyn's arms, crowed with joy. 'Like mine!' She lifted her shirt high, showing a pale, plump tummy—

And the birthmark of the Chosen.

TEN

It was like a splash of cold water on Red's face.

She had to give him credit, Auxter recovered before anyone else. 'Children! Arent has been baking all day, and she's a plate of sticky buns for you in the kitchens. Off with you, now.'

The boys needed no encouragement whatsoever. They sprang off like hounds on a scent. Evelyn released Brela, who ran after them. 'Wait for me, wait for me!'

Auxter reached for a staff that leaned on the wall behind him and struggled to his feet. 'Onza, as soon as you've dealt with the metal, come to the great hall. And spread the word, lad.'

The smith had retrieved his hammer, and was looking at his misshapen work with resignation. 'Might be a while.'

'Then set it aside. We've more important weapons to forge.' Auxter moved forward, fairly fast for a man with a pronounced limp. 'Evelyn, Red Gloves, come with me.'

'Auxter, I—'

'Not a word, Evelyn.' Auxter looked over his shoulder. 'And you, lass.'

Red raised an eyebrow.

'Keep your clothes on, eh?'

There was no time to respond to that. Auxter limped to the practice circle, and all activity ceased. The warriors stopped their sparring, and listened as Auxter issued commands, snapping out orders and messages for a half-dozen people. Red watched, impressed with the way he was obeyed.

Evelyn came to stand beside her. Red ignored her.

Once the warriors had scattered to do his bidding, Auxter waved the women on. 'Come.'

Auxter was not happy with the priestess, to Red's way of thinking. Not that she blamed him. The priestess was keeping too many secrets. Just as well Evelyn had been holding a child in her arms, or Red might have wrung her neck right then and there.

Auxter would've probably helped.

They followed Auxter to the big stone manor house and through wooden double doors into the great hall. Red looked around, impressed by the upper floor and the balcony. There were tables and benches scattered about, and the head table off to the side.

Auxter kept walking, toward the hearth at the other end of the hall. A fire was lit within, and Auxter made for it. One large chair stood square in the center of the furniture, facing the hall entrance. Not a throne, but certainly the chair of the head of the household, whatever he might be called.

Auxter sat in the chair, easing his leg out straight before him. 'Evelyn,' he said, patting the stool next to his chair. The priestess went where she was directed. He didn't offer Red a seat.

She wasn't surprised.

She planted herself before him, facing the hearth, her arms folded one over the other, her weight on her right leg. And waited.

Auxter eyed her closely. 'So. A chosen. And a warrior.'

'As you once were,' Red answered pointedly.

Auxter scowled.

Evelyn shifted on her stool. 'Auxter, I—'

'Have better sense,' Auxter growled at Evelyn. 'You might have warned me. Might have warned her, from the expression on her face. What were you think—'

People entered the hall behind Red, and Auxter broke off to call to one. 'Vembar, join us. Evelyn's brought news that wants discussion.'

Red turned slightly and saw a much older man shuffle into view, leaning on the arm of a slight girl. The girl was clad in a tunic and trous, with a dagger at her belt. She had straight brown, shoulder-length hair, just like Red's. The man was dressed in soft white robes, and moved slowly. Red figured him to be at least in his sixties, if not older. With the lass's help, he eased into one of the chairs close to the heat, next to Evelyn. 'What news?' He wheezed slightly, breathless from the effort.

'Vembar, may I make you known to Red Gloves?' Evelyn

looked at Red. 'This is Vembar, the Chancellor of Palins under the late King.'

Vembar returned Red's nod with regal dignity. No warrior here, that was certain. The man looked as if a strong breeze would carry him off.

'Vembar, Red Gloves is Chosen. She bears the mark under her breast.'

Vembar's eyes widened, but only slightly. The lass with him went white, her knuckles tightening on the back of his chair.

Vembar settled deeper into his chair, and looked back at Auxter. Something seemed to pass between them, but Red couldn't tell what the message was.

'I've summoned the others.' Auxter raised his chin, and gave Red a hard look. 'Time enough for Evelyn to tell this woman what she needs to know.'

'That would be good,' Red said dryly.

Evelyn flushed. She opened her mouth, probably to defend her actions, then seemed to think better of it. She straightened on her stool. 'For years, there have been tales of a Chosen One, born to restore the throne of Palins. But it was a tale told by simple folk, with no facts to support it. So it was ignored by the learned and those of the Church.'

She sounded like she was explaining and apologizing at the same time. Evelyn ran a hand over her hair, though not a strand was out of place. 'It wasn't until the Regent came to power that whispers began, of babes born and killed in the same night, for bearing the mark of the Chosen.'

More men entered the hall, but Red stayed focused on Evelyn as she kept talking. 'It wasn't until I chanced across a girl child of some six years old, bearing the mark, that I began to believe and hope. I managed to get her here, to safety.

'A week later, I learned of twins born with the mark. I rushed to their home, only to find the family slain.' She closed her eyes, and Red figured she prayed for the dead. 'Over the years since, I've found five living Chosen, all different ages.' She looked up at Red. 'You are the eldest.'

Vembar spoke, his voice a frail whisper. 'We believe that the prophecy is like the seeds of the dandelion. The wind carries the seeds, hoping that they will fall to the earth and flourish.' He moved his head to look at the lass by his side. 'So it is with the Chosen, each bearing the possibility of success.'

'Or failure,' Red pointed out. More warriors had joined them now, with a few women in the mix. Red hadn't missed the fact that they ranged around her now, their faces a mixture of curiosity and outright anger as they realized the meaning of the conversation.

'Now here you stand, bearing the mark of the Chosen,' Auxter said carefully, to ensure that his audience knew what the meeting was about. By now there were ten, maybe fifteen, in the circle about Red, and none of them seemed to be greeting the arrival of a Chosen with open arms and smiles.

'And the others?' Red asked.

'You've met the children. The boys and Brela all bear the mark,' Evelyn responded.

Red focused on the lass standing next to Vembar. 'As do you.'

The child lifted her chin. 'I do. I am Gloriana of Palins, eldest of the Chosen.'

'Not any more,' said Red calmly. She shifted her weight to her other leg as a growl arose from the group.

'How do we know that it's a true mark?' someone asked. 'It could be faked, to gain our trust.'

Red reached for her shirt yet again, and all eyes focused on the area beneath her breast. It would be nice if for once those expressions showed admiration of her form, not the birthmark. But not with this group.

'It's real,' Evelyn confirmed. 'I've checked it.'

Auxter grunted. 'So, you would step into a fully formed and well armed prophecy, and take a throne.' He leaned forward in his chair. 'But do you deserve it?'

Red had a good idea what was coming. She dropped her arms and shifted her stance so that her weight was balanced on both feet. 'If I so choose, I do.'

'Prove it,' Auxter barked. He tossed his staff to her. 'Lerew, Riah, Jaff, Taris.'

Red caught the staff as the four leapt to the attack.

'Auxter, they'll kill her!' Evelyn clutched at his arm.

'Not if she's any good,' Auxter growled.

Evelyn watched in horror as tables and chairs were pulled back, and Red was surrounded by four of the younger warriors, each with a wooden practice sword in his hand. Red stood in the center, twirling that staff and grinning like one whose wits were gone.

Evelyn would have stood, but Auxter reached over and tapped her knee sharply. 'Don't interfere,' he said softly.

One of the men, Taris, jumped forward with a cry, flourishing his sword in the air. Red dodged to the side, and tapped his wrist with the staff as he lunged past. His sword clattered to the ground.

Red twirled, placing one end of the staff between the legs of another man, tripping him up. She laughed and twirled again, using the staff to sweep the area around her. The other two opponents jumped back, narrowly avoiding the attack.

Evelyn held her breath, but Red flowed around them all without any apparent effort. She didn't avoid every blow, but she moved with the blow, absorbing the hit.

Not that they hit her often.

The others were cheering their fellows on, yelling advice and encouragement. Evelyn tried to relax on her stool, telling herself that this was just what warriors did.

'She's very good,' Vembar commented.

Auxter nodded. 'She's pulling her blows, going easy on the lads.'

Evelyn looked again, but there was no 'easy' to her eyes. It looked like they were really trying to kill each other. Red had Riah down on the ground, and was laughing as she used him to tangle Jaff's legs while he dodged her blows.

A familiar voice spoke from behind. 'They break my chairs, and I'll have their heads.' Evelyn looked over her shoulder. Arent was behind Auxter, with a tray of mugs and a grim look on her thin face. 'Ale?'

Auxter reached up and took a mug without a word. Arent served the others, then set the tray down and took her own mug in hand. 'So that's the new Chosen.'

'Word's out, then?' Auxter asked.

'Racing around like chickens on slaughter day.' Arent watched Red with narrowed eyes.

'She can get us the support of the High Barons—' Evelyn started, but Auxter cut her off with a look.

'Evelyn, how can someone so talented, and so smart, be so stupid?' Auxter asked softly.

Evelyn flushed up. 'She—'

'Aye, you've found a solution to a problem, Evie lass, but you've created more trouble in the bargain.' Auxter's gaze was on the fight, but his words were directed to her, and they were soft. 'We've spent five years working to building our forces, training Gloriana to take the throne, and teaching the others to treat Gloriana as the true Queen. The other children have been deemed her heirs. They know it, we all know it.'

A shout arose, and Evelyn looked over to see Red fall to the ground, somehow manage to roll under a table, and get to her feet on the other side, staff still in her hand.

Auxter continued, 'Now you walk in and produce another Chosen, and expect everyone to accept her with no hesitation.'

'She's Chosen,' Evelyn whispered back.

Auxter nodded. 'She is. And they will accept her, but it won't be as easy as lifting her shirt.'

'But—'

'Look at Gloriana,' Arent said softly.

Evelyn looked up at the older woman, then obeyed.

Gloriana's face was flushed, and there was anger in her eyes as she watched the fight.

A pit blossomed in Evelyn's stomach. Lord of Light, she'd made a terrible mistake. She looked down into her mug of ale. 'Auxter . . .'

'Enough!' Auxter bellowed. Evelyn jumped, startled by the cry, but the warriors merely stopped what they were doing, and turned to look at him.

'You can fight, woman. I will give you that.'

Red stepped out of the group, her color high, her breathing fast. 'So can they,' she offered, with a grin.

Auxter grunted. 'You are Chosen.'

Red planted the staff. 'If I choose to be.' She tugged on the edges of her gloves. 'I've yet to see a profit in it.'

Gloriana took a step forward, scowling. 'It's not about profit. It's about restoring the land and its people. It's about—'

Vembar shifted his leg to press against hers; Gloriana stopped talking and bit her lip. She glanced at the old man, then stepped back. Evelyn's heart went out to her – so earnest, so naive.

Evelyn sighed. That was part of the problem: Gloriana's youth and inexperience.

Red's eyebrow went up as the warriors pulled back stools and chairs to seat themselves. 'That's all well and good, but I'm a mercenary. We like to see a return for our efforts.'

'A throne, for one thing.' Vembar's voice was soft, but sharp.

'There *is* that,' Red acknowledged, taking a deep breath. 'Still, I've some thinking to do. And someone to talk to before I commit to this scheme.'

'Well enough.' Auxter held out his hand.

Red extended the staff toward him and placed it in his hand.

'On the morrow, then,' Auxter stated.

Red nodded, then gave him a grin. 'Any ale left?'

They walked in silence back to the grove, with three of the warriors carrying baskets and bundles of supplies. The birches seemed to glow with the last light of day, even though sheltered in the pines.

Evelyn began to chant, and once the door was open, the warriors started to carry the bundles through. 'Call for Josiah, and he'll tell you where to put them,' Evelyn instructed the men. 'We'll take care of them from there.'

Red stood by the stone, looking down at the dried sunflower head. More seed had been picked from it by the birds. The breeze had died down, but the scent of pine was still strong. The faint odor of manure from the fields was all but gone.

Red breathed in the air and tried not to think about much of anything for a while. Just to be, for a moment.

Evelyn cleared her throat, and Red looked up. The warriors were gone, the supplies all carried to the other side. But the priestess barred the way to the portal and stood there, glaring at her.

Not a good omen, to be sure.

Evelyn straightened her shoulders and lifted her chin. 'Before we go back, I want to know what your intentions are toward Josiah.'

'Excuse me?' Red asked, putting her hand on her sword hilt.

'I've seen the way you look at him.'

Red chuckled. 'I thought you were a priestess.'

'I'm sworn to chastity, not stupidity,' Evelyn said. 'As one of his few living relatives, I ask your intentions.'

Red tilted her head and studied the woman before her. 'Sister?'

'Cousin.'

'Ah.' Red nodded. 'That explains the "Lady High Priestess." '

To her surprise, Evelyn flushed red, as if embarrassed. 'No. We are second cousins. I don't bear the title as the result of birth. It was awarded to me by the Crown.' She pressed on. 'Josiah is dear to me, and I don't want to see him hurt.'

Red opened her mouth to give an earthy description of her 'intentions' . . . but the words didn't come. She closed her mouth, looked down at the ground, and studied the tips of her boots. A picture of Josiah rose before her: sitting on the well, his arms crossed over his chest, hunched as if in pain. Those wounded eyes . . .

'All I ask is that you are honest with him,' Evelyn continued. 'If it's for a bit of slap and tickle, well then . . .'

Red let the words slide past her. Being lectured on her love life by a priestess – the Twelve help her! Still, the idea of just a bit of fun with the man seemed wrong somehow. As if she already wanted more. She scowled at her boots. What was she doing, mooning over a man she hadn't even slept with yet?

'I don't know,' Red said abruptly. She looked up, realizing that she had cut Evelyn off in midsentence. 'I don't know what my intentions are.'

Evelyn drew in a breath, then let it out slowly. 'Don't hurt him. He's already suffered more than enough.'

With that, she entered the portal.

Red scowled at the portal. For the first time in a long time, she was at a loss. Over a goatherder. It was uncomfortable, and she didn't like it.

Still, there were . . . possibilities. And a good mercenary considers all the potential profit before selling her sword.

Red drew a deep breath, and stepped into the portal.

*

The hut was stuffed full of the baskets and bundles when Red and Evelyn squeezed in the door.

'There's no room for all this,' Josiah grumbled.

'There's need, though,' Evelyn pointed out. She moved to the bed to look down at her patient. 'He's sleeping,' she exclaimed softly.

Bethral nodded as she pulled a loaf of bread from one of the sacks. 'For the past hour.' She looked over at Red, and frowned. 'What happened to you?'

Red touched a sore spot on her cheek. 'Got to do some sparring while we were gone. Learned a few things.'

'Such as?' Bethral asked.

Red leaned against the door, and folded her arms over her chest. 'Oh, let us see. Things like I am not the only one to bear the birthmark of the Chosen.'

Bethral looked up, startled.

'Oh, that's not all,' Red purred. 'Josiah here hasn't told me all his secrets yet.'

Josiah's head jerked up.

'And the priestess has managed to assemble a rather large force of arms, and it's located in Soccia, no less.'

Evelyn's head jerked up.

'Soccia,' Bethral asked. 'Home?'

'Oh, yes.' Red scowled. 'Northern Soccia, by the look of it. Isn't that right, priestess?'

Evelyn opened her mouth, but Red wasn't in the mood for explanations. 'I know a shrine to the Twelve when I see it, birch trees and all. Not to mention the scarlets, a bird of our land, not of this. Oh, yes, Bethral, we can go home. Take our gear, our horses, and be gone in an instant through this lady's magic. Which is exactly what we are going to do if I don't get the entire truth, right this minute.'

ELEVEN

Red watched the priestess blush as red as a scarlet and look down at the floor. She started twisting her silver ring. 'It wasn't really a lie,' she hedged softly.

'Not really the truth, either,' Red snapped.

Evelyn didn't look up. 'Auxter's farm is in northern Soccia,' she confirmed. 'I didn't want you to just disappear without having a chance to talk you into helping us.' She glanced over at Josiah and looked away.

Red glanced at him as well. He stared back, his jaw set, almost defiant in the face of her demands. Good to see, actually.

'I told you every—' Josiah started.

Red cut him off, and pitched her voice high. ' "Unca 'Siah pops the door." ' She let her voice drop back to normal. 'That's what the littlest one told me.'

Josiah said nothing, and Red let the silence grow. Bethral's gaze went from face to face, but she didn't interfere. Evelyn was watching Josiah.

Red gritted her teeth and waited. If the man didn't say something soon, she'd have to—

'When Athelbryght was destroyed, I was damaged,' Josiah said. 'I told you that.'

'And I assumed that you were injured,' Red said. 'And you let me think that.' She could hear the faint sound of a goat bell outside, coming toward the hovel. She pressed her back harder against the door, and planted her feet.

'He was hurt.' Evelyn sat down, clasping her hands in her lap. 'When I found him in the yard, he was almost gone: cold, shivering, barely enough strength to breathe.' She raised her head, her eyes distant, seeing into the past. 'I started to pray there, in the rain and mud, desperate to aid him. But' – her voice trailed off – 'I could not.'

'The Gods didn't answer your prayer?' Bethral asked.

'No.' Evelyn looked back down at her lap. 'I thought that for a moment, thought that Josiah wasn't to be blessed, thought I'd sinned in some way, but—' She looked at Josiah.

'I cannot be touched by magic,' Josiah growled. 'Not by sacred magic, not by high. If I come into its presence, it goes out, like a candle. If I try to enter a portal, it "pops" and disappears.' His hands formed fists, knuckles white. 'Powers I once wielded with ease are gone.'

Powers he once . . .

Red narrowed her eyes. 'You were a mage?'

Josiah turned his back to her, facing the wall, his entire body trembling. Red studied every line of his frame as Evelyn spoke. 'Josiah was a mage of great power. His was a love for growing things and—'

'Stop.' Josiah's voice cracked.

Evelyn bowed her head, and they sat silent for a moment, as if someone had died. Of course, to Josiah's way of thinking, maybe he had. But Red's mind raced. 'In a land where magic is common, that makes you an incredible danger. And incredibly powerful. All at the same time.'

'Don't you think I know that?' Josiah snarled, spinning to face her. 'I could see, taste, touch, use the powers before. But now I'm blind, as blind as you are to the power that swirls around us. I can't even sense it. I'm a cripple.'

Goats were butting against the door now, but Red held the door closed.

'A powerful cripple,' Bethral noted, 'if you cancel magic in your presence. That would mean . . .' She looked at the man on the bed. 'If that's true, then how does this one stay healed?'

'Because once its work is done, the healing magic fades, but the results remain,' Evelyn said. 'If Josiah walked in during a healing, then all the work might be lost, but not after. Still' – she looked at Josiah – 'it's a curse. He can't be healed, can't walk through a portal, can't use the benefits of any magic.'

'That's true enough,' Red agreed. 'But from a warrior's point of view . . .'

'He could walk through a mage battle without being touched,' Bethral said. 'He could cancel magic locks or traps.'

'A pawn, to be used,' Josiah said bitterly. 'Or killed, when it can't be used, because of the threat it represents.'

'So that's why you've stayed here, hidden, alone, in this devastated land?' Red asked carefully.

'I deserve nothing less.' Josiah's voice was gruff as he turned to the supplies crowding the table. 'Evie, it's getting late. Don't you need to get back?'

Evelyn gave him a sorrowful look, then sighed. 'You're right, Josiah.' She focused on Red. 'I'd hoped to spend more time talking this over with you, before you make your decision.'

'We're not going anywhere.' Red said. 'Besides, I need to discuss this with Bethral—'

'Not really,' Bethral said. 'I've told you how I felt, and none of this has changed my view.'

Red glared at her, but Bethral gave her a simple shrug. 'I will follow you, sword-sister. It is your decision.'

'Thank you so very much,' Red snarled. 'That's so helpful.'

Bethral shrugged again. 'You are the Chosen One, if you so choose.'

Evelyn raised her hand to her mouth, and Red was certain she covered a smile. But when the priestess spoke, her voice was calm. 'I do need to return to the temple, since I've duties in the morning. Let me do another healing on our friend.' She rose from her chair. 'I asked Arent for some clothing for our guest . . .'

'These supplies need to be put away.' Josiah was unpacking one of the sacks. 'I'll get a meal started.'

'I'll go check the horses.' Red retreated from the hut as fast as she could. Too many bodies in that small area for her. The goats were clustered about the door as she left, but they followed her down the path.

The cold night air was a relief from the heat, and she sucked in a deep breath to clear her head. Beast and Steel were still in the paddock, and they raised their heads and nickered at her approach. Red went inside the barn, and gave their stalls the once-over. Sure enough, they needed tending.

Ah, well, the 'Chosen' had best get to work, then.

She hung her weapons close by, and started working. While her body did the mucking out, she thought about all the possibilities.

All the possibilities.

The all too familiar scents of a barn rose around Red as she started, but that didn't bother her. She welcomed the feel of her muscles moving, the sight of the stall getting cleared out. It pleased her to set things right again, using a simple shovel and the strength of her arms.

She'd thought Josiah insane when he'd told her about her birthmark. As if a bit of different-colored flesh made any difference. She snorted at the thought. For all the talk of prophecy, it took more than a birthmark.

But they'd built the beginnings, hadn't they? A source of supply, men, and arms.

It might work.

What a thing to accomplish, if she could. She, Red Gloves, little better than a 'lowlife,' toppling a throne and claiming a kingdom. She pictured herself on a throne and laughed out loud at the idea, the sound ringing in the huge, empty barn. She paused then, listening to the echoes of her own voice.

Athelbryght must have been a fair land, a prosperous one to support such a barn. She suspected that Josiah was a fair lord as well, generous with his people. His pain was a measure of his caring, that was certain.

There was strength there, within him. It took a strong man to survive what he had been through. Maybe not the strength of a sword, but Red knew all too well that the ability to swing a blade was not the full value of a man.

She paused in her work for a moment, leaning on the shovel. It would be a challenge, with no promise of success. Bethral was willing. Red grinned at that, since her sword-sister had always followed her lead and not always to Red's benefit.

There was a tempting profit to be made, that was certain sure.

But it would take time and effort, and she still had an itch she wanted scratched . . .

So Josiah wanted a Chosen, eh?

What would he be willing to pay?

Josiah walked toward the barn with an odd feeling of dread and anticipation. Whatever else she might be, Red Gloves certainly wasn't predictable. He'd probably find her in the foaling room, on one of the bunks, her hands behind her head, thinking about her destiny and the prophecy.

Instead, he found her wrestling with a wheelbarrow full of manure.

He stood in the doorway and gaped as she pushed it toward him. 'I didn't see a compost so I started one in the back.' She grinned at him. 'Not by where you chop wood.'

'Er,' was all he could say as she walked past him with her load. She was back in a moment setting down the empty wheelbarrow and picking up a shovel. He watched for a moment as she worked. 'You're mucking the stalls.'

'It needed doing.' She stopped for a moment. 'Odd that the goat stall seems awfully clean; you've no pile hereabouts.'

Josiah sighed, moving to look over the railing at the pile of straw where the goats bedded down. 'Whatever happened that day, the goats were caught up in it somehow.' He leaned against the wall, the rough planks catching at his tunic. 'They don't really eat either.'

Red frowned. 'I've seen them graze and chew cud.'

'But the grass and plants show no signs of grazing.' Josiah ran his fingers through his hair. 'They bear no young, give no milk, and don't seem to age. I don't know why, but that's how it is.'

Red chuckled, then returned to work. 'No mucking, then. A benefit to magic goats.'

'But they aren't magic,' Josiah said. 'Because they're around me all the time. Good company, though. In their own way.'

Red hefted up the last shovelful, then paused, giving Josiah a narrow look. 'They don't talk, do they?'

'No, no,' Josiah said.

Red hefted the handles of the wheelbarrow and left, muttering something under her breath about 'better not' and 'talking goats.' Josiah had to chuckle, in spite of himself.

Red returned, and between the two of them, they finished fast, putting down fresh straw. 'I'll leave the horses out a while longer.' Red said. 'Bring them in after we eat.'

Josiah put the shovel away. 'Evie's left.'

'I'll wash up and be right in.' Red tugged at her gloves. Josiah remembered Bethral's warning and made no comment.

He started toward the door. 'We can talk if you wish, if you've questions. I can give you the information you need to make up your mind.'

'Oh, I've decided,' Red purred.

Josiah stopped dead, the small hairs on the back of his neck lifting off his skin.

'There's a profit to be made here, Josiah of Athelbryght. A profit most mercenaries can only dream of.'

He closed his eyes as her voice moved over him.

'I'll do it. I'll fulfill your prophecy and restore the throne.' Red's voice was low, husky, and soft. 'But there's a bit more that needs to be added to this bargain.'

Josiah didn't turn . . . couldn't turn. He licked his lips, and forced the words from his throat. 'What more do you require?'

He heard her take a step, moving to stand just behind him. 'You, Josiah. I want you. Your body. In my bed, from now until the success of this "prophecy" or my death in the attempt.'

'But—' Josiah's brain was a complete blank. 'You – a throne – the prophecy . . .'

Red was right behind him. Even though they weren't touching, he could feel her heat, smell the sweetness of her body, even with the manure. Josiah felt the pressure all over his skin, as if he was naked.

Her murmur held laughter now. 'The throne is a profit to be had down the road. But I am a mercenary, and we like payment in advance.'

Josiah forced himself to take a step away from her. He turned, to find her standing there, her arms crossed loosely over her chest, her brown eyes dancing. 'You can't be serious.'

'I am,' Red said, then she hesitated. 'You're not a virgin, are you?'

'No!' Josiah sputtered.

Thank the Twelve. Red sighed with relief. She wanted nothing to do with a virgin. Too emotional. Too clingy. Too much time spent on what goes where.

Poor Josiah, he looked so befuddled. And in her own way, Red was just as puzzled. What was wrong with the man? She sighed, getting a bit impatient. 'Well, then, pay me now with your company. I'm not without skill.' She arched an eyebrow, daring him to doubt her.

'That's insane. Your wits have wandered off, looking for a home.' Josiah snapped. 'I told you that—'

'Oh, please!' Red scowled. 'You're asking me to commit my life to this cause. The least you can do is see to my pleasure as well.'

'I'm not—'

'Spare me.' Red rolled her eyes. 'No more talk of your worthiness or lack thereof. You are fair of form and healthy, Josiah.' *And far too long alone*, a thought she didn't voice. She watched Josiah's face instead, as his emotions passed over it. Desire, guilt, fear . . . 'All I ask is a bed partner for the duration of this "adventure."'

Josiah stood there, frowning, looking into her eyes. 'And if I say no?'

Red sighed. 'I will not force you, Josiah of Athelbryght. Even if the Way of the Twelve did not forbid such a thing, still I would not.'

'But it's a factor in your decision.' Josiah stated.

Red shrugged. 'It's only the truth, goatherder.'

'It is, isn't it?' Josiah said softly.

Red didn't quite understand those words, but she felt she'd gained an advantage somehow. She stepped closer, and couldn't help a sly smile as Josiah's nostrils flared and his eyes filled with desire. 'So what will it be, Josiah of Athelbryght?' she said softly. 'Your dream of restoring this land? Or your virtue?'

Bethral looked down at her purchase and allowed herself a faint smile. There was good reason to be satisfied with this day's work.

The man wasn't conscious yet, but he was sleeping naturally. Evelyn had advised her to stop giving him broth for now. She was hoping the man would wake up naturally fairly soon – tomorrow, if not during the night. Bethral took a moment to stand and stretch. She'd been by the bedside most of the day, and she felt it. But as much as she wanted to spar with Red, or take a good run on Steel, she wanted to be here when he opened his eyes. Those bright green eyes.

Bethral frowned. She wasn't sure why she'd lied to the priest, but it had been more instinct then intent. Her purchase held secrets, she was certain of that. And she felt oddly possessive of them, as if the copper piece she'd spent had given her that right.

The door opened, and Red blew in like a storm. 'What's to be had?'

'A haunch of beef, fresh bread, and baked turnips.' Bethral stepped toward the fire. 'The turnips are mashed, with some cheese and saffron.'

'Sounds good.' Red plunked herself down by the fire. 'I mucked the stalls, and I'll bed the horses after a while. Oh, and here's something. Magic goats don't shit.'

Bethral snorted as she cut meat from the haunch on the spit. 'Convenient.' She handed Red a bowl of turnips, and a slice of bread with meat. 'Where's Josiah?'

'Said he's not hungry.' Red smirked. 'He's in the barn. Said he needed a bit of time to think.' She took a bite and chewed with clear enjoyment. 'I was thinking we'd change the sleeping arrangements.'

'Oh?' Bethral asked casually. 'Is that what Josiah is thinking about?'

Red grinned. 'You might want to sleep here, so you can take care of your purchase, eh? Josiah and I can sleep in the barn.'

Bethral gave her a look, which Red ignored, choosing instead to stuff her face. 'How very considerate of you,' Bethral said.

Red swallowed. 'I thought so.' She took another bite.

'So, we're staying?' Bethral asked quietly.

The mischief faded from Red's face. She gave Bethral a solemn look. 'There's adventure and profit to be had here, Bethral. But it's not without its risks.'

'The greater the risk, the greater the reward.' Bethral nodded her approval.

Red nodded back, then looked about the hut. 'Any ale left?'

Bethral reached to fill her a mug. 'If he needs to think, why are you in such a rush?'

Red's eyes danced. 'Don't want him thinking overmuch. He'll just get confused.'

TWELVE

Josiah knelt at the hearth in the foaling room and stared at the cold ashes without really seeing them. He was still seeing Red's face when she'd . . .

So what will it be? Your dream of restoring this land? Or your virtue?

Josiah snorted softly. That woman was so different from any he'd known. She was like a force of nature, sweeping in with no regard for others, or decorum, or normal courtesy.

Lord of Light, he wanted her. His entire body thrummed at the idea. He was afraid of what that implied – afraid to trust her.

Snowdrop stuck her head in the door and bleated at him. Josiah looked back as all the goats followed, pushing through to explore the room. 'Don't touch her gear,' Josiah cautioned, as Brownie stuck his nose in the saddlebags. 'I wouldn't put it past her to gut you for it.'

Brownie pulled his nose back, grumbling.

Josiah turned back to the hearth and pulled kindling from the wood box, concentrating on his task. But the thought of Red filled his mind as he prepared to start a fire.

Maybe not so much like a storm, or a whirlwind. She was more like water, clear and cold. Crystal when still, then a raging torrent that swept everything in its path. A cool stream one moment, a flash flood the next. Water that slowly but surely filled all the hollow spaces in . . .

His hands stilled then, as guilt bore down on him. Staring at the kindling, he ran his thumb over the grain of the wood, feeling the roughness against his skin.

This was a mistake. He knew it was, that it could only end in pain. She'd win the throne or die trying, of that he was sure. If she won through, she'd go to Edenrich and sit on the throne as Queen, leading the kingdom to a bright future.

Leaving him in the ruins of the past.

He'd thought that was all that was left to him. But, may the Gods forgive him, he wanted her. He had but to close his eyes, and there she was, naked in the firelight, covered with soap, those red gloves her only clothing. He swallowed hard, trying to control his response.

Snowdrop butted his arm and pushed her head under his hand, looking to have her ears scratched. Josiah sighed, and obliged her. She flicked her ears in pleasure and settled at his side.

Josiah reached for the flint and tinder kept in the wood box, and returned to his task. The flint struck the steel, and sparks flew into the bits of thin wood and straw. A wisp of smoke started to lift as he blew gingerly. Josiah carefully fed more fuel to the tiny spark.

Red wasn't like the women he'd known before. Court women, interested in political advancement for their families through marriage, the farm women who labored with their husbands on his lands, the other mages that he'd known through the Guild. He'd had liaisons before, but only one that he'd thought was serious.

Who'd betrayed him, in the end.

Pain lanced through him. He'd trusted Elanore, and she'd betrayed him and the other High Barons.

There was something in Red's eyes, something honest. Her offer held no hidden depths. No commitment, no entanglement, no relationship. It was pure sex between two consenting adults, and no harm done.

The flames leapt up now, greedy and hungry, and he fed them a few large pieces of wood to chew on. Kavage butted his back, demanding attention, so Josiah sat on the edge of one of the bunks, and gave each goat its due. He relaxed as he murmured to them, stopping once in a while to add more wood to the fire.

When five goat heads turned toward the door, Josiah lifted his head and listened carefully. It sounded like Red was bringing the horses in for the night. He shifted, uneasy, and the goats stood up to mill about the room. But before he could do more, the door opened, and she was inside.

She met Josiah's eyes straight on, her own eyes sparkling. She smiled at him, a smile filled with anticipation.

At least until she saw the goats.

'Oh, no.' Red shook her head. 'No goats. Shoo! Shoo!'

She waved her hands, and waded into their midst to herd them out. But the goats would have none of that. They danced around, evaded her and the doorway at the same time, complaining bitterly.

'Out, you mangy beasts!' Red demanded. 'Out, out, I say!'

The goats ignored her, darting this way and that, bleating their protests.

Josiah burst out with a laugh in spite of himself. The fierce warrior, defeated by goats. He choked it off, sure she'd be offended.

Red's head whipped around to stare at him, but then she smiled. 'You could help, you know.'

Josiah stood, and between the two of them, they managed to get the goats into their stall for the night.

Josiah followed Red back into the foaling room, and closed the door. 'You told Bethral?' He turned around. 'That we would be sleeping—'

Red claimed his mouth with her own.

Josiah's face came alive when he laughed at her and the goats.

Red caught her breath as his eyes changed. The tilt of his head, the light in his eyes, his joy at her predicament. The sparkle in his voice as he laughed right out loud.

It was gone in an instant, replaced with the closed look that he usually wore. The pain had been chased away for only a breath or two. But she'd managed to banish that look, if only for a moment.

The thrice-damned goats were a handful, and it took both of them to herd them out and down to their stall. No way was Red having witnesses to this night, be they human or goat or powers that be. She'd plans for the evening.

One of which was not to give Josiah a moment to think.

He'd said just a few words before she made her move, but it was enough. His lips were warm and dry under hers, and tentative in their response. But she pressed herself against him, pushing him against the door, eager to explore, to taste. He was just as eager, warm and solid, and smelled faintly of marjoram.

She'd surprised him, but Josiah's arms came up to hold her, and she made her appreciation known with a soft moan, wrapping her arms around his neck.

He broke the kiss, moving his mouth to her neck, to trail kisses down to the bit of neckline revealed by her tunic. She moved her head to the side, giving him access, letting her own lips explore the soft skin behind his ear. The tingling sensation of his touch went right down her spine.

Red eased back, still in the circle of his arms, and started tugging at his tunic. He nuzzled her neck, burying his face in her hair. Her hands on his hips, she could feel the heat of his body through her gloves.

She placed her leg between his with calculated design, feeling his body respond when she brushed against him. He sucked in a breath, and she felt his chest heave as his arms drew her tighter.

She pressed in a bit more, then thrust against him slowly. His eyes went dark before they closed and he lowered his head to her shoulder. She started a gentle rhythm with her hips, and placed her lips to his ear. 'Surrender to me, Josiah.'

'I—' Josiah's face contorted, his voice a rasp. 'What about—'

Red chuckled, as she moved her hips faster. 'You first, lover.' She moved her mouth to the soft skin below his ear. She set her teeth in his skin and bit down, sucking at his flesh.

Josiah threw his head back and shuddered, his entire body convulsing against her. The door creaked as Red kept him upright, pressing him into the wood. She chuckled softly as he looked at her with eyes clouded with passion.

'You' – he licked his lips – 'I should—'

Red smiled, and leaned in to brush her lips against his. 'We've all night, lover.'

She tugged him away from the door, using his tunic. Josiah followed, his eyes fogged with something far more satisfying than pain.

Josiah couldn't help but stare at Red as she eased him down onto the bunk. She knelt on the floor before him, and carefully finished removing his tunic. He shivered slightly as the rough fabric rasped over his shoulders. She gave him a half-lidded look, with a soft smile. 'Warm enough?' she whispered.

He nodded, silent, unable to even voice the words. The fire had grown now, and her skin glowed in its light. Josiah was fair certain that the heat came more from her than from the flames.

Her gloved hands moved below the waist of his trous. She tugged, and he obliged, lifting enough that she could remove the rest of his clothing.

'Lie back,' she urged. 'I want to see you.'

Josiah moved back to stretch full length on the rough wool blanket that covered the bunk. 'Not much to see,' he said, considering his flaccidity with a rueful eye. 'I'm—'

'Five years alone, Josiah.' Red shrugged as she hung her sword belt over the end of the bunk, well within reach. 'Not unexpected.'

He watched as she moved to the door and blocked it with the blanket trunk. She returned to stand before him, and started to unbuckle her leather.

She pulled off the stiff leather jacket and carefully set it up on the top bunk opposite. Her gloved fingers untied the quilted underpadding, and slipped it off her shoulders. Josiah's breath quickened as the cloth moved over her skin to reveal . . .

He frowned. 'You're hurt.' There were bruises on her shoulders, and a spectacular one on her left shoulder blade.

Red seemed surprised at his concern as she glanced over her shoulder. 'Auxter's got some good men.' She lifted her brown hair off her back, and looked at the bruise as best she could.

'You could've asked Evie for healing.'

Red chuckled. 'The twinges remind me to move faster next time. Besides, that man needs her help more than I do.'

Her leather trous rode low on her hips, and Josiah swallowed as he watched her fold the underpadding and place it with the other garments. She moved with such grace, her breasts swinging gently. He caught her sly glance and his body responded.

Red's smile grew as she faced him and lifted her arms over her head. She stretched, arching her back, lifting herself up on her toes. Josiah's entire body twitched at the sight, a fact not lost on the warrior woman before him. There were scars, of course. He should have expected that, but it bothered him just the same.

Red relaxed from the stretch and sat on the bunk opposite to remove her boots. They were set together by the end of the bunk, her thick socks placed over them to air. Josiah chuckled softly, and she gave him a questioning look.

'It seems odd,' Josiah said. 'You're so neat.'

'Old habit,' she explained. 'A warrior needs to be able to find her gear in the dark, half-asleep.' She stood, and started to remove her trous. 'Can't do that if it's scattered about.' She skimmed the leather down without a second thought.

Josiah swallowed hard. She was so lovely, standing there, naked but for her gloves. She was smooth and sleek, moving with such grace that he didn't realize she was climbing into the bunk until she whispered 'Move over.'

He did, moving onto his side and shifting on the bunk until his back pressed against the wall. Red lay down on her side, facing him. 'Want you to do something for me.' Her whisper filled the space between them, in the soft shadows.

'What?' Josiah whispered back.

Red smiled, took his hand and guided it down, sliding it over her warm skin to rest over her heat. Josiah gasped at the invitation, and Red kissed his open mouth gently. 'Please, Josiah.' She pressed his hand down, and his fingers slid into her moist depths.

Red arched against the pressure, throwing her head back with a moan. Josiah caught her head, his fingers lost in the silk of her hair.

Soft movements from her encouraged him to apply a slight friction, ever so gently. Red's hips jerked, but she brought her leg up over his thigh, opening herself to him. She reached out and grabbed his hip, the leather of her glove warm on his skin. Her other hand pulled his head down to her breasts.

He was lost then, in a tangle of arms and soft skin. Josiah felt something loosen in his chest, as if a tight band had been cut, as he nuzzled and teased her with lips and tongue. Soft sighs and whispers urged him on, until Red bucked against his fingers, convulsing in pleasure.

She collapsed back on the bed, and they lay there breathing hard for a moment. Josiah laughed weakly as he brushed the sweaty hair off her forehead. 'I'm not sure we needed a fire,' he whispered. 'Not for warmth, anyway.'

Red gave him a sultry look. 'Not done yet, Josiah.' She moved then, arranging him flat on his back. She sat astride and guided him into her center without a word, then sat down, seating him fully within.

They both froze for a moment. Breathing. Adjusting. Feeling.

Gods, it had been so long. Josiah closed his eyes, feeling her heat spread over his body like a fever. It had never been like this, never felt like this before. He opened his eyes to see her face above his. Her eyes were unfocused, dreamy, and suddenly he wanted more. He reached up, and grasped her hips.

She focused then, putting her gloved hands alongside his head, her hair falling down around them. Her breasts swayed slightly, the nipples hard, tight buds.

'Your cycles,' Josiah breathed. 'Do we need to take care?'

She looked down at him with an odd look. 'There's no reason to worry, lover.' The ends of her hair floated softly over his chest as she shook her head.

'Well, then.' He tightened his grip on her hips, and thrust up.

'Yes, Josiah, Oh, yes,' Red moaned as he moved within her. She began her own dance then, matching his movements. Josiah's mind swam away into heat and light and exquisitely shared pleasure. He heard her cry out as he lost his mind and followed the light into darkness.

When he awoke, he found himself in the bunk alone, covered by the blankets. He turned his head and saw Red in the bunk opposite, curled under a blanket, a very satisfied smile on her face.

Josiah frowned, feeling a loss somehow. But then he sighed, rolled over, and returned to sleep.

Red hummed under her breath as she spread an extra blanket over Josiah.

He hadn't stirred when she'd eased off him, not even when she'd cleaned them both. He just lay there, sprawled all over the bunk, taking up every inch of room.

It was warm in the foaling room, but the fire would die as they slept. Red made sure he was well covered, from head to toe. She smoothed the blanket over his chest. Asleep, he looked younger, the lines of care eased, and that pleased her.

The love bite on his neck pleased her even more.

She added wood to the fire and checked the door. All was secure, so she shifted her sword belt to the other bunk and crawled under the blanket, turning to face Josiah.

She yawned, and stretched, sticking her legs out and pointing her toes. She pulled them back under the wool, feeling good. He hadn't been the most skillful lover she'd ever had, but there'd been something different with him.

A rush of pride filled her at the thought of her mark on his neck. A strong sense of satisfaction. A sense of power, too, at the way he'd responded to her touch. Red smiled, as she yawned again.

There was profit to be made here, a throne to be had. The odds were better than she'd first thought when Josiah had told her she was 'Chosen.' She chuckled at that. Her, a 'Chosen One.' This prophecy had a warped sense of humor, that was certain.

Her eyes drifted back to Josiah. Immune to magic. She studied his sleeping form, and thought about that for a bit. How could you use that to your advantage, against a mage? Would he 'pop' a mage's protective spell if he drew near? What was his range? Not being able to be healed, that was a problem. But in a battle . . .

She yawned yet again, gave it up, and settled down to sleep. There'd be work to do in the morning, what with the priestess returning for her answer. A group of people to convince, and a very young girl who needed to be won over. Questions she needed to ask, information she had to have.

She drew a breath, and set those thoughts aside. That was for tomorrow. Now was the time for rest, and dreams. Sweet dreams, if she could help it.

A picture of Josiah's face as she'd marked him floated in her mind's eye. She smiled again, as she surrendered to sleep.

'Profit,' indeed.

THIRTEEN

It was midday before Evelyn could escape from her Church duties and return to Josiah's hut. She wasn't certain that she'd had the right frame of mind during her prayers, but hopefully the Lord and the Lady would understand. She'd been distracted by the thought of trying to convince Red Gloves to follow her destiny.

All the arguments and points she'd thought to use were a jumble in her brain. With a wry smile, she admitted to herself that every Chosen she'd found so far had been a babe in arms, and there'd been no need to do more than get them to safety quickly.

Red was another matter.

She stepped out of the portal, into the ruined shrine, and then hurried along the path, intent on reaching Josiah's hut, mulling over the bait she might use to lure the mercenary. Wealth, that was a fact. Power, certainly. She'd mention the needs of the people, but she wasn't sure that would motivate her.

Evelyn sighed. Red had to understand how necessary it was, how important to Palins and the people. Lord of Light, Lady of Laughter, Red just had to listen . . .

The sight of the horses grazing by the barn, the goats cavorting nearby, did little to ease her fears. The women could be packing, getting ready to leave. Josiah was probably arguing with them even now. She heard voices in the hut, and headed that way.

Evie called out a greeting and opened the door, to find herself in the middle of a feast. The smell of frying pork and warm bread was welcome, but even more welcome was the smile on Red's face. Maybe the food would put her in the mood to consider—

'I'm in,' Red announced before Evelyn had taken a step within.

Evelyn stopped dead, the words she'd been prepared to wield scattered in her mind. 'Excuse me?'

'I'm the Chosen.' Red took a bite of pork, and waved Evelyn in. 'Shut the door,' she mumbled around her mouthful. 'You're letting in the cold.'

Evelyn obeyed, stepping within and closing the door behind her. 'You, you'll do it?'

Red smirked, apparently aware of the effect she was having on Evelyn. 'I said I would, didn't I?'

'Kavage, Evie?' Josiah asked. 'I'll warn you, it's very strong.'

'Never let Red make kavage,' Bethral advised.

'I'll keep that in mind,' Josiah said.

Something about his tone . . . Evelyn looked at Josiah, but he was avoiding her eyes, pouring kavage into a mug. 'Josiah, what—'

'You have your Chosen,' Red said swiftly, and Evelyn turned to look at her. 'A Chosen who needs information. Come sit, and answer my questions.'

That took a bit of doing due to the cramped quarters, but Bethral shifted to allow her to get to the hearth. Evelyn paused first to look at her patient, wrapped under a blanket, lying on his side. He appeared to be sleeping. 'He looks well.' She smiled at Bethral.

Bethral nodded. 'He took broth during the night. I had to clean him, but he never stirred.'

'Just as glad we missed those festivities,' Red said into her kavage.

Evelyn narrowed her eyes. 'We?'

'I've hopes he'll wake soon,' Bethral said as she sat on the edge of the bed.

Evelyn settled on the chair. Josiah reached over and handed her kavage. She looked at him, but he was still avoiding her gaze. 'What's going on, Josiah?'

Josiah turned his head to look at Red, and Evelyn sucked in a breath at the passion mark on his neck. 'Priestess I may be, but even I'm not that innocent.' She leaned forward. 'That's a—'

'That's none of your business.' Red cut her off firmly.

Evelyn turned toward her, ready to protest, but one look made her close her mouth. Red's eyes were intent and serious. Commanding.

Evelyn settled back in her chair, feeling the heat on her cheeks, and lowered her eyes. 'As you say.' She took a sip of kavage to steady herself, suddenly feeling very unsure. The dark fluid filled her mouth, hot and bitter. She wrinkled her nose.

Bethral chuckled, and handed her a wooden bowl with warm bread and pork.

'So,' Red said, sopping up meat juices with her bread, 'what do we have in the way of men, arms, money, support?'

Evelyn gathered her wits. 'We've built a core group at Auxter's farm. There's roughly one hundred men there, all trained to fight together. We've three mages, an excellent healer, and she has two apprentices.'

'Are you counted in that figure?' Red asked.

'No.' Evelyn shook her head. 'I'm not really a mage or a healer.'

Bethral and Red looked puzzled. Bethral glanced at the bed.

'I'm a priestess,' Evelyn explained, 'with prayers that bring magical healing. But I'm limited in how much healing I can do. A healer knows the ways of the body, and uses herbs and other remedies. In many ways, much more powerful than I am.'

Red tilted her head, and considered that. 'So, in a plague, for instance . . . ?'

'I'd be fairly useless,' Evelyn responded. 'I can save only a few, while a healer can save far more.'

'To those few, you'd be far from useless, Evie,' Josiah rumbled. 'And no healer could have aided our friend here.'

'True.' Evelyn smiled. 'And if I could reach one person sick with the plague, and heal him before it spread, then yes, that would be an effective use of my skills.'

'Can the other mages open those portals?' Red asked.

'Yes,' Evelyn answered. 'Auxter insisted that there be lots of avenues of escape from the farm.'

'Smart,' Bethral said.

'So.' Red set aside her bowl and took up a mug. 'One hundred men, brought together, trained together, and all loyal to their Chosen.'

'Who happens to be a young girl raised to believe that she was the one who'd triumph in glory and take the throne,' Bethral pointed out.

'From the look on her face, she's none too pleased about my advent,' Red added.

Evelyn leaned forward. 'We'll talk to her. Gloriana wants what's best for Palins. I'm sure she'll understand.'

Josiah spoke. 'Auxter's had the training of the children since their rescue. Gloriana's been taught to see the broader picture. She will understand.'

Red snorted.

Bethral looked doubtful.

'So, a base from which to build,' Red said. 'What more?'

'Horses, armor, weapons,' Evelyn said. 'We've not a lot of coin, but Auxter has provided what we need.'

'How nice of him,' Red said. 'Why so generous? Where's his profit, eh?'

Evelyn stiffened. 'Not everyone is involved in this for money.'

'That depends on how you define profit,' Red snapped back, her eyes sliding over to Josiah.

Josiah flushed.

'Red is just trying to understand the people involved, Priestess.' Bethral spoke gently, her voice warm and smooth. 'She needs to learn much in a short bit of time, and she has to ask rather than observe.'

Evelyn took a breath. That made sense to her. 'Auxter was a member of the King's guard who was injured in a skirmish, and pensioned off. He returned to his family's farm, but remained friends with the King. When the King died, he blamed himself.'

'Auxter was a loyal supporter of the King, for all that he was from Soccia,' Josiah added. 'He offered aid to Evie even before she found the first of the Chosen.'

'The farm had the added benefit of being isolated. Auxter's lands are far from Palins.' Evelyn played with the food in her bowl. 'We could build up a force without any questioning eyes.'

'What does the Regent know of this plan of yours?'

'Nothing.' Evelyn looked Red in the eye. 'If he knew of it, I'd be dead.' Her gaze drifted over to the bed. 'Or worse.'

Bethral shook her head. 'Word gets out, Priestess. You

mentioned that you'd talked to the other High Barons. They know, and you don't know who they've talked to.'

'I've been very careful,' Evelyn insisted. 'All my contacts have been with the High Barons alone, and privately. I've only talked about the Chosen. I didn't give any details of the farm. Only general information.'

'What about Dominic?' Red asked.

Evelyn shook her head. 'Dominic thinks little of my "projects," as he calls them. He thinks only that I heal the sick who appeal to me for aid, without thought of payment. He knows nothing about the Chosen.'

'Who knows about the children?' Bethral asked. 'Or that more than one person bears the mark?'

'No one outside the farm.'

'That's probably what's saved you,' Red said. 'You've been talking of vague plans, with a very young Chosen, and with no specific support. With everyone thinking Josiah is dead, then you're no real threat.' She leaned her head back, staring up at the roof. 'That will change.'

'It will,' Bethral agreed. 'Once you've started this, you must move fast.'

'We can keep this quiet,' Evelyn insisted. 'Surprise is essential.'

Red shook her head. 'Oh, we'll try, but you can't assume that the enemy won't learn of it. Once we start to approach the High Barons with news of my existence and trained forces behind me, word will spread to all the right ears, and all the wrong ones as well.' She stretched out her legs, and laced her fingers over her stomach. 'So all I have to do is supplant a twelve-year-old girl, get the support of her followers, flash my tits at the High Barons, and claim the throne.'

A hoarse whisper came from the bed. 'Now there is a tale worth telling, had I a tongue to tell it.'

Startled, Bethral twisted around, looking into the deep green eyes of the slave.

'You have a tongue,' Red said calmly.

'I do not. Those villains took consummate pleasure in removing it.' The man's voice was a rasp, and his hand moved under the blanket to touch his throat. 'I remember . . .'

'You are safe now,' Bethral assured him softly. It was so good to see those eyes focus on her face. She smiled at him as he stared at her.

'I suppose that is one way to view death.' He frowned at her. 'I am not sure I share the sentiment.' His gaze moved over the room, to focus on Evelyn. 'See, here is a priestess of the Gods of Palins, who will bring the holy light to this place and show us the shadows on our souls.'

Evelyn's eyes went wide and she stiffened in her chair. But the man didn't notice; he was looking at Josiah. 'There is Lord Josiah, High Baron of Athelbryght, dead these five years.'

His eyes met Bethral's again. 'You are one of the Angels of the Light, come to escort me to paradise.'

Bethral flushed a bit at that, as Red snorted a laugh behind her. The man looked over at Red and frowned. 'And you are' – he paused for a moment, considering Red Gloves – 'one of the Legion of the Damned, apparently.'

Red scowled. 'It's no wonder they cut out your tongue.'

'You're Ezren Storyteller,' Evelyn breathed, as if in prayer. 'Ezren Storyteller, Ezren Silvertongue.'

'Am I?' The man's face went blank, as if he was trying to remember.

'You told us his eyes were brown,' Evelyn challenged.

Bethral looked at the priestess. 'I did, and don't ask me why.'

Josiah was looking over at the man. 'Evie, are you sure? He's got the eyes, true enough, but—'

'Who could say?' Red pointed out. 'The man looks like a week-old corpse, with scarce enough flesh to cling to his bones. And no hair to speak of.'

A thin hand emerged from under the blanket, and the man ran it over his bald skull. He pulled back his hand and held it up, watching it shake.

Bethral reached out, and took his hand in hers. 'It's not as bad as she makes it out to be.' She tucked the hand under the blanket. 'Is Ezren your name?'

He stared up her, blinking, a puzzled look on his face. 'Do names matter in the afterlife?'

Bethral smiled again. 'You're not dead. The priestess has healed you, and given you back your tongue and your life.'

'It's him,' Evelyn insisted. 'He disappeared a year ago, and there were rumors that he'd been taken by Elanore's forces.'

Josiah stiffened. Red shot him a glance, then glared at Evelyn. 'Who is Elanore?'

Bethral ignored them, and sat on the edge of the bed. 'How are you feeling?'

'Amazingly well for a week-old corpse.' He closed his eyes with a sigh. 'Thirsty, in fact.'

'Who is Elanore?' Red asked sharply.

Bethral took up her own mug, and handed it to him. 'Here,' she offered.

He took it carefully. 'Tell me,' he whispered harshly, 'does she really bear the mark of the Chosen?'

Bethral nodded.

'How odd. I thought that nothing but a folktale, with no substance.' He sipped from the mug carefully, then made a face. 'I must be alive. Had I truly departed the world for the glorious haven of the afterlife, I doubt the kavage would taste this terrible.'

'Ezren Silvertongue is a storyteller,' Evelyn said. 'One of the best in the land. He can weave stories that bind his listeners to sit and listen for hours.' Evelyn leaned forward. 'What happened, Ezren? What do you remember?'

FOURTEEN

What did he remember?

He remembered . . .

Betrayal. Pain, such as he'd never known. Beatings . . . he closed his eyes, seeing blows he could not evade, feeling a whip cut into his . . .

'You're safe.'

That voice. He opened his eyes and looked up at her warm blue eyes, her halo of golden hair. The memories changed. He saw a flash of copper, felt the roughness of a warm blanket and moisture in his mouth. And her voice . . .

'*Who is Elanore?*' The brown-haired woman asked again, this time through clenched teeth.

He answered without a thought. 'Elanore is the High Baroness of the Black Hills, allied with Orrin Blackhart and the Regent.' The information was there, in his mind. He took a deep breath, and let the words flow out of him. 'A mage of considerable power, rumored to practice the blood rites. A lovely face that conceals a cruel, vindictive, and manipulative personality. She has not been seen in Edenrich in recent years. It has been bruited about that she was injured in the battle for Athelbryght, but I have not been able to confirm it.'

' "*Battle.*" ' The other man spoke with disgust 'It was a massacre.'

He would swear that man was Josiah of Athelbryght, but Lord Josiah had been killed, had he not?

Tiredness washed over him in a wave, followed closely by despair. He knew he was right, but he did not know *how* he knew. He closed his eyes, ashamed of his weakness. If he was not dead, then he was naked, in a lowly hovel with a priestess, two women warriors, and a dead man's twin.

He frowned. There were the makings of a story there . . .

'Ezren Silvertongue,' the priestess said again in a satisfied tone, and the name resonated in his head. Ezren. He supposed he might be Ezren.

'Evelyn, leave him be.' Josiah spoke again. 'Give him time.'

The blonde leaned over him, pulling the blanket up to tuck around his shoulders. 'What about some food? Do you think you could eat?'

Hungry. He was hungry. He had a tongue; he could . . .

'Yes, please,' he rasped out, trying not to sound too eager.

A warm wooden bowl was placed in his hands, with the smell of pork and fresh bread filling his nose and mouth. His mouth watered, and he paused for a moment, enjoying the sight and smell.

His hand shook as he helped himself. There was no way to maintain proper deportment, given the situation. But he forced himself to go slow and careful, so as not to make a mess. The bread melted in his mouth, and he could taste the meat juices on the back of his tongue as he chewed.

Lord of Light be praised . . . He swallowed, amazed at the sensation, at the feeling of being whole. He closed his eyes, consciously trying to capture the moment. One does not fully appreciate one's tongue until it is gone.

He opened his eyes, and found the others concentrating on their food. All but the woman with brown hair. She stared at him, her lips quirked up at the corners, studying him. When she caught his gaze, she raised an eyebrow.

'I find myself at a disadvantage.' His voice was harsh, although his throat felt well enough. 'May I ask where I am?'

'In what is left of Athelbryght,' she answered. 'You have the priestess to thank for the healing.'

The priestess shook her head. 'Thank the Gods, Ezren. It was their doing. I am merely their tool.'

'My thanks, regardless.' He paused for a moment. 'Your pardon, but your white hair . . . are you the Lady High Priestess Evelyn, of the Church of Palins in Edenrich?'

'I am.' Evelyn nodded at the other man. 'You know of Josiah of Athelbryght.'

Ezren gave a nod. 'I know of you from the Court, my Lord.'

Josiah returned his nod with a pained expression. 'Lord no longer, Ezren.'

Ezren raised an eyebrow, but acquiesced. 'As you wish.'

'I am Red Gloves, a mercenary out of Soccia,' the brunette said. 'And the Chosen. Want to see my tits?'

Ezren frowned at her blunt speech. This was the Chosen? The one to restore the throne of Palins? And her name . . . 'Why do you wear—'

'I am Bethral, mercenary and warrior, also of Soccia.' The blonde blocked his view with her body. He looked up, to see her give him a warning look. It appeared that gloves were not to be a topic of discussion. 'Eat, Ezren Silvertongue. You need to rest and heal.'

'There is a tale here, and I want to hear it.' His voice broke in his throat, and he swallowed hard. He remembered another voice, cloaked in darkness and pain. *'You'll die in chains, unable to tell my story, any story.'*

Bethral reached for another mug, and poured a clear ale into it. She pressed it into his shaky hand. 'This might be more to your liking than the kavage.'

'Ezren,' Josiah said, 'your confusion will clear as you recover. Give yourself time.'

'Josiah is right.' Evelyn gave him a rueful smile. 'You've been awake mere minutes, and I'm pushing and prodding.' She shook her head, and set her mug to the side. 'Auxter will be expecting us, and there is much to be done.'

'There is.' Red Gloves tossed back the rest of her kavage. 'I've an army to win to my side. Best we're about it.'

Evelyn stood and brushed crumbs off her robes. 'Red, Bethral, we need to move your gear to the farm.'

'Why so?' Red asked.

That caught the priestess by surprise. Ezren had the impression that Evelyn wasn't used to being questioned.

'So you can use the farm as your main camp. The men and supplies are—'

Red Gloves wasn't looking at the priestess. She was watching Lord Josiah. Ezren watched them carefully, certain there was more to this than met his eyes. He wasn't surprised when she cut the priestess off in midword.

'No. I will use the farm, certainly, but I'll return here in the evenings,' Red said in no uncertain terms. 'Every evening.'

Interesting.

'As you say,' Lady High Priestess Evelyn said in a non-committal voice.

'But we need to see Auxter, and now is as good a time as any.' Red stood, putting her mug with the other dishes.

'We can take Ezren, then.' Evelyn looked over at him. 'He'll receive better care at the farm, with many willing hands to aid him.'

Fear coursed through Ezren. The idea of more people seeing him weak and confused . . . it overwhelmed him. He didn't want to be seen like this.

'I think he should stay here,' Bethral said, to Ezren's relief. 'It's too much too fast. Let him regain a bit more strength before shifting him.'

Ezren sagged in relief as the priestess nodded in acceptance. He let his head fall back against the pillow, exhausted. His body shifted, and he squirmed slightly. 'Excuse me, but it seems I need some privacy.'

Bethral reached under the bed, and pulled out a chamber pot.

'No.' Ezren was taken aback. 'I would prefer . . .' He looked at Josiah.

Bethral put the pot down. Ezren had the feeling that he'd hurt her somehow. 'Of course,' she said softly.

'It's for the best,' Red said. 'I want you with me when I talk to Auxter.'

'We'll leave him in Josiah's care.' Evelyn moved for the door, as everyone made room for her to squeeze by them. 'Arent packed some clothing, and it's here somewhere, Josiah.'

'This bundle,' Bethral said, pointing under the table.

'Lady High Priestess.' Ezren's voice cracked as he sought her attention.

She paused, and looked back.

'Do not mistake my gratitude,' he said. 'But my voice? Will it return?'

She sighed. 'I don't know, Ezren. The power of the Gods gave you back your tongue, and I can try again on your throat. But I cannot say for sure that it will be as it once was.'

He lowered his gaze to the blanket, and listened as her footsteps faded away.

'You don't mind caring for him?' Bethral asked Josiah softly.

Ezren saw her glance at him, worry in her eyes. He smiled slightly, to reassure her.

'Not at all,' Josiah said.

Bethral followed the priestess out.

Red leaned against the table for a moment. Her eyes fixed on Ezren, and she waited for his full attention. 'Bethral has nursed you right along. Nothing of yours she hasn't seen and cared for. You be kind to her, eh?' Red straightened. 'After all, she's the one spent the copper to buy your carcass from the slavers.'

Ezren blinked, taken aback.

Red turned to Josiah. 'I'll be back, Josiah. Tonight.'

The man nodded. 'I understand, Chosen.'

Red gave him a look that Ezren could not quite interpret, and turned to go. There was definitely something between them, something more than the normal games between a man and a woman. Ezren frowned, trying to read more from their bodies, but Red was out the door and gone.

As Red left Josiah turned to him. 'Let's see to your needs, Ezren.'

'There is a tale here,' Ezren said. 'About those women. Tell it to me.'

Josiah handed him the chamber pot. 'I'll tell you what I know, but I don't know where to begin.'

Ezren struggled with the blankets, and Josiah reached to help. 'Tell me everything,' he demanded, as he got into position. 'From the start.'

'Well' – Josiah turned his back – 'it was raining . . .'

Who did this bitch think she was?

Gloriana pressed back against the stone wall of the upper balcony of the great hall. She'd heard the call to muster in the hall, heard that Evelyn had returned with Red Gloves and some blonde woman called Bethral.

Everyone not on watch had flooded in, filling both levels. Not everyone had seen this new Chosen yet although word of her appearance had spread fast. The description of the fight, and talk of the warning about her gloves had everyone shaking their heads.

Auxter and Vembar had called various groups into the hall at various times over the last day. Oh, they'd talked to her as well, explaining, rationalizing, trying to convince everyone how Red would bring their plans together, and how wonderful it was.

Gloriana had protested, but she'd been admonished. If she heard 'the greater good' or the 'welfare of the kingdom and its people' one more time, she was going to scream.

She'd hidden here, back against the wall in the shadow of the balcony. The leaders were gathered by the hearth, and Red Gloves faced the gathering. How could Aunt Evie sit there and let this happen?

Gloriana had seen Vembar looking around for her, but she'd remained hidden. He'd said something to Arent but then SHE'd started talking and everyone had fallen silent, settling back to listen.

The bitch stood there, calm and professional, and announced that she would act as the Chosen. Gloriana had secretly hoped that someone would stand up and refuse the woman who was taking her place, but no one did. Instead, they hung on her every word, like puppies eager for a stick. It made her sick.

And what about those gloves? Aunt Evie said she never took them off, and not to ask about them at all. Gloriana's eyes narrowed as she looked at Red's gloved hands. Maybe they were old and withered. Or maybe there were talons, and Red had been cursed for some terrible sin. Couldn't they see that she was some kind of criminal, not to be trusted?

Gloriana glared at Red. Why didn't the Gods strike her dead?

The blonde looked up into the gallery then, as if sensing her thoughts. Gloriana shrank even farther into the shadows as the woman swept the area for a threat. She was a mountain of a woman, big and strong and probably as dumb as a rock. Still . . . Gloriana was careful not to draw her attention.

Red Gloves stood there, so calm, so commanding, sword at her side, her arms crossed under those enormous breasts, and talked about the need to move quickly with the plans, and the further need to guard Uncle Josiah and someone named Ezren. About using Athelbryght as a base, so as to keep the farm a secret from the enemy. Of the work that needed to be done before they approached the High Barons for support.

Everyone fell all over themselves, offering information, giving advice, all talking at the same time. Like chickens scrambling for thrown grain.

Gloriana crossed her arms over her flat chest and glowered. It was so unfair! Just because the bitch was older . . .

Vembar chanced to look up then, and Gloriana was sure he'd seen her. He opened his eyes wide, then closed them, and shook his head as if disappointed. Gloriana flushed in embarrassment, and moved behind the pillar.

Men were forming a unit to set up guard duty in Athelbryght as soon as a portal could be raised. In her rage, Gloriana stepped forward and grabbed the railing. 'Why should we trust you, when you won't even take off your gloves? What are you hiding?'

Her voice rang out over the room, and everyone looked up at her. Gloriana's face was hot, but she wasn't going to back down. Her eyes were on Red Gloves, who stiffened and gave her a hooded look. Gloriana almost took a step back, away from those eyes, but she forced herself to keep still. The entire room seemed to hold its breath.

Red relaxed, 'We need to talk, you and I. Come with me.'

Aunt Evelyn stood up. 'Where are you going?'

Red gave her a considering look, and Gloriana held her breath, half hoping the sword woman would do something stupid.

'We are going to the shrine of the Twelve,' Red said. She looked back up at Gloriana. 'This is between Gloriana and me.'

Gloriana swallowed hard, sure that she was about to face her death. Red was still looking at her, but her voice rang out over the entire hall. 'Either the mark under my breast means that I have your trust in all things, or you might as well kill me now.'

They approached the shrine in silence, for which Gloriana was grateful. Red hadn't lectured, or scolded, or even threatened to kill her so far. She'd just led the way, and Gloriana followed behind, her stomach in knots.

'Lerew. Jaff.' Red called out. The men appeared from the

thickest pines, and Red dismissed them with a few words. They both looked over at Gloriana, and she gave them her nod of approval. Whatever was going to happen, she didn't want witnesses.

The men walked off, and they listened to the footsteps crunch through the needles, until the only sound was the birds around them. Red was staring at the rock, where the grain lay scattered about.

'Well?' the mercenary asked.

'Well, what?' Gloriana crossed her arms over her chest.

Red gave her an amused look. 'Do you really want to challenge me, child?'

Rage swept through her. 'It's not fair!' she cried, dropping her arms and forming fists. She spat out her words. 'You aren't even doing this for the right reasons.' She took a step forward, forgetting her fear. 'All you care about is money.'

Red raised an eyebrow. 'I am a mercenary.'

Gloriana glared at her. 'You're a better fighter than me, and older than me. There's nothing I can do about it, and it's just not fair.' The last few words burst out of her. Gloriana knew she sounded like a whining brat, and she flushed, hating Red even more.

But the older woman just nodded. 'You're right. It's not.'

Gloriana's shoulders slumped, and despair filled her. 'Vembar and Auxter tell me that all the time.'

'But we still expect it to be fair, don't we?' Red sounded oddly sympathetic. 'Even when you are older and know better.'

Gloriana looked at her, but there was no mockery in Red's expression as she continued. 'Gloriana, you are the next oldest of the Chosen. If I fail, it will be up to you to pick up the pieces and try again.'

Gloriana kicked at some of the needles, not looking at Red. 'I know.'

'I follow the Way of the Twelve. You know of this path?' Red asked.

'Yes,' Gloriana said. Great! A lecture. Just what she needed now, from this . . .

'You sound like a spoiled brat,' Red snapped. 'Look at me.'

Gloriana's head snapped up. The older woman was deadly serious.

'You know of the Twelve?'

Gloriana nodded. 'I do. I was raised to worship the Lord of Light and the Lady of Laughter, but Vembar has taught me about the faiths of other lands.'

'Then you know that we hold our oaths dear, and that an oath taken in a shrine to the Way is dearest of all?' Red asked. 'You would accept such an oath?'

'I would.' Gloriana nodded again, puzzled.

Red relaxed and flashed a smile. She stepped forward, and placed her gloved hand on the stone. 'Then, Gloriana, second eldest of the Chosen, hear now my oath to you and to the Kingdom of Palins.'

'They've been gone too long.' Worried, Evelyn paced before the great hearth, where Auxter and Vembar were playing chess.

Auxter grunted. 'Not that long. Sit down.'

'Evelyn, I'm getting tired just watching you,' Vembar said softly. 'Please sit before you wear me out, child.'

Evelyn plopped down in the chair next to his with a sigh.

'All will be well,' Auxter rumbled as he moved his queen. 'Have some faith in your Chosen, Evelyn.'

'Gloriana is so young,' Evelyn said. 'I trust Red; she bears the mark of the Chosen. I just can't—'

'Control her.' Auxter finished for her.

'She's not a tame one, that is certain.' Vembar spoke as he studied the board. 'Gloriana is better trained to sit upon the throne. But there's a war to be fought, and this Chosen can fight it.'

Auxter snorted, then gave Evelyn a sharp look from under his bushy eyebrows. 'You are well caught, Lady High Priestess. Either you trust her, simply because she bears the mark of the Chosen under her breast, or you don't. And if you don't feel that you can trust her, only time will convince you. Time we don't have to spare.'

'I trust her,' Evelyn protested.

'Then rest your feet.' Vembar advised.

'And your mind, Evie.' Auxter raised his head. 'What's that?'

Evie looked up to see warriors moving back into the hall. One came up to the hearth. 'They've just come out of the pines, Auxter.'

Auxter gave him a stern look. 'Report.'

'They're walking together. Gloriana is beside her, and they both look serious.'

Evelyn stood as Red and Gloriana made their way to the great hearth, followed by many more of the warriors. The first thing Evelyn noticed was the look on Gloriana's face. There was a new confidence there, a new maturity.

They both turned to face the room, and then Gloriana took a step forward. She stood tall, and lifted her chin before speaking. 'Red Gloves is the eldest Chosen, and is the one to lead us against the Regent. She has my full support.'

Red placed her hand on Gloriana's shoulder. 'Gloriana is my heir, should I fall in this effort. Together, we will restore the throne of Palins.'

Evelyn gaped, even as a cheer filled the room.

Red held up her hand. 'Save the celebration for our success. Right now, there is work to be done, and quickly.'

FIFTEEN

Warriors came out of the woods, from the direction of the old shrine.

Josiah heard them before he saw them. He'd left Ezren sleeping within the hut. The poor man had been muttering something about a hero's path as he'd drifted off.

Josiah had just started taking up a load of wood when the two horses had raised their heads, ears pricked forward. The goats had paused, too, and all heads turned in the direction of the shrine. Josiah dropped the wood and reached for his axe, turning to confront his attackers.

He came out of his crouch when he recognized Oris and Alad, Auxter's men. They raised their hands in greeting, and he walked forward to meet them at the door of the hut.

'Trouble?' Josiah looked over Alad's shoulder to see horses being brought out of the woods behind them, some still blindfolded from coming through the portal.

'We're to set a perimeter watch, Lord Josiah,' Oris said. 'And we're to clear your . . . home . . . so that the next group can get to work as fast as possible. Orders of the Chosen.'

'Which Chosen?' came a rough voice from the hut.

They all turned to see a brilliant green eye peering out of the slight crack in the doorway.

'Careful, Ezren.' Josiah moved forward.

The door opened wider to reveal Ezren, who sagged against its frame, his free hand clenching a dagger. 'I was uncertain.' He coughed. 'I thought perhaps . . .'

'They're friends. Oris and Alad.' Josiah reached out to steady the man. 'Let's get you back in bed.' He moved his body so that Ezren wouldn't see the men's horrified expressions at his condition. Ezren sighed, leaned into the support, and shivered.

Oris recovered first. He stepped forward, removing his cloak and offering it to Ezren. 'All due respect Lord Josiah, the Chosen has ordered that Ezren Storyteller be moved to the foaling room of the barn, with all the furnishings.' He placed the cloak on Ezren's shoulders and looked at the hut with a roll of his eyes. 'She's got plans for this place.'

'I say again' – Ezren stood up straighter, clutching at the edges of the cloak and pulling it tight around his body – 'which Chosen? Red Gloves or Gloriana?'

Alad grinned. 'Well, now, it would be the Chosen Red Gloves. Gloriana, the Chosen Heir, has announced her support of the Eldest Chosen in all things.'

'Plans?' Josiah asked, as even more men poured into the area, with horses and gear.

'Well, then,' Ezren said, 'she has accepted the call to adventure.' He reached for Alad's arm with a shaky hand. 'She has taken the first step on the Hero's Path.'

Alad took his elbow. 'Don't know anything about that, sir, but we've our orders.'

'Of course you do.' Ezren started toddling toward the barn, leaning hard on Alad. 'Now, tell me what happened, lad. Tell me what you saw.' He managed a few steps before he faltered. Josiah moved to catch him, but Alad anticipated the problem and scooped Ezren up in his arms.

'This is not necessary,' Ezren protested. 'I am perfectly capable of—'

Alad steadied himself, and started to walk toward the barn. 'Forgive me, Storyteller, but you are a bit of a load. The quicker I have you there, the more breath I have to tell you my tale.'

'Ah.' Ezren relaxed. 'Well, then . . .' Their voices grew faint as they left.

'Lady Bethral warned us about how he'd look,' Oris said, looking after them. 'But hearing and seeing are two different things.'

'He was badly abused, Oris,' Josiah said.

'Bastards.' Oris spat in the dirt. 'That's what we're about, then. Doing something about them.'

'Aye,' Josiah agreed.

'Here, lads,' Oris called to his men, 'let's get this place cleared out now. We've much to do, and little time to do it.'

*

Bethral came through the portal to find Josiah's hut in ruins. Men were tearing away the thatched roof and tugging down the mud-daubed walls. Others were already pulling apart the wooden frame. Bethral nodded in approval. They'd left the stone hearth standing, as per Red's commands.

From her glance about, it looked like all of Red's commands were being carried out. Men were at work on fences. Steel and Beast were with other horses, and from the looks of it, Beast was biting the others into submission, as usual. There were tents going up in the far field, with cooking fires well established.

Lord Josiah was seated at the well, his arms crossed over his chest, watching the men work with an unreadable face. She headed that way.

'Bethral.'

'Josiah.' She was not one to inflict a title on a man who didn't want one. 'Is Ezren seen to?'

He pointed with his chin. 'He's in the foaling room, forcing everyone he can get his hands on to tell him what happened at Auxter's.' He looked at the box under her arm. 'What is that?'

'Vembar asked me to give it to Ezren, with his compliments.' Bethral eased the box to the ground. 'He claims it's a portable writing desk, with supplies within, but I question the "portable."'

Josiah chuckled. 'Well, if there's one that needs it, it would be Ezren. The man is a walking book.'

Bethral settled herself on the well and sighed. Probably for the best that the green-eyed man was in the barn. He'd certainly be warm and safe there, until they could build a suitable place for one such as him. A man like that, a man of learning, would want his privacy. She'd find a space in one of the tents.

She looked about, studying the work on the hut. 'They've gotten a lot done in a short time.'

'Without so much as a by-your-leave,' Josiah grumbled. 'By the "order of the Chosen."'

Given his surly tone, silence seemed the best response.

Bethral watched as one of the lads working by the tents started their way. Josiah spotted him as well, and grumbled under his breath. 'They've been asking me questions all day: where to find

this, and what to do about that. They expect me to make decisions.'

Well, he was in a mood, that was certain. Best be about her
tasks, then. But she'd a message to convey to him, and she was
certain it would not be well received. Bethral leaned down, and
picked up the desk. 'There's to be a meeting in the morning.
Red, Auxter, and the other leaders. They will come here to break
their fast.'

'Here? Why here?' Josiah demanded.

Bethral stood. 'So you can be a part of it.'

That drew a grim look. 'I'm of no use to them,' Josiah
snapped. 'It's safer to stay at the farm.'

Bethral shrugged.

Josiah rolled his eyes. 'Order of the Chosen, I suppose.'

'Just so.' Bethral kept her voice pleasant and her face neutral.
'Evelyn has returned to the Church, and Red is eating with
Vembar and Auxter.'

'Fine,' Josiah growled.

'She said to tell you that she will return here tonight,' Bethral
added.

The lad came up to them at a run. 'Begging you pardon, Lord
Josiah,' he said. Josiah growled under his breath, but the fool
blithered on. 'Oris says to ask if we can dig the new necessaries
off behind the tents.'

'Ask the Chosen, why don't you?' Josiah snarled. He stood,
and stomped off down one of the paths. Bethral admired the stiff
and stubborn lines of his back, but they lost some impressiveness
when five goats took off after him, prancing and bleating at his
heels.

Open-mouthed, the lad stared at the retreating Lord Josiah.
He swiveled his head back and looked at Bethral. 'What do I tell
Oris now, Lady?'

Bethral sighed. 'Tell him that I'll come and talk with him. I
need to speak with the storyteller, then I will be there.'

'My thanks, Lady!' The lad ran off.

Bethral shifted her burden, and looked at the retreating back
of Lord Josiah Athelbryght. Poor man. He was learning what she
already knew so well.

Be careful what you wish for . . .

Josiah gritted his teeth, and ripped the weeds out of the soil, roots and all.

He'd fetched a hoe, but the marjoram needed tending, and he needed to rip and tear and hurt the weeds. Stones dug into his knees and sweat dripped off his face, but he didn't care. The dirt gave way under his hands, and the sweet scent of crushed leaves filled the air.

Who did she think she was? The place was flooding with people and horses. Had she given any thought to how dangerous that was? His home torn asunder, walls moving, everything . . . changing.

He sat back on his heels and wiped his forehead with his sleeve. The spring sun wasn't that hot, but he'd been working hard to clear this bed.

Damn her eyes. Damn her birthmark. He'd had five years of silence, and pain. Five years of penance – and it was all blown away in a moment.

His stomach churned. He closed his eyes for a moment, then spat to clear his mouth.

He wanted a Chosen. Wanted someone to avenge Athelbryght. But it was all moving so fast, and he'd never thought he'd be involved. Didn't she see him for the failure he was?

Josiah opened his eyes, and tore back into the weeds. Worse, he'd found himself giving orders, making decisions. He'd have taken charge as if nothing had happened. As if he hadn't made the mistakes that led to his people's deaths.

'You're upset.'

He looked up to see Red Gloves standing there, her hands on her hips. She tilted her head. 'Let me guess. You thought I'd wait five years to get started.'

Within her own head, Red laughed silently. So that's what Josiah's eyes looked like when he was furious. Snapping with energy, sparkling with life, heat, and anger.

Desire spiked through her. Who knew a dirty goatherder would create such heat deep within her?

'It's not safe here, and the land can't support these people,' Josiah snapped.

Red looked around at the herb beds, brimming with plants. 'You've been safe enough. And Auxter can support us for the short time we'll be here.' Red made a great show of heaving a deep sigh, giving Josiah a patient look.

He looked down at the soil beneath his hands.

'So' – Red drawled the word out – 'it's to be permanent, then, this burnt-out shrine? And all the lands about?'

'You could respect the dead,' Josiah growled.

'I do, as long as they don't take up too much time,' Red replied calmly. She chuffed out a laugh. 'Look around, Josiah. Hells, look at your feet. Even the earth knows. Those weedy things are growing like . . . weeds.' She had to chuckle at that, but Josiah wasn't sharing the laugh. Poor man. She really shouldn't tease, but it was far too much fun. Besides, he needed it.

'It's marjoram.' His tone was flat and joyless.

'Whatever,' Red said. 'Slow but sure, the land returns to life.'

'You're a cold bitch,' Josiah growled.

'No,' Red replied calmly. 'I'm the Chosen. One who will do the work, and not sit on her heels and wait for this prophecy of yours to do its will.'

Josiah's cheeks stained red at that, and he jerked to his feet. He had an inch on her, and tried to use it by towering over her, but she didn't flinch or step back. She looked him right in the eye. He opened his mouth in a snarl, but she cut him off. 'I face life head-on, Josiah of Athelbryght.' She spat. 'I don't flinch from the pain any more than the pleasure. That's life, and if you are lucky, there's joy in equal measure to the pain.'

'What do you know of pain?' Josiah growled. She was close enough that he could smell her, and her scent filled his mouth, making it water.

Red's eyes went flat. 'So you're the only one that's suffered, is that it? Well, my goatherder, I've had pain and some to spare, but I didn't hide in the ashes for five years.'

Josiah's hands formed fists, white at the knuckles.

'Weep yourself dry if you will,' she continued, 'but I'll not waste another minute. Bring it on – victory or defeat, either or, makes no never mind to me.' She shook her hair back off her face.

*

Angered beyond any real thought, Josiah reached for her. He grabbed her arms and yanked her close, not certain if it was to kill her or kiss her. Their eyes met, her cold passion meeting his hot fury. His lips curled back, seeking some scathing rebuke. Instead, he found their lips crushed together in a kiss, an open-mouth demand on his part.

She returned the kiss in equal measure. His shock was short, swept away by tongue-to-tongue wet heat.

His arm dropped to wrap around her waist, and with the other he grabbed her wrist, feeling the leather of her glove in his grasp. He pulled her down, into the depths of the marjoram, forcing her beneath him, pressing her to the ground.

Hands flew, clothing parted as the smell of crushed herb filled the air. They writhed there in the dirt, her armor melted away, and he used his leg to part her thighs, fumbling with his trous.

Frantic, furious, he entered her and thrust hard, pounding her into the earth, trying, striving for something just outside his grasp. Until he exploded in heat, rage, and pure sweet pleasure.

He collapsed on top of her, sprawled like a broken doll. His breathing was harsh in his own ears, and it took long moments before he could hear her breathe, too.

'Feel better, Josiah?' Red's voice was warm in his ear. She turned her head slightly and licked the curve of his ear.

He shuddered, then, at what he'd done. Swallowing hard, he tried to pull back. 'I . . . sorry. I took . . .'

Her laughter, clear and sweet, stopped him. 'You took nothing.' Her leather-covered fingers teased the hair at the base of his neck.

'I forced—'

'You think so?' She shifted slightly, and something pricked his side. A glance showed a dagger point pressed to his belly. 'I've been forced, my goatherder. Never again.' The dagger disappeared as quick as it came. 'But you took your own pleasure here and now, and owe me in return.' She carded her fingers through his hair, and showed him a sprig of marjoram. 'I prefer the softness of your bed before you pay me what is owed.'

He stared at her dumbly. 'They tore down my home.'

'No, Josiah. Come and see.'

*

She led him back through the herb beds toward the hut after they'd cleaned off. The goats danced at their side, pushing their noses into Josiah's hands, demanding attention. They tried it with Red, but she fixed them with a glare that put a stop to that.

Damn goats.

As she'd ordered, the hearth still stood, but the foundations had been laid around it for a wooden platform. Red nodded in approval at the tent over the platform. It was thick wool, nothing permanent but it would serve as a command center. The tent was in two parts; the wider area now held the table and as many chairs and benches as would fit.

The smaller area, by the hearth, had cloth as a divider, and held the bed. Josiah's old hut would now be his bedroom.

Their bedroom.

The warriors had cleared out of the area, and there were men moving about the tents, seeing to the fires at the end of a day. She could see Bethral talking to a group of riders, so the watch was set.

'You see?' Red asked, as she held the cloth aside. 'You've a bed, Josiah.'

'I'll bed down the goats,' Josiah said.

'I'll be waiting.' Red gave him a sultry look.

The fabric moved slightly in the light breeze. With a fire in the hearth, it would be warm enough. Red set about the task, well pleased.

Once the flames bit at the wood, Red moved about, taking off her sword belt and hanging it by the bed. Her packs were by the side, her bedroll on top.

By the time Josiah returned, she was naked on the bed.

And oh, so ready . . .

Josiah was sated and drowsy when Red stirred. He thought she'd a need for the necessary, but the sounds she was making caused him to open an eye. And then both of them.

She was setting out her bedroll in front of the fire.

'What are you doing?' Josiah asked. 'Come back to bed.'

Red turned her head and looked at him. She frowned, as if puzzled. 'Why?'

Josiah caught his breath. 'I—' He took a breath, uncertain. 'I thought you'd sleep with me. Isn't that what—' The words caught in his throat of a sudden. No. That wasn't what she was used to.

Red glanced down at her bedroll and then back at him, puzzled. 'I can guard from here, Josiah. If someone comes in . . .'

'The bed is more comfortable.' Josiah sat up in the bed, and the blanket slid down off his chest. 'And your presence beside me is part of the pleasure.'

It came and went in an instant, the merest flicker of longing in her eyes. But he saw it, and knew it for what it was. This woman – this lovely, hard, powerful woman – had never known comfort.

He'd bedded women before, and he'd always prided himself in seeing to his partner's pleasure as well as his own. But here was one who knew all the pleasure of sex, but none of the intimacy that can be shared between two bodies under a warm blanket.

Still, she hesitated.

'Please,' Josiah whispered.

She stood there, naked but for her gloves, then shrugged. 'As you wish.'

Josiah lay back down, and watched as she rolled the pallet up. For all her careful casualness, Josiah knew he'd unsettled her. She fiddled with the placement of her sword and dagger, laying them just so by the bed.

He held the blanket up for her as she slid back in beside him.

She gave him a knowing look. 'You just want me close at hand for a morning romp.'

'Do you blame me?' Josiah answered. 'Why pad across a cold room, when I can reach out my hands within the warmth of the blankets?'

Red chuckled, relaxing as she settled herself. 'I like a bit of play before breakfast.'

Josiah settled next to her, careful to let only their shoulders touch. 'We will both profit, my mercenary.'

Red yawned, and seemed to fall asleep between breaths.

Josiah watched her face in the firelight for a long moment.

Josiah awoke some time later, to find Red curled around him, her head on his shoulder, her gloved hand over his heart. He smiled, half-asleep, and covered her hand with his own. The red leather was warm under his fingers.

She was like a kitten, he thought muzzily. All teeth and claws when awake, but soft, warm, and purring while sleeping. He smiled faintly as he drifted back to sleep. A brown tabby, who'd played rough all day and now cuddled close.

Of course, it would be worth his life to call her so . . .

SIXTEEN

Ezren closed his eyes as he felt High Priestess Evelyn reach out and gently touch his throat. She was so close he could smell the incense lingering in her formal embroidered robes. It reminded him of services, the trailing smoke rising from the braziers as the sun streamed in the windows. He felt his body relax at her touch and the soft sound of her prayers.

It was warm in the foaling room, with a fire crackling in the hearth, but he still felt a chill. He'd slept well enough, even though someone had kept coming in during the night to feed the flames. When he'd woken, there'd been someone to aid in his ablutions.

Not the Angel of the Light, though.

Clean clothing, warm bread and butter, and a mug of hot kavage had made him feel better. One of the warriors had told him that Evelyn was on her way, so he'd been made comfortable on the bunk, and wrapped in blankets to ward off a chill. Far better treatment than—

No. His mind shied away, and he concentrated on the sensations of being healed, concentrated on the sound of Evelyn's prayers, on the slight tingle of warmth on his skin. He lifted his chin slightly, and took a long breath. How would you tell this in a story? What words would you use to get your listener to—

'There.' Evelyn's voice was soft.

He opened his eyes and saw her looking at him closely, her eyes questioning.

He swallowed, and took a breath. 'Lady . . .'

He winced as his voice cracked.

The priestess sighed, and stepped back to sit on the other bunk. It was just the two of them in the foaling room, for which he was grateful. He didn't have to hide his disappointment from her.

'Ezren, I'm sorry. I've done what I can,' Evelyn said.

'I am grateful for my life, Lady High Priestess,' Ezren croaked, pulling his blankets tighter around his body. 'But is there any possibility that . . .'

Evelyn reached for the kavage by the fire and poured a mug. The firelight caught her small silver ring and made it gleam. 'Your voice may yet return, with time.' She handed him the mug. 'More to the point, you need to rebuild your body slowly. Rest, food, time – those are your best healers now.'

He sighed, and sipped his kavage.

'Red has called for a council this morning,' Evelyn said. 'We'd like you there, if you feel well enough.'

'Here?' Ezren looked around the room, stuffed with supplies.

Evelyn shook her head. 'Red has a command tent set up outside.'

Ezren clutched the mug tighter. 'Who will be there, Lady?'

'Red, of course. Josiah. Bethral. Gloriana—'

'The young one?' Ezren considered that as Evelyn continued.

'Vembar. He insists—'

Ezren's head jerked up. 'Vembar of Edenrich? The late King's Chancellor?'

'Yes,' Evelyn said. 'Then there is Auxter, and his lady, Arent.'

'Of the late King's Guard?' At her nod, Ezren continued. 'I know Vembar, and I've heard of Auxter.' He looked at her closely. 'And I know why your hair turned white, Lady High Priestess.'

'I doubt there is much you don't know, Ezren Storyteller.' Evelyn smiled ruefully. 'We need that knowledge, if you would share it with us.'

'I am not sure, Lady.' Ezren hesitated.

Evelyn gave him a considering look. 'They know what you have been through, Ezren. You should not be ashamed of your appearance.'

Ezren reached up, and felt the scarred skin of his scalp. 'No, Lady, of course not.'

Evelyn said nothing, merely stood and reached for his blankets. 'Come. The sun is warm, but there is a bit of a breeze this morning. You can wear my cloak with its hood up.'

'Very well.' Ezren reached out to hand her his mug, then

started to wrestle his way from the bedding. 'Perhaps it *would* be best if I were there. We need to talk, Red Gloves and I.'

'Gracious Gods.' Vembar breathed out in horror. 'Is that Ezren?'

Josiah turned to see Evie emerge from the barn, Ezren at her side. The man was hunched, but he was walking under his own power. His face was still so very thin, almost skeletal.

'They warned you,' Arent said softly as she served Vembar some of the kavage. She blocked Vembar's view as she reached for the pitcher.

Vembar was a consummate diplomat and composed his face quickly. But Josiah knew he was shaken and trying to get himself under control.

'He looks a damned sight better than when Bethral bought him,' Red pointed out.

'Better?' Vembar drew a breath.

Bethral gave them all a glare, then rose to go to aid the couple.

'He's doing well, Vembar,' Josiah offered. 'But remember that his voice—'

'I do.' Vembar sat straighter. 'And I will have a care for my old friend.' He stood, took a few steps forward, and called to him. 'Ezren, my friend.'

'Vembar.' Ezren's eyes were bright under the hood. Bethral and Evie helped him to step onto the platform. 'I never thought to see you again, outside the presence of the Gods.' His voice crackled as he spoke.

'Or I, you.' Vembar stepped forward to clasp his hand warmly. He drew the man into a gentle hug, and then released him carefully. 'Let me make you known to these others. We can talk later.'

Bethral moved a chair behind him, but Ezren remained standing.

'Sit before you fall,' Red said.

'It is polite to remain standing during an introduction, Chosen,' Ezren replied. 'Lord Auxter, I have heard of you, from your time with the King.'

Auxter used his staff to stand. 'Allow me to make you known to my wife, Arent.'

'Lady.' Ezren nodded his head. Arent smiled and returned the gesture.

Josiah had to admire him. The man had been through a horrific ordeal, but he was acting as if this was nothing more than a simple garden party.

Red was standing next to Josiah, finishing her mug of kavage. The breeze came up and caught her hair, and it flared out gently. She reached out and tucked it behind her ear with a gloved hand.

Desire stirred in Josiah's groin, and he looked off into the distance. The platform they stood on worked well as a command tent, but it was little more than rough wooden planking, with Josiah's old table placed in the center. Once the wool sides had been rolled up, the goats had thought it great fun to climb on until Red had chased them off.

'And this is Gloriana.' Vembar held out his hand, and Gloriana came to stand next to him. 'The Chosen Heir and my student.'

'Lady fair.' Ezren reached out and kissed her hand.

Amused, Josiah watched as Gloriana smiled shyly and blushed. She curtsied with grace. 'Thank you, Lord Ezren.'

'I do not hold that title,' Ezren sighed, as he eased down into the chair. 'I am a storyteller, nothing more.'

'Or less.' Arent added.

'Gloriana, if you'd do the honors.' Vembar seated himself at the table.

Gloriana produced a large map, vellum by the looks of it. Josiah frowned, shifting so that he could take in the whole of it. Red moved to stand next to him.

Ezren leaned forward. 'This is old. It dates from before the King's death.'

'It was a gift from King Everard.' Vembar's voice trembled. 'I brought it with me when I fled the castle.'

Old and worn, it was still lovely, inked with colors that were faded, marked with the various baronies. Josiah's gaze fell on the outline of Athelbryght and he had to look away for a moment, the pain welling up from deep within.

Red noticed, but he looked away, avoiding her eye.

'Things have changed,' Ezren's voice crackled.

Auxter nodded. 'We know, Storyteller. All too well.'

'Tell us.' Evelyn settled herself in one of the chairs. 'Tell us what you know.'

Ezren frowned. 'My knowledge is old as well. At least a year old.'

'More current than ours, Ezren,' Vembar said.

'But you know—' Ezren started to argue, but Red cut him off.

'I don't,' she said firmly. 'Tell me, Storyteller. Start with the King's death.'

Ezren leaned back, tilting his head to see her from under the hood. 'Every story has its price, Lady.'

'So?' Red demanded.

Vembar coughed. 'It is the custom to pay a storyteller, Chosen.'

'Like a bard?' Red asked.

'Or a mercenary,' Josiah said under this breath.

Red shot him an amused look.

Ezren drew himself up under the cloak. 'I am no performer, Chosen. I collect and preserve stories. If you wish to hear, you must pay the price.'

Red gave him a narrow look. 'What is the price?'

'Answers to my questions.' Ezren's eyes gleamed green from the depths of the hood.

Josiah's eyebrows went up at that.

Red frowned at the frail man. For a long moment, there was silence, broken only when Ezren sighed and shrugged. 'Except about your gloves, Chosen.'

Red's face cleared. 'And my past, Storyteller. That's my story, none of yours. But I'll pay your price.'

Ezren nodded, and reached out to smooth the map with his hand. 'This is the land of Palins, in the sixteenth year of the reign of King Everard. The year that saw the death of the King, his Queen, and his heir.

'Now, the Crown rules Palins, but the lands are held by the High Barons, under an oath of fealty. The Crown retains the lands around the capital, Edenrich.' Ezren pointed to the map with a thin finger. 'There are . . . were . . . eight High Baronies: Athelbryght, Tassinic, Wyethe, Penature, Summerford, the Black Hills, Farentall, and Swift's Port.

'In the confusion after the deaths, the High Barons came

together to determine who would rule. Iitrus, Lord of the Merchant Guild, was named as Regent.

'A series of councils were held, all confused and contentious.' Ezren gestured with both hands. 'I will not go into details, but no agreement could be reached among the High Barons, due in large part to the designs of High Baroness Elanore of the Black Hills and the Regent. They were in league, and they turned that to their advantage.

'One dark night they sent assassins through the castle, after the High Barons and their advisers. The castle ran red with blood, but the plans failed in that they managed to kill only Josiah's mother and the High Baron of Farentell. The others escaped.

'Elanore and Iitrus then sent their forces against Farentell, squeezing it between them like an olive in a press, taking its people as slaves.

'This cut Palins in half, leaving the other High Barons at their mercy. Or so they thought.'

'It worked,' Auxter said. 'Worked brilliantly.'

'Except the High Baroness Elanore then made a mistake. Since Farentell fell so quickly, she also sent her forces against Summerford, hoping to subdue Athelbryght and Summerford at the same time. She led the attack on Athelbryght. Orrin Blackhart attacked Summerford.'

Bethral leaned over. She pointed to the Black Hills, and then to its borders with Athelbryght and Summerford. 'She warred on two separate borders at once?'

'She did,' Ezren confirmed.

Gloriana spoke softly. 'How was she able to attack on two fronts?'

'She used Odium, Lady fair.'

Red had never seen anyone's face go so white so fast. But Lady High Priestess Evelyn was as white as her hair and her robes.

'No!' The woman looked like she would keel over, but she sat straight and still in her chair. 'No, that can't be. Ezren, the Church would—'

The scarred man studied the map. 'Lady High Priestess, the Church supports the Regent, who in turn supports High Baroness Elanore. An uneasy, quiet alliance, but alliance just the

133

same. The Church turns a blind eye to slaves, since they have no rights as such. Although the people of Farentell never appeared in the slave markets.'

Evelyn opened her mouth as if to deny it, but Ezren did not let her. 'Lady, it is the truth.'

'Odium?' Bethral asked softly.

'The walking dead,' Ezren answered. 'The bodies of men and women whose souls were drained from their flesh.'

SEVENTEEN

Josiah sat down hard, and buried his face in his hands. Red saw the muscles of his back move as he fought to control his emotions.

Auxter gripped his staff and scowled. Arent stood behind him and laid a quiet hand on his shoulder. Red noticed that Auxter relaxed just a bit, the lines in his face easing. Red had a sudden impulse to do the same for Josiah, but the idea made her feel funny. He might not welcome such a gesture, and she felt awkward even thinking of it.

'I looked for those of Athelbryght wherever I found a slave market,' Evelyn whispered. 'Could they have sacrificed all the people of two Baronies?'

'You would be in a better position than I to know, Lady High Priestess.' Ezren's voice was gentle but firm. 'I know little of magic and its ways.'

'Lord of Light . . .' Evelyn still looked pale. 'I know nothing of the dark ways, Ezren Storyteller.'

Josiah lifted his head. 'No one practices those arts,' he rasped.

'High Baroness Elanore does.' Ezren's voice was firm. 'And Orrin Blackhart aids her in this. I've heard tales of men, women, and children herded into the Keep of the Black Hills, never to emerge.'

'It would explain the numbers,' Auxter said gruffly.

'What kind of person could do such a thing?' Evelyn asked. She glanced at Josiah and then looked down at her clasped hands.

For a long moment, there was no sound but the distant pounding of hammers. Red kept her questions to herself. She'd heard of undead, but had never fought them. A quick glance at Bethral showed she was just as puzzled. She'd need to know how to fight them, but that could wait. Auxter could probably tell her what she needed to know.

Ezren broke the silence. 'Elanore's attack went well, and Athelbryght fell. But word leaked back to Edenrich that Elanore was injured in the attack.'

Josiah jerked his head over to stare at the green-eyed man. 'She was injured?'

Ezren focused on him. 'I could find only two people who would even talk to me about it. And they'd both heard it from the friend of a friend.' He shook his head. 'I've no idea of its truth, nor the extent of her injuries.' The green-eyed man leaned forward. 'Do you?'

Josiah looked off into the distance. 'No.'

Ezren sat back, then looked at Red. 'Summerford rose to meet Blackhart and his army. But what Elanore and Blackhart did not understand was that while the High Baron of Summerford and the High Baroness of Wyethe despise one another, they each leap to the other's defense at the slightest hint of a threat. Blackhart could not face the combined forces, and retreated.

'So Elanore holds the Black Hills, and claims to hold Athelbryght. The Regent holds Edenrich. They split Farentell between them, although it is naught but empty land.'

'What of the others?' Arent asked. 'What did the other High Barons do?'

'Summerford and Wyethe fell back to their bickering when the threat was removed. Tassinic, Penature, and Swift's Port all hold to themselves, waiting to see who will prosper. Things were stalemated thus at the time I was . . .' Ezren's voice trailed off. There was a pause when the only sound was the wind. 'I don't remember.'

Red smoothed the map with her gloved hand. 'So which of the High Barons do you want me to approach first?'

'Auxter and I thought to approach the neutrals,' Vembar said, 'Tassinic, Penature, and Summerford. We'd try to convince them to aid our cause. We'd hoped to gain Wyethe as well. And if Lady Helene heard that Lord Fael was involved, she might be persuaded to join.'

Ezren frowned. 'Tassinic has links to the elves of the far south, being half-elven himself. What of Swift's Port?'

136

'Lord Royle thinks only of his ships. He'll not be pulled into this dispute.'

Red nodded and looked out at where the men were working. 'We can consider it for a while. It will take two weeks before we are ready.'

Josiah gave her a startled look, but it was Evelyn who spoke first. 'Two weeks? Why wait that long?'

'Two weeks to familiarize myself with the men and their skills.' Red quirked her mouth. 'We can work all day, and then talk all night about whom to approach and why. Ezren and Vembar know these people, as does Auxter.'

Auxter nodded his agreement.

'And Gloriana will sit in on these discussions,' Red added. 'She needs to be ready to take my place if I fall. Two weeks should see it done, and ready.'

Two weeks? That fast?

Josiah's hand trembled, and he closed it into a tight fist. It was going to happen. A Chosen would lead an army and restore the Throne of Palins.

Two weeks. He'd have two weeks. Two weeks until vengeance.

Two weeks of Red Gloves in his bed. Two weeks . . . but what then?

He swallowed hard, and consciously tried to relax his tight shoulders.

Red Gloves was not Elanore. They'd a clear agreement, and Red would hold to her word. He had no doubt of that. She'd laid it out plain enough, cutting through his doubts like the dagger-star of her birthmark. Straight to the point, and all the rules clear.

But at night, in their bed, after they'd enjoyed one another's bodies, he'd nuzzled the soft skin beneath her breast, and traced her birthmark with his tongue as she'd shivered at his touch. Skin so soft on a woman that hard. Who'd believe—

'More kavage?' Arent asked.

Startled, Josiah looked down to see an offered mug. He took it, more out of habit than want. He held it tight as Arent served the others, feeling at once cold and hot.

Two weeks.

'So.' Ezren leaned back in his chair and the hood of the cloak fell back, revealing his head. But the bright-eyed man didn't seem to notice or care. 'You have been called.'

Red raised her eyebrows. 'Called?'

'Called to your quest.' Ezren leaned forward. 'Josiah told me.'

'I also told you she didn't believe me,' Josiah reminded him. 'She crept away at dawn.'

'Crept?' Red scowled.

'Of course.' Ezren's hand was tapping the table. 'To be expected. The Chosen One, the hero in stories, often first refuses the call.'

'I thought his wits were gone,' Red replied as she reached for a chicken leg.

'Have you met your mentor yet?' Ezren's eyes glittered with curiosity.

Red talked through a full mouth. 'Excuse me?'

'A wise man or woman. One who acts as your teacher, to guide you past your fear.'

They all look at Red as she gnawed on the bone, grease on her chin. 'No.'

'Ezren,' Vembar started, 'perhaps your ideas about—'

'It is a common enough theme.' Ezren pressed Red. 'Are you sure?'

Red growled. 'Could we get to the point?'

'You have yet to cross through the first portal of this tale, Chosen One.' Ezren leaned forward. 'Where you commit to the quest, and cross the—'

Red turned her head slightly and smirked at Josiah. 'Oh, I'm committed to this little adventure.' She stood and stretched, lifting her hands over her head. Josiah caught himself admiring the shift of her breasts under her armor. Red relaxed and looked at them with a grin. 'So all we have to do is go there, meet this noble, show him my tits—'

'Breasts,' Josiah said.

'Competence,' Evie snapped.

Red shrugged. 'Call it what you will, that will gain his support.'

'One of the lads who makes armor has an idea for a way to

show your birthmark without you having to bare all, Chosen.' Auxter said.

Red laughed. 'It doesn't bother me, Auxter, but it will ease Evelyn's mind. Tell him he has two weeks. The weather will have settled into spring, and we can move troops about with ease. Two weeks.' She stood, wiping her hands on her trous.

'There is something else,' Ezren added.

Red drew a deep breath. 'What?'

'You must decide on an archetypal role for your leadership. As a woman . . .'

Red stilled. 'What of that?'

'A woman in power is typically found in one of three roles. The first is that of a virgin queen, all-knowing, untouchable, willing to sacrifice all for her people.'

There was dead silence. Josiah was starting to get a sick feeling in the pit of his stomach.

'You think I'm a virgin?' Red demanded, scowling.

Ezren seemed oblivious. 'Or the role of the woman betrayed, leading her people to avenge a wrong. The best example of this is Empress Penalla of Wensosa. We are told that she and her three daughters were raped by the forces of—'

Red's mug crashed down on the table. Her eyes were wide and fierce.

Ezren continued. 'Or you could take on the aspect of the great whore, a woman rapacious in her appetites, sleeping with everyone and everything, including livestock. The primary model in this case was—'

Red threw herself across the table at the man.

EIGHTEEN

Bethral had seen that white-hot temper flare in the past. She knew what was coming, and moved before anyone else could react. She met Red's charge, grabbed her wrist, and yanked it to one side, deflecting the blow.

Ezren came to his feet behind her, so fast that his chair fell, clattering on the platform.

Bethral took no further action. Red snarled as she tried to pull back, as if to strike again. Bethral didn't release her grasp.

'Red Gloves,' Josiah said.

Bethral didn't look away from Red. She just watched as the sound of Josiah's voice drew her sword-sister's attention. Red turned to look at Josiah, and then at Bethral. She blinked, sanity flooding back into her eyes. Bethral knew the anger was still there, but Red had regained control.

Red pulled away, and this time Bethral released her. Red came down off the table, glaring at the wrinkles she'd made in the map. She lifted her chin, as if daring anyone to challenge her. 'Two weeks. Get to work.'

With that, she stomped off and headed toward the herb beds.

Josiah followed, with the goats trotting behind him.

Bethral drew air into her starved lungs.

'Some things don't change, my friend.' Vembar spoke softly, leaning toward the startled storyteller. 'You still have no sense of self-preservation.'

Bethral looked over her shoulder at the storyteller. He was still standing, wide-eyed and shaken. Evelyn was retrieving his chair, so she hadn't noticed his condition. Bethral turned as if to help, hesitated, and then touched Ezren lightly on the arm.

Ezren came back to himself and turned to look at her. She raised her eyebrows in a silent question. He blinked, then gave a slight shake of his head.

Auxter heaved himself up out of his chair, using his staff. 'Quite a temper, that one. But she's right, there's work to be done. Evelyn, mind opening the portal?'

'Let me see Ezren back first,' Evelyn said.

'I will see him safe,' Bethral offered as Gloriana rolled up the map.

'When you are stronger, old friend, send word,' Vembar urged, as he was helped up by Arent. 'We will sit and talk for a while, shall we?'

'That would be good.' Ezren's voice crackled.

Bethral offered her arm, and he stepped from the platform. She could feel him tremble. 'Do you wish me to carry you?' she offered softly.

'Afford me a bit of dignity, Lady Warrior.' Ezren's voice was a bare whisper. 'I can make it.'

'If you falter, I will take you up,' she warned.

'All the more reason to struggle on,' Ezren growled.

They said no more as they walked. Silence seemed strange from this man, but Bethral knew he needed to keep his mind on moving, not talking. They made their way into the barn, and headed for the foaling room.

Beast and Steel were in their stalls, and Beast kicked the wall as they passed.

'Foul-tempered beast,' Bethral muttered.

'Like her owner,' Ezren said.

Bethral snorted her agreement as she opened the foaling room door. The small fire had burned down, but the room was still warm. Ezren sank into his bunk with a sigh, and removed the white cloak before pulling the blankets around him.

Bethral took the cloak. 'I'll see this gets back to Evelyn.'

Ezren looked up at her. 'I need to talk to Red Gloves.'

'I don't think that's a good idea,' Bethral said as politely as she could. 'It takes time for her to calm down.'

Ezren's voice cracked. Bethral looked at him with concern as he struggled for words. 'I have to tell her . . . what I have remembered.'

Red stomped off toward the herb beds, radiating fury.

Josiah followed quietly, the goats silently walking at his heels. He didn't hurry to catch up to her.

Once they were out of sight, past the trees, he watched as Red stomped up to one of the herb beds and kicked at a clod of dirt and grass. 'Muck.' She stood there, hands on her hips, and stared into the distance as he drew closer.

'It might help if you sparred with someone,' Josiah said.

Red snorted. 'Bethral thinks sparring's a bad idea.' She jerked her head back in the direction they'd come from. 'What would they say if they saw their Chosen go down, or get a black eye? Fine impression that would make on your High Barons, eh?'

'I've seen you fight. You're very good.'

Red shrugged, folding her arms over her chest. 'I'm not perfect, Josiah.'

Josiah knelt and started to pull out weeds in the onion beds. 'Ezren's right you know.'

'What, that I'm a whore?'

Josiah pulled out a few more weeds in silence.

'I know,' she growled into the silence.

Josiah sat back on his heels. 'When he told tales at the Court, everyone would stop and listen. Even the kitchen folk would crowd in the doorways, straining to hear.' Josiah looked up at the sky. 'I wonder if his voice will return.'

'What the hell was he talking about?' Red demanded.

'Ezren is more than a storyteller. He is also a student of stories. He feels that they are far more important than anyone realizes. But some of his ideas are . . . odd.'

'It's his knowledge I need,' Red grumbled, 'not his wild theories and ideas.' She thumped down beside him. 'Ah, muck.' Red looked like she wanted to spit something nasty out of her mouth. 'I'm going to have to apologize.'

Josiah kept his head down, and tried not to grin. His kitten preferred to use her claws, given half a chance. 'It's not that hard to say that you're sorry,' Josiah observed.

'Muck.' Red grabbed one of the pulled weeds and started to strip the leaves off. 'It seems to me, if you're gonna have a birthmark and be Chosen, it should give you special powers. Or knowledge. So that you can't make mistakes. What's the good of being "Chosen," otherwise?'

'I don't think it works that way,' Josiah said. He looked at her bent head, amused at the idea that Red would admit to doubts. As honest about herself as she was about others.

'Well that rakes muck, doesn't it?' Red made a face.

Josiah sat back and laughed.

Red smirked. She'd made him laugh, and that pleased her no end. She leaned over, and kissed him, bracing his head with her gloved hand. She pulled back when they both needed breath. 'I know what would make me feel better, goatherder.'

'Pity you had my hut torn down,' Josiah said. 'But there's always the herb bed.'

Red wrinkled her nose. 'I don't want to stink of onion, thank you.' She released his hair.

Josiah turned back to the weeds. Before she could suggest an alternative place, he spoke. 'High Baron Fael is one for the women, and he can't notch his bedposts for fear they'd collapse. He will, no doubt, want to bed you.'

His tone was too calm. He wasn't looking at her, but Red shrugged anyway. 'Whatever.'

At that, Josiah looked over at her. 'Will you?'

'If that's what it takes to bring him to us, then yes, of course, I'll bed the man.' Red frowned. 'What of it?'

Josiah looked away. 'Nothing.'

Red opened her mouth to respond, just as one of the younger warriors ran up.

'Chosen!'

'Yes?'

'The Lady Bethral sends word that Ezren Storyteller would speak to you, at a time of your convenience.'

'Go, and tell him I am coming.'

The warrior sprinted off.

Red stood and brushed off her ass. 'Just as well, no sense putting it off.' She adjusted her sword belt 'Are you coming?'

Josiah didn't look up. 'I've work to do here.'

Red frowned at him, but after a minute she shrugged and moved off.

*

A runner had been sent, and Lady Bethral had said that she would wait with him. Ezren warmed his hands by the fire.

He'd remembered.

A table, loaded with wine and food. A large hearth, with a bright fire. A request for a false story. A man, lunging over a table, going for his throat. 'You'll not tell this tale or any other.'

Bethral lifted her head at the sound of a knock at the door. She stood, as if to guard him from an intruder.

'Enter,' Ezren croaked.

Red Gloves walked in. When she saw Bethral, she smiled ruefully. 'No need, sword-sister.'

Bethral relaxed, and Red faced Ezren. She hooked her thumbs on her sword belt, and took a breath. 'Ezren Storyteller, I owe you an apology.'

Ezren shook his head, but Red pressed on. 'You'd done nothing to warrant an attack, and you were unarmed, besides. I ask your pardon, and pledge that it will not happen again.' Red grimaced. 'No matter how wild your ideas are.'

Ezren chuckled, but managed to keep a solemn face. 'I forgive, Chosen.' He gestured to the opposite bunk. 'But what is more important is what I have remembered.'

Red sat.

'Not all, mind.' Ezren spoke softly. 'But the reason I was taken and enslaved. I . . . he came across the table at me and . . .' His throat went dry.

Red leaned forward. 'What?'

Ezren patted the bed next to him, and Red shifted over. He leaned close, and started to whisper in her ear.

Bethral watched them from the corner of the room as she used a stone to sharpen her dagger.

Ezren had insisted that he would tell no one but the Chosen, and Bethral had insisted in her turn that she be present. She could see Red's profile as Ezren whispered, and Red's face was turning to stone as the words poured into her ear.

After a few minutes, Red stood. 'I promise you, Ezren Storyteller, that I will deal with this.'

'I will hold you to that promise, Chosen.' Ezren's voice seemed even harsher than usual. 'I will tell this story to no one else.'

'Agreed.' Red took a few steps, yanked the door open, and left.

Ezren sagged back into the blankets. The man looked drained to the bone. Bethral rose, and sheathed her dagger. 'You need to rest.'

Ezren yawned. 'She needs to listen. She does not understand the power of the story. Her story.'

Bethral helped him to lie down, removed his boots, and covered him with blankets as he mumbled about Red. Once he was settled, she looked down at him in resignation. His green eyes looked up at her, dulled and tired. Bethral sighed softly. 'In your tales, does the hero ever listen?' she asked.

Ezren blinked up at her. His eyes grew distant. 'I had not thought . . . of course they didn't have the benefit of my knowledge . . . but come to think of it . . .'

Bethral reached for the lantern, and doused the flame.

Ezren chuckled. 'Ah, Lady, you have me. Have you ever heard the Saga of the Daughter of Xy?'

'No.' Bethral took up her weapon and started to leave. 'You need to sleep.'

Ezren yawned. 'A wonderful story. Full of passion and drama. She did not listen, that is certain.'

Bethral paused at the door. 'Will you tell it to me?'

Ezren shook his head. 'I fear I will tell no more tales, Lady.' In the shadows of the fire, she saw his hand shift to his throat.

'Sleep, Storyteller.' With a deep sense of disappointment, Bethral pulled the door closed.

Seven days passed quickly. Seven days, seven nights . . .

Josiah had watched her over those seven days, moving among the tents, laughing and talking with the warriors. Laughing over a shared joke. Admiring a weapon. Helping repair a piece of armor, or teaching a warrior the proper way to wield a mace.

How did she do it? How did she know how to strike just the right tone? Red might not think it, but as far as Josiah could tell, she had yet to hit a false note with the men. She'd moved into their lives as if she'd always been there.

There were times that Josiah would stand and stare in disbelief at the way his world had changed.

The men were framing new buildings. Dead trees were gone,

taken down for fuel and fencing. Old paths were restored, and fences restored. Josiah wasn't sure where the livestock had come from, but there were cows in with horses. The goats seemed pleased with the company.

Josiah wasn't so sure.

How had she done it? How did she do it? She was an unstoppable force during the day. True, the others were involved. Evie, Auxter, everyone was involved in the work. But Red Gloves was at the center of it all, during the day.

But at night . . .

Josiah had to steady himself with a breath, to bring himself under control. His kitten was amazing in so many ways. The last seven days . . .

Connor was an apprentice armorer, and justifiably proud of his ability to work leather. He'd come up with an idea for a suit of leather armor for Red that would protect her and yet display the mark of the Chosen. He'd worked feverishly, and had finally brought the leathers for Red to try on.

Jaws dropped when she emerged from their sleeping area.

'You look . . . amazing.' Josiah swallowed hard and prayed he would not embarrass himself. He shifted in his seat, grateful to be seated at the table.

'Pity my breasts enter the room moments before I do.' Red said. She was standing in front of them, the leather creaking as she moved.

'More to the point, can you breathe?' Evie asked.

Connor's eyes had bugged out of his head. Josiah was certain the lad was going to start drooling. 'You look wonderful, Chosen.'

'Can you draw your sword?' Bethral asked.

Red reached for her weapon. 'I can, but—' She stopped moving and took a deep breath. 'Is there some reason this has to lace up the back?'

Gloriana frowned. 'What is the whip for?'

All eyes turned to Connor, who blushed. 'It adds to the effect, don't you think?'

Gloriana gave him a doubtful look.

'Oh, yes,' Alad blurted out, just a bit too eager. Red scowled at him, but Josiah could not blame the lad. She did look wonderful. He shifted in his seat again. His kitten was glorious.

The leather was brown, and molded to her like wet linen. The trous clung like a second skin and rode low on her hips. The top of the armor was of the same brown, but the leather was hardened. It was sleeveless, and laced up the back. The leather cupped her breasts, exposing their creamy tops. There was a hole, below her right breast, where the birthmark was displayed in all its glory.

Connor's loins had overridden his skill.

Red planted her hands on her hips, looking down. 'I can't see my feet.'

'Do you need to?' Auxter said.

Arent snorted.

'I can't breathe, much less swing a sword. And if I did try to swing a weapon, my nipples are going to pop—'

'But what a story, eh?' Ezren chirped.

All heads swung in his direction. Ezren's face might reflect innocence, but those green eyes sparkled.

Bethral raised an eyebrow. 'I don't know how you are supposed to walk in those boots.'

Red took a step. 'Throws my balance off, to be up on my toes like this.'

'Does nice things to your legs, though,' Vembar said.

Everyone looked at the older man, who gave them all a mild look in return.

Red laughed, then shook her head. 'Connor, this isn't going to work.'

The young man deflated before them. 'It puts the mark of the Chosen on display.'

'It does,' Red agreed. 'But I don't wear armor for looks. A few changes will put it right, Connor. And I want you to make a suit for Gloriana, as well.'

Connor sighed, and Red patted his shoulder. 'You still have a week, lad.'

A week. Josiah looked down at his folded hands resting on the table. The talk swirled around him as they talked about the changes Connor needed to make, but Josiah ignored it all. Seven more days, seven more nights.

'Josiah,' Red called.

Their meeting was breaking up, everyone milling about. Josiah looked up into Red's eyes as she leaned over him, her breasts shifting against the leather.

She arched an eyebrow, and gave him a sultry look. 'Wanna help me peel this off?'

Josiah's mouth went dry. He nodded, unable to speak.

Red smirked, and turned back to their sleeping area. Josiah took a deep breath, and followed.

Seven nights . . .

NINETEEN

Seven nights. Where had they gone?

Numb, Josiah leaned against the barn door and watched as Beast tried to take a bite out of the horse next to him.

'Beast!' Red snarled, and thumped the horse on the shoulder. 'Try that again, and I'll dine on horse meat tonight!'

That brought laughter from the warriors gathered in front of the barn with their horses and supplies. The fourteen days had come and gone. It was the fifteenth day, and the Chosen was ready to move.

Red was dressed in her new armor, very different from the last. Connor had modified it as she'd requested, and now the leather was combined with chain in a way that protected her fully, yet let her opponent know that she was a woman. There was a clever bit of leatherworking that allowed her to unlace it in the front and show her birthmark without baring all.

Bethral had been assisting Ezren to a chair just outside the barn doors, so that he could watch the preparations. Now, she wove between the horses and men and reached out for Beast's bridle. With a firm hand, she quieted the large black horse.

Auxter was already up and mounted. He arched an eyebrow. 'Foul temper for a trained warhorse.'

Red snorted as she checked the girths. 'This one's not trained for war. He fights when he wants, with no order from me. Bethral's the one that trains her horse.' She grinned. 'Beast and I have a mutual agreement.'

'Trust a mercenary to put it that way,' Josiah muttered under his breath. Or at least he thought he did. But Red heard. She turned her head and gave him that saucy grin.

Beast shook himself, as if agreeing with Josiah. Steel was in the paddock, dancing along the fence. The gray whinnied a protest, not wanting to be left behind. Josiah sympathized.

'Are we about ready, then?' Red asked.

The warriors around her responded as they loaded the last of their bags and gear. Evie was already mounted, her eyes closed and lips moving in preparation for her spell. They were almost ready to depart for Summerford, to meet with High Baron Fael.

Josiah folded his arms over his chest, and stared at the tips of his shoes. The goats were at his feet, watching the activity. He bit his lip. Fourteen nights . . . he'd had fourteen nights.

Red had picked these men herself. Ten men, with a captain. Auxter was going, as was Evelyn. Evelyn was needed in more ways than one. Red had gotten her to open a portal wide enough for the horses and riders, right outside the shrine in Fael's keep. It was a strain for Evie to hold open such a large portal, but she could manage it for short periods of time.

But Red hadn't stopped there. She'd made them all, herself included, train to ride a horse through the portal. No easy task, that . . . but what a sight it was when they rode through in formation.

Josiah had watched them do it over and over. He'd been at a distance, of course, but it was a sight to see.

They trained the horses, then Red pushed them further. She'd made Evelyn map the routes out of Summerford, and they'd gone over them until they were blue. Red had made it a practice of 'What if'? What if they were attacked? What if Evelyn was wounded or killed? What would they do, how would they react? What if they rode through the portal and into an ambush? They spent days reviewing and plotting, once the decision had been made as to which Lord to approach first.

Josiah had known, deep in his bones, that it would be Fael.

Red mounted up. Once she was in the saddle, Bethral released her hold on the bridle. Beast danced a bit, but Red controlled him easily. Beast wasn't a lovely horse in a classic sense, but he was the picture of strength. The horse's black coat shone, and Red had let his mane and tail grow out. Someone had offered to braid the tail, but Red had declined with a laugh. 'Beast hates to have it braided. Makes him even ornerier.'

Josiah wasn't sure that was possible.

Bethral threaded her way through the mounted men, over to the fence where Steel was still fussing.

Red laughed again, as someone complained about Beast.

Josiah tried to memorize the sight of her, there on her horse, her sword at her side. He'd had his nights, and kept their bargain, and now the Chosen would go forth and claim her throne.

Snowdrop bleated plaintively and butted his leg.

She was so damned lovely. And she was leaving.

Josiah's stomach was an aching pit, his mouth full of words he couldn't say. *Don't go.*

Don't sleep with him.

Lord Fael would try to bed her. Sweet Sovereign Sun, any man would. She was as lovely as a sharp sword blade, honed to perfection. More than anything, he wanted to claim some thing he had no right to. If he didn't say anything, she'd . . .

Josiah straightened, and took a step toward—

'Are we ready?' Red called.

Evie opened her eyes and gestured. The enlarged portal appeared. Red called out an order and the horses surged forward, then disappeared within.

Josiah took a few steps forward as the last rider vanished. A few more steps, and . . .

The portal 'popped,' whether by Evelyn's call or his presence, he didn't know.

Red Gloves was gone.

Steel neighed, complaining. Ezren watched as Bethral patted his shoulder. 'Easy, boy. Your herd will be back soon enough.' She tied the horse's head to the fence and picked up a hoof. 'Let's take a look at you.'

Ezren was quite content to sit in the sun and watch Bethral tend to her steed. His chair was well sheltered from any breeze. He had a cloak, and a blanket besides.

He watched as Lord Josiah stomped off with his goats. There went an unhappy man. Ezren was fairly certain Josiah had lost his heart to the Chosen, but he kept his tongue in his head. It would be a fine story, either way, but he suspected Red Gloves would not be pleased if he told it.

Maybe if he changed the names?

Ezren leaned his head against the barn wall and closed his

eyes. High Priestess Evelyn had told him to start walking about, to get some more exercise. He'd do that later. But for now . . .

'Your verdict, Lady?' he asked without opening his eyes.

There was a pause before Bethral spoke, and Ezren smiled, knowing full well he'd caught her out.

'You're doing well,' she said. 'The sharp edges of your bones have filled out, and there's more weight to you.'

'You talk as if I were a horse,' Ezren chided, without opening his eyes. 'Next you will comment on my flanks, or the look of my hocks.'

'My apologies, Story—' Her voice was soft and contrite.

'No matter,' Ezren chuckled. 'It is due to Lady Arent's cooking, I assure you. I would be well satisfied with bread and cheese, but she keeps piling meats and sauces on my plate until I burst. If I see one more potpie thick with meat and sauce, I swear I will—'

'Eat it.' Bethral finished his sentence.

Ezren heaved a much-put-upon sigh. 'Eat it.' He looked down at his hands, and the scarring on his wrists. 'I am quite sure, given what you told me, that in the past few months I would have desired this food above all else.'

'You don't remember?'

Ezren looked out over the fields to where the men were working on one of the fences. 'I remember being attacked.' He squinted a bit, remembering a flash of light on a copper coin and blue eyes promising his safety. But the less said about that, the better. 'I remember awakening in that hut. Nothing between. It is a story I do not know . . . or wish to remember.'

Bethral's gaze was on Steel's hoof. 'A mercy, perhaps.'

'Perhaps.' Ezren nodded agreement. 'Although no story should be lost.' He watched as she picked at the horse's hoof. 'Tell me of the Twelve.'

Bethral glanced over before returning to her task. 'I am not a follower, Storyteller. You should ask Red.'

'She is not here. Tell me what you know,' Ezren insisted. 'What is the way of the Twelve?'

Bethral released Steel's foot, and the horse dropped it down. She moved to the next and Steel snorted as she lifted it and braced it between her legs. 'What do you know of it?' she asked.

Ezren shrugged. 'Only that its followers do not believe in any gods.'

Bethral shook her head, pick in hand. 'That is not the full truth.' She looked over at him. 'What do you wish to hear? The story? Or the tenets of the faith?'

Ezren leaned back, and pulled the cloak tighter around his body. 'The story, of course.'

He caught her smile as she bent to her task and began to speak. 'Many, many years ago, a plague came upon the land of Soccia. None knew its cause, none knew its cure, and it swept over the land, killing all in its path. The people cried out to the priests for aid, but the priests were dying. They cried out to their lords and ladies, but the nobles were dying. They cried out to the King himself, but the Queen was dead, and the King was mad with grief. Finally the people, all the people, cried out to the Gods themselves, but the Gods were silent.

'Now the King and Queen had been blessed with fine sons and daughters, twelve in all. These Princes and Princesses went out among the sick and dying, and rendered aid in any way that they could. Each carried a staff as they walked about the land.

'The people blessed them for it, and would have worshipped them, but the Princes and Princesses would have none of that. Instead, they urged the ones they aided to aid others in turn, and so the land and the kingdom came to be reclaimed.

'It came to pass that the King emerged from his tower to find his people praising his children. Instead of pride or gratitude, something dark twisted in his belly. He summoned his guard, and had his children brought to the center of the capital, and declared them to be treasonous, plotting to take his throne. He ordered their deaths, there in the town square.

'The people cried out in despair, pleading for the King to spare his children, pleading for the Gods to intervene. But the King ignored their cries, and the Gods were silent. The Princes and the Princesses bowed their heads in obedience to their father and liege lord, and were executed in the square, their blood flowing over the stones.

'All were silent as the last died. The King opened his mouth to dismiss the crowd, but one man stepped forward, and took up the eldest prince's staff. "I will take up this man's staff and walk in his steps." With that, he faded back into the crowd. Then a woman stepped forward, repeating the words of the first, to take up the staff of one of the dead Princesses. And so on, until all twelve staffs had been taken up.

'The King screamed in anger, sending his guards to find the twelve, but they were gone. The dead were buried. The King took his throne. The priests reopened their temples.

'But the people did not return.'

Ezren frowned at that, but Bethral continued. 'Instead, they followed the way of the twelve who took up the staves and walked the world in aid of all men.

'Do not seek them in the halls of power, for they will not be there. Do not seek them in the temples, for they will not be there. Do not pray to them, for they cannot hear you. They are men and women who appear where there is work to be done.'

'You weave a fine tale, Lady,' Ezren said. His voice was rough, but he tried hard to keep his pain out of it. 'Red follows this faith?'

Bethral nodded with a soft smile. 'Some days better than others.'

Ezren laughed. 'So do we all, Lady.' He thought about what he'd heard for a while, as Bethral finished her task. 'What do you believe, Lady?'

'There is a great deal of wisdom in the way of the Twelve.' Bethral released Steel's hoof. 'But I follow the ways of my mother's people.' She patted Steel's neck, and the horse swung its head to snuff her hair. 'And you, Storyteller?'

'In Palins there is but one faith, that of the Lord of Light and the Lady of Laughter.' Ezren looked into the sky. 'These many years, the Church and the Archbishop have placed more emphasis on the Lord rather than the Lady. Other beliefs are tolerated, but not encouraged.'

Bethral shrugged. 'My beliefs do not require that I proclaim them, or draft others to them.'

'So there are no temples or churches in Soccia.'

Bethral gave him a sly smile. 'Once in a great while, a temple will open and the priests will invite all to a festival of worship, with food and drink for the taking. The place is packed to the rafters all day long, with many seeking to hear their words. The priests are all pleased by their efforts by the end of the day, but no one appears for services the next day.'

Ezren chuckled. 'They come only for the free meal.'

'Just so.' Bethral untied Steel, and let him out the gate to the pasture.

A sound caused Ezren to turn his head. A band of warriors headed toward them. The youngest grinned as they came closer. 'Lady Bethral, we are here to spar.'

'No.' Bethral gave them a steady look. 'I saw that halfhearted archery practice yesterday, when I was working with Jaff on his shield work.'

Ezren refrained from laughing out loud as the men all seemed to sag at once. 'Sparring is more fun,' one complained.

'It does no good to learn only one way or weapon,' Bethral answered firmly. 'So we will practice this day.'

'Standing around, shooting—'

'Who said that?' Bethral took up her picks and brushes. 'Go and get your short bows and quivers. We are going to set a course through the woods and run it, seeking cover and hitting small targets.'

That perked them up.

'The Chosen has started to move.' Bethral gestured to where the portal had been. 'Very soon, she will need our skills. And if I know Red Gloves, things will start to move quickly from this point on.'

Ezren shook his head and stood up carefully, fully intending to watch. 'Stories have a way of doing that, Lady Bethral. And usually when you least expect it.'

Red lounged in her chair her boots up on the corner of a well-worn wooden table, with a full belly, and a mug of ale in her hand. She was trying desperately not to let her face show the extent of her boredom.

It wasn't something she was good at, so she scowled into her mug. That she could do.

Lady High Priestess Evelyn was seated next to Red. She looked over with a mild expression, and raised one eyebrow.

Red lowered her boots to the floor.

High Baron Fael was an excellent host. He'd welcomed them

publicly, allowed Evelyn to present Red, viewed her birthmark with interest, and announced his desire to learn more of the Chosen. He'd invited them to sup with him, and now his hall was filled with men and dogs and the remains of a wonderful meal.

They'd been seated in all honor at the high table. High Baron told great stories of his hunts. Auxter was listening with keen interest, but the Lady High Priestess had a polite look on her face. Red was willing to wager that the woman was actually asleep with her eyes open.

Except for her boots-off-the-table look.

Auxter and Evelyn had tried to bring the conversation around to the Chosen, and Lord Fael's support. But the man managed to dodge every question, and parry with an observation about the hunt. But from his sly looks and soft smiles, Red knew she had his attention in other ways.

Red let her head loll back to observe the great hall they were in. High Baron Fael believed in showing the fruits of his labors, and many a set of antlers were hanging on the walls. A fair number of skins as well, to cut the drafts. Red admired them, but for some reason her mind's eye seemed to compare the hall to a small hut with herbs hanging from the rafters.

Red straightened, and scowled into the fire pit before her.

The men had been sent off to the barracks. Their host had taken pains to see to their comfort, true enough. But one more story of running down a deer and she would—

Red scowled at her mug again. Hard to get a man's backing if he was gutted on your blade.

Pity.

To give the man his due, he was a charmer. Lord High Baron Fael was a big man, easily as tall as Bethral. Broad at the shoulder, narrow at the hips. His reddish-blond hair was thick and wavy, and his eyes sparkled bright blue.

Here was a man, a warrior, who thought as she did. Spoke her language. A man who knew the difference between a cestus and a halberd and knew how to use them both. Handsome, charming – and certain sure, if his bed was as busy as Josiah—

Red cut that thought off.

As *they* said, then certain sure Fael'd be a skilled lover.

Here she was, wearing fine armor that almost seemed to breathe with her, light and comfortable. Her blades were sharp, her ale was cold, her belly was full, and her itch about to be well and truly scratched . . .

Except she wasn't itchy.

Red put a gloved hand to her mouth, and started to chew at the stitching on the side of the index finger.

She should be satisfied. Content. The Chosen, and acknowledged as such, damn it all to the very fire pits of the lower hells and back up the path. This polite banter would end, she'd be invited to his bed, and all would be well.

Wouldn't it?

Although if this polite banter went on much longer, Red planned to go bed down with the troops.

But at last, Lord Fael released his men from the hall, and waved his servants away. As the room cleared, he turned to them with a polite smile. 'Lady High Priestess, Lord Auxter, I wish to consider your words. Please, let me give you an answer in the morning. My servants await to escort you to your quarters.'

'Our thanks.' Evelyn rose, as did Red and Auxter.

'Stay, Chosen,' Lord Fael requested. 'I'd have further words with you.'

Red didn't bother exchanging glances with the others. She just nodded, easing back into her chair. 'As you wish, Lord Fael.'

The tap of Auxter's staff echoed in the room as he and Evelyn left.

'So, what makes you think you can restore the Throne?' Lord Fael poured them each another mug of ale, and leaned back in his chair to put his boots on the table.

Red mimicked his pose, just as relaxed and confident. 'Let me tell you about our plans.'

They talked well into the night, long enough that Lord Fael himself had to stoke the fire and add wood. To Red's surprise, he actually listened carefully, asking good questions and letting her explain her answers. Finally, he stood and stretched. She admired the movement of his tunic over his chest.

'The night grows late, Chosen. I'm for bed.'

She nodded, drained her ale, and stood.

Fael moved closer, to stand right next to her. He smelled of metal, oil, and sweat. He stepped closer, and tugged at the lacings on her armor. His breath on her cheek was sweet with ale. Not an unpleasant scent.

But not marjoram, either.

Fael moved closer, and Red tilted her neck to give him access. He nuzzled just under her ear. His fingers reached under the leather and stroked her birthmark, soft and warm against her skin.

'Would you be averse to my company this night?' Fael asked softly.

Had to give him credit for courtesy, at the very least. Red drew a breath . . .

TWENTY

. . . And hesitated.

'Lady?' Lord Fael asked.

Red stepped away from him, and shook her head. She almost didn't believe the words that came out of her mouth. 'I cannot.'

When she spoke, she realized that it was true. What used to mean little other than physical pleasure now meant something else. It had changed somehow. She'd just gotten Josiah's eyes to laugh. How could she cause them to fill with pain?

Lord Fael smirked. 'What? You aren't going to spread your legs for the cause?'

Her anger flared at the insult, and it was a relief. Anger was familiar. Something she understood. Red snarled, 'If I thought it would win your honest support and loyalty, I'd bed you. And leave you panting and stupid.' She put her hand on her sword hilt, but went no further. It wouldn't do to kill him. 'How do I know that your loyalty won't shift when another woman enters your bed?'

'A shared throne would be an incentive,' Fael replied.

Red pressed her lips together. 'There is' – she had to pause for a moment – 'there is someone else.'

Lord Fael gave her a look. 'You are bonded?'

'No.' Red shrugged, uncomfortable. 'But there is someone who would be hurt.'

'And that bothers you.'

'Yes,' Red growled. She didn't really want to think about that, but—

'You surprise me, Chosen.' Lord Fael sat back down. 'I'd have thought you'd do almost anything to win my support.'

Red thumped back down in her chair. 'So did I.'

'Who is this . . . man?' Fael asked.

'Lord Josiah of Athelbryght.'

Fael's eyes narrowed. 'You lie. Josiah of Athelbryght is dead these handful of years past.'

Red shook her head. 'He lives, isolated and alone in the ruins of his land.'

Fael sat back. 'Josiah was . . . is . . . a good man. A friend as well. Why didn't he accompany you? His presence—'

Red sighed. 'Call for more ale, Fael. This will take some time to explain.'

They sat by the dying fire as Red explained. Fael's eyebrows kept going up and up at her words, but he listened carefully and didn't interrupt.

When she was done, he leaned back again. 'You have trusted me with much, Red.'

She shrugged. 'If I'd have you as an ally, I must trust, Fael.'

'Yet you refuse me, for Josiah's sake.'

Red nodded.

Fael shook his head. 'Ah, Red. If I'd have done as you have . . . made the same decision.' He sighed. 'Well, what's past is past.'

That made little sense to Red, but they'd drunk more than enough ale that it might make sense to him.

'My servants will see you to your lonely bed.' Fael's tone softened his words. 'You've given me much to think on. In the morning, we'll talk. Maybe spar a bit, eh? And we will see.'

And with that, Red had to be content.

Lady High Priestess Evelyn was surprised by the knock on the door of her room. But she was even more shocked to find Red Gloves standing there, scowling, her arms filled with bedding.

'What?'

Red pushed past her and into the room. 'I'm sleeping here tonight.'

Evelyn looked out into the cold hall, then closed the door quickly to keep in the warmth. Red dumped the bedding before the fire, and started to take off her sword belt. Evelyn pulled her robe close around her body. 'I assumed that—'

'You assumed wrong.' Red knelt and started to arrange the blankets in a pallet.

The stone floor was cold under Evelyn's feet, so she crossed the room to stand on the small rug before her bed. She'd just finished her prayers before the fire, and been ready to crawl into bed. 'Fael won't give you quarters?' Evelyn asked softly.

'Fael's people made the same assumption that you made,' Red growled. 'There's no fire laid, no warming pans for the bed. I told them the floor before your fire was good enough.'

'And stomped off before they could protest I imagine.'

'Something like that.' Red set her swords next to the pallet. She stood, and started to work on the buckles of her armor.

Evelyn watched her. 'You could share my bed,' she offered quietly.

Red glanced over at the four poster, with its heavy curtains and thick coverlet. 'No, thanks. Close those curtains, and I'd feel imprisoned.'

'The floor is cold,' Evelyn said, 'not to mention hard.'

'Not the first time.' Red set her armor close at hand, but made no move to take off the quilted jerkin. She sat down on the pallet, and removed her boots. 'Better by far than standing around as gossipy maids giggle and fret over warming a room for me.'

'When on campaign, you never know where your head will lie.' Evelyn shook her head. 'That's what my father always said to me.'

'True enough,' Red muttered, as she crawled into the blankets.

Evelyn shook her head, stepping to stand between the fire and Red. The heat of the flames warmed her back. Red looked up, a question in her eyes.

Evelyn smiled, and with a gesture spoke a quiet prayer. She felt the stones beneath her feet respond to the magic, warming her toes.

Red's eyes widened.

'I think that will be more comfortable, wouldn't you say?' Evelyn asked as she padded back to bed.

'Useful, even if it's a priestly thing,' Red said, rubbing her hands over the stone floor.

'It should last for the night.' Evelyn took off her robe, pulled up her shift, and slipped under the covers. Warmth from the mattress and bedding surrounded her quickly, and she settled back with a sigh. Red was welcome to the floor, but Evelyn had slept on the ground far too often to refuse a bed. Nestled down, she pulled the blankets up tight. 'So, you did not bed Fael.'

Red lay on her back, her blankets pulled up to her shoulders. She looked up at the ceiling, and for a long moment Evelyn didn't think she was going to answer. But the words finally emerged, as if pulled from her by force. 'I did not.'

'Will he support—'

'Maybe,' Red said through her teeth.

'Maybe?' Evelyn asked. 'We need—'

Red rolled over to face the fire, her back to Evelyn. 'We'll talk more in the morning.'

'Why? Why did you refuse him?' Evelyn said sharply. 'You said before that there was no problem, that you'd sleep—'

'Because Jo—' Red snapped, then stopped. 'Because he doesn't suit me, all right?'

'Oh.'

'Enough talk,' Red said. 'Sleep.'

Evelyn settled down into the mattress and laid her head on the pillow. She left the curtain open so that she could study Red's back.

She'd been so busy lately, trying to balance her Church obligations with her work in Athelbryght. She hadn't really gotten a chance to get to know Red at all. She knew that Red was sleeping with Josiah, that much was certain, and she wasn't quite sure how that had happened. She hadn't pressed the point, since it was to their advantage to have Red . . . involved in their cause. But she flushed a bit, acknowledging to herself that the Lord of Light frowned on relations without a bonding. It was expediency, and she'd have to ask forgiveness for it when all was said and done.

Still, Red was so complex: one moment crude, the next showing her political savvy. And she absorbed information so quickly. Her leadership skills were the equal of Auxter's. And this . . . loyalty . . . to Josiah was another layer to consider.

All of their schemes were at risk now, if Lord Fael would not aid them. Yet she smiled in the darkness, oddly pleased. She liked Red the better for it, to be honest.

She closed her eyes. She'd have to leave it in the hands of the Lord and the Lady. For now, she was going to sleep.

With any luck, the Chosen wouldn't snore.

Josiah heard the shouts as he was about to bed down for the second night alone. The cry 'A portal's opening' had him up and struggling back into his clothes.

By the time he emerged from the tent, there were warriors, horses, and goats milling about in front of the barn. Lanterns had been brought, and greetings were exchanged as they dismounted.

Josiah spotted Evie first. It was easy enough to do, as her white hair and robes seemed to capture the light and glow against the darkness. She gave him a soft smile as he reached up to help her dismount.

'Fael is with us,' she said. She leaned in and whispered in his ear. 'You should see to Red. She has to be exhausted.'

Josiah looked about. Red was still mounted, and she raised her hand, calling for quiet drawing everyone's attention.

'We have Lord Fael's support,' Red said. 'But our appearance in his lands will set tongues wagging. It will not be long before the enemy knows of us, and our intentions. Set the watches,' Red continued. 'And everyone stay alert.'

A murmur of agreement arose, and then the men started to unload their horses and see to them. Josiah stepped to Red's side.

Beast turned his head to look at Josiah, but didn't seem to have the energy to bite.

Red looked down at Josiah with tired eyes. 'Do me a favor?' she asked softly.

Josiah nodded.

'Don't let me fall,' Red whispered. With that, she gathered herself up, and swung down from the saddle. She swayed when her feet touched the ground.

Josiah reached out, and set his hand in the middle of her back.

Bethral appeared, taking Beast's reins from Red's hands. 'I'll see to him.'

Red blinked at her, and her jaw worked as if she were stifling a yawn. 'I feel like I've taken on an army, single-handed.'

Josiah moved to stand beside her, and wrapped his arm

around her waist. It wasn't obvious, but he felt her sag against him slightly.

'Rest, then,' Bethral said. 'Ezren's awake and dying to know what happened, but I will tell him he must wait.'

'I'll talk to him,' Auxter said from behind them. 'I'll tell him enough to keep him happy until morning.' He headed toward the barn, thumping his staff as he walked.

Bethral tugged on the reins, and Beast went off, meek as you please.

Red sighed. Josiah looked down at her, his lips brushing her cheek. 'Can you make it to the tent?'

'Damned if I know,' Red said. 'I ache in places I didn't know I owned.'

Josiah snagged a lantern from one of the men, and got them started down the path. They walked in silence. He suspected that Red needed to think of nothing else but putting one foot in front of the other.

He waited until they were in the tent with the flaps closed before he asked, 'What happened?'

'Lord Fael is a bull,' Red replied.

Josiah tried to guide her to the bed, but Red resisted. 'No, not the bed. If I sink into that softness, I'll not get back up again for a while.' Red eased down into one of the chairs.

Josiah set the lantern off to the side. An image flashed before his eyes of handsome Fael pounding into Red, naked on a bed. His tongue stuck to the roof of his mouth, but he forced himself to speak. 'He was rough?'

'I'd say.' Red pulled off a boot, letting it drop to the floor. 'He wanted to do it all, let me tell you.'

Josiah winced, only to realize that Red was studying him out of the corner of her eye. He frowned at her, not quite under-standing.

Red shrugged and went on. 'He wanted to spar. First one weapon, then another. I matched him step for step, but . . .' She yawned. 'Then he wanted to watch me fight with his best man, so he could "learn my technique."' Red snorted. 'He probably needed a nap. And as if that wasn't enough, then he wanted to hunt, and not just deer. Oh, no. Deer and boar. Then a ride out

164

with his falcons, to have a go at pigeons. At least for that, you sit on a horse and the bird does the work.'

Confused, Josiah knelt, and helped her with the other boot. They'd hunted? Hadn't they slept together?

Red shook her head. 'Then nothing would satisfy him but a feast. With said deer and boar and pigeons on the table, mind. Overrich for my taste.'

Josiah looked up at her. 'Fael never did anything by half measures.'

Red grimaced. 'I guess not.'

'It was a test, then?'

'If so, I measured up.' Red wiggled her bare toes against the wood floor. 'Next time, I think I'll put gloves on Bethral and send her. She'd lay him flat, no trouble at all.'

Josiah opened his mouth, but there was a knock at the door.

Evie came in, a mug in her hand. 'I've brought a few things to help you.'

'What, no prayers?' Red asked with an arched eyebrow.

'Healing's of little help with tiredness,' Evie replied smartly. 'Besides, who's the one that doesn't like "priestly" things?'

Red yawned. 'True enough, Priestess.'

'Here's a tea that will help with the aches.' Evie pressed the mug into Red's hand. 'Don't complain about the taste. Just drink it.'

Red eyed the mug with resignation. 'It's going to taste like horse piss, isn't it?'

'You don't have to drink it,' Evie said with a sweet smile. 'Feel free to hurt all night, if you wish.'

Red wrinkled her nose, and emptied the mug in four swift swallows.

Evie produced a small jar from her robes. 'Here's a balm for sore muscles.' She handed it to Josiah.

'Is there enough for my whole body?' Red handed her the empty mug.

Evie gave her a sympathetic look. 'And it doesn't help that you slept on the floor of my room last night.'

Josiah jerked his head around to stare at them.

Red was looking at the jar, and didn't notice. But Evie was

looking right at him, with a soft smile on her face. Josiah's eyes went wide as he realized what she was trying to tell him.

Red looked up, and caught the exchange. Josiah opened his mouth, but Red looked away and growled at Evie, 'You snore, by the way.'

Evie gave her an arch look. 'If I do, I am sure it's quite attractive and ladylike.'

Red snorted.

'But yours aren't.' Evie smirked, and twirled away, her robes twisting around her as she disappeared out the door.

Red glared at Josiah as he stifled his chuckles. 'I don't snore.'

'Not that I've noticed.' He set the balm aside. 'You didn't sleep with Fael?'

Red looked at him for a moment, then looked away, reaching for the straps of her armor. 'I didn't.'

'He asked?'

'He did.' Red scowled at him. 'But I refused him. Just part of our agreement, goatherder. Now, are you going to help me with this, or not?'

With a sense of relief, Josiah moved closer and reached out. 'Let me.'

It took time to get Red out of her armor, and by the time the last piece was carefully set aside, her yawns were making her jaw crack. Josiah pulled back the blankets, and eased her onto the bed, face down.

Red sighed, her body seeming to melt into the bed. She said something that was muffled by the pillow.

Josiah reached for the balm, and dipped his finger in, letting it warm in his palm before spreading it on Red's shoulders. He kneaded it into her skin with soft strokes.

Red moaned, shifting slightly.

'Easy,' Josiah whispered, 'let me do this for you.'

Red settled then, and he continued to work the balm into her back and shoulders. He lost track of time as his hands glided over her body.

She blinked sleepily at him when he'd finished. He leaned down, letting his lips brush against her. 'You were teasing me, Mercenary.'

Red gave him a puzzled look. 'It really would have bothered you, wouldn't it?'

Josiah nodded, and reached out to stroke her hair. 'Why didn't you sleep with him, Red?'

She gave him a rare soft smile and whispered her answer. 'He didn't smell of marjoram.'

Josiah knelt there, staring at her, but Red had closed her eyes and drifted off. He urged her to turn over so that he could finish his work. Red did, but it was clear that she'd lost her fight with sleep. He made quick work of the rest, until the jar was empty and the fire had burned down.

He stripped then, and crawled in next to her, pulling the blankets up to cover both of them. Red shifted into his arms, and buried her face in his neck.

Josiah smiled. 'Sleep well, kitten.'

She snuffled against his skin. Not quite a purr . . .

Josiah chuckled, closed his eyes, and let her deep breathing lull him to sleep.

The noises of the camp awoke Red in the morning.

She blinked, letting her awareness grow slowly. It seemed fairly late, from the light. Josiah lay next to her, on his side, his hand covering her belly.

Red turned her head just enough that she could look at him. Those lines were eased in sleep. He looked younger, so handsome. His curls were unruly and getting long.

Why had she teased him? Red frowned, considering. To see his response, if she were honest with herself. She'd never done that with a bed partner before. Never done any of this before, this intimacy. Sharing a bed like this. She'd always taken her pleasure and moved on.

It was . . . comfortable.

Red stretched, pleased to find that she wasn't nearly as sore as she'd expected. Worth the taste of the tea. She grimaced as the taste in her mouth brought back the brew.

She slipped from the bed with regret, and managed it without waking Josiah. Pity there wasn't time for a bit of fun this morning. But the day was wasting, and she needed to be about it.

She pulled on a tunic and trous. She'd see about food first, for both of them. Bring it back here and wake Josiah. She smiled to herself at the outline of his ass under the linens. Perhaps they could make time for a bit of—

A cry jerked her head around, and she reached for her sword.

'A portal! A portal's opening!'

TWENTY-ONE

Red left at a run, sword in hand, headed for the area between the barn and the well. Warriors were there, facing a slight glow and the winds that seemed to come out of nowhere whenever a portal was opened. Evelyn explained that it was the air from two different places moving within the portal.

Red was grateful for the warning.

Her men held position as she ran to stand in front of them. A glance told her that her crossbow men were in position on the barn roof, as ordered. She could hear the others gathering, and questions called out behind her, but she ignored them. The portal was her focus.

A brief flare of light, and then it was before them, the familiar white curtains moving in the air. Red pulled her sword. They'd be met with open blade and a snarl.

Two men emerged from the portal, in armor but their weapons sheathed. They wore tabards that Red didn't recognize. Each stepped to one side, eyeing Red warily.

Red opened her mouth to demand answers, when another person stepped through. A young woman, almost stumbling, dressed in a green silken thing that showed more than it concealed. There were baubles, too: necklaces and rings and bracelets that clinked as she moved. Her long brown hair was in disarray, and her eyes were bleary. Red knew that look all too well. It spoke of a long night on the bottle. More than one bottle.

'You!' The woman tried to focus on Red. 'You're the bitch!'

Red narrowed her eyes.

The woman stomped forward, to push her face into Red's. Her breath was almost a weapon in and of itself.

'You're the one,' she hissed. 'You're the whore—'

Red hit her. Her gloved fist smacked the woman right on the chin.

The woman collapsed into a heap, the portal closing at the same time.

The two warriors stepped forward, reaching for their swords. Red snarled, 'Who is this fool woman?'

The answer came from behind her. Ezren was leaning against the barn door, wrapped in a blanket. 'The Lady Helene, High Baroness of Wyethe.'

In the stillness, Red looked over her shoulder, and raised an eyebrow.

Evelyn and Josiah were standing there. They both nodded in confirmation. Josiah looked concerned, but Evelyn had a look of disdain on her face.

Red turned back to look at the woman at her feet. 'Oh.' She lowered her sword. 'See to her, then.'

She walked back to where Josiah stood. Evelyn was taking charge, as the warriors lifted the unconscious woman from the ground.

'Invite her to breakfast,' Red called over her shoulder. She turned back to Josiah and gave him a smile. 'Wanna go back to bed?'

Josiah was looking over her shoulder, where retching sounds could be heard. 'It might be a while before your "guest" can join you at the table.'

Red reached out and took his hand, tugging him toward their tent. 'All the better, then.'

Josiah hadn't known that Red could be so deliberately cruel. Her plate was swimming with half-cooked eggs and fried turnips, and she ate with obvious enjoyment.

The others had joined in the meal, making room for the High Baroness at the table. Helene was hunched over, her head in her hand, trying to avoid looking at Red. The poor girl had a mug of kavage in her hand, and a sick look on her face.

'Some dry bread would help,' Evelyn said softly.

Red talked around her food. 'Can't you just . . .' She waved her bread in the air, a bit of egg dripping onto the table.

Helene swallowed hard.

Evelyn gave Red a knowing look. 'I took care of the bruise,

but there's not much I can do for the rest.' She looked at Helene. 'I certainly can't cure stupid.'

Helene winced.

'If only you could.' Red stuffed her bread into her mouth and swallowed as she reached for another piece.

Josiah frowned. He remembered a lithe little girl, heir to Wyethe, delighting in her studies of magic. But this Helene was sullen, embarrassed, and avoiding everyone's eyes, including Evie's. Clearly something had happened between Helene and Evelyn in the last five years.

And clearly Red had picked up on that. She was observing everyone closely as she waved her fork about. Josiah watched her take it all in. There were undertones here, and she was trying to figure it out without asking a question.

Swimming in uncertain currents, was his kitten—

Josiah cut that thought right off. His kitten? He had no right to so much as think that. 'Part of the agreement' was all that she'd said. He'd best remember that for the future.

Of course, she'd also mentioned marjoram.

Confused, Josiah leaned forward to take some more bread. Helene's eyes flashed in his direction and her sullen look deepened. 'Why didn't anyone tell me that Josiah was alive?'

'It was too dangerous,' Evie replied. 'I couldn't risk it.'

'I can keep a secret,' Helene snapped. She looked like a resentful child who hadn't been invited to a party.

Evie turned her head slowly, and gave Helene a disapproving look. She raised an eyebrow.

Helene blushed scarlet, and dropped her gaze to the table. 'I should just go,' she muttered.

'No,' Red said. 'There are things we need to discuss.'

One of the Guardians stepped forward, lifting his hand to rest it on the back of Helene's chair. Josiah wasn't certain, but it looked like his fingers brushed Helene's shoulder. 'Leave her be.'

Red looked up in surprise.

'I am Wolfe, Chief Guardian of Wyethe,' he continued. 'The High Baroness overreacted to some gossip that she heard, that is all.'

That had Red's attention. She leaned forward. 'What did she hear?'

'You slept with him,' Helene spat. 'You claim to be Chosen, and you—'

'Who? Fael?' Red asked. 'Who told you that?'

'I have my sources.' Helene lifted her chin. 'You slept with him to gain—'

'I didn't,' Red said.

Helene caught her breath.

'She didn't,' Evelyn said. 'She slept with me that night.'

Helene's head whipped around, her eyes wide.

Evie rolled her eyes. 'On the floor of my room, you stupid girl.'

'But,' Helene sputtered, 'but he sleeps with everyone . . . everyone.' Her eyes welled with tears. 'Everyone but me.'

Red looked at Evie.

'She was betrothed to Fael,' Evelyn explained.

'But he broke the agreement.' Helene started to sob. 'He—'

Red rolled her eyes.

Ezren leaned forward, and reached out to hand Helene a cloth. 'Wipe your eyes, Lady.'

'Ezren Storyteller.' Helene blinked through her tears. 'What happened to your voice?'

'Many things have happened in the last five years, Lady,' Ezren said with a sad smile.

'But what is past is past.' Red shoved her plate back. 'We all must deal with what is, not what we wish it to be. Pain must be faced.'

'And the answer is not at the bottom of a bottle,' Evelyn added.

'What do you know of pain?' Helene lashed out, tears in her eyes. 'My parents dead, my betrothal broken—'

'So you're the only one who's suffered?' Red snapped. 'Your people lost competent leaders and replaced them with a drunken child.'

Helene jerked in her chair, her eyes wide. Wolfe and her other guards stiffened, and Wolfe went so far as to put his hand on his sword hilt.

Red Gloves leaned back in her chair and raised an eyebrow. 'So, instead of bemoaning your pain, it's time to deal with the problem. I have Fael's support, and I've not shared his bed to get it. He, at least, cares for his land and his people.'

'Our High Baroness cares for us,' Wolfe growled. 'You go too far.'

Red never took her eyes off Helene as she spoke. 'Prove it. The resources of Wyethe are not infinite, even with Summerford's support. If Elanore and the Regent come against you again, they will wear you down eventually.' Red leaned forward. 'With your aid, I can restore this throne.'

'Because of a prophecy and a birthmark?' Wolfe growled.

'Because of organization, tactics, cooperation, and a birthmark,' Red fired back. 'And that grinds, doesn't it?' She grinned, then dived into the details. She outlined the battle plans, talked supply lines, explained threat points and pitfalls. Josiah noticed she looked at Helene and Wolfe, making sure both were taking in the information.

Wolfe was. Helene looked a bit dazed.

When Red finished, Helene sniffed, and cast a glance over her shoulder at Wolfe. Wolfe shrugged ever so slightly. Helene turned back, and straightened in her chair. 'I don't appreciate your insults, Red Gloves. But I will consider your words.'

'As you wish, Lady High Baroness.' Red stood. 'Return in the morning, and give me your well-considered, and sober, decision.'

Helene rose, using the table for support. Evelyn had her arms folded in her robes. 'Do you wish me to cast the portal for you?'

Helene shot her a glare, but her words were polite enough. 'No, thank you.'

'My men will see you to the shrine,' Red said, and nodded to Oris. 'Until the morrow.'

Helene took Wolfe's arm and left. Josiah moved closer to Red as they watched them leave.

Evelyn sighed. 'You were hard on her.'

'No harder than life itself,' Red said. 'She needs to think of someone besides her own self.'

'Do you think she will join us?' Josiah asked softly.

'If he will, she will.' Red took a last swallow of kavage. 'And that Wolfe is no fool. So three down, one to go.' She set the mug on the table, and studied it for a moment. 'You've said not to waste time on Lord Verice.'

Josiah nodded. 'His dislike of humans is well known. After

the death of King Everard, he cut off all contact with the Council.'

Evelyn tilted her head. 'There have been changes there, Josiah. But he still won't offer support that might endanger his people.'

'Takes only an afternoon to ask.' Red squinted at the sun. 'What's the harm in asking? Would Verice betray us?'

'No.' Evelyn shook her head. 'Of that I am sure.'

'Then let's pay a friendly visit, eh?'

There'd be no boots on the table in this place. Red had never seen so much cold white marble in her life.

And that was just the mucking elves.

The palace – and it was a palace – chilled her to her bones. The halls towered over her, and her boots rang as they walked with their escort of elven warriors toward their audience. Evelyn stayed beside her, seemingly unaffected, a source of warmth in this cold place.

Red had always thought of elves as nature-loving, roaming the forests with their bows, singing elven songs. But this building spoke of power, rigid and unforgiving.

Verice's coat of arms was a fierce eagle, wings spread, defiant and cruel. Clutched in its talons was a rose, but not a simple blossom. It was one of those large cabbage rose blossoms, with a few petals falling from the bloom. It held an aura of sadness, somehow. As if the eagle, for all its power, could not protect the flower.

They reached the huge doors, which swung open silently, with no hand to aid them. Red scowled and marched through.

Lord Verice was on his throne, his scowl even deeper than hers as he watched them approach. 'So, Lady High Priestess Evelyn, you bring me another Chosen. Older, I grant you, but no more solid than your prior will-o'-the-wisp.'

Evelyn was unfazed. 'Lord Verice, allow me to make you known to Red Gloves. She bears the mark of the Chosen, and the skills to see the Throne of Palins restored.'

Lord Verice sniffed.

Red said nothing. Given her temper, no good would come of it. Mucking elves. She unlaced the leather bit, showed him the mark, and then laced it back up again.

'I see no reason to change my position. I see no need for Tassinic to support—'

'Nonsense.' The voice was warm and light and joyous, such a contrast that all heads turned.

An extremely pregnant human woman waddled into the room, a warm smile on her face. 'Evie, it's lovely to see you!'

Lord Verice rose from his throne, his face grim. 'My Lady Warna, this is a formal audience.'

Warna smiled. 'I'd curtsy, my Lord, but more than like I would wobble and spoil the effect.' She spread her hand out on her belly. 'Besides, this is Evie.' She reached out her hand. Evelyn crossed over and hugged her.

'Warna, you look wonderful.' Evie stepped back to look. 'How do you do?'

'My Lord's heir is kicking. We are hungry, although I'm eating for at least two. I've sweets and kavage in my sitting room. Come.'

Verice raised an eyebrow.

Warna laughed. 'You can come, too, my Lord.' She took Evie's arm, and they turned and started to walk away.

To Red's surprise, Verice's granite face melted to a wry look of acceptance, and maybe just a hint of humor. He raised an eyebrow, and gestured for Red to precede him.

She returned the nod, and they walked down the hall after the women.

Lady Warna's sitting room was done in white marble, with wide, high windows that let in the sun. But here the marble was covered with a layer of . . . fluff.

Red blinked in the light. She'd never seen so many cushions, curtains, and bright colors. Pink ruled this room. Especially in the vases of large pink cabbage roses that seemed to be on every surface. The floor was covered with a thick carpet of greens and golds. The effect was cluttered, and rather glorious. Not Red's taste, but still impressive.

Warna sank slowly onto one of the padded seats. She settled in with a sigh, then smiled at her guests. 'Sit, sit. Verice, watch your sword. Don't knock over any more of my vases than you have to.'

Verice snorted, and sat on the edge of one of the chairs. He put a hand on his sheath, making sure it stayed under control.

Red followed his lead, careful not to sink into the softness. And she minded her sword as well. Wouldn't do to break anything.

A maid came in with a tray, a pot of tea, and small white cups of thin alabaster. Warna took one and a small cake, and bade the others join her. Red was careful with the cup, which felt so thin and fragile to the touch. The heat of the liquid warmed her fingers.

Warna smiled at her. 'So, you bear the mark? And are a warrior as well. Excellent.'

'Warna . . .' Verice growled.

She gave him a wide-eyed look, then smiled at Evelyn. 'The elven midwives give me a few more weeks before our heir arrives. I think I am going to explode any day.'

'You look well.' Evelyn took a sip of her kavage. 'If you'd like me to attend—'

'No,' Verice growled.

'There are some traditions that must be adhered to.' Warna smiled softly. 'I will be attended by elven healers.' She glanced over at Verice. 'But I thank you for your offer, Evie. It was kindly meant. Besides, you have other work to do.' Warna looked at Red. 'What support do you have at present?'

Red glanced at the woman, surprised. 'So far, I have Lord Fael's and Lady Helene's. And Josiah of Athelbryght.'

'Josiah!' Warna exclaimed.

Red sighed, and let Evelyn explain.

'Immune to magic.' Warna bit into her cake with a thoughtful look. 'There's a deadly weapon.'

Red gave her a grin. There was no fluff in that brain.

'And what strength of arms?' Warna pressed.

Verice coughed. 'You are so fascinated by such talk.'

Verice and Warna exchanged glances.

'I love to talk troop strength,' Warna replied, lifting her chin. 'Wait until I ask about the placement of the necessaries in her camp.'

Verice put his head back and laughed out loud.

Red looked down at her knees, a shaft of pure envy lancing

through her. They were clearly smitten, and Warna was so comfortable in her fluff and ruffles and pregnancy. Her genuine happiness was painful to look on.

'The point,' Evelyn said, 'is that we have the strength and a leader. Will you aid us?'

'My Lady has made her support of your cause clear,' Verice said. He set his cup of kavage on a table. 'But I am not convinced that the interests of Tassinic are best served by being drawn into this matter.'

Evelyn opened her mouth, but Verice cut her off with a gesture. 'I have heard your arguments, Lady High Priestess.' He glanced at Red. 'But you are a new factor.'

Red returned the look. 'I am no lass with no knowledge of the sword, or of what it takes to win a battle.'

Verice shrugged. 'Even so, why should I take this chance when neutrality serves me and mine just as well?'

'Verice . . .' Warna started to speak, only to give way to an enormous yawn.

'And that' – Verice nodded – 'means that my Lady needs her afternoon nap.'

Warna laughed. 'To be followed by my early evening nap.' But she made no protest when Verice rose and swept her up into his arms, frills and all.

'I'll grant you this.' Verice paused, Warna in his arms. 'I'll place my warriors at my border with Edenrich, to prevent encroachment on my lands, from either side. I'll not support one side or the other. Fight your battles as you wish. I will protect me and mine. Give my regards to Josiah. He is a good man. Now, if you will excuse us . . .' He swept Warna out of the room.

Evelyn stood, and Red joined her. 'That went better than I'd hoped,' Evelyn said softly. 'Now there is only one more High Baron to approach.'

Red nodded as the door opened and their escort appeared. 'Then let us be about it, Priestess. Time is not on our side.'

TWENTY-TWO

Red felt her shoulders ease as soon as they were through the portal and back in Athelbryght. She turned to Evelyn. 'We'll gather tomorrow, then, and work out the details?'

Evelyn shook her head. 'Tomorrow night is the earliest. Lord Carell doesn't like surprise visitors. I have to send a message through a portal first, asking permission to visit. Besides, I've Church duties tomorrow that can't be traded off.' She sighed.

'Do you think anyone suspects?' Red asked.

Evelyn gave her a tired laugh. 'No, they are used to me running about healing the "unworthy." Only Dominic has commented that I seem busier than usual lately. For all my vaunted powers' – Evelyn grimaced – 'they don't keep track of me that closely.'

'In the afternoon, then.' Red watched as Evelyn gestured at the portal. It seemed to flicker slightly, then the priestess stepped through and was gone.

Red stepped out of the shrine and hailed the guards. 'Anyone know where Lord Josiah is?'

'The herb beds, Chosen.' The lad grinned at her. 'Lord Josiah gathered up a bunch of slackers and took 'em off. Said he was gonna make 'em weed.'

'A fate worse than death,' Red grinned back. 'Thanks, lad.'

She headed that way, thinking of marjoram. Perhaps she'd scold Josiah for demeaning her warriors, release them from their servitude, and then she and Josiah could make better use of the herb 'beds.'

'Chosen!'

She looked over to see Auxter hailing her from the barn. Ezren was seated next to him. Red frowned, concerned. The man was sitting in a chair, half-naked, breathing hard. Auxter sat next to him, his staff leaning against the barn wall.

'Ezren,' she asked as she drew closer, 'are you well?'

Those green eyes flashed in a smile, 'Well enough, Chosen. What happened with Verice?'

'Ezren's fine.' Auxter chuckled. 'He's been chopping wood. Trying to gain strength.'

Bethral came around the side of the barn, with a bucket of water and a few mugs. She had a towel, which she handed to Ezren.

'Your idea?' Red asked Bethral.

Bethral nodded. 'We need the wood.'

Ezren snorted as he wiped his face. 'I'm certain the kindling I managed to cut will aid someone. Now, what happened with Verice?'

'Ah.' Red folded her arms over her chest, and told the tale as Ezren recovered.

He nodded at her words. 'To be expected.' He took a long drink of water. 'Now, would you say that word is out? About you?'

Red considered this. 'In the common ear, to be certain. In the ears of the powerful? I don't know. But word travels on the wind.'

'Talk works against us.' Ezren drew a breath. 'Let me make it work for us as well.'

'How so?'

Ezren reached for his tunic. 'I need ten or fifteen of your men. Older, experienced men. War veterans, if you have any.' He tucked his head into his tunic and struggled with the sleeves.

'What for?' Red asked carefully.

Ezren's head popped out of the neck of the tunic. His hair had started growing back, but there wasn't enough to be in disarray. Still, he ran his hand over it just the same. 'Why, to send them on leave to Edenrich and some of the other towns, of course. For an ale, and a meat pie, and a bit of gossip at a tavern or two.'

Red glanced at Bethral, who shrugged. 'I don't—'

Ezren's eye gleamed. 'They will spread the word that the Chosen has raised her banner and will soon issue the call to any man willing to serve Palins.'

'Banner?' Red pointed out. 'We don't have—'

'I will design one for you.' Ezren waved away her protest.

'The power of story, Chosen. For what is gossip but a tale told over and over?'

Ezren seated himself next to Auxter. 'Let me gather the men, talk to them, then have the Lady High Priestess open a few portals around the Kingdom. All I need is a few nights, and a few coins to buy a few rounds of ale for the thirsty.'

'It's a good idea,' Auxter rumbled. 'And I know just the men.'

'Is it too soon?' Bethral asked.

Ezren shrugged. 'It takes time for a tale to spread. But if it works, it may gather support in unlikely places.'

Red considered this for a moment. 'Do it.' She turned to go.

Ezren's voice rose behind her. 'You mean you are going to listen to me?'

Red smirked, but didn't stop. She had a goatherder to find. She walked quickly, not wanting further interruption. But when she caught her first glimpse of the group, she paused.

Sure enough, Josiah had the warriors on their hands and knees, pulling at the plants. She was pleased to see one of them posted as watch. She suspected they were trading off that duty to escape Josiah's eye for a few brief moments.

The watchman spotted her, and lifted a hand. She returned the greeting, and gestured for silence.

Josiah was on his hands and knees, patiently explaining to one of the warriors the difference between a wild onion and a weed. His voice floated over, warm and patient. She watched him for a moment as his hands moved, sorting out the plants and digging in the soil.

A man of the earth, of crops and livestock. A man reclaiming his lands and eventually his people. Josiah was living again, and although the pain still lurked in the depths of his eyes, there was light there as well.

Athelbryght would be restored, of that Red was certain. Josiah had already started to rebuild, even if he didn't realize it yet. He would need a woman beside him, to aid him in that task. Someone like Warna. Sweet and generous, plump and fruitful.

Red sighed, and looked down at the toes of her boots. It hurt to think of that. To think of Josiah . . .

Red scowled at her boots, then lifted her head and scowled at the hot, sweaty goatherder. How had this happened? A man of the dirt, a mucky farmer, for the sake of the Twelve! Who'd have thought it?

She . . . cared for him.

Red grimaced, then shrugged. What was, was. She'd act in accordance with the Way of the Twelve, as was right and proper. She had her path, he had his. No matter that it hurt. What was, was.

Josiah stood, and wiped his brow with the sleeve of his tunic. Red felt the heat rise in her body. She could almost smell him from here. Sweat, dirt, and marjoram.

Oh, she'd act in accordance with the Way, but in the meantime there was her profit to consider.

'Lord Josiah,' she called as she stepped out of the trees. 'What are you doing to my warriors?'

With a bit of scolding and teasing, she managed to release Josiah's victims back to their military duties and clear the area fairly quickly.

Josiah sighed as the last one scrambled away. 'I need their help, if these beds are to produce.'

'I've a different use for your beds.' Red gave him a sly look, moving closer.

Josiah arched an eyebrow. 'Verice didn't offer you his?'

Red pretended to shiver. 'The most we got was that he'd stay neutral. He has no care for either side.'

'He has no love of humans, that is certain.'

Red paused. 'But he's married to one.'

Josiah's mouth dropped open.

'Pretty thing, too, and very pregnant.'

Josiah stood there for a moment, shaking his head. 'I'd have thought it would take more than five years to change that heartless bastard. More like five hundred years. Ezren would say there was a story there.'

'Evelyn knows it.'

Josiah chuckled. 'And if I know her, she's not telling.'

'Just so.' Red shifted closer. 'Now, about your beds . . .' She lifted a gloved hand to stroke his face.

Josiah caught her wrist, and pulled her close, lowering his head to nuzzle her neck. Red smiled as his scent surrounded her, and tilted her head to give him access.

'There's a stream a short walk from here, with a pool big enough for two,' Josiah whispered in her ear.

'Within hail of the camp?' Red whispered.

'Yes,' Josiah said.

'Well, then.' Red stepped back, and tugged. 'Let's be about it.'

But Josiah still had her wrist, and an odd expression on his face. His thumb stroked the leather of her glove that covered the pulse point.

Red froze.

'When was the last time you felt another's skin?' Josiah asked softly. His eyes bored into hers. His thumb made a gentle circle on her wrist. She could feel the gentle stroke through the leather. 'When did you last feel someone's hair run through your fingers? Or the wetness of another's tears?'

'Josiah.' Red spoke sharply, and jerked her hand from his grasp. She rubbed away his touch. 'Don't.'

'I'm sorry.' Josiah made no move. He just looked at her, with eyes that held pain . . . for her.

Red looked away. 'So where's this path?'

He gestured and started off. Red paused, suddenly afraid. 'Josiah, you won't try to . . .'

Josiah turned and looked at her. 'No, I promise you, Red. I won't try to remove your gloves.' He held out his hand. 'You are safe with me.'

She relaxed, and reached out to put her gloved hand in his bare one.

The return message from Lord Carell was short and succinct:

If Lord Josiah lives, as you claim, then tell him to meet me at our old hunting camp, two mornings hence.

'Which gives us just enough time to get there,' Josiah pointed out. 'Carell has always been a careful man.'

'Well, I can't help,' Evelyn sighed. 'There's no shrine, and I can't travel with you. That's far too long for me to be gone from the Church.'

Red growled under her breath. 'I don't like this.'

'Take more of the men,' Bethral suggested. 'Little risk with a group of fifty or more.'

'Don't,' Auxter said. 'If Carell sees that large force, he will assume treachery. Besides, that many men will be too slow.'

The argument might have continued for days, but Red cut it off after an hour. 'We need to leave soon, so here is what we will do. Ten men will go with us. Auxter, Josiah, you will ride with me. We will—'

'I am going,' Ezren announced.

Red raised an eyebrow. 'I think not, Storyteller.'

'I think so, Chosen,' Ezren replied. 'I'm stronger, and able to sit a horse with no trouble.' He glared at her, his green eyes flashing. 'So far I have only heard this story. I want to see this part.'

'If he goes, I go,' Bethral added.

Red opened her mouth, then closed it with a snap. 'So be it. On your own heads. But if you fall behind, you'll return here, no arguments.'

Ezren bowed his head, then looked at her with a wide grin.

Red rolled her eyes. 'Oh, and no goats. We will lock them up in the barn.'

Josiah shrugged. 'You can try.'

It hadn't taken too long to provision and mount up. They'd ride through the afternoon, and camp overnight. Josiah was leading the way to a place on the border between Athelbryght and Penature.

'We used to meet there to hunt when we were younger. My father and Carell's father were fast friends,' Josiah said as he rode next to Red.

Beast lashed out, trying to bite Josiah's mount on the neck, but Red pulled the rein tight before he could connect. 'Stupid horse.'

'Uh-oh,' Josiah muttered.

Red's head snapped around. There were five goats on the trail ahead, standing there, glaring at her. The smallest one, a white one, looked a lot like Snowdrop.

'It can't be,' Red growled.

The goats ran up to them and started dancing around Josiah's horse, standing on their back legs to let Josiah scratch their ears. He leaned down in the saddle, and smiled as he stroked them.

'I guess the goats are coming.' Red rolled her eyes. 'I better not wake up with goats in my tent.'

She pointedly ignored everyone around her as they stifled their smiles.

The night passed quietly. Josiah enjoyed sleeping with Red in his arms. The goats had the good sense to stay out of their small tent.

In the morning, they mounted up and rode with a stronger sense of urgency. The hunting cabin was still a ways off, and they'd want to reach it before dark. Their path now followed close to the bog, and though the road was dry, the smell was all about them. Rotting plants and thick water. Josiah wrinkled his nose. When they'd hunted here before, the bog had been a healthy place, filled with green growth and fat prey. But now, the place seemed sickly.

Josiah shifted in his saddle, conscious that he hadn't ridden this much in a long time. He spurred his horse so that he was next to Red. 'How about we make a stop up ahead?' Josiah suggested. 'Ezren could use it.'

Red gave him a knowing look. 'He's not the only one, eh? Still, it's not a bad—'

''Ware!' Bethral's voice rang out from behind them.

Josiah's head exploded in pain. He had a brief glimpse of Red's face going slack just before unconsciousness claimed him.

TWENTY-THREE

Something tugged at her glove.

Red's eyes snapped open, eyes blurred by pain. She could barely see the man crouched at her side, her wrist in his hand as he pulled at her glove. He almost had it off.

She twisted her hand from his grasp.

The man jerked back in surprise, his mouth opening to cry out.

Red was faster. She grabbed his throat with her gloved hand and squeezed hard. He reached up, trying to pull her off. Red pulled him down, threw him to the side, rolling with his weight so that she ended up on top. She grabbed his hair in her gloved hand.

A simple matter to break his neck with a quick jerk.

Voices behind her. The sounds of panicked horses running. More enemies. There was a dagger on the man's belt. She pulled it free, hiding the movement with her body. Then she hunched down over his corpse, hiding the blade and holding her breath.

Another man, coming from behind, cursing. Red waited until he was close, then leapt up, slashing backward. She scraped his face with the blade as he came up behind her.

The man cried out and raised his hands to cover his face. She risked a quick look to try to locate others, then rammed the dagger into the man's ribs, angled for the heart. He dropped like a stone, his body sliding off her blade.

A cry of rage from behind warned her of a new attacker. She barely managed to dodge his sword thrust. This one was ready, armed and with a shield. Not so easy.

Red widened her eyes as if in fear, and clutched the dagger to her breast. She stepped back, careful of the bodies, and thrust out her empty hand to ward him off.

The man advanced, still careful, his shield and sword ready.

Red stayed silent, shaking her head and mouthing the word 'please' as she retreated. If he didn't buy it soon, she'd have to—

'Now, lass . . . no need to fear,' the man spoke softly.

Red stopped, and lowered her gaze. She wrapped her arm around her waist, and stood there, trying to shiver. Not hard, since some bastard had taken her boots.

'Give me the dagger, that's a good lass,' the man said, letting his shield drop just below his eyes.

Red flicked her eyes up and then away, shaking her head again. Fool. She was no lass, and couldn't he see the blood on the dagger? He just needed to drop his shield a little more, and—

His eyes gave him away. Red saw his thought and moved just enough to avoid his thrust. She snarled, showing her teeth.

The man grinned back, from the shelter of his shield. 'Nice try, bitch.'

Mucker. Red feinted, then darted to the left.

The man hung back, cagey, waiting for her to strike. Time was his friend, not hers. There might be others . . .

Red backed away, avoiding bodies, her eyes on the warrior.

He followed, intent on taking her.

Red turned and ran as fast as she could, up the road the way they had come. She heard him curse, and give chase. All to the good. There was a place just up the road that would work, if she could—

There, by the big tree where the bog had exposed the roots. She ran up, and put her back to it. The man, breathing hard, wasn't far behind. She snarled as he ran forward. She flipped the dagger so that she held it by the blade.

The man slowed, wary.

She threw the dagger.

He lifted his shield, covering his chest and face. She charged forward, running full tilt toward him.

The dagger clattered off the shield. He laughed, stooping to grab it, straightening up . . .

And she hit him, putting her shoulder into the shield, forcing him back, over the roots. He staggered and fell backward into the bog.

He splashed in, crying out, but the muck filled his mouth as he sank. His sword and the dagger were gone in an instant, and Red cursed the loss.

The man's hands were flailing weakly above the water, but the bog had him. She turned back, anxious to find the others.

When she reached the spot, Red stood, breathing heavily, listening. But there was nothing, no noise at all but the rush of blood through her body. She lifted her gloved hand to her head, and it came back full of blood. The pain was like a blacksmith's hammer, pounding and relentless.

She'd been stripped down to her padded tunic and trous. She wiped blood from her eyes, and looked around.

All she saw were bodies.

The bodies of men, strangers, horses. She blinked again, then stumbled over to a horse.

It was Steel.

Red staggered over. The big horse was dead, from multiple blows. The blood on his hooves meant he'd fought hard.

She didn't see Bethral.

She sucked in a breath. Auxter lay close by, his staff broken under him.

She stumbled to his side, but there was no need to double-check. The dust on his eyes told the tale. She gritted her teeth, denying the pain, and stumbled on.

Red searched, tallying the dead that she knew, and the ones that she didn't, trying to make sense of it all. All had been stripped, gear and weapons gone. She'd been unconscious for a while, then.

Her head throbbed, reminding her of her own injury. She returned, and tore some cloth from the tunic of one of the men she had killed. She pressed the cloth against the wound. Her stomach roiled at the feel, but she set her teeth and did it anyway. Wrapped tight around her head, it seemed to help the pain and stop the oozing.

She couldn't remember much, just Bethral crying out a warning, the goats bleating . . .

Josiah.

She jerked around, looking again, but he wasn't there. Bethral, Ezren . . . at least two of her warriors were unaccounted for. No goats. Some other horses, but not Beast. What—?

Red staggered back to the men, but the dead did not give any answers. Not until she found Jaff dead, his hands tied behind his back. His thigh had been cut, and the amount of blood told her he'd bled out from it. But that meant they'd taken captives. Where had—

The faint ring of goat bells echoed in the distance.

Her head jerked up, and she looked into the swamp. She held her breath, and listened.

There. Very faint . . . Red moved to the edge of the bog, and searched for a sign, a track, anything.

She found it then, a clear and obvious trail. Six men, with captives, heading deep into the bog on foot.

She looked for a weapon, any weapon, but there was none. She could check under the bodies, try to find a weapon, maybe some boots—

Bleating now with the bells, and getting fainter. A wave of urgency passed through her. There was no time.

She followed the tracks into the swamp.

The trail was clear; they were moving fast and making no attempts to hide their passage. Red moved as quickly as she dared, trying to stay on the higher ground, going into the muck only when necessary. It was cold and thick with slime.

She lost track of time and distance, but not the traces that she followed. That kept her moving. That and the faint sound of goat bells, getting stronger.

Finally she caught a glimpse of movement between the trees. The back of a man in a dark cloak who was holding up a dagger of some kind, chanting in an unknown tongue. Cursing, then—

Red heard Josiah cry out only to be cut off. As if—

She splashed forward, ignoring the noise she was making. Until an inner sense warned her, and she went down in the muck and crept closer to a bit of dry land up ahead.

The goats had gone silent.

She moved past a fallen tree to get her first clear glimpse of the area. There was an altar there, black and encrusted with moss. Behind the altar was a huge stone statue of a spider, its head cracked off the body, sunk half in the depths of the muck.

The air reeked of blood, mingled with the rot of the bog. The robed figure once again raised bloodstained hands before the statue, his chanting growing faster and more urgent. In his hands, a stone knife dripped thick with blood. Red swallowed hard as the stench filled her mouth.

She stayed down, taking in the five warriors clustered around the altar, pulling a body from its surface to throw in a heap. Part of her recognized one of Auxter's men. The other part saw the pile of bodies.

Josiah.

Red's heart stopped. His body was flung to the side, next to Bethral's. Face white, eyes open, a wide gash in his chest.

Deep within, Red howled. She clamped her mouth, to hold in the pain. *Later. Not now.*

Ezren's cries pulled her gaze back to the altar, where the five warriors were struggling with the smaller man, stretching him out, as the robed figure raised his knife again.

Cold fury filled her. She had no chance, but that no longer mattered. All she felt was rage and hate. Old friends. Good friends, who let strength flood into her battered body. Friends who would let her kill two, maybe three of the muckers before they cut her down.

Red closed her gloved hands in the muck, taking precious seconds to search for a weapon, any weapon. Deep within, she snarled, *You mucking prophecy, if you are ever going to help me, help me now!*

Her hand closed on a hilt.

Red took off running. It wasn't a sword, of course. She could see it from the corner of her eye, little more than a rusted dagger, its blade pitted with rust and holes. Just a jagged shard, really.

It would suffice.

They were still focused on the storyteller, who struggled fiercely, spewing insults and curses she barely understood. Red watched as time slowed, as her feet found purchase in the muck, moving faster than she thought possible.

Ezren spotted her between the bodies of his captors. His green eyes widened, and for a moment she feared discovery. But then he jerked his head around to face the mage as his captors spread his arms and legs on the altar. 'Damn you,' Ezren shouted. He spat in the man's face. 'Go ahead, foul monster, kill me! Kill me!'

The mage never hesitated. He plunged the blade into Ezren's chest.

Red reached the hillock at the same moment seconds too late. She launched herself forward and jammed the shard into the base of the mage's skull. Joy filled her as it crunched through his bones.

The mage didn't even cry out. His body just collapsed forward, to cover Ezren.

The guards were just starting to react. Red yanked the shard free of the mage's corpse, and attacked the nearest warrior. She went for his throat slashing for that soft flesh. She found her target, and she allowed his weight to pull her down, confusing the others and buying her a few precious seconds. As they started to move, Red stood, the dead man's sword in one hand, the shard in the other.

She screamed then, a battle cry of old, and launched herself at the next one. He fumbled at his scabbard as she moved in, thrusting her sword ahead of her. He dodged the blow, but he didn't see the shard until it was too late.

Rage filled Red, and she welcomed it. There was no thought beyond the parry and the thrust and she danced through the warriors with razor-sharp clarity. It felt as though they stood still and waited for her blows.

The bodies on the altar helped her, preventing the others from leaning over and attacking her. She kept moving, so that it was always between her and them as she fought.

She took one by leaving her side exposed for a moment and that cost her. The gash scored along her ribs, and burned like fire when she breathed. But so what? These men had killed her heart, and their deaths were hers to claim.

Red slashed again and again, pressing them back. There wasn't much room on this little island, and she used that to her advantage, letting the altar protect her as much as it could.

One stumbled, trying to avoid putting a foot in the muck. Red was on him in an instant, using the sword and the shard to slip past his shield and slice his gut.

That left one, and Red wasted no time. Her energy was fading fast, and he was the focus of her full hate. A few parries and she knew his measure. She could take him with ease.

A faint voice in the back of her head suggested offering him a surrender, to learn more of their attackers, and what they knew.

Red ignored it, and killed him with a few swift blows.

She stood there, breathing hard, using all her senses to check for more foes, but there were none.

Only the dead.

Red stumbled over to where the bodies lay. She knelt next to Josiah, and carefully set her weapons on the ground next to her. She reached out, drew him into her arms.

His face and lips were pale. Red tried to close his eyes, but they remained half-open, unseeing.

His body was a dead weight, and she cradled his head to prevent it from lolling around. She threw back her head, and keened her grief to the sky. The empty bog, cold and cruel, seemed to absorb the sound.

How long she knelt there, howling, Red could not say. Her face was wet with tears, her entire energy spent in the sounds coming from her throat. But some bit of sanity returned, and she found herself stiff and cold. Swallowing was agony, her throat rough and sore.

She didn't want to move, didn't want to draw another breath, but there was work to be done. An ambush to avenge, a betrayer to discover. She gently lowered Josiah to the ground, and scrubbed at her face with the back of her hand.

'Bethral, sword-sister,' Red whispered. She crawled over to where Bethral lay, cold and dead. She brushed a strand of blonde hair back from her forehead. Bethral's skin was white, and so very cold.

Red hung her head and grieved, trying to breathe, trying to control the tears. She dashed them away, furious at herself. She needed to get up, to move. She stood, slowly, her body cold and aching.

A few steps took her to the altar. Ezren lay there, his eyes closed, his face pale. The body of the mage was still slumped over him. Red yanked the bastard up and off, letting him drop to the ground.

The stone dagger was buried deep in Ezren's chest. Red sobbed, gasping for air. 'Thank you, Ezren Storyteller,' she whispered. 'You allowed me to avenge them, with the gift of your life.'

She reached out her gloved hand, and pulled the dagger from Ezren's chest. It slid out, coated in his heart's blood.

There was a rumbling sound from beneath the altar, as if a thousand horses were running toward her. Red staggered back, the dagger still in her hand. What in the name of the Twelve?

Pure light surged up from Ezren's chest, and exploded into the darkening sky. White and sparkling, it filled the air around the altar, spilling out and around them. The light – no, not light. It was power – pure, raw power that danced all about them. It took Red's breath away.

She stood, trying to focus as it seemed to circle the clearing like a shooting star, returning to hover over Ezren. It paused there, growing and churning. Red stared at it in astonishment. She'd never seen anything like it.

Ezren groaned.

Red dropped the stone dagger.

Ezren opened his eyes. As if that was what it was waiting for, all the built-up power poured down into the man, right into his chest.

Ezren cried out in pain, glowing with the power. He put his hands to his chest as if to stop the assault, but the light kept pouring into him until the man glowed as white as the High Priestess's robes.

The light disappeared, and Ezren sat up, his hand still pressed to his chest. He looked at Red, who stared back at him, stunned.

'What—' Ezren started to say, and then his gaze fell on the dead.

The poor man sucked in a breath, cried out hopelessly. He fell from the altar, flinging out one hand toward the dead. Light flared. Red had to cover her eyes, half-blinded by the whiteness.

The flare died. Red blinked, trying to clear her vision of the spots that floated before it. Ezren was seated on the ground, no longer glowing. But the altar had changed. White marble now gleamed behind him, and the statue of the spider was gone.

Red staggered to the altar. 'Ezren,' she said, still seeing spots, 'what—?'

'I don't know.' Ezren's voice cracked. His hand was pressed to his chest where the wound had been. 'What happened?'

Goat bells chimed behind them.

Red spun, bringing up her sword and shard. The blades flashed as her heart leapt in her throat.

Josiah was sitting up, surrounded by five goats, his hand at his chest. Bethral and the others, too, all stirred, sitting up and looking around as if they'd awakened from a bad dream.

TWENTY-FOUR

Ezren shivered, his teeth chattering. Josiah reached out to steady him. He could feel the man trembling under his touch. The goats pressed against them as they knelt on the bit of dry land, silent, as far from the altar as possible, seeking reassurance.

Josiah just wanted answers.

'Betrayed.' Bethral's voice was bitter. 'We were betrayed.' She threw another sword onto the pile that Oris and Alad had started as they stripped the dead.

'That's possible,' Red said. She stood guard over Josiah and Ezren, looking out into the bog. Josiah looked up at her. Red was covered in muck, and she had the oddest look in her eyes. Her gloves squished as she tightened her grips on the weapons she held, a sword and the rusted remnant of a blade. 'We need to move,' Red insisted.

Ezren wrapped his arms around his waist, still shivering. Josiah reached out, trying to rub some warmth into the man. 'What happened?' Josiah asked.

Ezren shivered harder. 'I . . . I—' His voice cracked and wavered.

'Later. It's not safe to stay here,' Red said. 'We were ambushed, that's all you need to know.'

Josiah frowned. 'I don't remember—'

'Not now.' Red cut him off sharply, looking him in the eye. Josiah's voice caught in his throat. Red's eyes were cold, hard, but underneath . . .

She was terrified, and the terror lurked just under the surface of her control.

Josiah frowned, but stayed silent. He remembered a warning, and pain, but nothing more. His chest was sore, his tunic ripped open in front, the material covered in blood. Everyone's was, except for Red.

What had happened?

Oris came over, his arm full of cloaks, which he draped around Ezren. 'We've found some armor for ourselves, but nothing to fit Bethral. There's swords and such, and boots to fit you.'

'Can we tell where they're from? Which barony?' Red growled.

Oris shook his head. 'Nothing I can see. They've coin, but not much. There's not much on the mage, either. But the gear is all good quality.' He looked Red in the eye. 'Auxter?'

'Dead.' Red grimaced. 'All dead.'

Oris closed his eyes but said nothing.

'Oris.' Red's voice was a rasp, but oddly gentle. Oris opened his eyes and looked at her. 'I am the Chosen, Oris,' Red said. 'The prophecy is alive in me.'

Oris stared at her, as if seeing her for the first time. Then he nodded. 'Aye, Chosen.' His shoulders straightened. 'I'll guard. Take what you can.'

Josiah watched as Red jerked her head in a nod, and walked over to the pile. Bethral and Alad were trying on bits and pieces. Everyone was careful to avoid the altar, gleaming white in the center of the hillock.

Ezren grimaced as he pulled the cloak tight around his body. Josiah took one of the cloaks as well, grateful for its thickness. The goats were warming him, but they were still silent. He reached out to scratch Kavage about the ears.

Bethral was helping Red with a chain shirt. The blonde had no body armor, but had strapped on greaves and bracers. Alad was taking the rest of the pile and putting it on a cloak. But Red said something, and he stopped and stood, leaving the stuff there.

Ezren moved away from Josiah, pushing past the goats, his eyes fixed on the gleaming white altar. Josiah watched, puzzled, as the smaller man reached out his hand, as if to—

'No!' Red was there, and she caught Ezren's wrist and pulled it back. 'Not a good idea.'

Ezren looked at her, dazed. 'But there's writing around the rim. I could—'

'We can't stay here, Storyteller.' Red gently pulled him away. 'We need to go now.'

Ezren shivered again, but he nodded and started to move away. Bethral came up behind him. 'Still cold?'

Ezren nodded. 'I can't seem to get warm.'

'You'll warm as we walk,' Red said. 'I'll take the lead.'

'What about this?' Bethral asked. She kicked at something on the ground. It slid over by Josiah's knee, a dagger with a blade that looked like it was some kind of black rock. There was blood on the blade. He reached for the hilt.

'Don't touch it,' Red snapped. She grabbed one of the extra cloaks, and tore a strip from it. 'Any extra pouches?'

Oris handed her one. Red used the cloth to pick up the dagger, and wrapped it well before stuffing it in the pouch. She handed it back to Oris. 'Carry it, but don't let it touch your skin.'

Oris nodded.

Josiah stood as Red started to move into the bog. 'You're going to have to tell us what happened eventually.'

Red said nothing as she moved past him.

Josiah watched her walk away. There was something terribly wrong. He glanced back at the altar. Whatever had happened had scared his kitten. Badly.

Oris, Ezren, and Alad followed Red. Bethral was waiting, and motioned for him to go ahead of her. Josiah gave her a questioning look.

Bethral shrugged. 'She'll tell us when she's ready.'

Josiah nodded, and followed the others.

Red watched as Oris looked at Auxter's body and heaved a great sigh. He leaned down, and pulled the broken halves of Auxter's staff from under the still form. 'Would that we could take him back with us.'

'We can't,' Red stated flatly, ignoring the man's pain. 'Wrap our dead in cloaks, and we'll hoist them into the trees. When it's safe, we'll retrieve them.'

Oris glared at her, but Red met his eyes and stared him down. He lowered his gaze and looked away. 'Aye, Chosen.' He gestured for Alad to help.

Red didn't give a damn and a half. They'd be hard pressed to get back safe on their own, much less hauling a dead body with them.

Josiah moved to help them, and Red's gaze drifted over his face. The image flashed before her of his open, dead eyes. She shivered, then forced those feelings down. Later. She'd deal with that later. Right now, they needed shelter and food.

Ezren was leaning against a tree. 'Bethral?'

Red turned, and saw Bethral standing over Steel's body. The blonde knelt, and pressed her hand on the horses's neck.

'Leave her alone,' Red snapped at him. 'She's praying.'

'Praying?' Ezren shivered, moving his shoulders as if in pain.

'For the soul of her horse. Leave her be.' Red glared at him. 'What's wrong?'

Ezren shook his head, his voice a raspy whisper. 'My skin is tingling, as if ants were crawling all over me.'

Josiah stepped closer. 'Let's see if we can get you warm.' He led Ezren toward a fallen log.

Bethral stood. Red motioned her over. 'Any chance you can tell me where they came from?'

Bethral shrugged. 'I'll try.' She moved off, circling the area, her head down as she studied the earth.

Oris and Alad were wrapping the bodies of their dead in cloaks, and hauling them into the trees. Wedged in the branches, they'd be all right for a few days, until they could bring more men here. Red snarled. She'd bring more men and hunt down the bastards.

Josiah and Ezren sat on the fallen log. The goats were gathered close about their legs. Red frowned, worried about the storyteller. He was clearly shaken, and drained of strength. They needed shelter, warmth, and protection from any others who might be in the area.

Bethral moved to stand beside her. 'How many did you kill here?'

'Three.' Red pointed them out. 'They'd looted everything, then started on me. I woke when the bastard touched my gloves.'

'Then I think they are all dead,' Bethral said. 'They lay in wait for some time, spread out along the path on both sides.'

'For us?' Josiah asked softly. 'Or was it chance?'

'I doubt that,' Ezren's voice cracked. 'They took everyone who didn't die in the initial attack to the altar but the Chosen.'

Red grunted. 'My head wouldn't be enough. No one knows what I look like. They'd need my body, in order to display the birthmark.'

Josiah looked ill. 'So they were after us.'

Bethral nodded. 'Best to assume so.' She pointed away from the bog. 'Looks like Beast went that way.'

Red snorted. 'Once I was down, he'd have run. Unlike Steel.'

Bethral jerked her head in a nod.

Alad came over, and held up a handful of arrows. 'Blunt tips, Chosen.'

'To stun,' Oris joined in. 'A well-planned ambush. They must have—'

'Later,' Red snapped. 'Night comes, and we need shelter.'

'We've cloaks,' Bethral offered. 'I say we cold camp this night, and move at first light. We can—'

The goats lifted their heads, and looked away from the bog. Their ears perked up. The warriors pulled weapons, gathering around Josiah and Ezren. They stood silent, listening.

Snowdrop bleated, her tail fluttering like crazy. She trotted off, followed by the others.

'Damn goats,' Josiah swore.

'No,' Red said softly. 'Don't say that.' She took a few steps after them. 'I'm going to follow. Stay here.'

She sheathed her sword, but kept the jagged shard in her hand. The goats were running now, prancing through the trees. Red kept them in sight, but stayed as far back as she could.

The goats danced through some brush that she had to skirt around. She carefully stepped to the edge of the woods, and looked out.

There was a fence there, and Beast, looking angry. He'd snarled his reins reaching his head under the bars to the grass beyond. Stupid horse. The goats were cavorting, pleased with their find.

Red stayed back, because Beast wasn't alone. There was a man – no, a lad – there, trying to free his reins while avoiding Beast's teeth. Beyond them, Red could see a steading in the distance, with smoke rising from the roof of the house, and a small barn beyond that.

Warmth and shelter, maybe. Red drew a breath and let it out slowly. She just had to be careful. Only one way to find out.

She stepped forward and hailed the lad.

Thankfully, the boy's mother was willing to shelter them. 'There's the barn, although the smithy's better for sleeping warm.' Larrisa pointed to a long building apart from the others. 'Light a fire in the forge and the loft heats up fast.'

Red nodded, grateful. 'Sorry for scaring the lad so bad.'

'Wasn't scared,' Therrin protested.

Larrisa raised an eyebrow. 'He shouldn't have been out there, Warrior.' She sighed, and Red could see the weariness in her face. The woman was plump, but there were tired lines in her face.

'Ah, Ma.' The boy blushed. 'Was trying to help the horse.'

Larrisa shook her head. 'As horse-mad as your father was.'

'Nothing wrong with running,' Josiah said. 'I'd have run from her, too, the way she looks.'

Therrin shot him a grateful look.

Red looked down at herself, and had to snort her agreement. Between the muck and the blood, she probably looked like death warm—

Josiah's dead face floated before her mind's eye, and she cut that thought off.

Larrisa looked them all over. 'Well, you do look a fright. You probably ran into them that killed my man a fortnight ago.'

Red stiffened. 'Them? There's more about?'

Larrisa nodded. 'Raiders. But we've stout walls. We can talk in the morning. You need to get that one warm, and now. There's water in the well, and I'll send out soap and what clothes I can spare.' Bethral wrapped an arm around Ezren, who stumbled forward. Oris and Alad followed behind.

Red tugged on Beast's reins. 'We'll put this one to pasture.'

Larrisa shook her head. 'Put him in the barn. Leaving him out will just draw raiders. There's feed enough, since all our horses but one have been stolen, and that one is ill. She's in the back stall.'

Bethral's head jerked around. 'Ill?'

Larrisa nodded, her face filled with pain. 'Something else we can talk about. It's nothing that she'll share with yours. Get warm and clean. I've two little ones to see to. I'll share what food I can.'

Red nodded, and tugged Beast's reins. He followed along, quiet as she could wish, and she was grateful for his cooperation.

The barn was big, with clean stalls. It took some doing, but Beast was too tired to put up a fuss. Red worked as fast as she could, but her body felt heavy and so damn weary. The wet leather of her gloves slid on the pitchfork handle, and she grimaced. No spares to change into, so she was stuck with them for now.

Josiah worked beside her, and she didn't look at him. Couldn't look at him. Not now. Later. Later, she could see him, feel him against her—

'Let me.' Bethral's hand grabbed the pitchfork. 'I'll finish in here. You two go get warm and clean. There's a bucket of warm water waiting in the smithy.'

Josiah sighed behind her, and set his pitchfork against the wall. 'Room enough in there for all of us?'

'We're sleeping in here,' Red growled. 'To protect the horse.'

Josiah shrugged. 'Wherever. I should sleep like the dead this night.'

Red turned white, and staggered.

Both Josiah and Bethral stared at her. Bethral reached out to steady her. 'What haven't you and Ezren told us, Red?'

Red shook her head. 'Later. When we're private.'

Bethral shrugged. 'Go. I will take care of this, and then join you.'

Red and Josiah walked out into the night.

Larrisa didn't have much, but she was generous with what she had. A thick porridge, with bread and butter. She'd sent the food out with Therrin. 'Ma says we'll talk in the morning.'

Red was too weary to insist otherwise. She'd barely been able to wash up, and had rinsed her gloves over and over, to get the muck out. They were damp now, but at least the smell was gone.

She'd thanked the lad for the food, and shut the door. Bethral returned, and they crammed into the loft, warm from the heat of the forge. There'd been no talk as they ate, just the passing of the loaf and dipping out porridge into the bowls.

But once bellies were full, eyes filled with questions. Red looked at Ezren, but he looked away, and shook his head. She snorted at a storyteller unwilling to tell a tale, but she could hardly blame him. 'I woke when someone tugged at my gloves . . .'

She continued, through the fight and the dash through the bog. She closed her eyes, unable to look at them as she told of their dead bodies, and Ezren's struggles on the altar. Of the power that had filled the air and brought them back.

There was silence when she finished. Josiah pulled up his tunic, to look at his chest. 'Not a mark, not a scar.'

'A vague ache,' Bethral said.

Alad looked down at the gash in his tunic. 'Don't feel any different,' he said with a worried look.

Oris coughed. 'Why didn't it bring the others back?'

Ezren spoke. 'Maybe because all I cared about was you. I saw . . .' He looked at Bethral, and then away. 'I saw all of you dead and I just wanted . . . to change it. To have you back.'

Enough talk. Red spoke up, setting aside her bowl. 'Josiah and I will sleep in the barn. Larrisa spoke of raiders, so . . .'

Oris nodded. 'I'll stand first watch. Alad can spell me.'

'Wake me, Alad,' Bethral said. 'I'll stand until dawn.'

Red opened her mouth to protest, but Bethral cut her off. 'No. Of all of us, you've had the worst of it. Whatever that magic did, we're not as tired as you. Sleep tonight.'

Josiah stood, and reached out his hand. Red looked up at him, and took it with a sigh, letting him pull her up from the floor.

'And tomorrow?' Bethral asked softly.

'Will have to wait,' Red replied as she eased open the door of the smithy.

The goats were waiting outside. They milled about for a moment, then trotted toward the barn, expecting them to follow.

The barn smelled of horse and hay. It might not be as warm as the smithy, but it was warmer than a cold camp in the woods. Josiah closed the door behind them, and bolted it. Red rigged a few tools to clatter over if disturbed, fussing until she was satisfied with the arrangement.

The goats bedded down in a pile of straw outside Beast's stall. Red paused, and reached down to scratch under Snowdrop's chin. The goat pulled back in surprise, but then leaned her head out and closed her eyes with a murmur of pleasure. Silly thing deserved more of a thanks, but it was the best Red could do for now. She reached out to the rest of them, and they clustered around, making little chuckling noises of pleasure as she gave them all a good scratch around the ears.

Josiah came out of one of the back stalls with an armload of horse blankets. He looked at Red in astonishment.

Red ignored him, patted Snowdrop, then headed up the ladder into the hayloft. She didn't have a sheath for her weapons, and the damn ladder looked as high as a castle wall, but she gritted her teeth and pulled herself up anyway. Josiah handed up the blankets, and then came up with one of the lanterns in hand.

Josiah hung the lantern from one of the posts, painting the loft in golden light and shadows. It took a few moments to arrange the blankets, but eventually they had a warm nest in the hay. Red stood there, trembling, all the emotion of the day threatening to spill out of her, all the pain, all the . . .

Josiah moved beside her, and slid his hand down her arm, covering her hand. 'Let it go, Red.'

Red looked down, and saw that she was clutching the jagged shard of a dagger. Josiah's warm fingers eased the weapon from her grasp. 'You can relax now,' he whispered. 'We're safe enough here.'

Red looked at him, at his warm, living face. He smiled, and eased her sword out of her other hand, placing both weapons close by.

Josiah moved then, to stand very close. He eased his hand up her back to rest between her shoulder blades. Red sagged, putting her head on his shoulder, and he took her weight with ease. She was content for the moment, breathing in his scent, as his other arm came up and wrapped around her.

Josiah's warm hands slid up under her tunic, rubbing her back.

Red just stood there for a long moment, listening to his soft breath and the beat of his heart. She closed her eyes, and didn't even react when he swept her into his arms and placed her on the blankets. 'You're falling asleep on your feet.'

She blinked up at him, staring at his wonderful living face. He smiled at her and shook his head. 'Let's get you out of these clothes. We'll be warm enough under the blankets.'

His warm hands eased her tunic off. The looted shoes slid off her feet with no effort, and her trous followed. He avoided her gloves, careful to make no contact with the leather.

The cooler air made her nipples tighten, but Red didn't reach for the blankets. She just stared as Josiah undressed, gazing at his warm, living flesh. With no mark on his chest, no scar to show. As if it had never happened.

Josiah didn't linger. He stretched out beside her and pulled the blankets up over them. Once they were covered, he pulled her close, making a face at the touch of her gloves. She drew back, but he shook his head, refusing to release her.

She sighed as he ran his hands over her arms and legs, sharing his heat with her, warming her chilled flesh.

'Sleep, Red.' Josiah's voice was soft and warm in her ear. 'I'm right here.'

She nodded, and closed her eyes. But the images that came were of the altar, of Josiah and Bethral dead on the ground, and Ezren screaming curses.

Her eyes snapped open. Her chest froze, the breath in her body trapped within. She reached out for Josiah, seeking reassurance. He was there, had to be there, beside her, and—

'Easy.' Josiah captured her frantic fingers with his own. 'All's well, Red. I'm fine.' He brought her gloved hand up to his chest. She pressed it there, seeking his warmth, the feel of his skin, the beat of his heart. But wet leather stopped her, and she moaned in frustration.

'What's wrong?' Josiah stirred beside her, propping himself on an elbow, concern flooding his face.

Red trembled. 'I need . . .'

'Whatever you need,' Josiah assured her, covering her hand with his own.

Red swallowed hard. 'I need to touch you.'

TWENTY-FIVE

Her wide eyes looked into Josiah's, frantic and frightened. Concerned, he pulled her to his chest, catching her hands between their bodies. 'Whatever you need, Red. We can touch. We are touching.' He moved his legs, rubbing his lower leg against hers.

'No,' came the soft, desperate response. 'More. I need to touch you.'

Puzzled, Josiah drew back. It took him a moment, but then he suddenly realized what she meant. 'You're going to take them off?'

Her eyes grew wider, and she shook in his arms. 'Ah,' he spoke softly. 'You want to, but you can't, can you?'

She shook her head, biting her lip. 'I want . . .'

'Hush.' He pulled her close, and released her hands so he could rub her back. She shuddered in his arms, more from shock than passion. He looked at the small lantern, burning softly on the beam. 'What if we blow out the lantern? Would that be enough? I couldn't see . . .' His voice trailed off as he saw her expression. Whatever demons drove her, they wouldn't let her take off those damn gloves. Unless . . .

He sat up, careful to keep her covered for whatever warmth the bedding offered. He reached over for his tunic, already torn in the front. He gathered the material in two fists, and tore off a wide strip. And then another, from around the bottom.

'What are you doing?' Red sat up.

Josiah didn't answer. He just tore a few more strips. 'Here. Wrap this around your eyes.'

Red frowned, but did as he asked.

'Can you see?'

She tilted her head a few times. 'There's a bit of light around the edges.' He wound another strip around. 'No,' Red said, 'I can't see a thing. But—'

Josiah took the strips off her head, and Red smoothed her hair back, giving him a puzzled look.

He smiled at her, glad to see some calmness back in her eyes. 'They're for me.' He offered her the strips. 'Bind my eyes, Red Gloves. Then bind my hands to the beams. Outspread, so I can't rub my face against them.'

Red's jaw dropped.

'I trust you.' He leaned in, kissing her soft lips. 'I won't be able to see, or get free. You can take off your gloves, Lady Warrior, with no fear.'

'Josiah,' Red whispered, as if unable to believe. 'You'd do this?'

Josiah moved, stretching out on the blankets, centering himself between the two posts. 'For you, Lady.'

Red got to her knees, and tied one end of two strips to each beam. Josiah extended his arms, and she tied the strips to his wrists. Josiah tested them, pulling hard. There was a bit of give in the fabric, but not enough to allow him to escape or to touch his face.

Red looked down at him, her face filled with wonder and a hunger he'd never seen. He lifted his head toward her, and she wrapped the fabric around his eyes. But she didn't stop with one strip; she secured him with three, tying them off. When she was done, Josiah put his head down. He opened his eyes, but there was only utter darkness. He closed them, satisfied that there'd be no chance he could see.

'Can you see anything?' Red demanded.

'No,' he replied, pulling at his bonds. 'It's safe, Red.'

She said nothing, but he felt her shift on the blankets. He gasped as he felt her lips brush over a nipple.

'You're certain?' she asked again. Josiah swallowed, and nodded, unable to trust his voice. The sensation was so different, not knowing when or where or—

Cold steel touched his other nipple.

Josiah jerked as the tip of a dagger pressed into his skin.

'You really can't see,' Red whispered.

'I trust you,' Josiah repeated, ignoring his racing heart. 'Whatever you need, Red.'

Silence was his only answer, as she sat beside him. Josiah tried to remember to take in air. He could feel her gaze on his skin, and his body responded. He did trust her, but there was something about being so vulnerable. So exposed. He drew another breath, and then felt her move.

She was drawing off her gloves.

The leather was wet, and he could hear her tugging at the fingers, loosening them in order to pull them off. He shifted on the blanket. He couldn't help but wonder. Were they disfigured somehow? Blackened and stained? Or maybe they were claws, hard and sharp, that would pierce his skin—

He jumped at her touch. Her fingertips were cold, and damp from the leather, but they felt normal against his skin. She placed them on his chest, just below his collarbone, and paused there. Her fingers warmed as she hesitated.

'Whatever you need,' Josiah urged her on, breathing deeply, trying not to struggle against his bonds. She needed this, needed to know that he lived.

Her hands pressed down now, palms over his nipples. Her fingers curled, and her fingertips moved over his skin with the barest of touches. He licked his lips, wanting more.

She explored his chest, tracing the lines of muscle, caressing the hairs. Josiah's breath came faster as her hands moved lower and lower still. Red made no sound, but Josiah could feel her focus on him, on his body, as she explored.

He was lost, lost in the darkness, lost in the feel of her touch. He moaned as she moved past his hips, stroking his thighs and the soft skin behind his knees. Silently, she rubbed his shins, then the tops of his feet.

'Touch me,' he asked, wanting more of her, but Red ignored him, retracing her path up his body until her fingers explored his neck and face. Softer than snowflakes, they touched him, fluttering over his cheeks and lips.

Josiah opened his mouth to plead, but Red covered his lips with hers, claiming a kiss. He could feel wetness on her face.

Red Gloves was crying.

He licked his lips, tasting the salt of her tears. 'Red—'

She moved then, wrapping her hand around him, guiding him into her depths as she straddled his body. He arched his back, thrusting up at the sudden touch, and slid into her wet heat.

She set the pace of their dance, and it was a slow one, each giving as much as was taken. Josiah climbed higher and higher as he strove to bring her with him. Unable to touch, all he could do was thrust, accepting the pleasure of her touch, her body, her mouth on his.

For one single moment, it felt as if they moved as one, then Josiah fell over the edge, crying out her name. In that brief instant, he thought she cried out his name as well, then all was lost in a bright swirl of pure release.

Eventually he stirred, and opened his eyes to find himself free, with Red curled at his side, her gloves on her hands. He shifted slightly, and kissed her eyes as she lay sleeping. Red stirred, but didn't awaken.

The tear tracks remained on her face, and he frowned at the sight. He stroked her face with his fingers, drying those tears. There was so much about his kitten that he didn't know.

Red roused slightly, and turned her head so that her lips brushed over his palm. Josiah smiled softly. Maybe he couldn't guard her body, but he could protect her heart, for as long as she allowed.

He settled down in the hay, making sure that the blankets covered them both completely. Red murmured a protest at the movement, then cuddled closer. He smiled at the beams over his head, and closed his eyes to sleep.

At dawn, Red was standing outside the barn, staring over sodden fields. It must have started raining in the night, for there was water puddled in the dirt of the yard.

Bethral, standing watch in the door of the smithy, had seen her emerge. She'd lifted a hand in greeting, but had not come over. That was fine by Red. She needed a moment to think.

She sucked in a breath of cool, wet air and glanced down at her red gloves. The leather looked the worse for wear, that was certain. They were drier, at least. Cleaner. She clenched both fists, and then released them, reassured by their familiar feel and presence.

Last night, Josiah had offered what it never occurred to her to ask for, offered his . . . surrender without hesitation. She couldn't have done the same. The very idea made her blood run cold. How could he trust that way? Trust her?

She closed her eyes, feeling once again the softness of his skin, the feel of his hair, hard muscle under velvet. She couldn't remember the last time she'd touched another that way.

She wanted to go back up in the hayloft, rouse her sleeping goatherder, and do it again.

She stomped that idea right down, mentally pushing it into the muck of the bog. Such gifts were rare, and not to be taken lightly or presumed on. By its very nature, it was far more valuable for its offering than in its taking.

But Twelve take it, she wanted more.

A sound drew her back, and she turned her head slightly to see the boy emerge from the house and head in her direction. He ran over, and bounced to a stop before her. 'Ma says to ask you to breakfast. She's cooked a haunch!'

Red gave him a nod. 'Tell Bethral.' She nodded toward the blonde. 'I'll wake Josiah, and we'll be in shortly.'

The boy didn't wait. He bolted over to Bethral, talking before he even reached her.

Bethral raised her head, and gave her a questioning look. Red nodded, then turned back into the barn to fetch Josiah. Might as well eat. They'd no gear, and it would take at least three days to get back to Athelbryght on foot, if they pushed. And Ezren didn't look near close to 'pushable.'

Beast was still asleep in his stall. Red frowned, considering, as she reached for the ladder. She could take Beast and make a run for Athelbryght. Leave the others here, sheltered as safe as they could be. But she rejected it before she'd climbed another step. It wasn't any safer to separate, and she wouldn't leave Josiah.

She huffed a breath as she climbed. They needed to be on their way, but they also needed food, and whatever information they could gather quickly. They might be able to buy supplies, maybe even horses with the looted coin.

No time for pleasure this morning. The dawn was a calm one, but Red knew that wouldn't last.

Nothing ever did.

Larrisa's face was glowing from the heat of her hearth. She shook her head as she carved a hunk from the haunch on the hearth. 'There's no horses to spare roundabout. I've supplies, and you're welcome to all you can carry.'

They'd been welcomed to her small kitchen, and a creaky wooden table laden with food. Red hadn't been the only one surprised at the bounty. Larrisa's three children were acting like it was a holiday feast eagerly staring at the venison.

'Sit, and fill your plates,' Larrisa urged. 'Therrin, help your sisters.'

Therrin sighed deeply, as if greatly put upon.

Larrisa gestured to Bethral. 'You may want to sit elsewhere. Farasa is a messy eater.'

Bethral laughed, and settled next to the smallest girl. 'What do you want little one?' The girl looked up with wide brown eyes and pointed at the bread and butter. Red had no idea how old they were, but they'd their fair share of adorable, that was certain.

Oris filled a plate, and accepted slices of meat from Larrisa. He took it to Alad, who stood watch outside.

'We can pay.' Red settled on a bench next to Josiah. 'We've—'

Larrisa shook her head. 'Better you than the thrice-damned raiders. Folks around here have decided to band together, and leave this place. The haunch would have rotted soon enough, so I put it on to roast.' Her voice was gruff. 'Eat, warriors. Then we can talk.'

For a few minutes, there was no sound but the passing of platters and the dishing up of food. Larrisa carved hunks of meat from the haunch, generous portions for all. Red ate, and watched as Josiah helped the littlest girl drink from her cup, making sure she didn't spill a drop. Therrin seemed torn, stuffing his mouth and looking at all of them. Red imagined he had a thousand questions, and they'd spill over eventually.

Oris took a second plate, and then a third, out to Alad. None of them held back, and Red could feel the meat filling the hollows of her stomach. Which left her with as many questions as the boy.

The boy burst out first. 'What happened to ya? Was you attacked?'

'That much is clear,' Larrisa chided. 'See to the kavage, Therrin.'

The boy jumped up for the pot by the fire, eager to serve. Red was sure he'd not miss a word. 'We were traveling toward Penature on the bog road when we were attacked.'

Larrisa shook her head. 'There's been problems with raiders for months, and no aid to stop them.'

Bethral caught Red's eye as Larrisa poured kavage. Raiders or an ambush? Had it been chance? Red shrugged. Given events, she was fairly sure they'd been targeted.

'This is a good bit of land.' Josiah spoke softly.

'It is.' Larrisa looked at him. 'My man was a farmer and horse breeder. He was killed when the raiders attacked, not four weeks past. Killed him and took the horses.' She looked down at the table. 'I've not the skill to lay in crops, and little hope to keep things going here. We've nothing left but a few pigs and chickens.'

'We could do it, Ma.' Therrin sat up straighter at the table, squaring his shoulders.

She gave him a soft look. 'If it were the two of us, we might. But the girls need tending, too.' She looked at the one sitting next to Josiah. 'Show me your arm, Cera.'

The girl lifted her arm, and pointed at a long red burn on the underside of her forearm.

'I left them for only a moment,' Larrisa said softly.

Farasa crowed, and banged the table with her spoon.

'We're leaving, Therrin.' Larrisa repeated. 'As soon as the others gather here, we'll be off.'

'Where to?' Josiah asked.

Larrisa sighed. 'Edenrich does not welcome folk, and I fear that wanderers are not welcome in Penature or Swift's Port. Athelbryght is in ruins. We've decided to risk the bog road and try to reach the Free City of Oxfair. We've heard that laborers are welcome—'

'We could stay, Ma,' Therrin announced, his mouth full of bread and his eyes full of pride. 'I can fight.'

Larrisa gave him a mother's eye. 'I'd rather it not come to that.'

Oris sighed, and pushed his plate back. 'Thank ye, Lady. I was very empty.'

'As to that, I've a favor to ask in return, if you would.' Larrisa spoke quietly.

'What aid do you need?' Red asked.

The fire crackled in the hearth softly as they waited for her to continue. Therrin got down and hugged his mom. Larrisa glanced out the window, toward the stables.

Bethral spoke. 'You said something about a sick horse.'

'Three weeks ago, my man was killed, and our horses taken. But one, a mare he had raised by hand, well . . . she was tied in the smithy and they didn't get her. She was Jeran's pride and joy. But since we buried him, the horse has not been eating, and I can barely get her to drink.' Larrisa stopped and swallowed hard. She wrapped an arm around her son's waist. There was total silence in the room. 'It needs doing, for the lass's not coming around. I won't let Therrin do it, and I can't . . . I can't . . .'

Bethral interrupted softly. 'I will aid you.'

Larrisa nodded. She drew a deep breath, then gently eased her son away from her. 'Therrin, take the little ones into the smithy loft and play with them for a while.'

Ezren stood. 'Perhaps a story,' he said. 'I have a few I can tell.'

Josiah rose, and swung the smallest girl off the bench and onto his shoulders. 'Let's go listen to a story.'

Oris stood. 'Lady Bethral, you'll need some help.'

In moments the room cleared. Red sat at the table and scowled, looking over the remains of the meal.

Apparently the Chosen had gotten stuck with the dishes.

Not in this lifetime. Red finished her kavage, then stood. She'd seen a whetstone in the smithy, and her blade needed an edge. Time enough for that while Bethral dealt with the horse.

She'd barely had the stone going before Bethral emerged from the barn and headed toward her. 'Is it done, then?'

Bethral cleared her throat. 'No.' She folded her arms across her chest, and shifted her weight. 'I've looked over the lass, and I think that I may be able to . . .'

Red snorted. 'Bethral . . .'

Bethral dropped her arms. 'Please, come take a look.'

Red grimaced. 'We've no time for . . .'

Bethral turned and started for the barn. Red followed, biting back the rest of her words. Oris was just inside the barn door. He and Bethral led the way to the back, where Larrisa stood, lantern in hand. In the faint circle of light Red could make out a horse tied against the far wall.

It was a huge horse. Brown and dirty, with an unkempt, shaggy coat. Head held low, hollows in the flanks, some sort of huge sore on the withers. Still, it stood taller than any Red had seen, with hooves so big she'd not dare to try to lift one. Size for size, the beast matched Bethral, what with her standing bigger than most men.

Bethral's quiet voice came from behind. 'Larrisa's willing to let me try to get her to eat.'

Red sighed. Never mind that they'd been attacked, and had no gear. Never mind that raiders were off in the woods. Never mind that there was a prophecy to fulfill, and their dead stuffed into trees. No, never mind all that. Bethral would sooner slit her own throat than walk away from a suffering horse.

Red smiled wryly. She'd known that within an hour of meeting her sword-sister. 'What's an hour more or less?'

Bethral's eyes lit up. As she'd known they would.

Oris spoke up. 'Larrisa says there's gear here we can go through, see if we can use anything.'

Red nodded. An edge to her blade wouldn't hurt. 'Go ahead and try. You might start by lancing that sore. It looks like it's gone sour.'

Bethral came up next to her. 'What sore?'

At which point, the sore moved and stretched and fixed a watery yellow eye on Red. It was a cat, the ugliest cat she'd ever seen − fur sticking out, black and brown and yellow and a mottled kind of green. A tail so bedraggled as to be an embarrassment. The creature stood on the withers of the horse as if it owned the beast, the barn, and all the lands around.

Red crossed her arms over her chest and snorted. Horses, goats, cats . . . Sweet Twelve, how about a few dogs and ponies to go along with them, eh?

Larrisa came forward, crooning to the mare. 'My man hand-raised her from a foal. He was going to keep her to breed and as an example of all the tricks he could teach to a prospective buyer. She was his pride and . . .' Her rough hand continued to stroke the beast, but her mind's eye was far and away in better and distant times. Red shifted from one foot to the other and coughed as a courtesy.

Larrisa sighed. 'She hasn't eaten since, and I can barely get her to drink.' She wiped at her eyes, and looked over her shoulder at Bethral. 'She's wasting, and I hate to see her suffer. I'm willing to let you try, but if you can't . . .'

Bethral nodded.

Red shook her head, left the barn, and went back to the smithy.

TWENTY-SIX

The blade of her looted sword wouldn't hold an edge. Red pumped the foot pedal, and swore under her breath as she set the blade back to the stone. She could hear the voices of the children, combined with those of Josiah and Ezren, overhead. Best not teach the little darlings any new words this day.

Oris came out of the barn, carrying two of the looted swords. 'Piss made, if you ask me,' he grumbled as he walked up. 'Want some help?'

Red nodded, and released the stone to him. 'Anything else in the way of supplies?'

Oris shrugged. 'A few packs, some cloaks at least. We'll need them for the trek.' He raised an eyebrow at her. 'I was thinking maybe Alad and I could—'

'We don't separate,' Red replied. 'Too many dangers that way.'

'Too many dangers any way,' Oris said, but he accepted her decision as he settled on the stool.

'What do you think of this?' Red pulled the shard from her belt. 'Any chance it could be worked?'

Oris gave it a dubious look. 'It's worthless rust, Chosen.'

Red grunted. 'Sharp enough when it needed to be.' She put it back under her belt. 'How's Bethral faring?' Red looked over at the barn.

'Talking to the horse, whispering in its ear.' Oris pumped the wheel.

'Whispering?' Red headed for the barn. That had better not mean what she thought it meant.

Bethral met her at the door, a slight smile on her face. Red stopped, suspicious. 'Well? What luck?'

Bethral's smile grew wider, and she stepped back into the barn. Red followed, and peered into the shadows.

The horse was eating out of a bucket and chewing like it hadn't a care in the world. The cat twined between its legs, back and forth, its sorry excuse of a tail straight up in the air.

The horse glanced at Red, turning its huge head slowly. Bethral must have spent the last hour cleaning and grooming. The mare's coat was a beauty, a deep reddish-brown with the dirt removed. Even with the hollow spots and the slight tremble in the knees, she held the promise of a fine mount.

Beast was hanging over his gate, snorting and demanding attention.

Red turned back to Bethral and saw her looking at the horse with pride. Red groaned, and rubbed her hand over her face.

Alad and Larrisa were talking in the tack room. The only other sounds were the chewing of the horse and something that sounded suspiciously like a purr coming from the cat.

Red glared at Bethral. 'What did you do?'

Bethral never took her eyes off the horse.

'Bethral.' Red waited until she had her attention. 'What did you do?'

Bethral looked down and shrugged. 'I cleaned her, brushed her.' She glanced at the ground. 'Talked to her.'

Red crossed her arms over her chest 'And?'

Bethral sighed. 'I promised her vengeance.'

Red groaned.

Bethral continued hastily. 'I explained my obligations . . .'

'Of course,' Red said.

'. . . and my duties to you, and they understand . . .'

' "They" being the horse and the cat?' Red asked.

'. . . understand that those come before all else, but should a chance arise . . .'

Red had a sudden vision of the horse wildly attacking some miscreant in a market square, with no warning or provocation.

'. . . and we prayed to bind our pledge . . .'

' "Our" being you, the horse, *and* the cat?' Red asked scathingly.

'. . . pledge and now all's well. She'll need only a day or two of feeding before she's ready to travel.' Bethral's voice was matter-of-fact.

' "A day or two?" ' Red snarled. 'Are you forgetting our—'

Ezren's head popped in. 'Are you finished yet?'

'No,' Red snapped, but it was too late. Ezren had seen the horse.

'Is that the horse?' He stepped within the door. 'Lady Bethral, you are amazing.'

Red made a rude noise. 'If that's what you call it. She's always picking up strays and lost causes.'

Ezren stiffened. 'I will take my leave, Chosen. The children will be glad of this news.'

Bethral's face was stony as the storyteller departed.

'Muck!' Red grimaced. 'Bethral, I—'

Bethral stepped over to the horse. 'I'd best water her.' With a tug, she urged the horse toward the yard. The cat padded behind, a disdainful look on its face.

Red snarled at it.

Larrisa and Alad came out of the tack room. Alad was dragging two heavy chests. Larrisa's face was lit from within by happiness, her arms full of gear. 'Where's Bessie?'

'Bessie?' Red choked. 'The horse's name is Bessie?' She looked out into the yard.

Bethral was taking the horse into the sun, one slow, careful step at a time. The horse's head was up, and Red could hear the excited children laughing from the smithy. Josiah swung the smallest girl up in his arms so that she could pet the horse.

The cat was back up on the horse's rump, looking self-satisfied. The sunlight on its mottled fur did nothing to improve its appearance.

'His pride and joy.' Larrisa smiled, and Red could see the beauty in her tired face. 'Your Bethral is special, that she is.'

'She's something,' Red muttered.

'Alad said she's in need of armor.' Larrisa pushed past Red.

Red gestured for Alad to precede her with one of the boxes. She picked up the other. They all stepped out into the sunlight. Red glanced at the fields around them, but they were clear. Oris was still at the wheel, keeping half an eye on their surroundings.

The children were laughing and petting the horse, the smallest one clinging to Josiah, reaching out her hand to pet its soft nose. The horse nuzzled them all, between drinks from the trough.

Alad dropped his box at Bethral's feet. She looked at him, puzzled.

Larrisa opened the box. 'Let's see if this fits you.'

Ezren heaved a sigh as he leaned against the post. Oris looked over, concerned. 'Something wrong, Storyteller?'

'No, no.' Ezren crossed his arms over his chest. 'I was just thinking how beautiful she is.'

'That's true enough.' Oris put the blade to the stone and pumped the treadle. Sparks flew as he sharpened the blade. 'Lovely carriage. And the deepest roan I've seen in a long time.'

Ezren gave him a withering glance. 'I meant Lady Bethral.'

'Ah.' Oris returned to his work, deciding then and there that he'd shut his mouth. The Storyteller was a complicated man, and it wouldn't do to offend. He'd been thinking there was something wrong since they'd left the bog, but he hadn't pressed the man.

Now, lovesick might be one explanation. Either that, or the man was bound up inside. A good dose of butternut oil would take care of the second problem.

Nothing was gonna help the first.

Oris lifted his eye from the stone for a moment, looking at the blonde warrior. A good one in a fight, that was sure, but to lose his heart to such a one? No thanks. Hells, he had to admire Lord Josiah for bedding the Chosen. The very idea made his manhood shrivel up. Now, a nice plump wife with a cheery smile, that was more to his taste.

His gaze went down to the blade against the stone, and Oris frowned at it. Better than nothing, but he could wish for his own steel back in his hand.

'What is that?' Ezren straightened.

Oris looked up. They'd opened that wooden box, and Larrisa was pulling out flannel bundles. The cloth in Alad's hands unfolded to reveal a piece of a suit of armor – plate, by the look of it. Oris stood, admiring its silver curve and its soft sheen. Even from this distance, he could see the quality. 'That's a suit of plate, I do believe.'

Now everyone was reaching down, pulling out pieces and unwrapping them. Oris walked closer for a good look, the storyteller right behind him. 'Gods, is that horse barding, too?' Oris asked as he peered over Alad's shoulder.

'Aye.' Larrisa looked at him, her worn face softened into a smile. ' 'Twas my man's.'

Bethral frowned. 'Larrisa, I can't take this. I did not . . .'

'No.' Larrisa smiled. 'He'd not have minded.' She looked at the horse. 'They were a grand sight, he and the lass, all decked out in it. A grand sight.'

Like kittens at cream, they dug it out of the trunks. Oris studied the pieces as they were held up. 'Not true plate. Looks like a mix of plate and chain.'

Larrisa nodded, as she held a piece up to Bethral's chest. 'Jeran wanted something he could move in.' She looked at Bethral. 'You've the size to wear it.'

Lady Bethral protested, but in a moment, she had more handmaidens around her than a virgin at a Goddess Wedding. Oris joined in, with everyone talking and laughing and trying to get the straps and buckles adjusted for fit. The padding underneath went on, a bit snug, and from there Bethral was slowly encased in metal, gleaming in the soft sun. When they had almost finished with her, they started putting the barding on the horse, their eagerness spilling over onto the beast.

Bethral frowned. 'Isn't that too much of a weight for her to take so soon?'

Larrisa shook her head. ' 'Twill be good for the lass. Won't hurt her none.'

Oris had to admit that the horse seemed to be enjoying the whole fuss. The cat snarled, and jumped down, strutting back toward the barn.

Finally, Bethral stood, in full armor, helmet on her head. The horse stood next to her, dressed out in full barding. Bethral took a breath, then mounted, pulling herself into the saddle with ease.

Oris winced. That flat chest plate must be pushing down on her breasts hard. But even with the poor fit, even with the tired horse underneath, they were a sight to behold, there in the sun.

The others had backed off, drinking it in. A full outfit like that was rarely seen outside of royalty. Oris had to admire the work. It was an impressive sight, and it deserved to be paid tribute.

Larrisa made a soft sound, and Oris turned to see her eyes brimming. He stepped closer, and laid his hand on her back. She smiled at him, and opened her mouth, but a yowl cut through the air.

Oris jumped when a dark streak ran from the barn and launched itself onto the horse, using its claws in the chain to pull itself up, not stopping until it reached Bethral's shoulder. The cat yowled, a high, angry cry.

'Raiders!' Bethral bellowed.

Oris spun, cursing. He had a brief glimpse of an archer, then dragged Larrisa down to the ground. Larrisa sprawled flat, crying out in surprise. She struggled to rise, but he pushed her flat, cursing himself for a thrice-damned fool. Them all out in the open, and the weapons in the forge . . .

Red cursed as she turned to see a large group of men charging their way, a few on horse but most on foot. She'd pay for her stupidity now, standing here, out in the open, nothing but a shard in her belt.

She'd pay. But the others—

Josiah scooped up the girls, and ran for the barn. Red saw Oris go down as she ran forward. Alad was behind her, at the forge, getting swords – but too late, too damn late, as one of the mounted raiders bore down on her, intent on riding her down, sword raised for a blow. She bounced up on her toes, waiting until the last minute to dodge, maybe get her shard—

A battle cry sounded, freezing her heart in her throat.

Bethral, mounted on the horse, charged past. Red drew in a breath, the small hairs on the back of her neck rising. For they were changed, those two, horse and rider. They glowed, the very image of perfection. Horse and rider moved together, smooth and powerful. There was no tiredness here, no ill-fitting pieces. And as fast as that flashed through Red's head, they moved on the charging raider.

Red had it in her to pity the poor bastard.

The man raised his sword, and they clashed together, but he had no chance, in leather, his sword a mere toy in comparison to the mace Bethral swung against him. Bessie slammed into the horse, knocking it off balance.

'Chosen!' Alad ran up, swords in his hand.

Red reached for one as Oris struggled to his feet. Larrisa scrambled away, toward the barn, screaming for Therrin.

Red, Alad, and Oris spread out, waiting for the rest of the band. Red knew that one mounted warrior would not hold them. She looked up as she moved into position, and realized that she was mistaken.

Bethral and her mount danced before the men, almost daring them to draw close. One stepped too close, and the horse spun and kicked, high and clean.

The man collapsed.

Bessie danced away, as if there was no burden on her back. The raiders paused, but they pressed forward, surging to get around them. Bethral kneed the horse, and Bessie lashed out with a hoof, catching one in the knee. He screamed in pain, and Bethral used her mace to drive him to the ground.

But a few of the men on foot slipped past, running toward Red and the others. Red screamed her own battle cry, moving forward to meet the attack with blade and shard. The others formed a line with her, intent on protecting the barn and the children within.

Red lunged in first, feinting. Her attacker's blade cut the padded quilting, just under her breast. Red showed her teeth as she rammed the shard home in his groin. It scraped against the bone, which made her smile as she pulled it free.

Red turned to aid Alad when Therrin ran from the smithy with a sword and a shield. Larrisa screamed as one of the raiders turned to meet this new threat, a vicious grin on his face.

Therrin held his shield high, taking the blow from his attacker's sword. Red wasn't close enough; no one was.

Bethral cried out, and then they were there, horse and rider. Bessie plowed the man into the mud, and crushed his head under a massive hoof.

Red turned back to the battle, but there wasn't one left. Oris and Alad had defeated their remaining opponents. All that was left was the stench of blood, and silence.

Larrisa ran to Therrin's side and fell to her knees, embracing the lad and crying.

The barn door opened slightly. Red noted that, but her attention was on the horse and rider. 'Bethral?' Red called out.

There was no response. The horse stamped its foot, dancing a bit from the rage of the battle.

'Bethral?' Red's voice rang out in the chill air of the yard.

Her head turned. Red caught her eye. And yet, not quite Bethral's eye.

Now the hairs on Red's arms joined the ones lifting on the back of her neck. There was a power there, surging through the two of them. It looked through Bethral's eyes, and smiled, as if secretly amused.

Red glared back.

The figure nodded toward the barn.

Red turned her head slightly, and stepped back.

Ezren was standing at the barn door, his eyes wide with fright. His hands were straight out before him, and they held fire, or rather, were wreathed in flames.

The storyteller stared at them, terrified.

'Ezren,' Red breathed, and moved forward.

'Is it safe?' Josiah's voice came from behind, and suddenly the flames were snuffed out, as fast as a candle in the wind.

Ezren stood for a moment, then collapsed to the ground. Josiah appeared behind him, leaning over to check the man.

Red turned back.

Bethral was gazing at her from beneath the helmet, with a puzzled look on her face.

Larrisa came over to Red, her arm around Therrin's shoulders. The boy was protesting bitterly, but his mom was crying with relief. Larrisa smiled, but then her smile froze.

Red gave her a look. What the hells?

Larrisa knelt down, pulling Therrin with her. As Red looked down, Larrisa raised her hand slowly and carefully and tugged at Red's slashed jerkin. She stared at the birthmark below Red's breast. Her gaze darted from Red's face to her chest and back.

Then, trembling, she reached for Red's hand.

'Larrisa . . .' Red really had no words as she shifted her blades and took the proffered hand. What could she say?

Larrisa swallowed hard. 'You are the Chosen of the prophecy.'

She clutched at Red's hand with damp fingers and stared up into her eyes. 'We'd heard you'd come.'

Red's throat closed and she nodded, more for a lack of words than anything else.

Therrin gaped at her, kneeling next to his mother, clutching his sword and shield.

Larrisa came up on her knees in the blood and the mud. She pressed her free hand against the mark. She lifted her face to Red. 'I, Larrisa, once of Penature, pledge my life to the Chosen, now and forever, binding my blood and the blood of my children to your service . . .'

It took time to sort it all out, time they didn't have.

Josiah watched as Red snapped orders, getting bodies disposed of, getting people moving. The girls had been very brave, going right up the ladder to hide in the hay, just as he'd told them to do. But it took their mother's voice to get them to come out of hiding, and many hugs before they settled down.

The raiders were stripped, their bodies dragged into the fields. Which was where their horses were found, and three pack horses as well. Alad discovered their stolen gear in the packs.

Josiah helped stand watch as Red dressed in her regular armor and buckled on her sword belt. She muttered under her breath as she did the same service for Oris and Alad, darting glances at Bethral and her horse.

Ezren claimed he was fine, and denied that anything out of the ordinary had happened. He'd just collapsed with relief. He mounted his horse with seeming ease, and stared at the surrounding area, claiming to be on watch, thus cutting short any talk.

Bethral stayed in her armor. It had been changed, fully fitting her curves. Josiah had pointed that out, but Red really didn't want to talk about that at all. She wanted them moving, as soon as possible.

But there were Larrisa and her children to consider. Josiah looked at the woman, who was loading one of the spare horses with their personal items. Oris and Alad had the girls on their horses.

'They're coming with us,' Red said. 'There's no choice.'

Josiah nodded. 'They can homestead in Athelbryght. Larrisa would be useful in the rebuilding.'

There was a silence, then Red looked over at him, as if seeing him for the first time. She nodded solemnly. 'That's very true.'

Josiah frowned, as he realized that Red's eyes were shadowed. 'What's wrong—'

Therrin came around the corner of the building, driving three pigs before him. 'Ma says to bring them with us!' His eyes lit up with excitement.

Red groaned.

Ezren looked over, a sly smile on his face. 'When I tell this story, Chosen' – he paused for effect – 'and I will tell it, someday.' His smile grew to a grin. 'When I tell the tale of the Chosen, I will leave out the pigs.'

Red snarled.

Ezren chuckled.

Red pulled herself into Beast's saddle. 'I've had more than enough mayhem, magic, and gods for one day.' She looked back as the others mounted as well. 'Let's be about it, shall we? I've a prophecy to fulfill.'

TWENTY-SEVEN

Gloriana stepped through the portal and into the darkness of the shrine in Athelbryght; from bright sun to cool shadows in an instant. A trip through the portal was usually a treat, but Gloriana's stomach wasn't churning with happiness or excitement.

She swallowed the lump of fear, and stepped forward into Aunt Evie's waiting arms.

'Gloriana.' Aunt Evie's voice was warm, her white robes soft and comforting. Gloriana buried her face in them. She felt safe, wrapped in the hug, and didn't look as she heard Vembar and Arent emerge from the portal.

'What word?' Arent asked quietly, in her firm, steady voice.

'None.' Gloriana felt Evie sigh as she spoke. 'Red and the others are overdue to the meeting, and no word has come. Lord Carell has people searching from his end, and I've sent a scouting party from here. We should know more soon.'

Aunt Evie's arms tightened around her, then eased her back. Gloriana looked into those kind eyes. 'Lord Carell is here, awaiting word,' Aunt Evie added, then hesitated. 'And I sent for more assistance. Lord Mage Marlon is here.'

'Marlon?' Vembar asked, leaning on his cane. 'I thought you'd kept him out of this.'

'I did, up to this point.' Evelyn nodded as she headed to the door of the shrine. 'But now . . .'

Her voice trailed off as she walked out.

Arent followed, and Gloriana turned to lend Vembar her shoulder. The old man gave her a smile. 'Relax, Little One. You bear the mark of the Chosen. You've the birth and the training, and you will make a wonderful Queen.' He leaned over, and put his hand on her shoulder. 'Display the mark, Gloriana. They need to see it when they see you. To be reassured.'

Gloriana gave him a weak smile, and nodded as she reached for the lacings. It was getting harder to display the mark without blushing. When she'd been younger, it hadn't bothered her. But now . . .

She undid the clever lacings, and fastened them so that the mark was displayed. Red had pointed out to her that it could be worse. 'What if it was between our cheeks? How do you display that, eh?' She could hear Red's voice in her head, and it made her feel better.

'Good.' Vembar smiled at her. 'That will reassure them that the Chosen still leads the cause.'

Gloriana had her doubts. Always before, it had been 'when.' *When you are older, when the High Barons support you, that's when you will lead us.* But now, Red Gloves had turned 'when' into 'now,' and if something had happened to her—

Vembar stumbled on the steps, clutching the door frame with a frail hand. Gloriana reached to help him. She needed to stop fretting, and focus on helping Vembar down the path.

Arent was standing outside, waiting. 'I'll do this, child. Walk with Evie.'

Gloriana looked into her face, seeing the strain there. Auxter was one of the missing, but Arent stood tall and patient. Gloriana wished she had that kind of strength.

Vembar reached for Arent's arm. 'Go on ahead, child.'

Gloriana walked forward alone. She was wearing the armor that Connor had made for her, as he had for Red Gloves. She was the Chosen Heir, and Red had insisted that she look the part, right down to the armor. But right now, all Gloriana knew was that there was a bead of cold sweat forming in the middle of her back, trickling down her spine.

Aunt Evie had waited for her, and they emerged from the trees together. Men were milling about the barn, keeping clear of the command tent. Evie walked steadily toward the tent, and Gloriana kept the same pace, as much as she wanted to run. All eyes were on them, and she could feel the weight of their stares.

Gloriana stiffened her shoulders as they drew closer to the men, and concentrated on not stumbling over a rock or root. She nodded to some of the warriors and gave them what she prayed was a relaxed smile.

It seemed to work. Men returned the nod, and then went back to their work, breaking up the stares to some degree. But even if they weren't looking at her, the responsibility was still there, pressing on her shoulders.

She breathed a small prayer to the Lord of Light and the Lady of Laughter. *Let Red Gloves be safe, let her ride into the camp at any moment, cursing and ready to take command.*

The command tent had its sides rolled up. Gloriana stepped onto the platform, where two men were waiting. One was a tall, handsome black man, with black hair and dark eyes. The other was seated, an extraordinarily fat man wearing a silk robe that swirled with color.

'High Baron Carell, let me make you known to Gloriana,' Evie was saying.

'Chosen?' The black man stood, his expression puzzled.

Gloriana stepped forward, and smiled. 'The Chosen Heir, Lord Carell.'

The fat man snorted. The black man gave him a frown, then smiled at Gloriana. 'A pleasure, Chosen.'

Gloriana gestured. 'Please, be seated. Have you been offered food? Wine?'

'We have, girl. Not up to the standards of Athelbryght, that is certain,' rumbled the fat man.

'Athelbryght will recover.' Evelyn spoke calmly, but Gloriana could tell she was irritated. 'Gloriana, this is Lord Mage Marlon.'

'Lord Mage.' Gloriana inclined her head.

Marlon sniffed. 'You have the bearing, chit, I give you that.'

'And manners,' Evelyn snapped. 'Are you so far gone that you can't rise to an introduction?'

Arent spoke as she aided Vembar into a chair. 'The chair would no doubt collapse when he plopped back down.'

Lord Carell grabbed a cup and quickly brought it to his mouth. Gloriana was certain he was hiding a grin.

Marlon barked out a laugh. 'Still as pleasant as ever, Arent.'

'What brings you from your hedonistic pursuits?' Vembar asked. 'I thought you'd retired to while away your days in de-bauchery and sloth.'

'This chit.' Marlon jerked his head toward Evelyn. 'With a wild tale of a prophecy come to pass. Nonsense, of course. An old wives' tale, told to drunks and fools. Believed only by the very stupid or the insane.'

Aunt Evie pressed her lips together.

Marlon frowned at her. 'Now I come to find out that Josiah lives, after five long years of mourning him.'

Aunt Evie flushed. 'There were reasons, good re—'

'Pfui.' Marlon scowled at her. 'And the so-called Chosen is missing—'

'And your scrying skills would be most useful,' Aunt Evie snapped. Gloriana looked at her in astonishment. Aunt Evie's cheeks were spots of red, and she was angry. 'I'll have a bowl brought and—'

'I've my own supplies at my worktable,' Marlon snapped back. 'No need to drag me into the Gods-forsaken wilderness with naught but well water and poor wine. What—'

A shout went up, and they all turned to look. A rider was coming fast. In mere moments, he pulled his horse to a stop before the platform. 'Lady High Priestess,' he gasped, 'they're coming, the Chosen and some others. They are coming behind me. We met them on the road and escorted them back.'

'Red Gloves is alive?' Evie asked, and Gloriana felt like her head would burst in the seconds before the scout answered. Relief flooded through her, right down to her toes, when he nodded.

'Aye, High Priestess.' The man grinned. 'Worse for wear, but alive.'

'My thanks.' Aunt Evie's voice regained some of its calm. She stood, her hands folded into the sleeves of her robe. A flash of disappointment passed over Vembar's face, but then he, too, looked pleased.

Gloriana watched as the group approached, surrounded by the escort sent to find them. Red was there, at the front, as was Josiah. But there were fewer men, and where had the pigs come from? She frowned, and stood to watch as the horses came to a stop before the platform.

'Impressive,' Lord Carell said under his breath.

Gloriana winced inside, but kept her face schooled. They looked tired and worn. She frowned, trying to see who was missing. Where was Auxter? Was that a cat on the back of Lady

227

Bethral's horse? Ezren Storyteller had a child on the saddle before him. There was a woman she didn't know, and a boy on a horse, holding a small girl.

The boy glanced her way, through hair that fell over his face. The little girl in his arms shifted and yawned, and the boy looked down and smiled at his burden. He had deep dimples in each cheek. He lifted his head, and Gloriana was caught by his eyes.

In the midst of the chaos, she couldn't help but smile back.

Evelyn's stomach settled down as Red Gloves rode into view with the others. She stepped forward, and watched as Red dismounted. 'We thought you were dead.'

Ezren Storyteller gave her a shadowed look. 'We were.'

'Later.' Red's voice was a growl. 'We'll deal with that later.'

Arent moved up to stand next to Evelyn. She scanned the group of men and horses. 'What has happened? Where is—'

Oris moved from out of the crowd. 'Lady Arent.'

Evelyn glanced over as Arent drew in a breath with a hiss. Oris was kneeling before her, a broken staff in his upraised hands. 'Auxter is dead.'

The entire group went silent.

Arent reached out trembling hands, and took the broken pieces from Oris. Gloriana moved forward to stand at Arent's side, her eyes brimming with tears.

Evelyn put her hand on Arent's shoulder, offering comfort. Arent stood silent for just a moment, then she turned to look at Evelyn. 'We will mourn him when this is done. Not before.'

'Agreed,' Red said, and the rest nodded.

'I thank you, Oris.' Arent's voice was clear. 'No easy task, to bear this news.' She held the staff close to her breast.

'I live to serve, Lady.' Oris rose to his feet, then swayed. Josiah reached out to steady him.

'Food.' Arent stepped off the platform. 'You need food and drink. Gloriana and I will see to it.' She strode off toward the cooking tents, calling out to some of the men in the distance. Gloriana followed, swallowing her tears.

'What happened?' Evelyn asked as the others began to

dismount. Josiah slid from his horse, and reached up to take the child from Ezren so that he could dismount.

Red spat in the dirt. 'The details can wait, but we were betrayed.'

'Not by me.' Lord Carell stepped to the edge of the platform. 'I've had no dealings with the Regent since the fool tried to tax my trade. I'd be damned before I'd give him money, men, or information. Fool doesn't understand that there's a free port just up the coast, and I'll lose the flow of commerce through my lands.'

Josiah handed the child back to Ezren. He turned to look at Carell with a grin. 'Learning wisdom in your elder days?'

'Elder days?' Carell scoffed. 'Who has the gray in his hair, old man?'

They stood and stared at each other for a moment, then broke into laughter. Lord Carell jumped off the platform and caught Josiah up in a hug, pounding his back. 'Josiah of Athelbryght! I never thought to see you again, my friend.'

Josiah pounded Carell's back. 'Or I, you.'

Red stepped onto the platform. 'If you're done, we've work to do.' She ran her gloved fingers through her hair. 'Oris, if you'd see to Larrisa and the children. Get them set up in a tent for the moment. And for love of the Twelve, do something with the pigs.'

Josiah and Carell stepped back, still grinning like loons. Evelyn smiled, but then she spotted Marlon staring at Red's gloves, opening his mouth, no doubt ready to launch one of his pithy comments. 'Red,' she said, moving forward, hoping to avert disaster, 'let me make you known to—'

Marlon turned toward her, a scowl on his face. But Evelyn was spared his wrath as his gaze moved over her shoulder, to focus behind her. 'By your mother's left tit!'

Evelyn glanced behind her, and saw Ezren standing there, a polite smile on his face.

'Aren't you an insulting bastard,' Red snarled, stomping onto the wooden platform.

'Not really,' Evelyn replied, trying to figure out what had upset the man. 'He is my father, after all.'

'Pfui,' Marlon snapped. 'What daughter of mine consorts with wild magic?'

Evelyn raised an eyebrow. 'Ezren is not—'

'Use the skills the Gods gave you, girl,' Marlon spat.

Evelyn snorted, but turned and whispered the words to activate her mage sight. She smiled reassuringly at Ezren, confident that—

Ezren glowed.

Evelyn jerked back instinctively at the sight of the raw, wild magic. Fear flooded through her. 'Storyteller, what happened to you?'

Ezren frowned. 'Lady High Priestess, I—'

'What does it matter "how"?' Marlon demanded from his chair. 'All that matters is that he has dared to violate the law concerning wild magic, and his life is forfeit. If you won't do the honors, daughter mine, then I will.'

Evelyn jerked her head around. 'Father—'

Marlon lifted his hand, and cut through the air with it, casting a spell toward Ezren.

'Father!' Evelyn protested, but it was too late. Ezren raised his hand to his throat, apparently unable to take a breath. 'Father, stop,' Evelyn demanded. 'We don't know—'

Bethral pulled her mace and advanced on the fat man. 'Release him, Wizard.'

Marlon growled at her. 'Stay back, Warrior. This is none of your concern.'

Bethral took another step, and Evelyn feared the worst, but Red's cry cut through the crowd. 'Josiah!'

Instantly, Josiah ran to Ezren's side. Ezren flung his head back, sucking in a deep breath of air.

Marlon cursed.

Red folded her arms over her chest, and gave him a sardonic look. 'Bad enough the enemy knows of us. Perhaps we should talk before we start killing one another.'

TWENTY-EIGHT

'Father, you can't kill him,' Evelyn said. 'We need him.'

They'd crowded onto the platform, lowered the cloth side of the tent, and set guards about to get as much privacy as they could. Bethral doubted that would be enough to stave off the curiosity, but it was an attempt. She'd put herself on one side of Ezren, mace in hand. High Mage or not, Marlon would not get another chance to bespell the Storyteller.

Not that she needed to worry while Josiah was seated close on Ezren's other side. But she'd not take a chance, either way.

'What the hell is more important than killing a rogue mage?' Marlon growled.

Red glared as she unbuckled her armor, and displayed her breasts.

Marlon rolled his eyes. 'Lovely. Evelyn, is this another one of your causes?'

Evelyn had two angry red spots on her cheeks, and wasn't looking too pleased. 'Father—'

'He's a rogue and a danger to us all.' Marlon lifted his staff and shook it at Ezren. 'Why didn't you just kill yourself? That is what the guild teaches you to do, for the love of the Lord and the Lady. Don't you remember your lessons?'

Ezren lifted his chin. 'I beg your pardon, Lord High Mage, but I've never had lessons.'

'He's not a mage, Father,' Evelyn said.

Marlon was speechless for a second, but he recovered fast. His eyes bulged and his jowls quivered as he roared, 'An untrained rogue?'

Ezren shrugged.

Marlon rubbed his hand over his eyes. 'I need a drink.'

Red glanced through a gap in the cloth. 'It's coming.'

'Not soon enough,' Marlon muttered. He shot a glare at Ezren. 'Tell me what happened.'

Ezren looked down at the floor. Bethral couldn't blame him, not wanting to relive the story. But he lifted his head and began to speak, his voice still harsh and rough.

Ezren started with the attack, with Red collapsing, and the warriors swarming over them. Bethral listened carefully, trying to figure out how they'd been overcome so easily, but Ezren lacked a warrior's eye. He just knew they'd been captured and taken to the altar deep within the bog.

Bethral remembered nothing of the attack – nothing, really, until she awoke at the altar, alive and well. It saddened her that she didn't know the details of Steel's death, but she knew the great horse had died trying to protect her. She'd a lock of his mane, and would say her farewell to his spirit when the time was right.

Ezren's recital ended with their awakening. His voice trailed off, and everyone sat quiet for a moment.

'You saw it?' Marlon was looking at Red. 'You have no mage skill, yet you saw it?'

'I did.' Red nodded. 'Like nothing I've ever seen. White and bright, like a thousand stars in a dense fog. I'd expected it to be hot, but it was more like . . .'

'Like what?' Marlon was genuinely curious.

'Joy,' Red answered, slightly embarrassed. 'It left me breathless with a sense of joy and delight.'

'And it didn't touch you?' Marlon pressed.

'No.' Red shook her head.

'But it touched you.' Marlon turned to Ezren, and considered him.

'It poured into him, like milk from a pitcher,' Red answered. 'His very bones glowed.'

'What do you remember?' Marlon asked.

Bethral watched as Ezren folded his hands before him, and the knuckles went white. 'I remember watching the others die. I remember being dragged to the altar, and struggling with my captors.' Ezren's voice was cracked, but it was almost as if he was reciting a poem. 'I saw the Chosen coming out of the bog, and all I wanted was to give her a chance to kill the monster.' He paused, and swallowed hard. 'I spit in his face, and he killed me.'

'You challenged him. Dared him to kill you,' Red said. 'The altar was bloodstained and had moss growing over it when they put him on it, but was pure white when . . .'

'And when you awoke, and saw the others?' Marlon pressed.

Ezren's head turned slightly, and Bethral saw a flash of green before his gaze fell to the floor. 'I just wanted it not to be true. And then it wasn't.'

Marlon shook his head. 'I'd give a lot to see that altar and know what the engravings say. Were there any walls, or other ruins?'

Red shook her head. 'There was only the stone spider that disappeared.'

'I have the knife,' Bethral offered.

Everyone turned and looked at her.

Ezren swallowed hard at the sight of the stone knife, still wrapped in the ragged cloth. Marlon had Bethral put it on the table in front of him, and used a dagger to move the cloth aside to display it.

'Flint,' Marlon muttered. 'The handle is some kind of antler.'

'I didn't clean it,' Bethral said.

Marlon grunted, and continued to use a dagger to move the rag about. There was dried blood on the rag, but the knife's blade was completely clean.

Marlon lifted both hands in the air, and started to chant softly. Ezren felt the hairs on the back of his neck rise, and he saw Red lean back in her chair, away from the mage. Marlon's eyes began to glow white.

The mage studied the blade. 'There's no taint of any kind of magic on the blade.' He looked up, letting his gaze travel over Red. 'None on the Chosen.' He shifted his look to Bethral, Oris, and Alad. 'But you three have been touched by wild magic.'

Bethral and Oris took that in stride, but Alad shifted uneasily.

'Josiah,' Evelyn asked, 'step away from Ezren for a moment.'

Ezren felt his stomach clench, but nodded his head at Josiah when the man turned and looked at him. His skin tingled as the big man moved away. Bethral shifted her weight, as if uneasy.

But all that happened was that Marlon looked at Ezren, then looked away just as quickly. The light about his eyes flickered slightly. 'A bonfire, that's what he is. I can barely look at him.' He gestured, and the glow was gone from his eyes. 'Describe the mage.'

'Dead,' Red said with satisfaction.

Ezren closed his eyes, forcing the image to appear before him. He did his best to describe the man and the robes he wore, right down to the small gold hoop in his right ear.

Marlon pursed his lips. 'Well, whoever he was, he was a damn fool. Working blood magic on a wild magic site.' He tilted his head, and considered. 'He may not have known it was wild magic he was dealing with. Hard to believe anyone, even a blood fiend, would be that stupid.'

'There have been rumors that the Regent has been hiring blood mages,' Ezren said.

'Which shows that the Regent is also a damn fool.' Marlon glared at Evelyn, then shifted his gaze to Bethral. 'Put that away,' he commanded, pointing at the stone knife.

Bethral obeyed.

'Maybe the altar was designed to hold wild magic.' Ezren stopped when Marlon, Evelyn, and Josiah all shook their heads.

'That's like saying you wove a shirt for a fish,' Josiah said softly. 'The wild magic is found in the wild places, not where men have tamed the land. It's dangerous.'

'There are other dangers, nephew.' Marlon focused on Josiah. 'Just what happened to you?'

Josiah sat back in the chair next to Ezren and began to tell his tale.

Red didn't like this one bit.

'Just do it, daughter.' Marlon had turned his chair to face the field. Josiah had been sent to the center of the field, where he stood with the goats grazing around him.

'Father,' Evelyn was clearly upset. Red was sure she saw the woman's hands trembling before she tucked them in her sleeves, out of sight.

'We both know you can, and I have to watch what happens.'

Marlon sounded almost smug. 'How can it go against your beliefs to aid your cousin, eh?'

Evelyn's fists clenched at that, and they came up in front of her. The High Priestess cried out something, and to Red's horror, a pillar of fire appeared to their left, swirling in the weeds, burning the greenery at its base. With a gesture, Evelyn sent it moving, heading directly for Josiah.

Red watched, speechless.

The flames swirled and leaped as if eager to burn his flesh, but within touching distance they were gone, with only the scorch marks to show where the pillar had been.

One of the goats raised its head and bleated, as if to protest the interruption.

'Do it again,' Marlon said, his eyes aglow.

Evelyn shot him a glare worthy of a firestorm. Red shifted back, fairly certain that the flames were going to appear in Marlon's lap this time.

But once again the flames danced in the field until just before reaching Josiah, when they disappeared.

'That's enough.' Marlon released the spell on his eyes. 'You can come back, Josiah.' He returned to his chair and settled his bulk within it.

'By the Incorruptible Twelve, what was that?' Red demanded, her eyes wide.

'Ask her.' Marlon gestured to Evelyn.

Evelyn glared at him before turning to Red. 'Suffice to say that those spells are destructive, and I do not choose—'

'Do not choose?' Marlon shouted.

An uneasy silence reigned for a moment, until Red decided that she needed to change the subject. 'What did you learn about Josiah?' she asked.

'Easy enough,' Marlon said, picking up a wineglass and scowling into it. 'I'm surprised Evelyn didn't figure it out for you. She might have, if she worked at it harder.'

Red scowled.

Evelyn set her jaw. 'If you'd enlighten us, Father.'

'Fair enough.' Marlon looked at Josiah as he came onto the platform. 'It's not so much that Josiah destroys magic. He has somehow become attached to the land, to Athelbryght itself. Any magic that Josiah touches is absorbed back into the land, restoring it.' Marlon rolled his eyes. 'I am not sure what to make of the goats.'

Red looked at Josiah as he took the words in. 'Uncle, is there any chance that my powers would be restored?'

'Damned if I know, Josiah.' Marlon's face was full of pity. ' "Maybe" is all I can offer. Maybe once the land is fully restored.'

Josiah sighed and looked over the fields, his eyes distant.

'Meanwhile' – Marlon looked at Ezren – 'you are a nightmare. What every mage scholar has talked about for years. An untrained rogue with wild magic.'

'Help him,' Evelyn said.

Marlon looked at her in astonishment. 'How? He doesn't even have the basic skills needed to manage magic, much less the wild flavor. He hasn't absorbed his lessons through his mother's nipple, like you did.'

'It can be taught,' Evelyn insisted.

'Why me?' Marlon demanded. 'You could—'

'Because as the head of the Mages' Guild, you trained mages for years. You are his best and only hope.'

Marlon snorted. 'Even if I can teach him the basics, daughter dear, it is a temporary measure at best. Eventually he will lose control, and then what? A danger to all who surround him.'

'Not if he stays close to Josiah,' Red said.

'Use Josiah like a wet blanket on a fire?' Marlon took a sip from his glass. 'That might work, but eventually it will not be enough. Risky for Josiah as well, since the strongest fire can blaze hot enough to burn wet wool.'

'Give him some basic training, Father,' Evelyn asked. 'Enough that he can learn some small control.'

'We don't even know if that will work,' Marlon grumbled as he eyed Ezren. 'It's wild magic that fills his soul, not the mundane.' He narrowed his eyes, and considered Ezren. 'Still, it might be educational.'

Evelyn seemed to be holding her breath.

'Very well, then.' Marlon straightened in his chair. 'Ezren, what does it feel like when the magic builds within you?'

'I . . . it's hard to describe.' Ezren squirmed in his chair, looking at each of them.

'I can help,' Marlon said. 'You know how it feels when you really have to piss?'

Red's mouth dropped open. Bethral blinked in surprise, but Evelyn just rolled her eyes. 'Father, I don't think—'

'It's how we teach the children,' Marlon said loftily. 'Just as you teach a child not to soil his nappies.'

'It is, Evie,' Josiah said apologetically. 'You didn't go to a formal mage school, so you wouldn't know.'

'Magic's like peeing?' Red asked.

'Pissed your trous lately?' Marlon asked, ignoring Evelyn's indignant sputters.

'No, you rude pi—' Red growled.

'Because you learned when you were a babe. Your body knows – you know – and barring illness or extraordinary circumstances, you are in control. The urge that builds up, you delay, do a bit of a dance, eventually you gotta go or pee your pants.' Marlon focused on Ezren. 'He can't, because he's never learned. He doesn't recognize what his body and the magic are telling him.'

Red looked at Ezren, who had the faintest bit of red on his cheeks. He lifted his chin in defiance. 'I am certain I can learn.'

Marlon gave him the eye. 'Maybe. You can learn the feelings, what they mean. But can you learn control? Especially when you are angry, or startled, or—'

Red snorted. 'So all the high-horse mages are just those who can hold their water longer than others?'

Marlon stopped, and gave her an offended look. 'If you don't mind. Guild secrets.'

Red quirked her mouth, but she managed not to laugh out loud.

Much later, Marlon, Red, and Evelyn were seated at the table. The cloth sides of the tent were rolled up, and the last bit of sun was disappearing behind the hills.

'Josiah may have lost his skill, but not his knowledge. He can help Ezren.' Marlon sighed. 'But it won't last, daughter.'

'It's dealt with for now,' Red growled. 'We've other worries that need seeing to.'

Marlon snorted. 'Your cause is—'

'Thank you for your assistance, Lord High Mage,' Evelyn said stiffly. 'I am sure you wish to return to your home.'

Marlon gave her the eye. 'Without sharing the latest gossip of the Regent's Court?'

Red raised her eyebrows. 'You have access to the Court?'

'I do,' Marlon said. 'As Guildmaster, I am frequently invited to the Regent's table.'

'And just as frequently, you decline the invitation,' Evelyn said.

'The Regent has not held many Court feasts of late.' Marlon looked at Evelyn sideways. 'Seems he's heard tell of a Chosen raising an army against him, one who wears red gloves and wields a sword as most women wield a needle.'

Red shrugged. 'Not unexpected that he learned of me. Once word got out, I knew it would make its way to his ears.'

'But there's no talk of your involvement, daughter,' Marlon said. 'Just the usual complaints that you give away your services to the poor.'

Evelyn smiled slightly. 'Mother always said that it wasn't right to charge for prayers.'

'You know the Archbishop, Evie. He'd charge per blessing and double on holy days if he could,' Marlon pointed out.

'True enough,' Evelyn sighed. 'But that is a problem for another day.'

'You might not hear if there was suspicion against her,' Red pointed out. 'She is your daughter.'

Marlon shook his head. 'Don't think me a fool, Red. I've other ears. I'd know. I may not approve of her foolish ways, but I'd know of a threat to my daughter.'

'Father, it would help if the Guild withdrew its suppor—'

'At the time, the Regent seemed the only option – you understand that, don't you?' Marlon glared at Evelyn.

Evelyn looked down at the table. 'I am sure it seemed so at the time, Father.'

Marlon sighed. 'I may be the Guildmaster, but mine is not the only voice in the decision. I will consult with the others.'

Evelyn said nothing.

Marlon looked at Red. 'Josiah is as much a weapon as your sword is. In many ways, far more powerful.'

'He's a man, not a weapon,' Red snapped. 'A man who will be needed to rebuild this land.'

Marlon studied her face, then gave a satisfied nod. 'Well, then, I will return to my comfortable lodgings, and leave you to it.'

Red stood. 'We'll see you to the shrine.'

'What for?' Marlon asked. He turned his head to Evelyn. 'Stay alive, daughter.'

Evelyn gave him a sad smile. 'I'll try, Father.'

'Don't you need to open a portal from the shrine?' Red asked.

'Oh, please,' Marlon scoffed. He snapped his fingers and disappeared, chair and all.

'Father loves to show off,' Evelyn apologized.

'He can do that?' Red looked at her, shocked. 'Just "poof" and he's there? Or gone?'

'He isn't head of the Mages' Guild because of his charming personality,' Evelyn pointed out. 'He's the most powerful mage in the Kingdom, and the only one who can do that.'

'Fine. Wonderful.' Red stood. 'I've a prophecy to fulfill. Let's be about it, shall we?'

TWENTY-NINE

He was losing her, and he wasn't sure why.

Josiah paused, leaned on his shovel, wiped sweat from his forehead, and looked around him, letting the land distract him. As uneasy as he was about Red, this work filled him with a sense of satisfaction.

Soon after their return, Red had sent a party to retrieve the dead they'd been forced to leave behind. Larrisa had gone with them, and spread the word to her neighbors that there was safety to be found in Athelbryght. Red had told her to pass the word to those she trusted.

Families had started to arrive with the supplies they could carry, and their animals in tow. Many had lived in Farentall before the battles had ravaged that land. They all were looking for a safe place.

Red had taken one look, and thrown up her hands. She'd given the task of settling them to Josiah. 'You know the land,' she'd said, with an odd guarded look on her face. 'You figure out what to do with them.'

Though it was late in the spring, Josiah had set them to glean what they could from the land. The fields about the camp would be worked by all, to ensure a decent crop for the fall.

The livestock had been combined, and soon the herds would multiply. Josiah was pleased, although he always had to explain anytime someone tried to milk his goats.

Larrisa had aided him in sorting the wheat from the chaff, helping him figure out their skills and abilities. They'd worry about the establishment of homesteads once Palins was restored and Red was on the throne. In the meantime, they'd search to find what new life was returning to Athelbryght.

Already there were fish and eel in the river, and someone had reported deer on the farthest fields at dawn. Arent was still supplying them from the farm in Soccia, but with any luck, if they planted in the fall, they'd be self-sufficient come this time next year.

One of the lads came by with a bucket of cool well water, and Josiah gratefully accepted a drink. Another few breaths and he'd get back to work.

His gaze moved toward the barn and the command tent, where there was a bustle of far different activity. For the last week, Red had done nothing but organize men and arms, sending messages and conferring with the High Barons. Josiah had tried to join in the councils, but more than once his curse had canceled an important spell or portal. Besides, he really didn't have an interest in troop movement, try as he might.

Red had chased him off. Oh, she'd smiled as she'd done it, but Josiah knew that the Chosen was putting distance between them. Not at night. Lady of Laughter, the nights were full of their lovemaking, and his body pulsed at the thought of this evening's tryst. But the heat between them was different, and Josiah was fairly certain he knew why.

She'd exposed herself to him – let him see into the depths of her heart. To a warrior such as herself, that would be frightening. Josiah chuckled, feeling a bit smug. His kitten was startled and afraid, her fur puffed out and teeth and claws displayed.

But the nights – she was just as eager as he, and more often than not, it was his kitten who reached for him in their tent. Of course, once she took the throne—

Josiah stopped in midthought, not letting himself finish the idea. He'd have her as long as he could, Lord of Light willing.

Their forces were almost ready, he knew. Another few days, and she'd leave to join the forces massing to attack Edenrich.

Another few days . . .

'Lord Josiah!' The cry came from behind. Josiah whipped around to see Lerew running toward him.

She was losing him, as she'd known she would.

Red looked toward the fields where Josiah was working as she waited for the next messenger to arrive. A moment of peace in the organized chaos that is a military campaign. Bethral and Oris stood nearby with horses, also awaiting the next messenger.

Josiah had tried to look interested as they pored over the maps and discussed the routes that the warriors would take from the various baronies, but more than once his eyes had strayed to the fields around them. Red smiled at the memory. The refugees had been a good reason to send him off to do the work he was best suited for. Every night, in their tent, he'd talk of plants and grain and births among the cattle and sheep.

She'd lie back on the bed, content for a while just to watch and listen to him. Odd that he didn't bore her with his talk of crops and livestock. She enjoyed watching his face as he talked, alight with interest, enthusiasm, and plans for the future. He was so sexy, padding about the tent, folding his clothes, crawling into bed . . .

Red sighed. She wouldn't be able to do that for much longer.

She looked at the maps spread over the table. The armies had been moving for some time now, and it wouldn't be long before they'd be massed, waiting to move on Edenrich. From every report, they'd be ready sooner, rather than later. She'd know in the next hour or so.

As much as she wanted to remain at Josiah's side, they couldn't move soon enough for her. Time wasn't their ally. The Regent knew of the Chosen with the red gloves, might even know of the force gathering to stand against him. The sooner they moved, the less time he'd have to counter them.

Red glanced over to where Gloriana was studying a map, comparing the counters with the papers before her. She was intent on her work, and dedicated to the cause. Gloriana certainly looked the part of the Chosen, wearing the armor that displayed her birthmark.

Red studied the girl carefully, satisfied with what she saw. Gloriana looked so young, her shoulder-length hair brushing the map as she leaned over the table. She'd do, to follow in Red's footsteps if necessary.

Of course, one never knew with the young, until they were tested in the fire. But Red thought Gloriana would survive, when it came down to it.

Movement by the shrine caught her eye, and she saw Ezren leading a group of men talking and gesturing. The men were all dressed differently: some prosperous, some plain, and a few down on their luck. She'd let him have full rein over his plans, and didn't ask too many questions. He seemed very earnest that his scheme would be helpful, but only time would tell.

She stretched, reaching up and standing on her toes. It would be good to finish this, good to—

She heard a cry, and turned to see Josiah and his workers running for one of the distant fields. They were moving fast, and she couldn't tell . . . were they being attacked?

'Oris,' she called out, and pointed.

Oris pulled himself up on his horse, as Bethral did on Bessie. Red ran from the platform and mounted as well, and set Beast to a gallop. Damn fools, if there was trouble, why didn't they run toward her, and not away? Where were the cursed sentries?

Fool goatherder! She kicked Beast into a gallop and pounded through the fields.

Josiah didn't know whether to laugh or to cry. He knelt in the soil, examining the tiny green leaves on the twisted, gnarled vine.

Others milled about, talking and laughing and checking the other rootstocks. But Josiah just stared at the tiny growth, and felt something ease in his chest. He'd never thought it possible.

The thunder of hooves brought his head up. Red pulled Beast to a halt, scanning the area and glaring at them. 'Where's the attack?'

Josiah looked up into Red's eyes, filled with concern and worry. His heart swelled with joy, with gratitude, with love for the woman who had ripped his scabs off and started the healing. He just grinned at her – looking like a fool, he was sure. 'No attack, Red. Come and see.'

She dismounted, and threw the reins to Oris. Bethral stayed mounted, her armor gleaming silver in the sun.

'Fool goatherder,' Red grumbled as she knelt. 'Scared the life out of me. I thought you were being attacked.' She nudged one of the goats away with her knee. 'What is this?'

Josiah smiled at her, using his fingers to display the leaves. 'The vines. They are coming back. Athelbryght is coming back.'

Red gave the vine a dubious look. 'If you say so, Josiah. Not much to look at, though.'

'Not yet.' Josiah stood, brushing off his knees. 'But in a few years . . .'

Red quirked her mouth, and gave him a doubtful look.

Josiah laughed, the joy welling up inside him. He reached out, took Red in his arms, and swung her about. The goats kicked up their heels, bleating and dancing about. Red squawked a protest, but there was a sparkle in her eyes when he set her back on her feet.

'The grapes will come back, Red, wait and see.' Josiah grinned. 'We'll make wine again, wonderful wines that dance on your tongue.'

'Wine to make a bard weep?' Red asked, repeating what she'd heard him say.

Josiah looked at the smiling faces of the men and women talking and laughing around him. 'Aye, Chosen.'

She smiled, but there was something in her eyes. Something haunted. Josiah reached out to her, but Red pulled back. 'I've one last dispatch to consider.' She turned back toward Beast. 'We'll eat in the tent tonight. Just the two of us, eh?'

'Yes,' Josiah said softly, but Red just mounted and rode away.

Their meal was a simple one. They ate on the bed in an easy silence, which suited Red just fine. She relished the food, and the light of the sun as it glowed on the tent walls. She'd managed to bathe before they ate, and was wearing some worn trous and a tunic from deep in her pack. Old, but comfortable. No armor this night. The guards were posted about the camp, and Bethral had trained them to within an inch of their lives. They were safe enough.

And her plans for the night did not include smelling like oiled metal.

She watched Josiah as they shared the food. He ate absent-mindedly, lost in thought of vines and grapes, no doubt. She smiled, and he caught the look as he reached for the last of the kavage.

He smiled back. 'What are you staring at?'

'The vines are not the only things growing, Josiah. You need a haircut.' She set her mug aside.

He shrugged, putting a hand up to his neck. 'I usually cut it when I can feel it on my neck.'

'Let me,' Red offered. She leaned over, and drew her dagger.

He gave her a smile, and she moved behind him, running her gloved fingers through his curls. She pulled the hair out with her fingers, and carefully started to trim it. 'So soft,' she whispered as the silky locks clung to the leather of her gloves.

'It will get everywhere,' Josiah warned.

'We can shake out the blanket.' Red smiled at the back of his head. She loved the contrast, the black strands with the dusting of silver. 'Your hair shines like Bethral's armor. Silver in the black of night.'

Josiah sighed under her touch. 'I'm afraid there's more of the gray than the black.'

'Silver,' Red corrected him. She continued to work, but she made sure that her gloved fingers stroked the back of Josiah's neck once in a while, the barest of teasing touches. He shifted a bit but made no protest.

She worked around to the front trimming back the curls just enough so that they framed his face. She couldn't resist stroking his lips with a gloved finger.

He looked at her with hungry, smoky eyes, the gold flecks gleaming in the depths.

Satisfied, she sat next to him on the bed, gathered her hair in a fist, and pulled it over her shoulder to see the ends.

'Do you want me to . . . ?' Josiah asked.

'No need,' Red said. 'I've done it this way for a long time.' She trimmed the ends, and then released the hair so she could gather it on the other side. With careful strokes, she cut it short so that it fell just to her shoulders.

Josiah was busy brushing the hair from his tunic. She stood, and they made short work of gathering the bits on the floor. Josiah went out to shake the blanket.

Red sheathed her dagger and pulled off her boots. Josiah returned, and together they smoothed the blanket over the bed.

He stood across the bed, and looked at her. 'So, Chosen.'

'Josiah,' Red breathed, 'take off your tunic.'

Josiah stepped around the bed, and walked to her side as he pulled the garment over his head. Red reached to help him, kissing him as soon as his lips appeared under the cloth. She tossed the tunic aside.

Josiah returned the kiss hungrily, and Red leaned in close, enjoying his warm, wet mouth and teasing him with her tongue. Breathing in his scent she moved closer, enjoying the feel of her tunic caught between their bodies.

Josiah put his arm around her, pulling her closer, deepening the kiss. Red broke the kiss, tossing her head back with a chuckle. She pushed back, escaping from his arms, and pushed him down on the bed.

Josiah sat. 'Doesn't seem quite fair, that your tunic—'

Red pulled her tunic over her head in a single move. She grinned at Josiah as he took her in. 'Mercenaries don't play fair, High Baron.' She reached down, and skimmed out of her trous as fast as the fabric would allow.

She kicked the clothing to the side, and climbed on the bed to kneel behind Josiah.

She pressed herself to his back and reached around to stroke his nipples. Josiah moaned, and put his head back. An awkward angle, but Red kissed him as she reached around to untie his trous. 'Stay like that, Josiah,' she whispered in his ear. 'Don't move.'

He felt her soft breasts press against his back, felt her arms come around his waist. He tried to obey her, tried to stay still, but his body had other ideas.

Her gloved hand dipped between his trous and fevered skin, moving lower and lower. He arched up into her touch, and Red chuckled at his frustrated efforts.

Josiah growled and turned to grab her. Red fell back, laughing, her arms stretched above her head, her breasts quivering.

He moved then, up and over her, pinning her to the bed. Now it was her turn to moan and arch up against him, but he denied her that touch. Instead, he took her nipple in his mouth and teased it between his teeth.

Red reached down, and they struggled for a bit, each making demands that the other would not meet. Finally Red fell back, sweaty and spent, giving him a mock glare. 'You have an obligation here, Lord High Baron.'

'Which I will meet, Chosen.' Josiah nuzzled her neck. 'If not now, there is always the morrow. I will satisfy, that I promise. But when? Well . . .'

The play left Red's eyes. 'I leave at dawn, Josiah. We have only this night.'

Josiah pushed himself up, bracing himself on his hands. 'I thought you wouldn't be ready for at least another week.'

'No.' Red shook her head. She reached up and stroked his face. 'Fael moved fast, because the weather has held. I leave in the morning, with Bethral, Evelyn, and our warriors.'

Josiah looked at her. 'Tomorrow, then. It begins tomorrow.'

Red nodded. 'It does.'

'And finishes,' Josiah asked urgently, 'when?'

'When it does, however long it takes.' Red sighed. 'The best plans change to meet the circumstances.' She stared into his eyes. 'If I had my way, I'd stuff you through a portal to Soccia. Instead, I'll leave men here to guard you.'

'And the refugees,' Josiah said pointedly.

Red shrugged. 'Them as well.' She hooked a gloved hand behind his neck. 'Don't you have something you need to do, 'Siah?'

He smiled down, and shifted his body between her legs. 'I think so, Chosen.'

'Best be about it, then.' Red pulled his mouth down to her, and kissed him.

He shifted again, entering her heat slowly, taking his own time to enjoy the sensation. Red moaned, flexing her hips to take in more, but Josiah held firm, using his mouth and hands to stroke and tease.

She hissed when he was fully seated and, moving her hands down, pulled him closer. Josiah resisted her, setting his own pace. A long, slow, steady stroke. He watched her face as she flushed, lost in her passion, as her body twisted beneath his. Her eyes closed, her head thrown back, he watched as she fell from the height he had taken her to.

Josiah stilled, waiting. Her wet heat rippled around him, and he breathed deeply, not wanting to give in to the demands of his own body. He was rewarded when her eyes fluttered open, and she gave him a lazy smile that turned to surprise when he pressed down. 'Josiah,' she breathed, responding to his demands.

He kissed her then, demanding her surrender, speeding up his thrusts until she clung to him, almost sobbing from the pleasure. Red threw her head back and cried out his name, and this time Josiah followed, losing his own awareness to the pulse of her body.

When they recovered, breathing hard, their bodies entangled, he reached out and brushed her hair from her face. Red smiled drowsily and snuggled close with a murmur of satisfaction. He moved his lips to her ear. 'Sleep, kitten.'

Her eyes flew open, and she stared at him, wide-eyed. 'Kitten?'

Josiah swallowed hard. 'I . . . you . . .' He dropped his head back on the pillow. 'Just go ahead and kill me.'

Red shoved over, and straddled him, pushing his wrists down on the bed. 'What did you call me?'

Josiah looked up into those lovely eyes. They weren't glaring at him, or sparking with fury. She almost seemed . . . embarrassed.

There was a flush on her cheeks, and he'd swear that she was more pleased than not. He gave her a careful look. 'I enjoy holding you, and when we come together, the way you curl up next to me, I . . .' He shrugged as best he could. 'You look like a kitten. All sated and soft next to me. Like you are about to start purring.'

She gave him a searching look, as if almost afraid to trust him. His smile widened slowly. 'You like it.'

She pursed her lips, pressing him further into the bed, shaking her head in denial. 'Don't call me that in front of other people.'

He bucked his hips up, and knew she could feel him responding to her. 'Of course not.'

Her mouth quirked up, and to his delight, the smile spread to her eyes. 'I mean it, Josiah. I'll . . .'

'What would you hurt, Chosen?' He moved his hips again. 'Seems to me you have a use for all the important parts. My face, perhaps?'

She leaned in and kissed him thoroughly, until they both broke it off, breathless and hungry.

'My chest, perhaps?' Josiah asked.

Red moved down, and kissed his chest just above his heart.

Josiah closed his eyes at the touch of her soft lips. He chuckled as he felt her move again. 'Or perhaps you'd cut off my—'

Red swallowed him whole.

With a cry, Josiah shattered into sharp shards of wet hot pleasure.

It was the camp sounds that woke her.

Red opened her eyes as soon as she roused, but didn't move. She was wrapped in Josiah's arms, curled by his side, his breath on her neck.

They were starting to bring the horses out of the barn, to ready them for the journey. Saddles being put on horses blended with the jingle of tack. She could just make out Bethral's voice talking softly. Probably telling Bessie what they were doing that day. Bethral seemed to feel that the horse should know as much as the rider.

She should be up and about the day.

It was the day, after all. The beginning of the conflict, the start of the battles that would place the Chosen on the throne.

What did it say that she'd rather stay in bed with Josiah?

She sighed softly, not wanting to rouse her goatherder. Now it really started, and they would have to be careful. With no knowledge of who had betrayed them, or what information the enemy had, it would be difficult to make any plans.

As if sensing her unease, Josiah shifted slightly. Red smiled. He'd looked so happy over those tiny leaves, his eyes gleaming bright in the sun.

She withdrew from his grasp slowly, easing off the bed. He was sprawled in the linens, and she made certain that he was well covered against the chill.

Her gear was arranged as she'd left it, and she dressed quickly. She moved quietly, so as not to waken Josiah. Kitten, eh?

It was embarrassing, but it delighted her, warming her heart deep within.

Her weapons strapped on, she paused when she realized that the shard was nowhere to be found. She looked under the bed, but it was not there. For that matter, she wasn't sure of the last time she'd seen it. She shrugged. It wasn't like it was really useful, after all.

Still . . .

Her gaze drifted back to the bed, where Josiah lay, curled in the bedding. Something clutched deep in her chest.

By the Twelve, she didn't want to go. Didn't want to leave this man.

Red stood by the side of the bed, watching Josiah sleep. She leaned over, checking again to make sure the blanket covered his shoulders. She drew in a deep breath, taking in his scent. Quickly, before she could change her mind, she leaned down and let her lips brush his hair.

She took up her boots, and left the tent.

There was work to be done.

THIRTY

Evelyn's heart raced as she watched the rest of their warriors emerge from the portal. She couldn't help but shift in the saddle. Her horse shifted as well, tossing its head in protest. She tightened the reins with sweaty palms, and calmed her mount. But she couldn't control her anxiety.

Red Gloves gave her a glance out of the corner of her eye. 'Nervous?'

Evelyn took a deep breath. 'Of course.'

Bethral chuckled.

They were watching the portal from a distance as the men came through in formation. Red had insisted on being the first through, and she'd placed herself where she could be seen as they formed up.

They were to ride for Radaback's Rill. Evelyn had never been to the valley where the stream was located, but it was said to be lovely. Ezren had told her the story of the place. It was nonsense, of course, but still, one had to wonder . . .

Evelyn took another deep breath, trying to calm herself and focus on what was happening around her.

Bethral sat astride Bessie on the other side of Red, the picture of calm, armored strength. She carried the furled banner, the standard of the Chosen that Ezren had insisted on. Bethral and Bessie stood as one, unmoving, steady as a rock.

Evelyn shifted in the saddle again.

'Try to look a bit more confident, Lady High Priestess,' Red said with a wry smile. 'It would help if you didn't squirm.'

'Five years,' Evelyn said. 'Five years, I've worked for this. Since the day I rescued Gloriana and took her to Auxter.'

More men came through the portal.

'I've used resources, gathered people, all in the hope of

restoring sanity to Palins.' Evelyn looked at the Chosen. 'I've every right to be worried.'

'Waste of energy,' Red said.

'What if no one has answered the call to arms? What if one of the High Barons has betrayed us?' Evelyn took the reins in one hand, and rubbed the other dry on her robes. 'Months of planning come down to this hour. How many warriors will be there? Will you have enough warriors to challenge the Regent?'

'We'll know soon enough,' Bethral answered.

The last of the men came through the portal, and Evelyn closed it with a gesture. Oris came up, wearing a grim smile. 'We're ready, Chosen.'

'Lead the way, Oris,' Red said.

Oris turned his horse, and signaled the men to move. He took the lead, sending out riders as scouts.

'Well, Lady High Priestess, the answers await. Let's go find out, shall we?' Red urged Beast to a walk.

Evelyn followed. 'I'll pray as we ride.'

'That, too, is a waste of energy,' Red called over her shoulder.

'Still,' Evelyn muttered under her breath, 'it can't hurt.'

The ride was a swift one. Red might not have been worried, but she wasted no time, setting a swift pace to the meeting place. Evelyn said her prayers as they rode, asking the Lord and the Lady for aid in their cause. There had to be enough men, there just had to be. After all the work, the effort, the miracle of finding an adult Chosen . . . the Gods must be blessing their purpose.

A shout caught her attention, and Evelyn looked up to see Oris at the top of a rise just before them, waving them on. Red and Bethral rode forward, and Evelyn urged her horse to follow. She had to know . . .

Red and Bethral topped the rise and sat there, looking down into the valley.

Evelyn kicked her horse forward, pushing between Oris and Red. The rise sloped down into a wide valley.

A valley filled with men and horses, wagons and tents.

Evelyn sat frozen in astonishment.

The valley brimmed over, it held so many. Heads were

starting to turn their way as their own warriors moved up behind them.

Red Gloves sat on Beast, looking smug.

More movement below, as the word spread like a wave through the crowd. Warriors emerged from their tents, looking in their direction, shading their eyes. Evelyn watched in amazement, not quite daring to believe. Perhaps this was the Regent's army, and they'd—

'Unfurl the standard,' Red commanded.

Bethral unfurled the cloth, and the standard of a white dagger star on a red background snapped out fluttering in the breeze.

As the cloth flared out, loud cheers erupted from below, and grew into a roar. Tears filled Evelyn's eyes as relief swept through her. She could see the men reacting, opening their mouths to bellow a welcome. They pulled their swords, held them over their heads, and hailed the Chosen.

In response, Red stood in her stirrups and drew her sword, holding it over her head to flash in the sun.

The cheers deepened, resounding through the valley.

Evelyn's breath caught in her chest, and she whispered a quiet prayer of gratitude.

'Well enough.' Red settled back in her saddle and took a deep breath, which made Evelyn believe she hadn't been as calm as one might think. After sheathing her sword, Red twisted her hair up and donned her helmet. 'Let's be about this, shall we?'

She urged Beast down the rise, and broke into a gallop. Bethral and Evelyn followed, through the camp of cheering men to a command tent in the center of the valley.

'Amazing,' Lord Fael said as he brought them into the command tent. 'And they keep coming. Apparently word has spread like wildfire of the coming of the Chosen.'

'Ezren Storyteller,' Bethral said.

'Probably.' Red looked around as the others gathered about the central table, satisfied with what she saw. 'But this means more men that we don't know, and no one can vouch for.'

'And which one will want to stick a knife in your ribs,' Wolfe of Wyethe offered. Lady Helene sat quietly beside him at the table, dressed sensibly in decent armor. Wolfe's influence, no doubt.

Red nodded. 'So I'll keep the warriors from Auxter's farm as my personal guard. I know and trust them.'

'Makes sense,' Fael agreed.

'The Heir is safe and well hidden,' Red told them. 'She's young, but ready to step in if I fall.'

'Let us hope it doesn't come to that,' Lord Carell said.

Red grinned. 'I'd prefer it.' She pulled out one of the maps and spread it before them. 'Now, let's talk troop movements. Lord Fael, Lady Helene, we need to depend on part of your forces to keep Elanore and her army from crawling up our ass.'

'There's been no movement on her part,' Wolfe offered. 'She uses Odium, and they are slow and do not hide their passage.'

'Keep it that way,' Red said. 'Stay between her and our rear. That also puts you in a position to reinforce from behind if needed. Now, as to our course. I think that—'

The talk went on for an hour or so, and finally Evelyn stood and shook out her robes.

Red raised her head. 'Leaving?'

Evelyn nodded. 'I've sunset duties at the Church. I need to pass the word to the healers that we are moving. I've made arrangements that they will join us in the next few days.'

'That's not a good idea, Evelyn,' Red said quietly.

'It's dangerous, I grant you that,' Evelyn said calmly. 'But it's also the last chance to see if there is any gossip or rumor. I will be gone only a few hours.'

'Have a care, Lady High Priestess,' Red warned. 'If something happens, there will be no rescue.'

Bethral's head jerked up at that, a frown on her face. Red glared at her, knowing the signs. 'I mean it. This venture is not so secure that I can afford to rescue one at the price of success.'

Bethral held her eyes, then looked away.

'I understand, Chosen.' Evelyn smiled. 'But I've walked under this threat for five years. One more night makes little difference.' Evelyn looked at the map. 'The next shrine you encounter is here.' She pointed it out on the map. 'I'll be there at dawn, with a corps of healers and perhaps more information.'

*

He'd lost her. Josiah sighed. She'd left without saying goodbye, and there'd been no word—

'Oh, please,' Ezren scoffed. 'You sound like a lovesick lass, abandoned in a tale.'

'There's been no word,' Josiah pointed out.

'There has been plenty of word,' Ezren responded. 'The messengers come on a regular basis. They are moving into position now; there is no real fighting going on yet.' Ezren got a smug look on his face. 'And it would appear that my stories have helped them to gather forces.'

Josiah sighed.

'Your complaint is that there has been no form of personal correspondence,' Ezren continued. 'But they are both warriors, focused on a conflict.'

'Both?' Josiah asked, giving Ezren a look out of the corner of his eye.

'I meant Red Gloves, of course.' Ezren set a candle on the center of the table. 'Now, go over this with me again.'

'As you wish.' Josiah moved his chair as far from Ezren as the platform allowed. The goats gathered around him, and settled down at his feet. Ravage and Dapple were chewing their non-existent cud. Fog sat next to him and leaned against his leg, looking for a good scratch.

Josiah obliged.

'I can feel it when you move away.' Ezren's gaze was unfocused. 'As if it were dancing on my skin.'

'Like a cool breeze after you've worked up a sweat?' Josiah said wistfully.

'Exactly so.' Ezren frowned. 'I'm sorry. Does it bother you to talk about . . .?' He waved his hand around in the air.

Josiah paused for a moment, unsure how to answer. Fog put her soft gray head on his knee. Finally he looked over at the storyteller. 'Does it hurt to think your voice may not come back?'

There was a long pause, as Ezren's eyes glittered. 'Very much so.'

Josiah sighed. 'It feels as if there is a hole in my chest. I was so used to the power, so used to . . .'

'As if a part of your heart is gone,' Ezren whispered.

Josiah nodded, and they sat silent for a moment.

Josiah stirred first. 'But you need help, and if I don't teach you, you could kill someone.' He leaned back in the chair and crossed his arms over his chest. 'Magic is a force in our world, Ezren. Like the power of a flowing stream, magic is there if you can see and feel it. It can aid, it can harm.'

'Yes, yes . . .' Ezren focused on the candle. 'How do I light it?'

Josiah rolled his eyes, then grinned. 'I said the same thing at my lessons.'

Ezren grinned back, his green eyes flashing.

'But you're dealing with wild magic, Ezren.' Josiah's smile faded. 'It's the difference between riding an old, tame saddle horse and riding a wild stallion.'

Ezren focused on the candle again. 'Marlon said I had to bleed off the magic. Not let it build up.'

'True,' Josiah said. 'Very well. Focus on the candle. Feel the power building within you, gradually, carefully. Reach out with the power and send it to the wick. Think of fire, and heat.'

The goats lifted their heads.

'Think of a spark,' Josiah continued in a soft voice. Ezren was leaning forward, his fists clenched tight. 'Just like you are striking a flint, but using the magic, not stones.'

A trickle of smoke rose from the wick, just a thin wisp of gray. Brownie let out a bleat.

'Good, good.' Josiah leaned forward. 'Keep your focus.'

The goats disappeared.

Suddenly, the candle was engulfed in a tower of flame that roared up white hot. Ezren's chair tipped over with a clatter, and he fell to the floor. The flames reached up, growing higher and higher—

Josiah jumped forward, and the flames went out with a puff.

He helped Ezren off the floor, and they both looked at the fabric above them. The flames had burned a hole clear through. The edges of the fabric were still smoldering. There was a scorch mark on the table where the candle and holder had been.

Ezren gasped for breath. 'The magic got excited and lost control.'

The goats were about their feet now, bleating with worry. Josiah reached down to scratch random ears. 'That's the problem.

Magic doesn't have a personality, Ezren. It doesn't have emotion. It's a tool.'

'It didn't feel that way,' Ezren insisted. Snowdrop butted his knee, and he staggered slightly.

'Maybe we should just focus on—'

'Riders!' came the call from the woods.

Josiah turned. Ezren turned with him, looking out as warriors ran from the barn.

'That's odd,' Josiah said. 'The day's messengers have already been and gone.'

The sunset prayers had just concluded when one of the young acolytes came up to Evelyn. 'Lady High Priestess, the Archbishop requests your presence in his chambers.'

Evelyn didn't let her expression change as she removed the heavy sacred vestments and placed them on their hooks. A summons from the Archbishop wasn't that unusual. One of the Court sycophants had probably overeaten and needed her to ease his suffering.

Of course a good dose of butternut oil would work better than any of her magics. But try telling a Noble Personage that bit of priestly wisdom.

Evelyn nodded to the lad, and folded her hands into her sleeves as they left the robing room. The Archbishop's chambers were not far, and the acolyte was eager to complete his assignment. Evelyn followed him into the room, only to find Dominic standing there with a few of the other healers, clustered about the Archbishop's desk. They all had worried looks on their faces.

The Archbishop just looked peevish.

'Lady High Priestess, we need your services.' He spoke in a solemn, stuffy tone. 'Word has been sent that the sweat has broken out in a small village to the west, on the border of Summerford.'

'A plague?' Evelyn frowned. 'Are they certain?'

'The report seems to indicate a small outbreak.' Dominic spoke with a sniff. 'A small village hardly warrants our services. Surely the local healers could deal with this.'

The Archbishop sniffed his agreement. 'Still, it's best to stop it early, before it spreads any further. Lady High Priestess Evelyn can use her skills to go to the local shrine quickly, and assess the situation.'

Evelyn folded her hands into her robes, and prayed for patience. The Archbishop would send her because he wouldn't have to hire the services of a mage. And she'd go, gladly. The risk of plague was not to be ignored, and if she could heal the sickest, the illness could be stopped before it spread. It was an hour or two's delay at the most. 'Where is the shrine, Holy One?'

'Dominic has the details, Lady.' The Archbishop fixed her with a look. 'Go swiftly, and return with news. Do not drain your powers to the dregs, trying to heal all and sundry.'

Evelyn bowed her head. 'As you wish, Holy One.'

The bad news arrived at dawn even as the scouts reported the first sight of the enemy forces.

Red clenched her jaw as Alad knelt on the ground before her, head down, trembling and trying to get the words out. Bethral stood beside him, her hand on his shoulder, using that voice of hers. But if he didn't start making sense soon, she'd shake it out of him.

They were outside the command tent and a crowd was beginning to gather. All trusted men, thankfully.

Alad's wounds were minor, but they spoke of a hard fight, hand-to-hand with the enemy. His gaze lifted no higher than her boots, his entire body radiated pain, and each sentence plunged a blade into her heart.

'They took him, Chosen, took 'im away from us. We're so sorry. We tried, honest we did, but—'

Bethral laid a hand on Alad's shoulder, and handed him a waterskin. 'Drink.'

More of the High Barons gathered about, as did Vembar and Gloriana. The army continued to move past. Scouts were waiting to give their reports, but Red Gloves was focused on the man in front of her. She wanted to scream at him, but she stood instead. Silent. Waiting.

She was going to explode in a minute, venting her fury. It wouldn't help, wouldn't get her any information any faster, but it was like a burning itch that had to be . . .

'Start at the beginning.' Bethral gave Red a glance, as if telling her to be still. 'What happened?'

'Last night, after supper.' Alad gripped the waterskin in both hands. 'Riders came. We thought they was messengers at first but they wasn't. The patrol gave warning, but it wasn't enough. They came in hard, and we fought. Even the settlers, they fought too. And then the Storyteller—'

'Ezren?' Bethral asked.

'Lady,' – Alad looked up at her – 'it was like nothing I'd ever seen. Some of the kids, they was playing by the barn, and the attackers was riding toward 'em. Lord Ezren, he came out of your tent, throwing fire hither and yon, screaming at them, shaking with fury.' Alad's eyes were wide. 'They was charred black.' He looked at Bethral. 'The attackers, and their horses, too. The kids ran screaming, and then something happened, because Lord Ezren' – Alad sucked in a breath – 'Lord Ezren, his eyes rolled back up into his head and he fell over, like the life went right out of him.'

Bethral went still. 'He's dead, then?' The questioning tone in her voice wasn't hopeful.

'He's alive.' Alad darted a glance at Red. 'But that's why we didn't notice right away—'

'Josiah?' Red growled, controlling her anger. Concealing her fear.

Alad nodded, and looked back down at the ground. 'They got him. We thought we'd beaten them off, but they got to 'im, and got 'im away.'

'You stupid mucker,' Red spat. 'How hard is it to protect one goatherder?'

Alad hunched his shoulders. 'They rode off with him, Chosen. Toward the Black Hills. They took the southern road.' He shot her another glance. 'There's no shrine for miles that way.'

Fear clutched deep in Red's gut, fear such as she hadn't known since she was a child. She gestured to the warrior with the maps, and reached for the one she needed.

'You're not thinking . . .' Vembar was leaning on his cane, frowning at her. 'You can't be thinking to rescue him?'

'Chosen.' One of her guards stepped forward. 'The priest Dominic wishes to speak with you.'

Bethral's head snapped around to stare at the man.

Red snarled, 'This can't be good. Is he alone?' At the guard's nod, she answered, 'Bring him, then.'

'What can it mean?' Helene asked, her eyes wide.

'It can mean only one thing,' Red said. 'That the Lady High—'

Dominic swept into the circle of warriors and horses. The cool, snooty persona was gone. This elf was shaken and afraid.

'Well?' Red asked.

'Evelyn is taken, and I may have played her false.' Dominic looked about, as if unable to believe his eyes. 'I can't believe that she planned all this and didn't—'

'What happened?' Red demanded.

'A rumor of plague,' Dominic answered. 'In a remote village on the Summerford border. The Archbishop sent us there to determine if the sweat had broken out. But when she opened the portal, and we stepped through . . .' Dominic looked away. 'She realized it before I did, and pushed me back. It closed in an instant. There was nothing I could—'

'How did you play her false?' Bethral growled.

'I was at Court shortly after I met you.' Dominic looked sick, as if something was eating away at his guts. 'Someone said something about red gloves, and I might have mentioned . . .'

'Me,' Red said grimly. 'When was she taken?'

'Two hours, maybe a little more. It took time to find someone to open a—' Red's glare cut him off. 'It was Elanore's people,' Dominic said softly. 'I saw that much. And not far from the keep, either.'

Carell had out the map of the Black Hills. Bethral moved to look over his shoulder. 'Where?'

Dominic's long, thin finger pointed. 'Here. We were supposed to be here. But it opened here.'

'Miles from Athelbryght,' Fael noted. 'That's deep in the Black Hills.'

'There's no hope of a rescue,' Red said. 'They'd have taken her into the keep by now.'

Bethral looked at the map. 'But a small team might . . .'

Lord Carell snorted. 'No hope for her or Josiah. We'd best just—'

Red jerked her head around and glared at the man. 'There's hope for Josiah yet. They'd not get far with a captive, and the shrine is far from—'

'Red,' Carell warned.

'You can't go after Josiah,' Vembar said. 'You are the Chosen, and you must lead this army. The first encounters with the enemy are crucial. You can't—'

Red snarled, 'Don't tell me that I can't—'

Vembar scowled, the wind whipping at his white hair. 'Which do you now choose, Chosen?' Vembar asked. 'For you have a decision to make. Your destiny? The welfare of these warriors, sworn to your service? Or Josiah of Athelbryght?'

THIRTY-ONE

Hot goat breath on his cheek brought Josiah back from pain and darkness.

He wasn't sure he was grateful. His head was pounding, his mouth was full of grit, and Snowdrop had planted a front hoof right on his foot. Dapple was up on two legs, his hoofs scrabbling on Josiah's thigh, as if he was trying to climb up.

Opening his eyes wasn't much better. They felt thick and gummy. He seemed to be hanging from something . . .

Blinking to clear his vision, he shifted to stand on his feet, the tent around him swaying madly. His hands were bound above his head, and he looked up to see a tree . . .

That didn't seem right.

He was standing, at least, and that eased the pain in his arms and shoulders. But his hands hurt now that the pressure on them was gone. They burned, tingling from the lack of blood.

Josiah drew a deep breath, and then another. The goats about his feet muttered and bleated, pressing close. Dapple returned to all four legs, but he didn't stop complaining.

Josiah closed his eyes, and willed the pain in his head to go away.

The pain did not respond.

The attack; it came back to him then. He remembered being surrounded by horsemen, but the rest was a blur. There was enough light to see by in the tent, but whether it was morning or afternoon was a mystery. He moved his fingers, trying to loosen the ropes, and looked around for answers.

The tent was around the tree. That made more sense. It was big, and held luxuries that you wouldn't expect in a tent. A carpet on the grass, padded chairs, a table with bottles and bowls of something. An odd sight, especially when you were tied to a tree.

Josiah closed his eyes again, and rested his head against his arm. The goats were still pressed close to his legs, but they'd quieted down now. He could make out some sounds from outside, but no real words.

He spat on the carpet, trying to clear his throat. The tent must have been thrown up recently, since the grass around the carpet was fairly fresh. He wasn't certain if that was a good thing or bad—

A rustle of cloth was all the warning he had. The tent flap pulled back, and she was standing there, lovely as ever.

'Elanore,' Josiah rasped.

'Josiah.' Elanore stepped within, letting the flap close behind her. She hadn't changed at all: still regal, still beautiful, in formal court attire. Her gathered skirt swirled on the grass, and Josiah caught a faint hint of her perfume. She was lovely, and perfect, and she left him cold.

Elanore smiled at him, her perfect red mouth warm and inviting. She gave the goats a passing glance, looking a bit puzzled. But then her gaze returned to him, and she moved forward, reaching out as if she wanted nothing more than to touch him.

Josiah pressed back against the tree, wanting nothing to do with her. The goats flinched back as well.

Elanore's face fell. 'Josiah,' she said softly, 'there's so much to say, so much I need to tell you.'

'What is there to say?' Josiah scowled, and spat again. 'You destroyed Athelbryght, and—'

Elanore's concern slipped a bit, her eyes flashing with anger. But just as quickly it was gone, and her face once more filled with sorrow. 'Oh, no, Josiah. You don't know the truth, beloved.' She turned to the table, and picked up a crystal goblet. With elegant movements, she filled it to the brim, then turned to face him. 'Here. Drink, beloved. Let me explain.'

With a pleading look, Elanore advanced, offering the goblet to Josiah's lips. She extended her hand, took another step – and then her lovely face melted away, leaving small eyes peering from scarred flesh, and bare wisps of hair on a bald head.

It happened so fast that Josiah couldn't hide his reaction. His head snapped back against the tree, his eyes wide.

Elanore stopped, puzzled. But then her face seemed to reflect his horror. 'What—' She dropped the goblet and her hands went to her face, covering the worst of the scars. Her eyes widened, stretching the scarred skin around them. 'No, no, no!' Her cries faded as she fled the tent.

Wounded. Ezren said she'd been wounded in the battle for Athelbryght. Josiah shook his head. Elanore had always prided herself on her beauty. But now . . .

Josiah held his breath, listening intently, but he could hear nothing. The goats relaxed, settling at his feet, avoiding the spilled wine. Josiah looked down at Kavage. 'Well, doesn't this just rake muck?'

Kavage burped up some cud.

'I don't suppose one of you could get a knife and cut me loose,' Josiah suggested.

The goats ignored him.

'Well, then, I guess I'm on my own.' He looked up and started to work at the ropes that bound him.

He had them looser by the time she returned.

Josiah looked at her closely when she reentered the tent. Her beauty was back, perfect in every way. But Elanore's angry eyes held no caring concern now. She stopped just inside the tent. 'How did you do that?'

Josiah remained silent. He stilled his hands, not wanting to give away the progress he'd made.

Elanore was staring at him, and at the goats. 'All this time, I thought you dead.' Her face was blank, almost frighteningly so. 'When word came, I could scarce believe it. I had to find you, to see you, to tell you that I still love you.'

'You used me to lay claim to Athelbryght,' Josiah grated. 'Elanore, you destroyed my people, my land, and my life.'

'No, no, beloved. I never intended to destroy.' Elanore's smile was gentle and perfect, but her eyes were cold and dead. 'I just wanted to combine our lands, our people. The men I sent, the mages, they made a mistake. I never wanted—' Elanore drew closer, her hand outstretched.

'Unless you want your face to melt away again, I suggest you keep your distance,' Josiah snarled.

Elanore snatched her hand back. Her face changed, taking on a look of cunning and greed. 'How did you do that, Josiah? What happened to you?'

'You did.' Josiah wasn't going to give her any help. He needed information, though. 'They said you were wounded . . .'

That lovely face twisted. 'I'd linked with the mages that I sent to Athelbryght. There was a backlash through the link, and—'

'Linked?' Josiah glared at her. 'So you saw the battle, saw the attack through them. You knew what they were doing, damn you.'

Elanore smiled, a slow, wanton smile. 'You have no idea, Josiah, of the sheer pleasure power can bring. To feel them die, to feel that energy, that—'

Sickened, Josiah looked away.

Elanore kept talking, almost crooning. 'They were to subdue you, and bring you to me, Josiah. You had no real battle magics; it should have been fairly easy.' Her voice sharpened. 'But somehow, when you stayed conscious enough to prepare a final blow, you had power that I'd never sensed in you before. And now . . .'

Josiah looked back at her. Elanore's eyes had narrowed, and she was studying him closely. 'Now it seems you have a new power. A power I need to understand.'

She gestured, and her eyes began to glow. 'How did you manage to live through that final strike? And how did you drain—'

A shriek pierced the air, a cry of defiance and rage. 'Athelbryght! Athelbryght!'

Josiah's head jerked up. 'Red!'

'She's set a piss-poor watch, that's for sure,' Red growled. 'Sloppy.'

She'd crawled through the brush to get a view of the enemy camp. Tattered tents hastily set up, in no particular pattern. Nothing to brag about, certain sure.

'We can take advantage of that,' Riah whispered. He lay next to her in the tall grasses. 'There's plenty of cover to hide us as we circle around.'

'He's in the tent in the center. The one set up around the tree.'

Onza's eyes were glowing softly with his spell. He lay next to Red, being careful to keep low.

'You see him?' Red asked sharply.

'No.' Onza shook his head. 'It's more what I don't see. There's a lot of magic down there, but not in the central tent.'

Red grunted. 'Makes sense.' She turned to Alad, who lay next to her in the bushes, his face streaked with dirt. 'Take ten men, circle around to the far side, and attack when you hear my battle cry.' Red focused on the tent. 'Riah, you and your men attack from here.'

'She's got more of those undead than humans,' Riah pointed out.

Red nodded. 'Kill the men first, then we'll concentrate on the undead.' She looked over at Onza again. 'You use your magics from a distance, eh? We need you to get back.'

Onza nodded.

She turned back to Alad. 'You remember what Evelyn told us about Odium?'

Alad nodded. 'Go for the arms and legs. Crush the spines. Don't bother with thrusts to the chest or belly. We remember.'

Red nodded. 'Go, then.' Alad and his men faded back into the woods. She watched them move, then turned to Riah. 'Take your men, and do the same.'

Riah nodded. 'And you?'

Red stiffened. A woman in a fancy court dress was coming into view, headed for the main tent, the one with the tree in the center. 'I'm going after Josiah.'

Josiah had no more said her name than a blade appeared in the side of the tent, slicing through it with ease. Red stepped through, dagger in a defensive position. She took in Josiah with a glance, and then focused on the woman opposite him.

'The whore of the Black Hills, I presume?' Red asked.

Elanore screeched, and flung out her hands. Flames shot from her fingertips, headed for Red, who darted behind Josiah. The flames licked close . . .

And then popped out of existence.

Josiah almost laughed out loud.

'Who are you?' Elanore demanded.

Josiah felt gloved fingers on his, then a touch of cold steel. Red's voice came from behind as she sawed at the ropes. 'I am the Chosen, bitch. And this man belongs to me.'

Elanore clenched her fists in front of her chest. 'No, no, no—' She shook with fury, a rage that Josiah didn't understand. 'He's mine, mine – you hear me?'

'That's not what I heard,' Red popped her head around Josiah's shoulder to look at Elanore. 'I heard tell you weren't very juicy.'

Elanore shrieked, gestured, and rained fire down on them.

Red pressed herself against Josiah, and they watched as the flames danced around them. 'Always thinking, aren't you?' Josiah whispered.

Red didn't take her eyes off the enraged mage. 'Yup. And she's not.' Red's breath was a warm puff on Josiah's ear. 'She's burning herself out, and where's all that power going, Josiah?'

'Athelbryght,' Josiah whispered. He looked at Elanore, who was chanting and gesturing, throwing everything she could. A gale wind rose about them, swirling through the tent, tossing chairs and bottles around. But not a breath of wind touched them.

'You had to be this tall,' Red muttered. Stretched on tiptoe, she sawed at the ropes with her blade. 'Keep an eye on her.'

'She's going to kill us,' Josiah said calmly.

'Not with magic.' Red kept working. 'If she gets close, I can kill her. But I can't leave your protection and—'

Elanore screamed again, her fury rising even as she stopped to take a breath. The gale wind faltered and dissipated.

'What's the matter, Elanore? Too old, too slow?' Red taunted. 'Or is it that time of the month, love? Or maybe you no longer bleed, eh?'

Elanore's face mottled with red, and she raised her hands again, as if to strike. But she seemed to reconsider. She called out something, and there was movement at the tent flap.

'Damn.' Red stepped in front of Josiah, pulling her sword.

Two men came in, moving slowly, their skin gray and their eyes staring blindly. Odium. There was a stench about them, a putrid smell of rotting flesh.

'Kill her,' Elanore demanded. 'Kill her!'

Josiah yanked at the ropes, trying desperately to free his hands. They strained where Red had cut into them, but still held him captive.

The Odium shuffled forward, and Red snarled. She waited, at the ready, until the first one moved forward, swinging its club.

Red dodged to the side, and sliced down, cutting into the arm, pulling the blade back to try to inflict as much damage as possible. The Odium ignored the wound, and stepped forward, raising its club—

Only to crumble to dust at Red's feet.

Red laughed. 'Well, that was certainly clever, whore.' She danced back a bit as the other Odium made the same mistake.

'Red Gloves. I've heard of you, bitch,' Elanore spat. 'What are you hiding, whore? Talons? Scars?'

Red's fury flared in her face, but she kept a grip on her weapons and stayed close to Josiah. 'Do you use those creatures for other things, Elanore? They might not mind a dry bit of puss—'

'Gutter scum!' Elanore screamed. 'I'll have your gloves and your tits on a platter.'

'That's as may be, but I have what you will never have again.' Red swiftly turned her head and kissed Josiah.

Josiah blinked at the press of her lips, but the kiss was fleeting. Red was keeping her eye on her opponent.

The woman turned to the table, apparently looking for something to throw. Red twisted about, and charged, sword and dagger at the ready.

It was a feint on Elanore's part. She turned toward Red, and flung out her hands. Magical force slammed Red Gloves back through the air to crumple helpless at Josiah's feet.

Elanore cackled, picking up Red's dagger. She moved closer, her face once again melting into a horror. She leaned down, and tugged at Red's glove.

'No!' Josiah said. 'Elanore, don't—'

Even as Josiah struggled against the ropes, Elanore ripped the glove from Red's right hand.

THIRTY-TWO

Josiah roared. He yanked downward, breaking the ropes that bound him. Elanore had one startled moment to look at him before he lunged forward, grabbing her by both arms.

She looked up at him in horror. 'No, don't . . .'

Josiah shook her, furious beyond words. 'Damn you! The Lord and the Lady damn you to darkness and despair.' He forced her back, away from Red's body. She struggled, dropping the dagger. Her face was in agony, as if his touch was . . .

He was draining her.

With a fierce gladness, Josiah pinned her against a table. He held on tight and stood there, breathing hard, as Elanore struggled in his grip. He couldn't see the magic, but he knew he was hurting her, absorbing her carefully hoarded power, maybe draining any that were linked to her.

Elanore sank to her knees, and he followed her down, keeping his grip. Her perfume filled his lungs, cloying and sickly sweet. Memories came back to him, a wave of disgust. Had he ever really loved this woman? Josiah grimaced, but he did not let go.

Elanore's mouth worked, but no words came out. Her struggles weakened as he pulled her power from her.

Josiah leaned over, putting his lips by her ear. 'She's right, you know. She has my heart.'

Elanore's ruined face crumbled then, and she sobbed out a ragged whisper. 'Please, Josiah. Please don't . . .'

Josiah stood there for a long moment, his eyes closed, then he cast her from him, letting her fall to the carpet. Elanore lay there, crying weakly.

A sound from behind. He spun, and saw Red rousing, her eyes opening, coming conscious, staring in horror at her bare hand.

Her perfect, pale hand.

*

Nonononono. Red threw her head to the side and squeezed her eyes closed. No, please, no, not that—

'Red, Red, it's all right.' The voice was the softest of whispers, but it was as a lash on her back. Red jerked away, scrambling back as best she could with one hand in the air. Nonononono . . .

Warm arms wrapped around her and held her tight. A hand grabbed her wrist. 'Easy, kitten.' The voice sounded puzzled. 'I don't understand—'

She'd trusted him. He was her uncle, her only remaining family. She'd followed him everywhere after her parents died, right through the doors of the brothel, to be sold to the madam. 'You'll whore for her, and be damned,' he'd said. 'They'll pay high for one so young,' the madam had said.

'Red, listen.' The voice was soft and warm in her ear. 'I'll put the glove on, but you have to open your fist.'

She'd been damned. Used, and misused, bound and helpless, hurt and damaged past caring, past hope. Made to serve, made to touch, made to pleasure with her hands. Disgusting things, nasty things.

Strong arms held her close, and pressed her face into the shelter of a warm chest.

She wept and cried and begged, but it went on and on and on. Until the night they'd had at her hard and fell asleep, leaving her with one hand loose and a blade close.

'Oh, kitten,' the voice breathed. 'You're trembling like a leaf in a storm. Kitten? Can you hear me?'

They'd paid, all of them – the men, the madam, the whores as well. They'd all paid in one night, a small girl and a sharp blade had seen to it. She'd crept down halls and into rooms, silent, careful, until all that was left was to leave.

'It's on, Red. It's covered. Open your eyes, kitten. It's safe to look.'

She'd left, with a sharp blade, some coin she'd found, and gloves to hide her horrible, horrible hands.

Hands that had done nasty, disgusting things.

Hands that had slain the men who had hurt her.

Hands that had killed her uncle, lying in the next room with another of the whores.

She'd never look at her hands again, and would kill any who tried. Any who—

Red's eyes snapped open.

Josiah's face was close to hers, his brown eyes filled with caring. She was in his arms, cuddled close on the floor, and he was holding her hand, now covered with a glove.

Her dagger was on the floor next to them.

Had he seen them? Seen her shame?

She'd never look at her hands again, and would kill any who tried. Any who—

'There's fighting outside,' Josiah said softly. 'We can't stay here.'

Red blinked, trying to clear her head. She'd—

She'd never look at her hands again, and would kill any who tried. Any who—

Josiah stood, and offered his hand. 'Are you all right?' he said, frowning, his eyes filled with . . .

She'd never look at her hands again, and would kill any who tried. Any who—

. . . love.

She stared at him, seeing it for the first time. Seeing it for what it was. They'd shared their bodies, yes, but Josiah was sharing something else. He was sharing his heart.

Red shook with fear, and swallowed hard.

Josiah shifted, and she saw Elanore collapsed on the other side of the tent, starting to rouse. Her throat was dry, and it rasped as she tried to speak. 'What—'

Josiah stood. 'I drained her. She won't be working magic anytime soon.' He reached down, and pulled Red to her feet.

Red let him pull her up, then stood there a moment, staring at her gloved hands.

She'd never look at her hands again, and would kill any who tried. Any who—

She reached down and picked up her dagger, looking at the bright, sharp blade.

She'd never look at her hands again, and would kill any who tried. Any who—

She looked up into Josiah's eyes. Brown, with gold flecks, filled with—

She'd never look at her hands again, and would kill any who tried. Any who—

She could not kill him.

Her body quivered, every old instinct telling her to kill the man who had seen her hands. But the new instincts, the new feelings, the ones she felt for him and only for him, cried out against it. She saw again his dead face in the bog, felt the grief that had overwhelmed her.

Josiah stared at her with concern, the goats at his feet.

Red shook her head, trying to clear it. 'Battle – fighting – outside.'

Josiah nodded. 'I'll go look.' He stepped to the flap and lifted it. 'A few Odium, from the look of it. I'll just . . .' The flap fell as he left.

Red frowned, looking after him. Then she turned and focused on Elanore, who was struggling to stand. A threat, a threat to herself.

And Josiah.

Red moved to stand over her, her dagger in her hand. Elanore looked up, her face a tearful ruin, her hands clutching the fabric of her dress.

Red scowled at her. 'And what do I do with you?'

Elanore's eyes sparkled with hate.

'Did you see my hand?' Red asked.

Elanore's eyes went wide, and she stared at the blade before her. 'No.'

Red relaxed slightly. 'I believe you.'

Elanore snarled, 'It doesn't matter what you do with me. My magic will renew, and I'll kill you then, and all you care for, until Josiah is mine again. I'll be back, Chosen.' She spat on Red's boots. 'Put me in a dungeon, or a high keep, or a lonely prison cell. I'll be back, and more powerful than ever.'

'No, you won't,' Red said calmly.

Elanore tilted her head up and spat a curse.

With a swift slash of her dagger, Red sliced her throat.

Elanore collapsed, and Red stood over her, dagger in hand, and watched to make certain the bitch died.

Red ran outside and into Josiah's arms as he tried to come back into the tent. 'They're still fighting,' he whispered. 'I listened for a bit, and I think your men are close. Did you bind her?'

'She's not going anywhere,' Red said hastily. She kept a hand on his arm as she stepped past him and looked around. She could hear the sounds of fighting coming from around the tents. She drew her sword, and made sure the bloody dagger was not in Josiah's sight. 'Let's see if we can help.'

Josiah nodded, and followed as she moved between the tents. The goats trailed behind silently.

Riah was fighting an Odium, who'd managed to grasp his sword arm. Red ran forward, aiming for the neck of the creature, and Josiah followed right behind her. The Odium crumbled to dust, its magic drained.

Red checked her swing. 'You know, that takes all the fun out of it.'

'Speak for yourself, Chosen.' Riah was breathing hard, with gashes on his arms that ran with blood.

'We'd better see to those wounds,' Josiah said.

'Later,' Red ordered. 'Let's find out—'

A sudden noise, and both she and Riah were on their guard, taking a protective stance beside Josiah.

Alad came around one of the tents, Onza at his side. He smiled when he saw them. 'We finished the last of them. The Odium are destroyed, Chosen, and the living have fled.'

Red and Riah relaxed. 'Our men?' Red asked.

'No losses, no major wounds.' Alad grinned. 'We can loot—'

'Do it. Take whatever supplies you find.' Red sheathed her sword. 'I've an army marching on Edenrich, and I must return. I've an hour's hard ride to get back to a portal. You're going to have to bring Josiah to me overland.'

They all nodded. 'We'll keep him safe, Chosen.' Alad said with a serious face.

Red took a step closer, and stared hard into his eyes. 'Don't bother coming within sight of me if you don't.'

Alad swallowed hard, and jerked his head in a nod.

Red stepped back, satisfied. 'Send someone for the horses. Don't bother with the dead, but see to the wounded and get moving within the next hour. Don't linger here.'

Riah jerked his head at Onza and they started off.

'What about Elanore?' Josiah asked. 'We'll need to—'

'No,' Red said. 'She's dead.'

'She's what?' Josiah turned in shock.

Red ignored him. She turned to Alad. 'Get moving as fast as you can. Take any extra horses you find. You'll need them.'

Alad saluted her, and trotted off. Red couldn't blame him for wanting out of the line of fire.

Josiah took a step toward the tent, but Red caught his arm. 'Don't,' she warned.

'What' – Josiah looked back at the tent — 'did you do?'

Red brushed her hair back off her face. 'What had to be done.'

'You killed her.' Josiah looked down into her eyes. 'She was helpless, and you—'

'Helpless, my ass,' Red snorted. 'She was a threat, one that I would not leave behind me. I wasn't about to give her another chance to try to kill us.'

Riah came up with Beast. Red turned from Josiah's angry face, and took the reins. 'And don't tell me that she was too weak to hurt us, or that she deserved a fair chance, or, Twelve help me, a trial of her peers.' Red pulled herself up into the saddle.

She looked down into Josiah's stunned face. 'I've an hour's ride to get to a portal, goatherder. We can debate the quality of my mercy later.' She leaned down and put her fingers under his chin, to claim his mouth with a kiss.

Josiah pulled his head away, taking a step back.

Red straightened and contemplated the man. Anger simmered in his brown eyes, the gold flecks almost glowing. She knew full well he was upset because he was, at the core, a good man. An honest man, of quiet strength and gentle compassion.

Everything she wasn't.

'Chosen, we are ready.' Onza and two other men were there, mounted as well.

Red pulled Beast around. 'Alad, get Lord Josiah on a horse. If he gives you any problems, chain him to the saddle.'

Alad's eyes widened.

Red kicked Beast and rode off before Josiah could say another word.

THIRTY-THREE

Vembar watched with pride as the Chosen directed the establishment of a fortified camp for the night. Astride her black horse, bathed in the light of torches, clad in her armor and helmet, she made his heart swell with pride.

He hadn't thought to live this long, and he prayed to the Lord of Light for his doubts. His prayers had been answered, all but one. To see her take the throne, and be crowned. And there was a chance, a chance that it would happen soon, Lord of Light be praised.

A cloaked warrior came up beside him. 'You trained her well.'

'She'll make a great queen.' Vembar gave the warrior a sidelong glance. 'Someday.'

Red looked at him from the shadow of her hood. 'One never knows, elder. Only time will tell.'

'True enough.' Vembar turned back. 'Josiah?'

'Safe.'

Vembar arched an eyebrow. 'Elanore?'

'Dead.'

'Well done, then.' Vembar shook his head. 'But I still think you made the wrong choice, Red Gloves. And I told the same to your sword-sister.'

'Bethral?' Red asked sharply. 'Why?'

'We've had a message,' Vembar said calmly. 'From Blackhart. He sent for parley, and the Lady Bethral chose to go to the Black Keep.'

'If he doesn't kill her, I will,' Red growled.

Bethral rode into the Keep of the Black Hills alone, as requested. She carried no weapons, only a simple white flag on a branch, also as requested. However, she and Bessie were wearing their armor. She wasn't that stupid.

Red was sure to disagree when she heard about this little adventure.

Presenting an image of calmness was no problem as she was passed through the gate of the lower wall. The warriors of the Black Hills were respectful enough. The Odium that stood at their sides all had the same vacant expression. Those creatures made her queasy, truth be told. She ran through the methods of killing them as Bessie trotted along the winding road to the upper wall.

The road was a fairly long one, and if her eyes strayed over the defenses once in a while, taking note of their strength and nature, what harm in that, eh? She'd had hopes of rescuing Evelyn, but not much more than that. This fortress would be hard won, and the forces of the Chosen had other things to do. Still, Blackhart's message had offered a truce and an exchange. Bethral had to explore the possibility. The Lady High Priestess had saved Ezren Silvertongue, and there was an obligation on Bethral's part.

She arrived at the gate, and was admitted to the courtyard before the main doors. A guard stepped forward – a human, thankfully. He was clad in plain tunic and trous, with no weapon. 'I am to watch your mount, Lady Warrior.'

Bethral nodded, and dismounted, keeping her peace flag. She handed the reins to the man, and then reached out an armored hand to place it on Bessie's neck. 'Ward.'

Bessie shook herself, and seemed to relax, as if about to take a nap. Larrisa had gone over all the tricks her husband had taught the horse, and this was one of them.

The doors to the castle opened, and Bethral strode forward, the peace flag in her hand like a sword.

The place was dark, as if built of shadows and black marble. There were Odium lining the corridor, apparently placed there on guard. In the confines of the hall they had a definite odor about them. Bethral kept her face blank, but tried not to breathe too deeply.

The darkness stretched on, lit only by torches placed far apart. Bethral wasn't certain, but it seemed to her that her armor was almost glowing in the dark shadows of the place.

The doors ahead opened by themselves, revealing a throne

room filled with torch light. Bethral strode forward at the same pace, not stopping until she stood before the throne.

To her relief, Evelyn was seated on the throne, her hands and feet chained together, looking small and vulnerable. Her eyes opened wide when she saw Bethral, then narrowed in concern. There were some stains on her robes, especially at the knees, but Bethral couldn't see any injury.

Then again, she knew damn well that some of the worst hurts can't necessarily be seen.

Two robed and hooded figures stood just behind the throne where Evelyn sat. But Bethral focused on the man standing at the bottom of the dais, one foot up a step, dressed all in black. A handsome bastard, that was certain, with black hair and eyes. His face was pale, as if he'd not seen the sun for quite some time.

He arched an eyebrow, well aware of her scrutiny. 'Lady Bethral, I assume.'

'Blackhart,' Bethral replied. 'You asked for a parley.'

'I did.' Blackhart gestured to the throne. 'You see the Lady High Priestess, as promised.'

Bethral looked at Evelyn. 'Lady High Priestess, are you well?'

Evelyn sighed, and shrugged. She pointed to her ear, and shook her head.

'A precaution, nothing more.' Blackhart gestured toward where the robed figures stood. 'She can't hear you, nor can she be heard. She's well, I assure you.'

'I'd like to hear that from her,' Bethral said pointedly.

Blackhart smiled. 'I am certain you would, but the Lady High Priestess's skills are highly spoken of, and while the chains about her wrists suppress magic, I'd prefer she didn't speak.'

Bethral gave him a mild glance. 'Not a good beginning to a parley, Lord.'

Blackhart smiled charmingly. 'Then let me draw your attention elsewhere.' His smile disappeared. 'We've learned that Lady Elanore is dead, slain at the hands of the Chosen.'

That was interesting news. Not wanting to acknowledge her ignorance, Bethral just shrugged.

Blackhart's eyes narrowed. 'What do you know of the Odium?'

'How to kill them,' Bethral said promptly.

Blackhart nodded. 'Then what would you say if I told you that Elanore created the Odium that guard this place?'

Bethral shrugged again.

'And the magic that creates them dissipates upon the caster's death.'

Bethral raised an eyebrow, and looked around the room. 'Then she's not dead.'

'She is dead.' Blackhart stepped off the dais, and walked closer to Bethral. His voice dropped to a bare whisper. 'They should be so much dust on the floor. And while they are obeying me and my warriors, I do not know who really controls them.'

'What do you ask of me?' Bethral said softly.

'I will disband the Black Keep's army, provided my men go free with their armor and weapons and gear.' Blackhart looked grim. 'They've kith and kin in these hills, and they will need every piece of it to survive.'

He turned his head to stare at Bethral. 'I will surrender the Keep to you, although little good it will do you. I cannot clear it of the Odium within. I've already tried. I can only release my men, and see your Priestess to you safely.'

'Why?' Bethral asked, more for time to consider than anything else.

'A keep full of undead that I can't control, a High Baroness dead, your army at the borders, and my people caught between.' Blackhart arched an eyebrow. 'I'd have thought my reasons fairly obvious.'

'Very well,' Bethral agreed. 'But you must be held accountable for your crimes against Palins, Lord Blackhart. I will require you to surrender yourself to me. They may go free. You may not.'

'Done.' Blackhart handed her a set of keys. 'You may free her.'

He gestured toward the robed figures, and they retreated as Bethral advanced. Evelyn was shaking her head, as if to clear it of the spell effects, as Bethral approached.

'Are you well?' Bethral unlocked the wrist chains first. Odd to see that the Priestess still wore her star sapphire ring. Prisoners didn't normally keep jewellery for long.

'Well enough.' Evelyn looked at her with wide eyes. 'What—?'

'Can you work magic?'

'No.' Evelyn shuddered, rubbing her wrists. 'Whatever those

chains are, they've drained me completely. I'll need rest before I can do anything.'

Bethral handed the keys to Evelyn and gestured for her to free her legs. She turned slightly, watching the room. Blackhart was talking to a group of the hooded warriors, who then darted off in all directions.

Blackhart looked their way. 'Leave with her,' he suggested. 'You can do nothing with this place.'

'I'm free?' Evelyn whispered.

Blackhart gave her a long look, then jerked his head in a nod. Bethral helped Evelyn to stand as Blackhart continued. 'I will give the orders to my warriors, and then I will emerge from the gates and surrender myself. Your men will let my people pass?'

'I will give the orders myself,' Bethral replied, as Evelyn took a few shaky steps. 'I have your word?'

Blackhart gave her a grim smile. 'For what it is worth, Lady.'

Evelyn's head jerked up at that, and she focused wide eyes on Blackhart. For a long moment they looked at one another, then Evelyn advanced, folding her hands into her robes.

Bethral followed, first grabbing the chains on the floor. At best they might aid Ezren. At worst, she'd use them as a weapon.

Evelyn walked forward, pausing to study Blackhart's face. 'I thank you, Lord—'

'No.' Blackhart gestured. 'There's no time. Go, and quickly.'

Evelyn made no move to obey.

Puzzled, Bethral reached for her arm. 'Lady High Priestess, we must go.' She took her by the elbow, and urged her forward.

'I will be at the gate within an hour.' Blackhart was looking at Evelyn as he made the promise.

Whatever had passed between them, there was no point in lingering here, and every reason to leave. Bethral took the chains and the High Priestess, and left the throne room, marching down the long, dark hall. The torches still burned, the Odium still stood watch. 'Did he hurt you?' Bethral demanded.

'No,' Evelyn said, breathless. 'Why are we—'

'Elanore is dead,' Bethral said softly, not breaking her pace. The chains were wrapped around one hand; the white banner was in the other.

'No, she's not,' Evelyn insisted. 'If she was, the Odium would collapse. Although how she had the time and power to create so many is beyond me.'

'That's the point,' Bethral said. 'She may not have.'

'Then who . . . ?' Evelyn wondered.

Bethral shook her head, and hurried their pace to the courtyard. The man was still there, and Bessie came instantly alert when Bethral emerged from the building.

Bethral wasted no time in mounting, pulling Evelyn up behind her. 'Hold on, Priestess,' Bethral commanded.

With a clatter of hooves, Bessie turned and cantered through the gates and down the road. Bethral urged the mare on, noting the movement of people in the barren land between the walls. Blackhart must have planned this for days. From the looks of it, people were prepared to flee the Keep in droves.

Once out the main gate, Bessie galloped to where their forces stood waiting. Bethral pulled to a stop, and called for one of the warriors to help Evelyn down. 'Take her to the shrine in the village, and get out of here,' Bethral ordered.

'The village?' Evelyn said breathlessly.

'Deserted when we came through,' Bethral snapped. 'We've a mage waiting to open a portal.'

Evelyn shook off the hands of the warriors around her. 'I'm fine. I want . . .'

The gates opened behind them.

Everyone went on guard instantly. Bethral turned Bessie to face the gate, grabbing her mace from the warrior who held it for her. Evelyn was pushed to the back, and warriors formed up in front of her.

They needn't have bothered. The wave of people emerging from the keep had no interest in them. They swarmed down the road, some on horse, some in wagons, some on foot – all wearing black cloaks, all fading into their surroundings like shadows.

'Let them pass,' Bethral called, and no one raised a hand.

From horseback, Bethral could see others emerging from hidden doors in the walls and following faint paths into distant woods. She kept a sharp eye for betrayal, but none was evident. The only thing here was fear.

Finally, the wave ebbed, and then stopped. At the last a troop of seven mounted men emerged, moving slowly down the road to the gate. Blackhart was in the lead, apparently looking about for stragglers.

Just shy of the gate, he pulled his horse to a stop and spoke with the man to his right, seeming to argue for a moment. Whatever the talk, Blackhart won. They clasped hands, and then the six mounted men galloped off through the gate and turned to the north.

Blackhart waited for a moment, then urged his horse forward. When he reached the lower gate, he stopped and gestured to the side. An Odium shuffled forward.

'Guard,' he demanded in a loud voice.

The figure stood there.

'Guard,' Blackhart said again.

This time, the figure nodded its head. 'Gaard,' came a dry, empty voice.

Bethral heard Evelyn gasp in horror. 'Odium don't speak,' she whispered. 'They can't . . . they can't!'

Blackhart rode forward, and the gates closed behind him. He kept his horse at a walk and drew up next to Bethral. With a flourish, he handed her his sheathed sword. 'We'd best be on our way.'

Bethral nodded, and gave the orders. Willing hands lifted Evelyn back onto Bessie. Bethral felt her shift, looking toward Blackhart, whose hands were being roughly secured.

Blackhart wasn't looking at the men around him. His eyes were fixed on the High Priestess. Bethral felt her shift again, and knew full well that Evelyn had looked away.

Something had passed between those two, but there was no time for speculation. With one last look at the Black Keep, Bethral gave the order to leave.

It was ten days before Josiah and his escort joined the army of the Chosen. And that was just the outer edge. It took another full day of riding to reach the command center, and Red's tent.

Josiah slid off his horse with a weary sigh. They'd had no problems on the road, but it had been a hard ride nonetheless. He ached.

'This way, Lord Josiah.' One of the young guards headed

toward the command tent, and Josiah followed. Alad and Riah were right behind.

The huge tent was filled with tables and maps. The men who surrounded the tables were all talking at once. Red stood in the center, at the largest table, considering the map before her as two men described the movements of the Regent's forces.

He could tell that she'd sensed his presence the moment he stepped in the tent. She didn't react, didn't turn her head, but Josiah knew.

The men finished their explanation, and she dismissed them with thanks and a nod. Only then did she turn and look at him.

She tilted her head, her unbound hair falling to her shoulders. 'What, no chains?' she asked Alad as she looked at Josiah.

'Not necessary, Chosen.' Alad's tone was formal. 'We'd no trouble on the journey.'

'You made good time. I thank you for bringing Lord Josiah to me safely. I'm sure you are tired—'

'Not too tired to fight, Chosen,' Riah blurted out. Alad nodded his agreement.

Red smiled. 'Oris was hoping you'd feel that way. He's got positions waiting for you. Again, my thanks.'

They nodded to both her and Josiah, and left the tent.

'Sit.' Red gestured to a chair without looking at him. 'There's kavage, if you'd like.'

Josiah eyed her closely as he sat. She ignored him, studying the maps before her, so he was free to look at her. Lord of Light, she was beautiful. Maybe not in the classic sense, but she had her own sharp beauty. She was at ease in her armor, her sword and dagger on her hips. Strong and confident. His mouth suddenly went dry. To break the silence, he looked at the table, at the maps and notations. 'How does it go?'

Red shrugged, again without looking at him. 'Well enough.' She moved around the table, away from him. 'We've cut the supply lines to Edenrich, and while Swift's Port is not aiding us, they are not sending aid to the Regent, either. He's made a few forays against us, and was lucky once, but we got our people out with reinforcements. He's working up his courage to confront us. It won't be long now.'

'Red, I—' Josiah started.

Red cut him off. 'Evelyn was taken.'

'What?' Josiah asked. 'Who?'

'Elanore's forces,' Red replied. 'She's safe. Bethral parleyed with Blackhart for her release.'

'Why did he offer a parley?' Josiah demanded.

Red looked at him finally, her eyes steady. 'He learned that Elanore was dead. Apparently the Odium in the Keep are under someone else's control. He released Evelyn unharmed and surrendered himself so that we would let his people flee the Keep and the countryside unmolested.'

Josiah drew in a long breath.

'I'll send for food,' Red said. 'And a messenger to Evelyn. You will want to talk—'

Josiah stood. 'I don't want to talk to her, I want to talk to you.'

Red gestured at the map. 'I'm really very busy, you know. The prophecy and all.'

Josiah snorted, and moved around the table. 'As if you believe—'

'The western scouts, Chosen.' A voice came from outside the tent.

'Enter,' Red called before Josiah could protest.

The tent flooded with men just off their horses and brimming with news. They started to move maps, eager to report. Red leaned over the table, intent on every word.

Josiah growled under his breath, and got some kavage. Food could wait. He wanted to talk, and talk they would, if he had to wait all night.

Twelve, she wanted him.

All he had to do was walk in the tent, and her hunger was there. It had been nine long nights since she'd seen him last, and she'd ached for him each and every night.

He looked tired, but well enough otherwise. The scouts had spotted them earlier, so she'd known when he would arrive. She thought she'd been prepared, but it was harder than she'd ever imagined.

Red listened as the scouts spoke and gestured at the maps. She noted the information, but her mind wasn't really on it.

She had to distance herself from him, and it had to start now.

She'd thought about keeping him in her bed until the final battle. But that was unfair and unwise. He was a distraction. A pleasant one, to be sure, but dangerous all the same. She needed to be focused on her plans, and not on him. It hurt, a physical pain deep in her chest, but she set that aside.

The scouts were finishing, and she was nodding and making the right responses. But Josiah was still there in the background, a mug of kavage in his hand and a look of determination on his face.

But she was just as determined. Best to cut right to the heart of it and make it quick. Josiah of Athelbryght had his own destiny to fulfill.

As she had hers.

Josiah waited patiently. Red gave him a glance as the last scout left the tent. She arched her eyebrow as she spoke. 'We've a staging area a distance away, where Gloriana and Vembar stay as safe as I can make them.' Red pushed her hair behind her ear, still looking at the map. 'I've had a tent prepared for you there. Evelyn will wish to see you as soon as possible. I'll summon an escort—'

'Red,' Josiah said, and she stopped talking, darting a glance at him. When he realized that she wasn't going to speak, he moved closer. Red gave him a cool glance. 'And where will you sleep, Chosen?' he asked.

'Here, of course. I must stay close, in order to—'

'You're afraid,' Josiah said softly.

THIRTY-FOUR

Red stilled.

'You can expose your breasts to anyone without hesitation,' Josiah continued, 'but you can't expose your emotions, can you? Any more than you can show your hands.'

Red glared at him, but he raised a hand to stop her. 'You were right to kill Elanore. I see that now. I'm sorry. There's nothing to be afraid of, kit—'

'The bitch was defiant, spewing hate and threats. Her death was quick, which was more mercy than she deserved,' Red growled. 'The Twelve teach that we build our own hells in the afterlife. May she burn long and hot in the fire of her own making.'

'Don't try to change the subject,' Josiah said. 'Red, I—'

Red shook her hair back then, her lips pressed tight, her hand on her sword hilt. 'Our agreement is at an end, Lord Josiah. A larger profit awaits me now.'

Josiah stood, and started around the table, staring into Red's eyes. 'You're afraid that I—'

The tent flap lifted, and Ezren stepped in. Josiah stopped, not recognizing the stranger with the new growth of auburn hair over his pate. But then those green eyes flashed a welcome. 'Josiah,' Ezren said with a smile. 'I heard you had arrived. How good to—' The storyteller paused, looking at the two of them with concern. 'I have interrupted. I beg your pardon.'

'No need.' Red picked up her helmet from the table. 'I've work to do. Please see that Lord Josiah is escorted to Gloriana's tent.'

'This isn't over, Red Gloves,' Josiah warned.

She looked at him then, and he saw the determination in her eyes. 'I've a war to win, Athelbryght. We will have time to discuss this later.' She turned and left without another word.

*

Two dusty days later, Red sat on Beast and cursed the whole business. The Regent wasn't stupid, nor were his men. She looked down into the valley before the city walls, and surveyed the placement of their forces. The Regent's army had emerged from behind the city walls at first light, and Red had formed up accordingly. But he'd more men behind those walls, and fresher cavalry. Red wasn't at all certain of the outcome, but the odds were not in favor of the Chosen.

Horns blew as instructions were relayed and the formations changed as a result. It would have to do, at this point. Finally, they'd have this out, here and now.

She secured her helmet and checked her weapons, for she had no intention of sitting this one out.

One comfort: Josiah was well back, safe as he could be made. The warriors with him had orders to flee at the first sign of defeat. She'd have started Josiah off to Athelbryght before this, but the man flatly refused to go. All he wanted to do was talk.

Red smiled grimly as she adjusted her scabbard. There'd be no talk with the goatherder. She'd managed to avoid him so far. If all went according to plan, she'd be free of that soon enough.

Bethral sat beside her, carrying the red and white banner of the Chosen. They'd exchanged a few words about what her sword-sister had done, with Red raging and Bethral as calm as you please. In the end, Red couldn't argue with the results.

The breeze snapped the cloth of the banner back and forth above their heads. Bessie snorted in anticipation, and Beast was just as eager. A fair day for a battle, win or lose. Red focused back on the battlefield.

Evelyn sat on the other side, clad in brown leather armor that she'd produced in the last few days. Red could have sworn that it was older, showing signs of wear. The Priestess seemed at least to know how to put it on.

Evelyn had demanded a place at her side. 'If you go down, I can do something about it. I've done it before.'

Red had given up arguing with her. On her own head be it.

Gloriana was well to the rear, with her own set of guards. Ezren and Vembar were with her. If Red fell, she'd be summoned to take command.

It was done. The work, the worry, the toil of the last few weeks came down to this. A fierce gladness filled Red. She welcomed this battle, no matter the end. It was time to take her place in the front lines.

Movement caught her eye, and she looked sharply to the south, where a force had appeared. By the Twelve . . . those weren't her men. Had the Regent—?

'Riders,' Bethral noted, and Red turned in the saddle to see a group of warriors riding toward them, carrying no obvious banner but wearing the coat of arms of a black eagle, its wings wide, carrying a large cabbage rose.

The riders pulled up next to them. The lead warrior pulled off his helm, and gave them all a grim look.

Red raised an eyebrow. 'What brings Tassinic to the field, Lord Verice?'

Verice gave her a sardonic look. 'My Warna is delivered of two healthy babes. I have a fine son and a lovely daughter.' He caught Evelyn's look. 'They are all well, Lady High Priestess.'

Evelyn smiled. 'That's good news.'

'And,' Verice continued, 'the children both bear the mark of the Chosen.'

Bethral and Evelyn's mouths dropped open. Red threw back her head and laughed.

Verice raised an eyebrow, but the corner of his mouth was raised slightly. 'The Regent now threatens me and mine, Chosen. My forces are yours; our swords, at your command. Is there room for us in your plans?'

Red smiled with fierce delight 'Oh, yes. And the plans have just changed!'

Josiah sat on his horse at the farthest point of the valley, straining to see what was happening.

The Regent had placed his forces carefully before his gates, and Josiah had been told that there were more warriors within the city. Red's attempt to break through was a desperate gamble to avoid a lengthy siege, but one that all had agreed to.

Now the armies faced one another, and even from this distance Josiah could hear the roar as thousands of men screamed their defiance, taunting each other with insults and threats.

Horns echoed faintly, and Josiah's heart leaped to see the banner of the Chosen unfurl and charge the enemy. The line of warriors behind her followed, streaming across the ground, moving together. Red's banner marked her location to friend and foe, Bethral by her side. Evelyn, too. He swallowed hard, and watched as the two armies clashed, the banner engulfed in the struggle.

The sounds of the fight were faint, and Josiah strained to hear. But it was his eyes that captured the story. Within a few breaths the Regent's army surged forward, overrunning their opponents.

'No,' Josiah could barely believe how fast it happened. One minute the army of the Chosen was advancing; the next, they were fleeing the field. The red and white banner was gone, and . . .

'It's a rout,' one of his guards said. 'We'd best go now.'

'No,' Josiah said, but then the gates of the city opened, and more men began to stream out on horseback, giving chase. 'Lord of Light,' Josiah prayed. He couldn't make out Red's banner anywhere. But he saw the banner of the Regent emerge, meaning that Iitrus had finally left the shelter of his walls to take the field and hunt down his enemy.

'Now, Lord Josiah.' The warrior closest placed a hand on the bridle of his horse. 'We must leave now—'

Red's army continued to run as the line of warriors streaming from the city gate trickled. Josiah couldn't turn his eyes from the defeat, couldn't look away.

Kitten . . .

Horns sounded. All heads swiveled to look to the south. Warriors were sweeping out of the woods, horsemen with lances and the banners of—

'Tassinic,' Josiah breathed softly. What had brought Verice to Red's side?

'They've flanked them,' someone pointed out.

Josiah watched as the line of elven horsemen smashed into the flank of the Regent's army like a wave. Suddenly, the routed men turned back and attacked.

'Gods, she is a cagey bitch,' one of the warriors said. 'It was a feint.'

Planned? She'd planned that?

As if from nowhere, the banner of the Chosen flared out once again, and headed for the Regent's.

The Regent's warriors seemed confused, and they milled about for a moment before turning to make a run for the gates. But it was far too late for that. Red had arrived, and Josiah could almost hear her battle cry from where he stood.

Within seconds, the Regent's banner fell to the ground. Josiah's heart swelled with a sense of joy and peace. He didn't have to see it to know that the Regent was dead on Red's blade.

The warrior next to Josiah grunted in satisfaction. 'All over but the shouting, now.'

'Can we go—' Josiah gathered his reins, but everyone around him shook their heads.

'It may be all over,' the warrior said grimly. 'But the shouting takes a while.'

They'd won, but not without death, not without loss. Josiah looked out over the field of battle and saw more than the dead and dying. He saw his Athelbryght burned, his people dead and taken. Even as the army cheered around him, he knew well the cost.

Word had spread that the Regent Iitrus had taken the field toward the end, and in the swirl of the battle, he'd been killed. Josiah had no doubt the man was dead at Red's hand.

Gloriana rode beside him, with their escort. He could see her swallowing hard as she looked around.

The command tent was empty, to Josiah's surprise. Gloriana saw his face as they entered. 'Red told me that after the battle is when the leader must truly lead. "Easy to get people to follow you into combat. Hard to get exhausted, wounded people to see to each other and clear the dead."' Gloriana's voice hitched. 'That's what she said.'

Josiah looked at her strained face, and opened his arms.

Gloriana ran over, sobbing. 'So many, Unca 'Siah. I thought it would be glorious, but it's awful.'

'I know, child.' Josiah hugged her close, and let his own tears flow there, in the privacy of the tent.

*

'That's the worst of it,' Red said.

Night had fallen, and the campfires were being lit. She'd worked her way around the camp, seeing to the survivors, letting them cheer the Chosen, gleaming in her armor and helm. She had taken the surrender of Edenrich and the Regent's army. Criers had been sent into the city, announcing to all and sundry that she'd enter the city on the morrow, to claim the throne.

She looked across the valley, at the command tent. It glowed in the night, with people coming and going. Josiah would be there, with Gloriana and the others. She could almost feel him. She'd summoned the leaders to the tent for an evening meal and council.

Red rolled her shoulders, trying to relax. She'd more to do this night, before she could sleep. A promise to keep, a few announcements to make. Red grinned at the thought. Aye, just a bit more work to do. She patted Beast on the neck, just as three horses came up, bearing Evelyn, Ezren, and Bethral.

THIRTY-FIVE

Evelyn drooped over her horse, tired but exhilarated. It seemed this day would never end, and yet there was so much still to do before the morrow, when all her hard work and efforts would see Red Gloves take the throne of Palins.

When Bethral and Ezren had appeared to fetch her, she'd assumed they'd head toward the command tent. But instead they'd ridden to the top of the rise, to the small shrine. Red stood there, with five warriors.

Bethral and Ezren dismounted, and handed their reins to a warrior standing close. Red handed them both black cloaks. 'Come.'

'Where are we going?' Evelyn dismounted as well, taking a cloak and following them into the shrine. 'Shouldn't we be—'

'There's something we need to see to, first,' Red told her. 'There is a shrine to the Lady of Laughter in the White Tower, yes?'

Evelyn stilled, her eyes wide. 'Yes, but—'

'Just outside the Regent's chambers,' Red said. 'I want you to open a portal to that shrine.'

'I haven't dared,' Evelyn said quietly. 'I'm sure it's guarded, and—'

'We will deal with any guards,' Red said. 'Open the portal.'

Evelyn frowned, and opened her mouth to argue, but Red glared her down. So she drew a deep breath and concentrated, casting the portal spell. It had been years since she'd been in that shrine, but it was a lovely one, filled with paintings of the Lady, laughing and joyous.

Evelyn opened her eyes as the light flared and then the curtains appeared, moving in a breeze only they seemed to feel. Red gave the portal a grim look, took up a small metal lantern, and stepped through.

Ezren followed, and Bethral gestured for Evelyn to go ahead.

The shrine was empty and dusty, as if long unused. Probably for about five years, to Evelyn's way of thinking. The font in the center was dry, but she could still make out the silver stars painted on the blue ceiling to mimic the evening sky.

Red held the lantern high, and stepped to the door, listening. Bethral followed, and stood silently as the portal closed.

Red turned to Ezren and nodded. He eased the door open and slid into the corridor. Evelyn started when she heard low voices, of Ezren and at least two others. Bethral advanced with her mace, but Red shook her head. They both waited at the door. It was on the tip of Evelyn's tongue to ask what was going on when Ezren appeared. 'Come,' he said quietly.

Red opened the door, and gestured for Evelyn to follow her. Once in the corridor, they walked a few feet to another door. Evelyn recognized the doors to the Old King's chambers. She frowned. Rumor had it that the Regent had taken these rooms for his own.

Bethral stayed back, watching the corridor. There were guards at the far end, but they seemed to be ignoring their party.

'No need,' Ezren explained. 'They know what we are about.'

'It's sure to be locked,' Evelyn insisted as she focused the lantern on the door.

Red pulled a ring of keys from her cloak and unlocked the door.

'Where did you get those?' Evelyn asked.

Red gave her a hard glance. 'Off the Regent's body.'

'Oh,' Evelyn said, but Red was already through the door, and gone. The Priestess sighed, and followed.

The rooms hadn't really changed since she'd last seen them. More cluttered, that was certain. She stood in the center of the room, and stared at the treasures tossed idly aside. A white mink cloak thrown over a chair. Wine bottles on every table. Pouches with gold coins and gems spilling out. Evelyn shook her head at the mess, but something about the bottles caught her eyes. She reached out—

'Priestess,' Red called from the bedroom.

Evelyn went through the second door, into the King's bed-chamber. There was the huge four-poster bed with velvet curtains that she remembered so well, having healed the man more than once.

There was a woman seated on the bed, dressed in a thin nightgown, clutching a . . . Evelyn moved closer. A doll. The woman was holding a doll, and rocking back and forth. Her hair was long and thin; her skin, pale.

Ezren knelt before her, talking softly. She looked at him with wide blue eyes. When she shifted on the bed, Evelyn heard the clink of a chain.

Evelyn froze as Red reached under the blanket and pulled out a chain that ran from the bedpost to the woman's ankle. She moved to Ezren's side and looked at the woman closely.

Ezren looked up, and gave her a weak smile. 'Priestess—'

The woman's nightgown was open at the neck, and Evelyn could see a mark in the light of the lantern. 'A Chosen,' she breathed.

The woman looked at her, her eyes distant. She was rocking the doll back and forth, and humming softly.

'Only this Chosen has been raped and abused by the Regent,' Ezren said with a gentle tone and fierce expression. 'Trying to get her with child.'

Sweet Joyous Lady. Evelyn swallowed hard, then whispered a spell and reached out to touch the woman's hand. The woman stopped her rocking, and flinched away.

Evelyn smiled, held out her hand, and waited.

Curiosity replaced the woman's fear, and she reached out to gently lay a finger on Evelyn's ring. Evelyn slowly turned her hand over so the woman could see the white star sapphire. The light caught the stone, and the star appeared on its surface.

The woman's eyes went wide, and she looked up at Evelyn. 'Star,' she said with wonder.

'Star.' Evelyn squeezed her hand gently, then focused into the woman's body. She drew a deep breath, sickened at what she found. She pulled back, and opened her eyes. 'Her mind is gone.'

The woman pulled her hand away, and then reached out to touch Evelyn's hair. She smiled, then cradled her doll again.

'Iitrus kept her here,' Ezren sighed, 'trying to get a child with the mark, in order to place the child on the throne. He wanted me to tell a story about her, so that—'

'Is there somewhere you can take her, Priestess?' Red asked. 'Somewhere safe?'

Evelyn nodded. 'There's a shelter to the east, where they care for poor souls whose wits the Lady has taken.'

'She needs to disappear,' Red warned. 'She looks older than I am, Evelyn. That could be a problem if she fell into the wrong hands.'

'But you've won.' Evelyn frowned.

'The war, High Priestess,' Red said with a snort as she unlocked the chain. 'But there is still much to be done. It will take time and work to secure the throne. And there are those who would prefer a puppet. If you can't secure her safety, it were better if she died.'

Ezren looked sick. 'She's right, Lady High Priestess.'

'I'll hide her,' Evelyn insisted. 'I'll take her this moment, through the portal.'

Ezren stood, and swept off his cloak, placing it on the woman's shoulders. He urged her to stand, and he and Evelyn walked her to the door.

Bethral stood by the door to the corridor, guarding. She didn't turn her head as they came up behind her. 'All's clear.'

'I'll arrange for more time.' Ezren slipped out, headed toward the guards at the end of the hall. Red moved to follow.

'Wait.' Evelyn took a step to the table. She reached for one of the bottles and held it up to the light. 'Look at this.'

Red smiled when she saw the label.

They'd gathered in the command tent. The tables were full of food and drink, cleared of their maps for now.

The lantern light glowed on happy faces. Red looked at each one of the Lords and the Lady Helene. Fael was gesturing widely with his knife, describing a fight. Oh, there were currents there, but for this night they'd come together in fellowship.

Verice sat next to Vembar. Seemed they shared memories of past years and were exchanging tales. Oris, Alad, and Onza were there as well, their chairs clustered together, they seemed a bit overawed. Gloriana sat near Arent, whose joy was tempered with sorrow for Auxter's death. Red had mentioned a state funeral, but Arent had refused. They'd honor him with the rites of the Twelve, once things had settled down.

Evelyn glowed, there was no other word for it. And Josiah . . .

Red smiled. Apparently someone had found some fancy dress, and he'd been stripped of his normal tunic and trous. He looked fine in the deep blue, with silver trim to match the silver in his hair. But she couldn't say he looked terribly comfortable.

He'd stared at her all through the meal, saying nothing out loud. But his eyes spoke, and she knew he planned to confront her later.

Not if she had anything to say about it.

She looked down at her plate as a pain stabbed through her heart. She didn't flinch, just let it sweep over her. When she knew she could, she lifted her head to smile at one of Ezren's quips.

Once the food had been eaten, the talk grew more serious. Red knew it was time.

She rapped the table sharply. 'I've something special to share.'

Servers came out then, bearing the bottles she and Evelyn had found. One was placed before Josiah, who picked it up with reverence. He held the bottle in both hands. The label crackled as he ran his thumb over it. He looked at Red in a daze. 'This is from Athelbryght.'

'They all are.' Evelyn leaned over. 'I think they're all the same year, Josiah.'

Josiah nodded absently. 'It's one of the reds we laid down during Everard's reign.'

'We should save these,' Ezren said as he admired one of the other bottles.

'No.' Josiah lifted his head and looked straight at Red. 'We should drink them. To honor our past and pledge to the future.'

Red gave him a wry smile and a nod.

The bottles were opened, and glasses were filled. Red lifted hers high. 'To Athelbryght.'

'To Athelbryght' was chorused, and everyone drank.

There was a pause as they appreciated the taste. Red breathed in the wine, and let it sit on her tongue. It was a wonderful rich red.

'A wine to make your mouth laugh,' Ezren said.

'Aye.' Lord Carell stood. 'A fitting wine with which to salute our Chosen. To Red Gloves!'

'Red Gloves!' the company responded, and everyone drank.

Red smiled, and lifted her glass in response. But as the others refilled theirs, she gestured to a warrior by the tent flap. Almost as one, the servers set their bottles down, and slipped away. She had made arrangements for privacy from this point on, for she had things to say not for the ear of the common man.

Red waited as the bottles were passed, and then stood. 'All has been accomplished now, as Evelyn set out to do, so many years ago. On the morrow, the army will march into Edenrich, and the Chosen will take the throne and be crowned as the new Queen.' She paused, and caught Ezren's eye, just to make sure he was listening. 'But it won't be me.'

She drew a breath, conscious that it was almost over. The faces about the tent were stunned, confused, and bewildered. All but one.

So she said it again, just to be clear.

'I will not take the throne of Palins.'

THIRTY-SIX

Gloriana smiled, and gave her a nod. The rest of the room exploded in questions.

Red almost laughed out loud, but she buried her laughter in her goblet, swallowing the last of the wine. She placed the goblet on the table, and put both hands on her hips. 'Quiet!'

They all closed their mouths.

Red shook her head, bemused by their reactions. 'Let me say again that I will not take the throne.' She looked at Evelyn. 'That was always your plan, or destiny's plan, not mine.' Red sat down, shaking her head. 'I'm not going to sit there.'

'But' – Evelyn blinked at her – 'if not you . . .'

Red gestured to the end of the table. 'Gloriana, of course. You've trained her well for this moment, and she will serve this land better than I would.'

She leaned back in her chair. 'In the morning, Gloriana will ride into Edenrich, wearing the armor of the Chosen and a pair of red gloves. She will be welcomed and cheered as Red Gloves by all who see her.'

'The army—' Lord Fael started.

'The army saw a woman in the same armor, with her helmet on, under the banner of the Chosen,' Red explained. 'The warriors who had daily contact with me were of Auxter's training, and they are more loyal to Gloriana than to me.'

Vembar was staring at Red as if he'd never seen her before. 'You planned this.'

'Of course,' Red said. 'Gloriana will plant her pretty ass on the throne, and remove her gloves, announcing to all that Red Gloves is no fit name for a queen. Henceforth, she will be known as Queen Gloriana, the Chosen of Palins. The city will ring with rejoicing.'

Ezren recovered his wits. 'But you are the true Chosen.'

Red shook her head. 'Please. Where is the profit for me in a throne?' She avoided looking toward Josiah. Instead she leaned back in her chair. 'Can you see me then, seated on the throne, dealing with squabbling Guildmasters without lopping off a few heads? And the paperwork of a kingdom – Sweet Twelve, you'd drive me mad in the bargain.'

Red looked at Evelyn. 'Not to mention the religious problems. Gloriana worships the Gods of Palins. Can you see the Archbishop blessing and crowning my head with holy oils and prayers after I tell him to stick his Gods up his ass?'

Red pointed at Fael. 'And what about a marriage alliance? Would you marry me to some poor bastard of a nubile lord?'

Fael snorted.

Red turned serious then. 'And when it came right down to it, I chose to place my own interests' – she glanced at Josiah – 'over saving the land and the people. Despite the protests of a learned and elder adviser.'

'Not that eld,' Vembar said mildly.

There was silence for a moment, as everyone looked at Gloriana, clearly weighing the possibilities.

'The child is a better choice for the throne than I am,' Red said, 'because the land and its people would ever be her first concern. She is trained in statecraft and diplomacy, and surrounded by trusted advisers.'

Ezren looked dazed. 'But the hero returns from his adventures with the treasure for his people.'

'And the treasure that I bring you is the girl. Trained to power and the throne, she will be a better queen then I ever will.' Red smiled at him. 'Your story is still there, Ezren Silvertongue. Only now it's about a young lass who meets her teacher' – she pointed at Vembar – 'and her adviser' – Red pointed at Evelyn – 'and gathers the forces she needs to take the throne.'

The room exploded in talk and argument. Red quietly sat down.

Josiah was staring at her, and she quirked her mouth in a smile. He was confused, and he seemed to search her eyes for answers. Red looked away.

She let the argument rage for a bit, then stood. 'We'll finish this in the morning. I, for one, am exhausted. Seek your beds.'

They stood, and started to move out. Red waited for Josiah to draw close. She leaned toward him, taking in the smell of his skin and the faintest touch of marjoram. 'I'll come to your tent. Wait for me.'

He looked at her, then nodded, and went out with the others. Red sighed. Just one last thing to do, then she could sleep.

She looked around, and found Vembar still in the tent, standing by his chair. When he caught her eye, he lifted his glass. 'To the greatest Queen that Palins will never have.'

Red smiled as he drank, then left the tent.

The camp was settled for the night as Gloriana walked past sleeping warriors to the picket line where Beast was tethered. She gripped the red leather gloves she'd found on her bed.

Red was saddling Beast in the dark, at the very end of the line of sleeping horses. There were saddlebags at her feet, and a cloak over them.

Gloriana walked closer, making no effort to move silently. Red glanced up, then returned to her task. Beast didn't seem too pleased that he was being saddled, and Red was wrestling with the buckles.

'You're really going to do this,' Gloriana said softly.

'I told you I would,' Red answered just as quietly. 'Swore you an oath, if you remember rightly.'

'But why leave?' Gloriana asked. 'You could stay and—'

'Ah, no.' Red shook her head. 'Ezren would probably say something about a hero's sacrifice, but the truth is, I have to go. It wouldn't work for me to stay.'

'But you could change your name, and—' Gloriana stopped as Red gave her a serious look.

'Thank you, Gloriana. It means much to me that you want me to stay.' Red gave her a wry smile. 'But I know how power works. You need to step into my shoes completely, and I need to be gone. Or the true story will be known.'

'Then at least take this.' Gloriana held out a fat pouch that clinked with coins. 'A mercenary should make a profit.'

Red smiled, reached into her saddlebags, and pulled out another fat pouch. 'Truth be told, I saw to that already. I took gems from the Regent's chambers; they're lighter than gold. But

299

another will not go amiss.' Red took the coins, and stuffed them in her saddlebags. 'Now, put on your gloves, girl.'

Gloriana sighed. Carefully, she pulled the red gloves on, one at a time.

Red nodded. 'I'm not sure I'm doing you any favors, putting you on a throne, child. There will be problems, not the least of which is the state of the countryside and your people.'

Gloriana straightened her shoulders. 'I'll start with abolishing slavery. And the coinage. The people need to know that they can trust the Crown's coin and its justice.'

Red rolled her eyes. 'Better you than me.'

Gloriana hesitated for just a moment then flung her arms around Red, hugging her tight. 'Thank you, Chosen.'

She turned, and started back to her tent. And her own destiny.

'You're really going to do this.' Bethral's voice came from the darkness. She emerged from the shadows, her armor gleaming faintly.

'I am, sword-sister.'

'Where will you go?' Bethral asked as she walked closer.

Red shrugged. 'Where I will.'

'Not alone.' Bethral dropped her saddlebags next to Red's. 'I'll saddle up Bessie and—'

'It will look better if you stand beside Red Gloves when she takes her gloves off and claims her throne.'

Bethral frowned. 'I'd thought to go with you.'

Red smiled, and crossed her arms over her chest. 'Now who's avoiding the call to adventure?'

Bethral stilled.

'Go ahead,' Red said softly. 'Tell me that those green eyes mean nothing to you.'

Bethral's shoulders slumped. 'There is no chance there, Red. He's a man of learning with a mind like quicksilver. A man used to the world of the Court and its intrigues. There's no room in his world for a woman of the sword.'

'All I know is that if you leave with me, you've given up any chance,' Red pointed out. 'Are you ready to do that? Are you sure?'

Bethral hesitated.

'Never before have you hesitated to follow me.' Red chuckled. 'Seems to me that someone recently told me that I should chance the uncertain road.'

'I don't know—' Bethral paused, and looked back at the center of the camp. Then she turned back to Red. 'But I won't know unless I stay.'

'Be well, sword-sister.' Red extended her hand. Bethral took it, and Red pulled her into an embrace, mindful of Bethral's armor.

The big blonde picked up her gear, and with a last salute, faded into the night.

Red mounted, and sighed. 'At least there's a moon, Beast.'

The tired horse grunted, and started to walk toward the forest. Red figured she'd travel for a few hours, then camp for the night. That should take her far enough away to be undisturbed, and before Josiah discovered—

The sound of goat bells came from behind her.

Red cursed silently, and pulled Beast to a stop. The goats came up around her, their bells chiming as they moved.

'I waited.' Josiah's voice was a rumble.

Red sighed. 'I'd hoped to avoid this, goatherder. What gave me away?'

Josiah walked up to stand at her stirrup. He was still wearing his finery, and the silver trim caught the light. 'Evie came to tell me you asked her to open a portal, and she refused.'

Red scowled. Damn the priestess.

'You are really leaving?' Josiah questioned. 'Leaving the throne, the wealth, the power' – he looked at her hands – 'the red gloves?'

Red smiled and looked down at her new gloves. 'I am.'

Josiah placed his palm against Beast's neck. The goats moved closer, clustered about him. They all stared up at her, their eyes intent. 'You could be queen of this kingdom. Should be—'

'No,' Red said sharply. 'That was your plan, never mine.'

'But—'

'You didn't listen,' Red snapped. 'This life is not for me, and you know that, in your heart. There is no joy, no freedom, no profit in a throne. Not for me.'

'So you will go? Where?' Josiah demanded.

301

'Where I will. Not where a prophecy would place me.' Red shrugged. 'I've no real plan. A mercenary can find work.'

'In Palins?'

'No. I have to go from here. If I stay, even with a new name, it would cause problems. It must be a clean cut.' Red looked into the distance. 'Swift Port, perhaps.' She scowled at Josiah. 'Does it matter? I'll go where the wind takes me.'

'What if we need you? How do we—'

'You won't.' Red shifted in the saddle. 'Gloriana has good advisers to see her throu—'

'What if I need you?' Josiah asked.

Red sucked in a breath, and looked at him. They stared at one another for some time in silence. But Red was stronger than that. She quirked the corner of her mouth. 'You don't, Lord Josiah, High Baron of Athelbryght. I've taken pains to see you set where you should be. At the right hand of the queen, to aid her in restoring her land. She needs your wisdom and strength. And you have no need for a mercenary, Josiah of Athelbryght.'

The goats muttered.

Josiah opened his mouth, but Red was done. 'Enough.' She let her frustration show on her face. 'If you want the truth, I am barren.'

Josiah stared at her.

'Foolish man. In all this time that we shared our bodies, did I take precautions?'

Josiah opened his mouth. 'I never thought. There are herbs . . . I assumed that—'

Red barked a laugh. 'True enough, but I'd no need. I'm barren, Josiah. Unable to bear a child.'

'How did—' Josiah cut off his words.

Red glanced at her gloves, then shook her head. 'A long tale, and dull in the telling. Suffice to say that it's true.' She tightened the reins. 'Enough of this. You are Lord Josiah, High Baron of Athelbryght. You, too, must be about the business of securing and restoring your lands. Get yourself a wife, man, to bear the heirs you need.'

Red took one last look at him. A man standing strong and straight, his eyes clear and brown, looking a bit puzzled. She knew what she had to do. She tossed her hair back. 'Get back to your tent, Noble Lord, before you catch your death.' She spurred Beast forward. Beast wouldn't be able to run long, just long enough for her to lose the goats and their herder.

Now lost to her forever.

THIRTY-SEVEN

The stars were out in the night sky before Red made camp in a thick grove of pine with a stream close at hand.

Beast was weary, and so was she, in body and heart. She got them both water, then built a small fire. Just enough to brew some kavage. There was hardtack and dried beef in her pack. A bit of something in her belly, a nice long sleep, and she'd be over it.

Over the longing that was building in her chest.

The copper pot looked as cheerful as it always had, sitting in the coals, tiny bubbles forming in the water. She'd had that pot for years, a quiet companion on her travels. It was just the right size for enough kavage for her and Bethral, and it easily fit in a pack.

Red sat on her pallet and stared at the water, not really caring if it boiled or not. It was just something familiar to do, a welcome task before she crawled into her bedding and tried to sleep. She wasn't thirsty, and she didn't want kavage.

She didn't know what she wanted, truth be told.

No, that wasn't the truth, either, and she'd picked a muck of a time to start lying to herself. Red sighed, and left the pot to its own devices, stretching out on her pallet and staring at the stars.

Beast was hobbled nearby, eating tiny leaves off the bushes that sheltered this clearing. She could hear him rustling the branches and chewing.

The night noises around them were normal. A few twitters in the trees and the quiet rustle of tiny creatures scurrying in the leaves on the forest floor.

Deal with your pain. See it for what it is, understand its source, and, having acknowledged it, choose to bear it well. Pain is part of life, as much as joy and happiness.

Red grimaced. There were times when the Way of the Twelve

was an enormous pain in the ass. It would be far easier to ignore her pain, or pretend that it didn't hurt. Or just lie here and sob until she wasted away into nothing.

With a deep breath, she closed her eyes and pictured him.

The moment was there, in her mind's eye, his head thrown back in a deep laugh, then the slight tilt of his head, that rare smile gracing his face. His eyes dancing.

She knew now. Knew what those eyes looked like filled with joy, filled with pleasure and life.

The night was still, and she took a deep breath of pine-scented air. Oh, yes. She knew now, and she also knew that it would more than like haunt her every moment for the rest of her life.

Red looked at the stars, took a deep breath, and then spoke aloud, for all the mice to hear. 'I love Josiah of Athelbryght.'

There was no thunder, no lightning, no heaving of the earth. The world about her was unchanged, the trees not at all impressed. But deep within, Red felt the truth, and she had to close her eyes as the pain welled up in response.

She loved Josiah of Athelbryght. She loved his bright eyes, his gentle strength, his quiet pain. She wanted the man in her life, her bed, her world. She wanted to be his world, by his side, protecting him. Loving him.

Beast snorted at something on the ground, then shifted to graze on another branch. Red tensed and held her breath, straining to hear . . .

She was listening for damn goat bells.

Scowling, she turned on her side to stare at the pot.

The water was still not boiling.

Red flopped on her back and felt for her weapons, making sure they were still in easy reach. Then she folded her hands over her stomach, and looked into the night sky.

She loved him, and that was that. She'd fulfilled her agreement. There was a Chosen on the throne of Palins. She'd a pouch of gold and a fistful of gems for her trouble, and her freedom. She'd lost Bethral, true, but Bethral's path was in a different direction. That was how the world worked, wasn't it?

She'd accomplished her other, quieter goal as well. The pain in Josiah's eyes had been banished, replaced with a sparkle. She'd had the pleasure of his body and company, but now his path was in a very different direction, as different as one could get. Adviser to the Throne, Lord High Baron, the man needed to be about his work. Plenty to do there, not to mention his need to get an heir. A fat, fertile farm wife, restoring her lord and his land with her . . .

A fat, fertile farm wife. One who would fill Josiah's heart and bed, and make him bread and bear him children. Athelbryght would live again.

Babies, vines, crops . . . the man would do well.

The tears welled up again, and Red cursed her stupidity. She sat up abruptly, wiping away the tears with the palms of her hands. At least she knew that she'd had the healing of him, whatever woman wormed her way into his heart. She'd always know that the joy in his eyes was there because she'd put it there first.

Small comfort.

But she'd done right by him. He'd healed and grown, and she was no small part of that. Leaving him to flourish was the right thing to do.

Enough of this. She glared at the little copper pot, but the water just sat there. 'In the morning, I'm going to find a tavern, and get my itch scratched but good.'

The pot made no comment.

That was what she needed. A bit of bed fun with a warrior or two. Get the smell of Josiah's skin out of her head. Replace those memories with others, lots of others if need be.

Except it wouldn't work.

Red cursed again, out loud, a blistering oath. It wouldn't work. She wanted Josiah and only Josiah, damn him. She could hunt up the strongest warrior she could find, rub marjoram all over his skin, and hump him until the bed broke – and it wouldn't work.

She couldn't replace Josiah. Couldn't look to find him in another. She was well and truly doomed. The pain sat like a lump beneath her heart, and she breathed through it, trying to move past it.

Ah, well. Pain was a familiar enough companion. She'd borne it before, and it hadn't killed her. But this . . . it was like all the color had drained from the world and her life.

A glance at the pot, which still wasn't boiling. Red snarled at it, at life, at truth.

Muckers all.

She'd enough funds to go where she pleased. She couldn't stay in Palins. Soccia was no place for a mercenary. Too fat, too peaceful.

Swift Port had that fleet of seagoing ships. She'd seen the ocean once, and had waded out to see if the water was really salty. She'd never been on the water in one of those big vessels. The idea of open water, and wind filling the sails, might appeal.

Beast snorted.

Well, that was a point. She'd have to give up her horse, and who knew what it was like on one of those boats when the waves picked up, eh?

She could go to the Black Hills. Go fight the Odium and other dark monsters that filled those hills. She'd have to change her name, of course. Red Gloves was no longer hers. She looked at her hands, at the new black gloves that she wore. They looked odd. Out of place. It would take time to get used to them.

Black Gloves wasn't going to work.

Gloves, maybe?

She thought about that for a moment, but decided against it, puffing out a breath in frustration. It wasn't like she could remember her birth name, if she'd even had one. She'd always been Red to every—

Kitten.

Red felt the heat rise in her cheeks as she heard Josiah's voice in her head. The ache in her body was sorrow, but it was also need. She took a deep breath, letting the pain sweep through her.

Kitten the mercenary. That would impress them, eh?

Still . . . she rolled on her side, and blinked at the fire. Cat, maybe? Katerina? That had a nice ring to it. Katerina the mercenary.

She blinked, as exhaustion washed through her. She'd decide in the morning.

She got up, and saw the water bubbling merrily in the pot. With a sigh, she used her glove to draw it off to the side, and dumped the ground beans into the water. The kavage would be cold and strong when she woke, and she'd need it to get on her way and put a few more miles between her and . . .

Red settled under the blankets, and watched as the tiny fire died.

Cold and strong. Laughter bubbled in her throat as she pulled the blanket about her shoulders. Cold and strong. As her life would be.

Cold . . . and strong . . . and empty.

Red woke when a cold, wet nose nuzzled the back of her neck. With a shriek, she leaped to her feet, sword and dagger at the ready.

The goats scattered, bleating, as they ran to hide behind Josiah. He was mounted on a horse, and looking irritated.

Breathing hard, her hair in her face, she glared at him. 'Where are the damn bells?'

'I stuffed them full of moss,' Josiah said calmly.

'Sweet Twelve.' Red breathed hard, trying to calm her racing heart. 'You scared a year's life out of me, and then some.'

'Serves you right.' Josiah dismounted. He had on plain tunic and trous, with none of the trappings of his office. 'Do you have any kavage?'

Red looked at the scattered fire and the overturned pot. 'No.'

Josiah sighed. 'Well, then, if you start the fire, I'll see to the horses. Which way to the water?'

Red pointed toward a path through the trees, and Josiah tugged at the reins of his horse. 'I'll come back and get Beast.'

She watched as Josiah walked off, her heart starting to calm in her chest. The goats were glaring at her. She put her hands on her hips. 'Well?'

They proceeded to bleat at her, as if scolding, as they moved about the camp, taking up positions around her. Red knelt to see to the fire, feeling as if she'd been taken prisoner. By a band of magic goats.

By the time Josiah returned, she had the fire going, and the little copper pot full of water was in the coals. Her heart started to beat faster at the sight of him.

Josiah had washed his face and hands in the stream. He looked clean and tousled, his curls in disarray. The goats settled around

308

them as he arranged his gear in silence. He set his saddlebags on the other side of the fire, and used the saddle blanket as a pad to sit on. Without a word, he dug out some cold meat pies, a handful of raisins, and a loaf of bread.

Red took a portion gratefully. Far better than what she had in her pack. They ate in silence as the water cheerfully started to boil in the pot.

Josiah yawned as she added kavage to the water. 'Lord of Light, but I'm tired.' He rolled onto his back, and laced his fingers behind his head. 'What with chasing you all through the night.'

'Josiah—' Red said. 'What are you doing here? I told you—'

Josiah answered, his eyes closed. 'Oh, yes. You told me how it would be, didn't you?'

'I' – Red glared at him – 'I did. You have responsibilities, Josiah of Athelbryght.'

'I do.' He nodded, his eyes still closed. 'But how would it look to be an adviser to the Queen, with five goats at your feet all the time?'

Red snorted back a laugh.

Josiah turned his head, and looked at her with a smile, his brown eyes warm. 'I never liked Court life, Kitten. Never spent any more time there than necessary. But you had it all planned for me, didn't you?'

Red scowled. 'You can't follow—'

'Yes, I can.' Josiah sat up, and glared right back. 'I can follow you, my mercenary. Or we can go home. To Athelbryght. And build our new lives together there.'

Red shook her head. 'Josiah, you are a High Baron. You need—'

'You,' Josiah said. 'All I need is you. By whatever name. By whatever path. All I need is you.'

''Siah.' Red closed her eyes to the hope in his. 'I can't give you children.'

Josiah shrugged. 'So? The goats don't breed. Did it occur to you that I might be sterile as well?'

Red blinked.

Josiah stretched out, looking slightly smug. 'There are the other Chosen children to consider. They'll need a home and land.

I've known them since they were babes, and I'd be proud to pass my heritage to them.'

''Siah . . .' Red sighed.

'It's not like you asked, Kitten.' Josiah's voice was a rumble. 'After all, allow me to point out that I have goats. Magic goats.' He sighed dramatically. 'What woman in her right mind would have me?'

Red quirked her mouth up. 'The goats are a definite problem.' She leaned over to scratch Fog under his chin.

'And what about protecting my lands?' Josiah pointed out. 'The lands need to be warded, and I'll need a fighting force. Those warriors are not going to take orders from me very well.'

Red remained silent.

'And then,' Josiah continued in his deep voice, 'there's the small problem that I've lost my heart to you.'

Red blinked back tears. 'I've got these gloves, 'Siah.' She held out her hands, showing him the black gloves.

'I'm a broken mage without power,' Josiah pointed out. 'With a scarred barony whose people suffered because of my failures. We both have pasts.'

Red nodded, silent.

'Someone once told me that you can't live in the past. That you have to deal with your pain and move on. Our pasts won't change. What can change is what we do now, with each new breath we take.'

Josiah looked at the sky. 'Now, if you don't come over here and kiss me, I'm afraid I'll have to do something drastic.'

Red moved slowly, on all fours, coming around the fire to stretch out beside him. Josiah opened his arms, and Red folded into them, tears running down her cheeks.

Josiah kissed the tears away as he pulled her close. He claimed her mouth with quiet strength.

When they ended the kiss, he cradled her close, putting her head on his shoulder as he eased the blanket over them. Red sighed, breathing in his scent and the faint touch of marjoram. She felt her bones melt into his heat, the pain in her heart ease. It felt so damn good to be in his arms, and they weren't even naked.

'So, my mercenary,' Josiah rumbled, 'where shall we go?'

'I wonder,' Red whispered in his ear. 'You drained all that power from that whore. I wonder what that did for your lands.'

'We could go see,' Josiah said. 'Although I think the land started to heal the moment you pounded on my door, Kitten. I know I did.'

Red lifted her head, shifting a bit so that she looked into those brown eyes with gold flecks that gleamed in the firelight. 'Josiah, I want—' She caught her breath, suddenly afraid.

Josiah raised his eyebrows, inviting her confidence but waiting patiently.

Red licked suddenly dry lips. 'I want to try to take off the gloves.' She clutched him close. 'With you, only you. When we love.'

'As you wish,' Josiah said softly. 'We will heal together, you and I, shall we?'

Red nodded, her fear fading away. She put her head back on his shoulder. 'Together.'

The sky above was filled with stars, the night clear and cool. They lay in silence for a moment, cuddled under the blanket.

Red quirked up the corner of her mouth, and lifted her head enough to brush her lips against Josiah's ear. 'Profit, indeed.'

Josiah's laugh startled the goats, and Red rejoiced to see his brown eyes dancing with joy and love.